The Imagined Arctic in Speculative Fiction

The Imagined Arctic in Speculative Fiction explores the ways in which the Arctic is imagined and what function it is made to serve in a selection of speculative fictions: non-mimetic works that start from the implied question "What if?" Spanning slightly more than two centuries of speculative fiction, from the starting point in Mary Shelley's 1818 *Frankenstein* to contemporary works that engage with the vast ramifications of anthropogenic climate change, analyses demonstrate how Arctic discourses are supported or subverted and how new Arctics are added to the textual tradition. To illuminate wider lines of inquiry informing the way the world is envisioned, humanity's place and function in it, and more-than-human entanglements, analyses focus on the function of the actual Arctic and how this function impacts and is impacted by speculative elements. With effects of climate change training the global eye on the Arctic, and as debates around future northern cultural, economic, and environmental sustainability intensify, there is a need for a deepened understanding of the discourses that have constructed and are constructing the Arctic. A careful mapping and serious consideration of both past and contemporary speculative visions thus illuminate the role the Arctic has played and may come to play in a diverse set of practices and fields.

Maria Lindgren Leavenworth, Professor of Modern English Literature, Department of Language Studies, Umeå University.

Routledge Studies in World Literatures and the Environment
Series Editors: Scott Slovic and Swarnalatha Rangarajan

For more information about this series, please visit: www.routledge.com/Routledge-Studies-in-World-Literatures-and-the-Environment/book-series/ASHER4038

The Imagined Arctic in Speculative Fiction

Maria Lindgren Leavenworth

Routledge
Taylor & Francis Group

NEW YORK AND LONDON

First published 2024
by Routledge
605 Third Avenue, New York, NY 10158

and by Routledge
4 Park Square, Milton Park, Abingdon, Oxon, OX14 4RN

Routledge is an imprint of the Taylor & Francis Group, an informa business

© 2024 Maria Lindgren Leavenworth

ISBN: 978-1-032-40966-5 (hbk)
ISBN: 978-1-032-40968-9 (pbk)
ISBN: 978-1-003-35558-8 (ebk)

DOI: 10.4324/9781003355588

Typeset in Sabon
by Newgen Publishing UK

Contents

Acknowledgments

Many colleagues and friends have helped me in the long process that has resulted in this book, and whether you asked needed questions about ideas, read chapters in various stages of completeness, or suggested books I should include, I am grateful. I especially appreciate guidance from the anonymous reviewers of the first draft of the manuscript, and inspiration from the ever-supportive Speculative Fiction Network. Special thanks go to Virginia Langum for reading, to Van Leavenworth, my True North, for reading and thinking with me, also beyond this project, and, most of all, to Heidi Hansson and Anka Ryall who led me to the Arctic.

Introduction

Aesthetics, Instabilities, and Imaginings

When Victor Frankenstein starts narrating his tale to Robert Walton in the frame story of Mary Shelley's 1818 novel, he promises depictions "of powers and occurrences, such as you have been accustomed to believe impossible" (24). In the 1831 edition of *Frankenstein* is added: "Were we among the tamer scenes of nature, I might fear to encounter your unbelief, perhaps your ridicule; but many things will appear possible in these wild and mysterious regions" (31).[1] The untamed setting in which Frankenstein tells his tale is, of course, the Arctic. Perceived of by ancient Greeks and Romans as located at the end of the world, the Arctic was thought to be home to the long-lived Hyperboreans, mentioned, for example, in Herodotus' *Histories* (ca. 450 BCE) and limned in Pindar's *Tenth Pythian Ode* as living "remote from toil and strife" (Morice 125). Pytheas of Massalia brought home a more realistic image a century later: that of the island of Thule in the far north. Although the northern extent of his journey is debated, he reached the edge of a semi-frozen ocean and described a sun that never sets. In early modern Europe, as explorers from several nations sought a trading route to Asia, images were circulated that on the one hand emphasized a ghostlike icescape, on the other suggested that the Arctic was the passageway to a tropical paradise. Maps such as Olaus Magnus' 1539 "Carta Marina" shows Arctic islands surrounded by fantastical sea creatures, and Margaret Cavendish's proto science fiction novel *The Blazing World* (1666) imagines a utopian world, reachable through the North Pole.

Shelley's frame story is far less fantastic than these early narratives and the science fiction of *Frankenstein* is rather seen as residing in the account of reanimation nestled within it. However, even if wholly or partly imaginary versions of the Arctic were complemented or gainsaid by first-hand descriptions via exploration that intensified in the eighteenth and nineteenth centuries, speculation in Shelley's novel is not confined to Victor's experiments. The original publication of the novel falls in the same year as two British expeditions departed for the Arctic: one, led by David

DOI: 10.4324/9781003355588-1

Buchan, attempted to sail the waters between Svalbard and Greenland that were rumored to be ice free, the other, led by John Ross, aimed to locate the Northwest Passage. Neither was successful, and large portions of the Arctic remained unmapped in the European imagination. The nineteenth-century accounts at hand also, Chancey Loomis notes, continued to promote "inherited images" through which the Arctic landscape is presented as "vaster, more mysterious, and more terrible than elsewhere on the globe" (96). It was thought to be, Loomis continues, "a region in which natural phenomena could take strange, almost supernatural, forms, sometimes stunningly beautiful, sometimes terrifying, often both." The combination of imprecise geographical knowledge and these repeated references to awe-inspiring peculiarities make the Arctic the logical destination for Walton with "a belief in the marvellous" (Shelley 22), and it is a place which Shelley can fill with her own imaginings.

Aesthetics of the Arctic sublime echo in periods that follow, but they are tempered by accounts from further geographical and scientific expeditions, and complicated by geopolitics. Searches continued for the Northwest Passage, the coastlines of the Arctic Ocean were (sometimes erratically) mapped, and new records were set for coming furthest north. When tourists increasingly started seeking out Arctic destinations in the mid to late nineteenth century, the broad perception of the Arctic as forbidding to the outside visitor or requiring extraordinary endurance was questioned, and increasing numbers of female travelers in the latter period also helped destabilize the image of the Arctic as a testing ground for an exclusively male heroism. Parallel to and influencing aesthetic shifts and imaginings, twentieth-century issues clustered around the exploitation of natural resources and war, extending both literal and figurative mappings. The Arctic became a nexus in rushes for minerals and oil, a seemingly inexhaustible larder for fish and wild game, and a strategic military location in World War II for both land-based transports and for predicting weather that could affect the battlegrounds of Europe (Emmerson 122–124). The Cold War period "ushered in an age of contamination" making the Arctic "an atomic era battlefield" (McCannon 263) and saw increasing amounts of pollution drift towards the high latitudes. Forms of appropriation of Arctic areas have also resulted in cultural and geographical disenfranchisement of Indigenous peoples. Among them are dislocations of Sami communities between 1920 and 1940 resulting from boundary disputes between Norway, Sweden, and Russia (McGhee 249), and the High Arctic Relocations taking place in the 1950s, in which the Canadian Government moved several Inuit families from Northern Quebec and Baffin Island to Ellesmere Island and Cornwallis Island (Marcus). With the founding of the Arctic Council in 1996, in which members from the eight countries that are wholly or partly situated in the Arctic were joined by six participants representing Indigenous groups, past and ongoing effects of colonial practices have become increasingly visible (Keskitalo). And how the Arctic is entangled with or enmeshed in broader contexts is underlined by its contemporary function as a global barometer gauging climate change: the vulnerability of the area is becoming a concern also for people who do not reside there.

Despite the Arctic's migration from the periphery of knowledge to a position in which a general awareness of the area grows and in which specific aspects highlight it as central, the area contains and produces peculiarities that continue to constitute a pull on the imaginations of authors writing about the material space of the Arctic, and more generally of the north, from an outside perspective. Physical dangers posed by intense cold, darkness, the threat of moving or amassed ice, the impossibility of correctly measuring distances or even distinguishing land from ice, often drive the plot in works of fiction, but the Arctic is established as a multifaceted antagonist in non-fiction also. Effects on visitors' psyches, predominantly madness caused by isolation, are recirculated, as is the disorientation produced when the validity of sensory impressions taken for granted south of the Arctic no longer hold. Optical illusions and atmospheric phenomena that produce ghost ships and mountain ranges, loomings caused by ice refraction that elevates or lowers what is seen, parhelia and paraselenae—mock suns and moons—that upset the heavens, "serve as caution against precise description and expectation," Barry Lopez notes in his travelogue *Arctic Dreams*, and as "reminder[s] that the universe is oddly hinged" (24).

Notions of otherworldliness and reverie abound in critical works that address how perpetuated discourses compete with or complement the busyness and heterogeneity of the Arctic. Robert McGhee traces images of the area through history, noting that "stories, the true and the false, have gradually accumulated to form the vision of a distant and fantastic Arctic . . . . not so much as a region as a dream" (10), Margaret Atwood concludes that "[t]urning to face north, face the north, we enter our own unconsciousness [and] the journey north has the quality of dream" ("True North" 33) and Graham Huggan demonstrates how "the Arctic has served as a free-floating idea that . . . moves energetically—as if to mirror the volatility of its own surroundings—between dream and nightmare states" (72). Peter Davidson maintains that the north represents "an escape from the limits of civilization" (21) and that it is "always a shifting idea, always relative" (8), which opens for a wide variety in representations, and Sherrill Grace makes a similar point: the north as a construction "is multiple, shifting, and elastic; it is a *process* [and] above all, Other" (16).[2] Fraught with political, cultural, and environmental tension, the vast Arctic is neither a museum, nor a larder. Mindful of this historical and contemporary background, the critics above gesture to discourses permeating both fiction and non-fiction, written mainly by authors not indigenous to or residing permanently in the Arctic. These discourses often highlight the area's stereotypical function as an emblem of the unfamiliar, as an empty stage on which to enact a battle between human and nature, or as tendering promises for adventures that modernity has made impossible elsewhere. These fantasies and their affordances for speculative fictions form the bases for this book. My intention is not to solidify sometimes faulty perceptions but examine the traction they still provide in reiterations, manipulations, and subversions, as well as investigate myriad alternatives to them.

The Arctic is a sea surrounded by land, a geological 'instability' that in some ways contributes to likewise unstable descriptions and impressions. Even definitions of what constitutes the Arctic vary between scientific fields and because of political agreements, but commonly the Arctic Circle at 66° 33'N constitutes the southern boundary, delimiting the midnight sun and the polar night. "[E]xact demarcations," however, Anka Ryall, Johan Schimanski, and Henning Howlid Wærp maintain in the introduction to *Arctic Discourses*, are less important "than the cultural notions surrounding this area as representing a generalized North. The question is not where the Arctic begins, but where we think and have thought that the Arctic begins" (xii).[3] North as a direction is also dependent on the subject's perspective and position: "wherever it is located, it points always to a further north, to an elsewhere," Davidson notes, adding that "there have always been as many norths as there have been standpoints from which to look northward" (7, 21). Sometimes, even the boundary between north and south is only figurative and Arctic imagery is worked into depictions set in non-Arctic environments. Schimanski and Ulrike Spring refer to "arcticity," denoting how artefacts transposed to other areas can still "be immediately recognizable as Arctic" (59), whereas contributors to the anthology *Arcticness* use the titular term to capture "the quality of *being*" Arctic also in places outside the geographical region (Medby vii). As I am mainly concerned with outside views, my own use of "the Arctic" is relatively uncontroversial; it is a term coined by outsiders (for this reason sometimes avoided by Indigenous peoples), and it does not distinguish between heterogeneous localities. Although I will substitute the broad "Arctic" with specific placenames where this is important for the argument, my interest predominantly lies in larger discourses connected to the Arctic as both place and idea.

In focus in this book is how the Arctic has been and is imagined in speculative fiction: non-mimetic works that start from the implied question "what if?" The geographical instabilities and the ways in which the Arctic invites fantasies give rise to what-if-questions that run the full gamut from being incrementally removed from the world as we know it to giving fully fledged supernatural answers to past mysteries. That is, questions range from what if the northern polar ice cap melts slightly faster than predicted, to what if the majority of Sir John Franklin's crew were killed by a fourteen-foot-tall ice monster? A wide definition of speculative fiction encompasses works of fantasy and science fiction with no or weak ties to the world as we know it, but the speculative fictions addressed in this book all have locations in the actual Arctic (or in some instances Subarctic) as a setting, and authors reiterate or subvert what is known about these locations (or the Arctic broadly) at the time of writing. The speculative fiction analyzed is born out of already-existing situations, relations, and circumstances, that is, I am interested in the function of the actual Arctic and in how this function impacts and is impacted by speculative elements.

Shelley's Arctic frame story in *Frankenstein* is my point of departure for an interrogation of discourses, themes, and motifs that in various ways are recirculated, negotiated, or contested in a selection of speculative short stories and novels, published between 1818 and today. And her Walton embodies the outside status, his initial dream of "the region of beauty and delight" (15) illustrating, precisely, the imagined Arctic. "The pole that fascinates him," Francis Spufford argues, "is a pure book-learnt construction of the imagination . . . a space cleared on the map for him to fill with daydreams of discovery" (58–59). This elastic construction, gleaned from poetry and novels as well as from documentary texts, in an extended sense informs all the fictions in my sample. Characters are often temporary visitors to the Arctic, arriving with hope or with trepidation conjured up by images and stories encountered at home. Their preconceptions form their view of the Arctic; the Arctic, in turn, transforms their identities and notions of home. The majority of the authors in my sample are similarly not from nor residing permanently in the Arctic. Where what can be called an inside perspective appears, focus is still on constructions based on ideas of the periphery or the unknown. With a few exceptions, the works I discuss are by Anglophone authors, the selection on the one hand reflecting my own academic belonging, on the other indicating that it is within Anglophone speculative fiction that we see a consistent and increasing preoccupation with the Arctic. My selection, then, is not exhaustive, but illustrates salient themes in the output of speculative texts using the Arctic as a setting.

Authors from Indigenous cultures, to whom the Arctic is home rather than Other, are consequently not featured to a great extent in my discussions. This should not be read as signaling a lack of speculative fiction from Indigenous authors, on the contrary, Marek Oziewicz notes, "speculative visions of the world formulated from a postcolonial or minority perspective . . . . often articulate multicultural reality better than the historically white and predominantly Anglophone non-mimetic genres." The diversity in the output is illustrated in compilations of Indigenous speculative fiction such as *So Long Been Dreaming* (edited by Nalo Hopkinson and Uppinder

Mehan, 2004) and *Walking the Clouds* (edited by Grace L. Dillon, 2012). The recent anthology *Taaqtumi* (edited by Neil Christopher, 2019) gathers horror stories set in the Arctic, written by northern and Indigenous authors Aviaq Johnston, Ann R. Loverock, K. C. Carthew, Jay Bulckaert, Repo Kempt, Gayle Kabloona, Richard Van Camp, Thomas Anguti Johnston, and Rachel and Sean Qitsualik-Tinsley. Representing a blend of traditional and modern storytelling, the stories address past relocations as well as contemporary climate threats, and feature both old and new monsters.

The texts analyzed in this book are primarily aimed at an adult readership, even though boundaries sometimes blur. Adventure fiction of the kind that I address in Chapter 1 for instance, with Jules Verne as a common source of inspiration, is in style and content likely to appeal to a young audience as well. In the main, I have opted to not discuss books and short stories that explicitly target children or young adults, but there are a number of themes and ideas that recirculate regardless of demographics. In the recent anthology *The Arctic in Literature for Children and Young Adults* (Hansson, Lindgren Leavenworth, and Ryall 2020), speculative fictions are represented by Sami author Máret Ánne Sara's novels *Ilmmiid gaskkas* (2013) and *Doaresbealde doali* (2014) which Lill Tove Fredriksen approaches with a focus on how stories familiar to Indigenous readers are utilized to reflect contemporary ecological concerns. Importantly, Sami children's books are rarely categorized as fantasy, even though they often rely on a blurring of boundaries between the imagined and the real; as Fredriksen argues "in the Sami oral tradition, it is not difficult to enter the mythical and supernatural world or to return to the 'real' world . . . . and the demarcation between humans and other creatures" is less than clear-cut (135).[4] Tiffany Johnstone addresses the illustrated children's books *A Promise is a Promise* (1988) and *Hide and Sneak* (1992) by Inuit author Michael Arvaarluk Kusugak in which protagonist Allashua's encounters with Qallupilluit and inuksugaq work as cautionary tales but with an added focus on "the dangers that come with the displacement of Inuit knowledge" (132). My own chapter in the volume investigates how the Arctic is represented "as a stage on which to enact contemporary concerns" specifically connected to environmental issues: resource extraction in Marcus Sedgewick's 2009 *Revolver*, climate change in Rebecca Stead's 2007 *First Light*, and species extinction in Sarah Beth Durst's 2009 *Ice* (Lindgren Leavenworth, "Orientation and Disorientation" 227). By moving along a spectrum of texts with variously strong connections to the actual world, I address how the Arctic works to complicate characters' physical and existential orientation. Affinities between works aimed at children and young adults and those targeting an adult audience are thus numerous, but especially pronounced in depictions of climate change: a discussion I enter into in Chapter 3.

Since I am foremost concerned with visitors' descriptions of the Arctic, it follows that the majority of the examined texts in part are fictional travelogues and thus take their place in a long tradition in which fact and fiction (or at least exaggeration) are blended. The eastern travels depicted in the fourteenth-century *The Book of Sir John Mandeville* and *The Travels of Marco Polo* have Arctic counterparts both earlier, in what is quoted from Pytheas' journeys in Strabo's *Geographica* and Pliny's *Natural History*, and contemporary in Jacobus Cnoyen's summary of the lost *Inventio Fortunata*, which imagined the North Pole as a black rock surrounded by a whirlpool.[5] But also for travelers from the Subarctic, such as Saxo Grammaticus, the far north was a periphery both geographically and conceptually. Northern Norway "teems with peoples of monstrous strangeness," Iceland is "noteworthy for marvels, both strange occurrences and objects that pass belief," and monsters prowl the Scandinavian forests, he notes in the preface to *The Danish History* (published around 1200). In Old Norse myth as well as in the Finnish *Kalevala*, the underworld and the world of death lie to the north (Davidson 30). Fantastical elements become more pronounced with the distance from the traveler's home, and flourish when the periphery of the known world is reached. The structure of the travelogue: departure, encounter, and return, characterize many of the texts I address, but the last stage is sometimes missing, leaving the intrepid explorers (or the hapless victims of winds and whirlpools) in the Arctic, potentially for good.

As these examples solidify, exploration was, unsurprisingly, touted as a male affair, and to an even greater extent than other geographical areas, the Arctic seemed to require but also call forth what was regarded as particularly male qualities: bravery, endurance, and hardiness. Shelley's Walton has progressively "inur[ed his] body to hardship" by work on whaling ships in the North Sea during which he "voluntarily endured cold, famine, thirst, and want of sleep" (17). In both body and mind, he changes from the poet he has been at home to a more masculine explorer: that is the only way he will survive in an Arctic that promises no comforts. In the denouement of *Frankenstein*, Walton, his crew, and Victor are locked in the ice, and with mutiny threatening, Victor addresses the crew, berating them for their lack of courage and fortitude in the face of imminent danger. Instead of being remembered "as men who had not strength enough to endure cold and peril" they are encouraged to "be more than men" (217) and to conquer the ice. Victor continues: "This ice is not made of such stuff as your hearts may be; it is mutable and cannot withstand you if you say that it shall not." Spufford reads in this passage "an invitation to beat the Arctic by out-freezing it, and abandoning the change and flow—the *mutability*— of emotions" (61). To the "male" qualities required, then, is added checked affect; like women, emotions are to be left at home.

The Arctic as an exclusively male domain is a pervasive fantasy, setting the stage for encounters between man and nature but ignoring the practical reality that women have inhabited, visited, and explored the Arctic, and, also from a distance, contributed to the cultural, social, and economic constructions of the area. Critical literature on the heterogeneous Arctic pays heed to the fantasy and its apparent exclusion of women, but also amply demonstrates the impact of women's participation in or negotiations of a variety of discourses. Works such as Lisa Bloom's *Gender on Ice*, concerned with the intersection of nationalism, gender, and race, effectively shows how the desired "blankness" (2) of the Arctic helped construct an American white heterosexual masculinity: "the epitome of maleness" (6), in stories of exploration, but also how this stereotype throws other identities—non-white, feminine, queer—into relief. With literary examples ranging from *Frankenstein* to Robert Michael Ballantyne's adventure fiction, Jen Hill examines "a genealogy of polar narratives" (4) to similarly argue for the Arctic as an imaginative ideological space of importance to masculine identities, while still illustrating women's role in British empire building.

Depending on the nature of the journey (exploration or tourism) and on the attitude of the journeying subject (to conquer or to entertain) the Arctic landscape is often heteronormatively coded as a formidable male foe or a dangerous, alluring female, with gendered descriptions sometimes shifting mid-narrative. However, in a previous analysis of Michelle Paver's *Dark Matter* (a novel revisited in Chapter 2), I have suggested that the Arctic emerges as a queer space. As a representative of a normative approach, Paver's protagonist expects to be challenged or enticed by a stable Arctic, but instead experiences a series of increasingly destabilizing moments that upset taken-for-granted boundaries and restrict his movement. With inspiration drawn from Sara Ahmed's discussions in *Queer Phenomenology* (2006) I argued that "queer moments are produced by the actual as well as the supernatural Arctic: they distort perspectives and highlight a continuous resistance emanating from place" (Lindgren Leavenworth, "Abnormal Fears" 463). Approaching "conceptual problems" from the perspective of realistic travels, but similarly connecting them to lack of boundaries, to the upset of norms taken for granted elsewhere, Lopez notes that they are produced by "a fundamental strangeness in the landscape itself" (12). The queerness of the Arctic landscape, consequently, complicates the visitor's ability to orient her- or himself and the effects are extrapolated in speculative fiction.

My discussions in this book, then, have a consistent focus on imaginative responses to both fluctuating and static images of the Arctic. To readers with an already active interest in and knowledge about the actual Arctic, I hope to establish how speculative fiction contributes specific imaginings that in different ways engage with Arctic discourses, that is, how works in the wide genre in particular ways respond to expectations and add new Arctics to the textual tradition. To readers of speculative fiction, I hope to illuminate the specific function the Arctic fills, and how the historical, ideological, and cultural complexities of the vast region productively, but sometimes also problematically, are woven into works. From the starting point in Shelley's *Frankenstein*, where the Arctic is the only place fit for the telling of the fantastic tale, to contemporary works that engage with the vast ramifications of anthropogenic climate change, the ways in which the Arctic is imagined or what function it is made to serve illuminate wider lines of inquiry informing the way we envision the world and humanity's place and purpose in it.

Frames and Contexts

What most readers come away with from *Frankenstein* is the tale of hubristic creation and the Creature's revenge on its maker, but the frame story has received increasing attention in recent debates around effects of anthropogenic climate change; echoes of Victor's and Walton's parallel attempts "to penetrate ground that seems unredeemably dead, searching for a core of vital warmth unseen before" (Griffin 59) resound in works depicting how human impact and exploitation have altered the world in geologically salient ways. The Arctic frames the story of life created from dead matter, creating a particular vantage point from which to gauge the varying levels of speculation in Shelley's novel, and my readings of Arctic speculation more broadly are surrounded and sustained by critical works that provide context and traction. The scholarship around Shelley's text is vast, helping me to illuminate its connections to science and exploration, and informing my analyses of monstrosity in particular, but discussions by Beth Newman, Andrew Griffin, and Spufford are especially helpful for teasing out the precise function of the frame story.

Newman places *Frankenstein* besides Joseph Conrad's *Heart of Darkness*, arguing that similarities regarding the narrative format make the reading of both like "peeling an onion" (144). In *Heart of Darkness*, the unnamed narrator listens to Marlow aboard *Nellie* on the Thames, its waters "crowded with memories of men and ships," among them Franklin, *Erebus*, and *Terror* (Conrad 4), and relays the story that plays out along the Congo River. Walton's letters in Shelley's novel turn into a written-down account of Victor Frankenstein's story, itself including the Creature's account of experiences with the DeLacey family, and then returns to the epistolary format. In analyses of the links between the works, Newman maintains that Conrad's novella "makes meaning something that happens on the margins, along the edges of a narrative, as much as something that

we discover within it" (141), and Walton's narration, made in a geographical margin, is "addressed to someone absent from the narrative situation,
someone removed in time and place" (144). Griffin similarly works with
two texts, investigating the role of ice and fire in *Frankenstein* and Charlotte
Brontë's *Jane Eyre*, demonstrating how in the former, the Creature's initial linkage to fire is inexorably turned into a strong connection with ice,
established as the focal element via the frame story, and finally to a "syn-
thesis of both in his dramatic suicide-by-fire at the North Pole" (51).[6]
Walton's letters in this way establish that the narrative both begins and will
end in the icy Arctic. To Spufford, "the outer rind of *Frankenstein*" importantly sets up the similarities between Walton and Victor Frankenstein, specifically their adherence to " 'Promethean science', the period's heady sense
that the powers of nature might be appropriated for humanity" (59), and
the differences in how they are penalized for overstepping bounds: death
in Frankenstein's case, failure to conquer the Arctic in Walton's. Although
Walton might be "only an extra in the main drama of the book," these
parallels and divergences are significant, Spufford argues, to identify the
broader ramifications of pronouncedly male science and the importance of
the northern periphery as an antithesis of a feminine-coded "warmth of a
home" (60). All three critics thus draw attention to how the Arctic of the
frame story is used to establish a sense of Otherness, a geographical reflection of the strangeness of the story within it.

From these responses to *Frankenstein*'s narrative frame, I now move
into acknowledgments of how other critical works frame and accompany
my own discussions. How the Arctic has been represented in British documentary and literary works is well-trodden ground but moving beyond
the common temporal focus on the nineteenth century, Spufford's *I May
Be Some Time: Ice and The English Imagination* effectively outlines
"exploration's imaginative history" (8).[7] *Jane Eyre* fills a slightly different
function here than in Griffin's discussions: it is instrumental in a charting of
how images of the Arctic were disseminated to a wider public.[8] The course
runs through "a factual appendix:" Captain Edward Sabine's account
of Greenland birds, appropriated and expanded by Thomas Bewick in
History of British Birds, which then migrates into "the collective consciousness of an age, via a famous novel" (8). Through Jane Eyre's perusal
of Bewick, the reader encounters images of Arctic locations—an "epic roll-
call of the coldest and loneliest places on earth, in all their frigid glamor"
(Griffin 50)—and of how these transform in a child's mind. Between a
cold windowpane and the curtain she draws around her, Jane forms her
own images of "death-white realms" and they make her "happy at least in
[her] own way" (Brontë 6, 7). The speculative potential of Bewick's work
is underlined by Jane's interpretation of the illustrations; they limn, to her,
"marine phantoms," "object[s] of terror," and "mysterious" happenings

(6). Although this scene represents but a detail in Spufford's comprehensive account, it contributes to establishing how polar exploration "became a subject for debate, a resource for metaphor and slang, and a powerful mobiliser of emotion . . . . signs that a domain had been found for it *in here* as well as *out there*" (46, 47). Although Spufford's focus is on how the cultural landscape of Britain is impacted by polar discourses (and vice versa), his analysis of the imaginative preoccupation with the Arctic resonates more broadly.

The migration from periphery to center—the out there moving in here—can be productively understood against considerations of how the Arctic in the fictions in my sample lies to the side of more stable constructions of place. Siobhan Carroll's discussion about atopias in *An Empire of Air and Water* provides a fruitful model through which to understand its function. With a focus on the time period 1750–1850, Carroll involves an array of fictions in examinations of atopias defined as " 'real' natural regions . . . which, because of their intangibility, inhospitality, or inaccessibility, cannot be converted into the locations of affective habitation known as 'place' " (6). While atopias such as the polar regions are reachable and real, they are situated in both literal and figurative peripheries, producing a difference in relation to the stability of home. They abut but also contrast to the familiar and as such are eminently suited to speculation. Not available for direct colonization, the Arctic cannot be incorporated into the British empire (nor in other constructions of state) and the visitor's impact is transitory and impermanent; as Carroll notes in connection with both poles, they have "a disconcerting tendency to reassert" themselves and remove signs of conquest (20). The unstable location that the Arctic constitutes needs to be translated to make sense, and both travelogues and fiction perform this work—like Spufford, Carroll draws attention to how ideas about the Arctic move from outside to inside without fully transforming atopia to permanently livable place.

Similarities between the polar atopias are noted also by Elisabeth Leane, who carefully delineates imaginative constructions of the far south in *Antarctica in Fiction*. She takes an interest also in texts that have a seemingly weak connection to place. "Even—perhaps especially—when Antarctica seems marginal to a literary text," she argues, "it is worth exploring the meanings (themselves the accumulated product of previous representations) that the continent brings to the text, and the meanings that are in turn bestowed upon the far southern regions by each new literary context" (5). These layers of meanings and previous representations often overlap with those produced in connection with the Arctic and are illuminated when Leane moves into considerations of speculative fiction. Fantasies of the extraction of great riches, the discovery of forgotten civilizations or entrances to subterranean worlds, the polar area as a repository of the past, and anxieties concerning ecological changes are remarkably similar, regardless if you are looking north or south.[9] Both Antarctica and the Arctic have become increasingly accessible both literally and figuratively, opening, Leane suggests, for a cultural turn that diversifies perceptions.

In examinations of responses to and depictions of contemporary environmental collapse, Astrid Bracke examines postmillennial fictions clustering into four "narratives" that in various ways "reflect [an] awareness of climate crisis and participate in the construction and renegotiation of the stories that surround it" (1). Where Bracke in the econarratological approach in *Climate Crisis* focuses on "the polar" as one of the narratives that relay and construct stories around accelerated warming, I have the Arctic as the common denominator (the narrative) and address climate change as one of the discourses speculative fiction draws from and contributes to. There are thus methodological affinities between our projects and productive overlaps in approaches to environmental upheavals and the role the Arctic plays. Bracke's emphasis is on fiction that is not overtly connected to the central topic of climate change but that nevertheless "participates in a reconceptualization of climate crisis discourses" (6). As this crisis now permeates debates, social, economic, and cultural changes follow in its wake, and climate change is reflected in a number of other processes connected to human existence. Like both Leane and Bracke, I examine texts that sometimes are only tenuously linked to the Arctic, but nevertheless tease out what the Arctic means and how it functions in stories about monstrosity, romance, discovery, and melting polar ice.

I share with Shane McCorristine an interest in "constructions of the Arctic as a strange and spectral place" (9) and his recent *The Spectral Arctic* has as its focal point the disappearance of the 1845 Franklin expedition—its two ships HMS *Erebus* and HMS *Terror* and 129 men—and the imprint it made on its contemporaneity, on ensuing rescue operations, but also on authors attracted to the lack of closure today. Clairvoyants, mesmerists, and ghosts played important roles not only in the actual search for the missing expedition, but in how images of the Arctic were disseminated by thitherto excluded demographics (many of the clairvoyants were working-class women) and circulated among new groups in British society. McCorristine's careful readings of what has previously been regarded as ephemeral narratives illustrate "a gradual breakdown in cultural authority over the Arctic" (29), so that explorers' renderings of both landscapes and what they saw as required characteristics to survive and succeed come to coexist with stories by people who, importantly, had never been to the Arctic. The departure of *Erebus* and *Terror* is a pivotal moment in the history of British, naval exploration, and the expedition's disappearance is a pivotal moment for the imagination. Even though criticized, questioned, and negotiated, the last Franklin expedition features crucially into both real and imaginary forays into the Arctic.[10] Also in my sample, the fate of this expedition reverberates, and authors invent both fantastical adventures for survivors and answers to what befell them in the ice. But the discourses which the Franklin expedition is part of, and some which it originates, are so intimately connected to the Arctic that brief references crop up also in novels with no connection to exploration history. In Sarah Moss' *Cold Earth*, for example, which centers on a small group of archeologists in Western Greenland, one character disconcertingly ponders "how the Franklin survivors cooked their colleagues" (255), thus referencing evidence that the lost expedition was forced to resort to cannibalism. Images of the heroic explorer are often modeled on Franklin or his second-in-command Francis Crozier, and the science and practices of expeditions broadly, such as notations of latitudes and longitudes, the taking of measurements and samples, and processes of naming "conquered" lands, are incorporated also in widely speculative fictions. Longstanding ideas of the open polar sea that underlie many expeditions both pre- and postdating Franklin's are fertile for the imaginings of lost continents or cultures, discovered by the fictive explorer, and sometimes it is the very idea of exploration that constitutes a pull; the protagonist in Paver's *Dark Matter*, for example, refers to both Roald Amundsen and Ernest Shackleton as role models in his search for his lost masculinity and a sense of immediacy.

The imaginative history of exploration, the perception of the Arctic as atopia and as narrative, underline how the area is constructed by what Ryall, Schimanski, and Wærp identify as particular Arctic discourses that "overlap and intersect" (xi). These mobile spheres of meaning influence and design different aspects of works and "Arctic discourses and literary discourses . . . join to create texts and forms in which the literary becomes the Arctic or the other way around." Especially in periods when little is known about the world's far north, the literary discourse, as broadly signifying imagination, takes precedence, but also in more recent times, fiction can "make peculiarly visible the gap between the empirical experience of location and the mental exercises that invest sites with meaning" (Carroll, *Empire* 12). Although *Frankenstein* is a consistent presence in critical work on the literary Arctic and part of discourses around exploration, science, transgressions, and punishment, the specific affordances of speculative fiction remain to be comprehensively mapped.

The Speculative Spectrum

The Arctic harbors a host of contradictions and impossibilities that invite speculation. The cold and ice are in both literal and figurative ways seen as arresting development, while, conversely, rapidly rising temperatures cause the quickest and most serious alterations in the Arctic. Fantasies of circumpolar lands give way to ideas of the open polar sea; anything is more exciting for the imagination than the ice that is covering the Highest Arctic. The region, Sara Wheeler maintains, "attracts fiction to its facts with remorseless zeal" (18), a fusion of the real with the imagined seen already in the earliest stories and reports. Similarly, Carroll' study of eighteenth- and nineteenth-century texts shows that in writings on the Arctic broadly—by past and contemporary visitors as well as critics— the area emerges as "a geo-imaginary region where the line between fact and fiction often appeared hopelessly blurred" (*Empire* 22). In Carroll's discussions, speculation connotes risky monetary ventures and imagined geographies, but she remarks on the "genealogical link between polar texts and the spaces depicted by 'speculative fiction' in the twenty-first century." The intertwining of meanings of speculation as they appear in the Arctic context conjures up particular imaginative responses: it is, I argue, in speculative fiction, that the extremes and paradoxes of the Arctic are most effectively depicted as works are consistently linked to real conditions and concerns but stretch and manipulate this link in various ways. The perceived stasis gives rise to stories about ancient species slumbering in the permafrost and place-bound ghosts, whereas melting ice makes the area a useful starting point or main setting in speculative climate fiction or (post) apocalyptic narratives. The blank space of the Arctic as well as peculiarities connected to specific localities and landscapes lend themselves to fantasies about what hovers between known and unknown.

I designate all the selected primary sources, very briefly introduced in this section, as speculative fiction, but it should be noted that the definition that I start from has a fairly recent history, developing as a response to the perceived limitations and prescriptions connected to the genres of science fiction and fantasy in particular. Rather than a genre, speculative fiction is, in Oziewicz's effective overview, better understood as "a fuzzy set field of cultural production" in which texts in different media are grouped together by thematic resemblances rather than by adherence to strict categorizations. The inclusive term has since around 2000 come "to refer to the entire field in ways that challenge the dominant consensus about fault lines among various non-mimetic genres, canonical and upstart alike." Speculative fiction consequently evades entrenched views about categorizations and instead embraces both genre hybrids and works whose representations are only incrementally removed from the world as we know it. Also helpful is the earlier definition by R. B. Gill in which speculative fiction embraces "works presenting modes of being that contrast with their audiences' understanding of ordinary reality [with] key emphasis . . . on speculative representation of what would happen had the actual chain of causes or the matrix of reality-conditions been replaced with other conditions" (73).

These broad definitions are advantageous when examining how the Arctic as a real-world place functions in non-mimetic fiction and are suited for approaches to themes and discourses. Oziewicz's stress on "resist[ance to] stratification . . . especially rankings from masterpieces to failures and the pitting of genre fiction against literary fiction" also means a foregrounding of "the system of relations within the field rather than [of] individual works themselves." In my project, this means that award-winning novels are set next to pulp short stories, and that works that would traditionally be seen as belonging to the genres of horror and science fiction are placed along-side examples of romance and climate fiction. Rather than tracing chrono-logical lines of thoughts, each section in the chapters revolves around an aspect coming to the fore in writings about the Arctic: an event, issue, or a question that speculative fiction can help address, complicate, or answer.

To exemplify: in Chapter 1, I group three narratives together that respond to the disappearance of the last Franklin expedition. The selected texts not only illustrate the breadth of the large body of works published in the aftermath of the disappearance but also engage with the gaps in explor-ation history in very different ways. In the pseudonymously authored nov-ella, "The Extraordinary and All-Absorbing Journal of Wm. N. Seldon" (1851), three crewmembers leave an optimistic Franklin; he is hypothesized as being alive and well off the routes of rescue operations, and the men can pursue romantic adventures away from the frozen-in ships. Dan Simmons' *The Terror* (2006), which would traditionally be categorized as horror, introduces a monstrous being that systematically hunts and kills the crew, thus explaining their disappearance. And sections from Ed O'Loughlin's post-modern *Minds of Winter* (2016) extrapolate ideas that Crozier survives the ordeal without distancing the narrative too far from known history. From the common denominator—the vanishing of the expedition—the authors take inspiration from a number of sources and discourses, par-ticular to the time of writing and to the purpose of their texts. When seen together, they illustrate how the field of speculative fiction performs spe-cific cultural work in filling the silences and gaps in documented history. Each of these texts also returns in my discussions of other salient aspects in writings about the Arctic: I use the novella in a discussion about discovered civilizations in the Arctic, *The Terror* in analyses of both monsters and representations of Indigenous beliefs, and chapters from *Minds of Winter* both in my examinations of ghosts and in concluding remarks about strat-egies employed when writing the Arctic.

The distinct forms or modes of these examples, and the different discourses they are inspired by and contribute to mean that they illustrate varying levels of speculation. In analyses of processes of "subcreation"—J. R. R. Tolkien's term for an author's construction of a fictional world—Mark J. P. Wolf suggests that aspects of texts can be placed along a spectrum of speculation in which "the 'secondariness' of a story's world . . . becomes a matter of degree, varying with the strength of the connection to the Primary World" (25).[11] The idea of a speculative spectrum is helpful not only to address works' variously strong ties to Primary World discourses but also for purposes of delimitation and clarity. At the furthest speculative end of Wolf's spectrum are works that in a genre context are defined as High Fantasy, depicting a fictional world with no ties to Primary World events, people, or locations. In her proposed taxonomy of fantasy, Farah Mendlesohn's category "immersive fantasy" is aligned with Wolf's radical secondariness; works within this category present cohesive fictional worlds in which fantastic elements are unquestioned and unexplained (59–113). Since representations of the Primary World Arctic are the reason behind my own selection, none of the works I discuss can be designated as pure fantasy: the speculative spectrum employed is slightly narrower. This does not, however, mean that the depicted Arctic is not in itself speculative: the inherent Otherness of the region, as noted, constitutes a pull on authors' imaginations and is manipulated to different ends. Along with other elements, the Arctic can also assume a fluctuating position on the speculative spectrum, commonly starting off positioned close to the Primary World, and ending up (temporarily or permanently) with very weak ties to it.

The degrees of secondariness in my material can further be usefully understood via affinities with other taxonomies such as Tzvetan Todorov's delineations of the fantastic, the marvelous, and the uncanny. In a departure from what is normally understood by fantasy and the fantastic, Todorov's usage targets works that present a recognizable world in which magic or the supernatural intrude. "In a world which is indeed our world, the one we know" he explains, "there occurs an event which cannot be explained by the laws of this same familiar world" (25). The character who experiences the intrusion and effects of the inexplicable, and importantly also the reader, must decide on an explanation, pushed towards either a marvelous or an uncanny solution. In the marvelous mode, the supernatural or magical turns out to be an integral part of the fictional world, confirmed by the narrative itself, and in the uncanny, the supernatural is commonly revealed to have psychological explanations such as characters' dreams or hallucinations. The fantastic is experienced as a moment of hesitation between belief and disbelief in the supernatural and "it may evaporate at any moment," Todorov argues (41). The fantastic hesitation experienced by the reader and by the character(s) accordingly ends when the supernatural event is decided to have a marvelous or uncanny explanation, yet some texts "sustain their ambiguity . . . even beyond the narrative itself" (43). In her engagement with and expansion of Todorov's taxonomy, Rosemary Jackson thus concludes that "the purely fantastic text establishes absolute hesitation in protagonist and reader: they can neither come to terms with the unfamiliar events described, nor dismiss them as supernatural phenomena" (27). In my sample, Arctic locations and conditions combine with the particular situatedness of characters to produce, in both characters and readers, this ambiguity, this inability to either reconcile or dismiss the inexplicable. John Burnside's *A Summer of Drowning* (2011) and Eowyn Ivey's *The Snow Child* (2012) are particularly effective examples, but the Otherness of the Arctic—in details as well as more broadly—evokes the possibility of the fantastic in other works as well.

In my discussions, a Todorovian radically uncanny explanation is commonly less relevant than a marvelous or a fantastic since it negates the representation of an actual Arctic within the narrative. Anna Adolph's 1899 novel *Arqtiq: A Story of the Marvels at the North Pole* is not considered, for example. Its speculation includes a civilization at the North Pole inhabited by a telepathic and gender-equal people, but the narrator wakes up at the end of the narrative, revealing that the encountered strangeness has been "a dream" or possibly "a grand inspiration" for a future adventure (Adolph 79). The Arctic in this novel remains a dreamed-up concept: "the laws of the world . . . remain what they are" (Todorov 25). In my sample texts it can sometimes be debated whether recounted experiences manifest anxieties of a troubled mind, but I am in these cases concerned with dreams dreamt in the Arctic, or with disturbances produced by specifically Arctic conditions. Ghost stories often invite a reading of effects of hauntings as uncanny, for example in Paver's *Dark Matter* (2010) in which the protagonist's nerves fray because he is all alone in the Svalbard autumn dark. In Arthur Conan Doyle's "The Captain of the 'Pole Star'" (1883) and Moss' *Cold Earth* (2009), ghosts predominantly haunt one character, but effects of the supernatural appearance increasingly influence a wider group, and in Yrsa Sigurðardóttir's *I Remember You* (*Ég man þig* 2012), a group of visitors to an isolated part of Iceland jointly come to the realization that the place is haunted. In these instances, ghosts cannot as easily be explained by the strain on the individual character's psyche but manifest in ways that push speculation further, ending in a possibly marvelous explanation.

Marvelous beings, confirmed by the story as supernatural, appear after journeys into the Arctic in my sample fictions. Among them are Algernon Blackwood's titular creature in "The Wendigo" (1917), Stefan Spjut's trolls in *Stallo* (2012), and Adam Nevill's old god in *The Ritual* (2011). Beings like these, but also the human doubles in Bracken McLeod's *Stranded* (2016), exceed the physical or existential laws of the Primary World and leave concrete traces in the fictional world, at least in its northern periphery. Equally disturbing to the fabric of reality as marvelous monsters are narratives that extrapolate contemporary climate change in apocalyptic or postapocalyptic future visions. These scenarios are represented by Marcel Theroux's *Far*

North (2009), Lily Brooks-Dalton's *Good Morning, Midnight* (2016), and, again, Moss' *Cold Earth*. Respectively, the end of humanity is represented gradually, suddenly, and ambiguously, and in all three novels, the Arctic "on the rind of civilization" (Brooks-Dalton 5) functions as a last outpost. Among other radically speculative imaginings are the material fusings of human and animal minds in Sam J. Miller's *Blackfish City* (2018) and Vicki Jarrett's *Always North* (2019): novels that illustrate affordances of speculative fiction when envisioning new approaches to and new linkages between the categories of human and other-than-human.

Novels grouped around time-specific hypotheses, science, and climate change illustrate gradients in the level of speculation. Late nineteenth- and early twentieth-century narratives in which authors engage with the idea of the open polar sea can lie relatively close to the Primary World end of the speculative spectrum. The main speculative element in Verne's *The Voyages and Adventures of Captain Hatteras* (*Voyages et aventures du capitaine Hatteras* 1866), for example, is that the feat of claiming the North Pole leaves permanent traces in the novel's approximation of the Primary World. Pushing speculation further, Robert Ames Bennet's *Thyra: A Romance of the Polar Pit* (1901) and Vidar Berge's *Den hemlighetsfulla nordpolsön* (1902; in my translation *The Mysterious North Pole Island*) envision successful ends to disastrous Primary World expeditions by letting their fictive travelers discover forgotten lands and lost civilizations around the North Pole. In Mary E. Bradley Lane's *Mizora* (1880–81) and William Bradshaw's *The Goddess of Atvatabar* (1892), action moves underground, to societies that are ideal, respectively because of politics or opulence. In these lost-civilization novels, representations of the Arctic cleave to discourses highlighting barrenness and hostility; atopic spaces that need to be quickly traversed in order for the discovery to be made and the real adventure to commence. Regardless of the level of speculation, the cultural work performed by these novels fills what is perceived of as empty space with meaning and provides an alternative geography for the high latitudes.

Specific Arctic conditions set the stage for seemingly scientifically supported contemporary speculation in novels in which humans, animals, or pathogens survive impossible conditions or (re)appear as the polar ice melts. In Juris Jurjevics' *The Trudeau Vector* (2005) deadly algae are thawed and used to protect the isolation of an Arctic research station, whereas pathogens of the 1918–19 influenza pandemic survive in the permafrost in Robert Masello's *The Romanov Cross* (2013). James Rollins imagines how ancient mammal/amphibian hybrids lying dormant in the ice are awakened by the activities of scientists in *Ice Hunt* (2010). Although the joint starting point for these novels is the preserving abilities of ice and cold, the effects of thaws spread them out across the speculative spectrum: algae and viruses survive in dormant states in the Arctic also in the Primary World, with accelerated warming threatening to release them, whereas Rollins' grendels require a more committed suspension of disbelief.

Climate change is foregrounded in several of the contemporary texts in my sample and imagined developments in the Arctic illustrate extrapolations to various degrees of today's situation. On the speculative spectrum closest to the Primary World end, Laline Paull's *The Ice* (2017) depicts a very-near future and features small details that set the fictional world off from the real. The "what if?" explored in this kind of text is thus reliant on a small temporal shift as it focuses on a scenario of polar ice caps melting only slightly ahead of predictions. Tobias Buckell sets his novel *Arctic Rising* (2012) in 2050 and imagines new global power structures following the complete disappearance of Arctic ice; in his acknowledgments, Buckell hopes that the book will be published "before [his] 'science-fictional' plot idea . . . isn't quite so shocking" (339). A more dystopic view is found in Emmi Itäranta's *Memory of Water (Teemestarin kirja* 2014) in which Arctic Finland has transformed into a hot, moist, and bug-infested place where each day means a struggle for access to fresh water.[12] The varying futurities in these novels are combined with characters' attachment to the Arctic: the Arctic as a temporarily visited space or as a home to which there are deep emotional ties influence attitudes to climate change and the agency to combat it.

The Arctic is thus the constant in my meanderings through depictions of a warming or dying planet, of spaces for conquest and adventure, of ghosts, monsters, and improbable romance. In the majority of the works, there is a trajectory starting in approximations of the author's Primary World and moving to the Arctic, and the speculation and secondariness that increase by every degree north the fictional travelers move requires adaptation. In a few examples—the novels by Burnside, Spjut, Theroux, Itäranta, and Miller; in Michel Faber's "The Fahrenheit Twins" (2015) which I discuss as exemplifying speculative indigeneity—the Arctic is a place of belonging which forms characters' identities, but these Arctics are either epistemologically or climatologically unstable, necessitating further change. The imagined Arctic is thus a construction also to characters that call it home.

A brief look at formulations around various local Gothics helps illustrate the speculative potential of northern places and spaces more broadly and how discussions about the uncanny, slightly differently conceptualized than in Todorov's taxonomy, zero in on "disturbing, vacuous area[s]" (Jackson 63). Be these areas figurative or literal, they have particular bearing on how atopic space transforms (or not) into place. Cynthia Sugars describes the first stages in the search for and formation of a Canadian national identity as "a haunting by an absence of haunting" (15), but develops how a Romantic, European Gothic enters the Canadian imagination, populating it with old fears which need to be negotiated and inflected to accommodate the challenges and affordances that were always already there. Yvonne Leffler and Johan Höglund note a late nineteenth-century emergence of a particular Nordic Gothic with strong ties between the supernatural and local landscapes and a rather late, but effective, turn towards the Arctic in Nordic twentieth-century fiction (18). In previous formulations about Scandinavian Gothic, Leffler foreshadows the centrality of the environment, arguing that "[t]he mind" of characters in Gothic fiction "is invaded and taken-over by the Nordic landscape and the wilderness" ("Gothic Topography" 49). With focus on visual narratives, Lorna Piatti-Farnell identifies a specific Arctic Gothic in which "the landscape [functions] as a Gothicised agent of fear and dread . . . also through its connections to folklore, memory and historical hauntings" (77), and Anita Lam notes how the traditionally separated Gothic affects of "horror and terror can metamorphose into each other" when narratives are set "in the frigid cold of an inhospitable Arctic environment" (191); both existential and corporeal sources of fear combine. The Arctic landscape is in these latter formulations an agent setting specific processes in motion; processes I see also in works with stronger ties to the Primary World.

The polar atopias are also connected via Gothic imagery. Katherine Bowers notes an extension of the Arctic Sublime in nineteenth-century fiction in which the poles share a "disorientating alien quality" as their size and perceived antagonism test the resilience and abilities "of the so-called civilised mind" (72). Writers of Polar Gothic—Bowers' examples are Samuel Taylor Coleridge, Shelley, and Edgar Allan Poe—are joined by how they depict "ice [as] a negative space, which gives rise to supernatural beings that reflect the self: the albatross, Frankenstein's creature, the Polar Spirit." Also using Coleridge and Poe as examples and with a starting point in Julia Kristeva's notion of the abject, Leane finds the Antarctic Gothic in narratives set "on the edge of established social conventions," which include depictions of sublimity challenging "the rational mind," and recurring motifs of "the monstrous, the infernal, the Satanic" (59). In Poe's *The Narrative of Arthur Gordon Pym of Nantucket*, William Lenz notes, the Antarctic Gothic presents a "reversed world" where life may be death and death life; "a region from which there can be no verifiable report, a purely imaginative realm of symbol, supposition, and superstition" (35) in which the individual can only confront and scrutinize him- or herself. The imagined Antarctica becomes "a stimulus to new perceptions" (37). Although a distinction sometimes needs to be made between Arctic and Antarctic Gothic due to the difference between populated and unpopulated landscapes, and although the far south "is metaphorically and literally the underside of the world" which makes it more apt to function "as the world's subconscious, harbouring our deepest fears" (Leane

19), processes of filling figuratively vacuous areas with meaning intersect, and representations of polar spaces align. Also in speculative fiction about the world's far north, there are imagined entrances to actual or symbolic underworlds, consistent challenges to visitors' rationality and thereby their tales, and a resistance emanating from the landscape that makes it productively difficult to categorize. Repressed or subconscious fears are brought to the surface also in the Arctic, and monsters prowl the icescape: the far north too brings needed stimulation to the Gothic imagination.

When the geographical scope is abandoned, elements of the Gothic find their way into fields such as eco-gothic and globalgothic. Work within the former identifies "an ecologically aware Gothic" (Smith and Hughes 1) which, like the national variants, can be traced back to Romanticism and its preoccupation with often troubled relationships between humans and nature, but also looks forward to how ecocriticism's focus on place can benefit re-readings of traditional Gothic works. The contracted term globalgothic "mark[s] the confluence, in globalised space, between divergent cultural traditions" (Byron 4), and Fred Botting and Justin D. Edwards note how large-scale events, among them terrorism and climate change, have eroded not only previous paradigms of power, but differences between center and periphery. "Gothic conventions situate terror as happening 'out there'" they maintain, "its position is elsewhere, outside the self, something that takes place away from the security of the homely [but] binary models of terror and proximity" no longer hold (21). From terrors and horrors in confined Gothic locations, befalling a limited cast of characters, the tropes that now return in familiar guises signal unsettling changes that have a global effect.

As a field of cultural production, then, speculative fiction is becoming increasingly important when addressing immediate concerns and heterogeneity; as Oziewicz remarks, "non-mimetic genres may be potentially more adequate than the so-called realist literature to address contemporary global challenges and [highlight] diverse perspectives, traditions, and experiences." With effects of climate change training the eye on the Arctic, and as debates around future northern cultural, economic, and environmental sustainability intensify, there is a need for a deepened understanding of the discourses that have constructed and are constructing the Arctic. A careful mapping and serious consideration of both past and contemporary speculative visions is thus warranted to understand the role the Arctic has played and may come to play in a diverse set of practices and domains.

In the first chapter, I examine the Arctic as a site of alternatives: to history, with emphasis on the disappearance of the 1845 Franklin expedition, to geography, in texts that present the area around or beneath the North Pole as home to lost civilizations, and to ontology in novels that trouble the boundaries between real and imagined. I am broadly concerned with the peripheral position of the Arctic and with possibilities opened up by discourses of both figurative and literal instability. In Chapter 2, focus is on how the Arctic becomes an actual or symbolic repository for the past. Firstly, I address narratives in which ghosts in particular ways are tied to or produced by place, paying special attention to how the Arctic enables or hinders the specters' visibility and legibility. Secondly, I investigate the function of peripheral but manifest Arctic monsters teasing out how the Arctic produces or harbors these marvelous entities, and how the monstrous presence affects the Arctic. Thirdly, I discuss pseudoscientific novels in which the melting ice brings pathogens as well as hibernating beasts back to life. Another function of melting ice is foregrounded in the environmental focus of the third chapter. I look at texts that envision temporally close or distant human-driven climate change, investigating how the Arctic oscillates between being perceived as atopic space and affectively connoted place, and how this fluctuation impacts attitudes to the environmental degradation. I also examine depictions of more-than-human entanglements, which find a specific form in the Arctic, and discuss the affordances of speculative fiction in general when thinking through and establishing new paradigms for human thought and behavior. Melting Arctic ice leading to a flooded planet is complemented with other forms of secular apocalypse, and I investigate how authors imagine the end in the Arctic, or the end starting in the Arctic. My focus is throughout on how speculative Arctics contribute to a vast, multifaceted construction, but it is, importantly, also a construction to characters (Indigenous or later settlers) who call the Arctic home. Negotiations of this construction are highlighted in the concluding chapter where I also draw out linkages between discourses and time periods, exploring strategies employed in both imagining and writing the Arctic.

I address, then, two centuries of speculative fiction set in the Arctic, the selection bookended by Shelley's *Frankenstein* and Jarrett's *Always North*, respectively concerned with the promethean and protean sciences of appropriating knowledge and transforming matter (organic and geological). Although there is a consistent engagement with the Arctic in the nineteenth century, reflecting intense polar exploration, speculative fictions cluster around the turn of the century. Twentieth-century novels set in the Arctic, influenced by the region's strategic military location, are more commonly found in the war, spy, and thriller genres and are not overtly speculative.[13] The speculative genre of science fiction rather develops in the twentieth century in magazines of the pulp variety. To map all the short stories with connections to the Arctic in publications such as *Amazing Stories*, *Astounding Stories*, *Wonder Stories*, and *Startling Stories* is a project in itself, but texts briefly alluded to in my discussions, published between the 1920s and the 1970s, illustrate that themes and motifs from previous time periods continue to circulate, among them the journey north in quests for lost civilizations, or prefigure later foci such as epidemics starting in the far north and the threat of meting polar ice caps. In the last few decades, there has been a return to the Arctic in speculative fiction, coinciding with a heightened interest in the area generally, but specifically with how the Arctic threatens to become a ghost itself due to climate change. Moving from peripheral to central, the valuable but vulnerable area becomes of global import, and authors take contemporary environmental changes as a starting point for discussions about species extinction (or revival), the collapse (or construction) of societies, or the end (or beginning) of the world.

Notes

1 References to Shelley's novel will henceforth be to the 1831 edition.
2 All formatting in quotations corresponds to the original.
3 Or, as Lopez puts it, "part of the allure of the Arctic has always been the very imprecision of its borders" (282).
4 Fredriksen's observation connects to broader implications of designating works as speculative: what makes a work speculative from the European and North American perspective I employ may resonate very differently with Indigenous readers. Simultaneously, perceptions of time, apocalypse, and first contacts in many Indigenous worldviews may make them appear immediately speculative in the eyes of the outside reader. Grace L. Dillon exemplifies how "[n]ative slip-stream" while seemingly speculative in depictions of "time travel, alternate realities and multiverses," regularly features in fictions by Indigenous authors but importantly "models a cultural experience of reality" (3, 4). Potawatomi scholar Kyle P. Whyte, similarly, draws attention to how Indigenous concepts of time may read as speculative without being so; rather "spiraling time" that imagines the present coexisting with the past (ancestors) and the future (descendants) is particularly apt to address questions of accountability and action (229).
5 Impacting early maps of the far north, little evidence exists of the fourteenth-century *Inventio Fortunata* as the text in which it is summarized (Cnoyen's *Itinerarium*) is similarly lost. A letter from cartographer Gerardus Mercator to the astronomer John Dee, dated April 20, 1577, includes one of very few references to and quotations from Cnoyen's summary. In a translated and annotated transcription of this letter by E. G. R. Taylor, is the following description: "In the midst of the four countries is a Whirl-pool . . . into which there empty these four Indrawing Seas which divide the North. And the water rushes round and descends into the earth just as if one were pouring it through a filter funnel. It is 4 degrees wide on every side of the Pole, that is to say eight degrees altogether. Except that right under the Pole there lies a bare rock in the midst of the Sea . . . . And nothing grows thereon, for there is not so much as a handful of soil on it" (60).

6 Jane Eyre's trajectory is the opposite, "moving unsteadily but with increasing control toward the proper use of fire" (Griffin 53).

7 Robert G. David's *The Arctic in the British Imagination, 1818–1914* (2000), and Jen Hill's *White Horizon: The Arctic in the Nineteenth-Century British Imagination* (2008) exemplify the interest in the period, and with primary sources such as school textbooks, advertisements, paintings, and news items (David) and fiction and poetry (Hill), both engage with the function of the Arctic in the context of British imperialism. Janice Cavell's *Tracing the Connected Narrative: Arctic Exploration in British Print Culture, 1818–1860* (2008) explores competing narratives of polar exploration in a vast array of texts, and Russell Potter carries out a similar analysis based on panoramas, art, and photography in *Arctic Spectacles: The Frozen North in Visual Culture, 1818–1875* (2007).

8 The main title of Spufford's book signals how central Robert Falcon Scott's walk to the South Pole 1911–1912 was to the cultural imagination. It illustrates the apex of a long history of polar obsession, and Lawrence Oates' last words before leaving the tent for the last time epitomize the unselfish heroism of the ideal.

9 Similarities confuse both artists and critics. Leane includes an illustration from William Kingston's *At the South Pole* (1870) in which members of a naval expedition are attacked by polar bears, and notes that critics have placed *Frankenstein* in Antarctica and John W. Campbell's novella "Who Goes There?" (1938) in the Arctic (13). I can add to these examples Jules Verne's inclusion of Arctic penguins (flying to boot) in *The Voyages and Adventures of Captain Hatteras* (1866, 397) and Johan Höglund's placement of the action in the Arctic in the adaptation of Campbell's novella in John Carpenter's horror film *The Thing* (126; both the 1982 film and its 2011 prequel are set in Antarctica, albeit filmed elsewhere).

10 Travel writers are joined by authors who imagine the Franklin disaster in fictionalized accounts, among them Gwendolyn MacEwen's verse play *Terror and Erebus* (1965), Robert Erdric's *The Broken Lands* (1992), William T. Vollman's *The Rifles* (1994), and Dominique Fortier's *On the Proper Use of Stars* (*Du bon usage des etoiles* 2008). John Wilson imagines the fate of cabin boy David Young aboard *Erebus* in *Across Frozen Seas* (1997), a novel directed towards a young adult audience, and both Andrea Barrett and Greer MacAllister envision the trials of rescue operations (male and female, respectively) in *The Voyage of the Narwhal* (1998) and *The Arctic Fury* (2021).

11 Tolkien's discussion is found in the essay "On Fairy Stories" (1947).

12 Itäranta wrote the English and Finnish versions of the novel simultaneously, and the novel is sometimes discussed as an example of Young Adult fiction.

13 Examples of war and thriller novels include Alistair MacLean's novels *HMS Ulysses* (1955), *Night Without End* (1959), *Ice Station Zebra* (1963), *Bear Island* (1971), and *Athabasca* (1980). Hammond Innes utilizes the glacial areas of Norway as a setting in *The Blue Ice* (1948), whereas Jack Higgins' *East of Desolation* (1968) takes place in Greenland. Clive Cussler places several of his

Dirk Pitt novels in an Arctic environment (*Ice Berg* 1975 and *Deep Six* 1984), and Desmond Bagley sets his spy thriller *Running Blind* (1970) in Iceland. Although elements such as newly invented weapons, imaginary agencies, and not yet realized modes of transport thread the line of realism, novels like these do not fall within my designation of speculative fiction.

1 Alternative Worlds and Histories

In the first letter to his sister Margaret Saville, sent from a wintry St Petersburg, Walton conveys his expectations of the area he is about to venture into, "never before visited . . . never before imprinted by the foot of man" (Shelley 16). The Russian December chilled by air coming down from the Arctic gives him a "foretaste of those icy climes" and produces passionate visions (15). However, he finds "that the pole [as] the seat of frost and desolation" is impossible to imagine; instead, the midnight sun that will shine over the landscape once he undertakes his journey in the spring and summer ought to transform it into a "region of beauty and delight" that tenders a promise of easy passage "to a land surpassing in wonders and in beauty every region hitherto discovered on the habitable globe" (15). It is not only beauty that is promised by this delightful Arctic but discoveries that will benefit humankind, such as the workings of the magnetic north, fuller understandings of the movements of heavenly bodies, and the identification of the Northwest Passage—"that fata morgana of Arctic navigation" (Holland and Huggan 101). This Arctic is revealed a fantasy, and Walton accomplishes none of the scientific feats. The open seas he has imagined are substituted with ice that immobilizes his ship and the possibility to see and observe is obscured by fog. Instead, of course, Walton's discovery consists of spotting Victor Frankenstein on the ice and his feat becomes relaying the story of life created from dead matter and the punishment that follows: wondrous enough it would seem.

Still, Walton's formulations gesture to imaginings of an Arctic where many things are thought possible because of the dearth of concrete information, or because information pointed in different, often irreconcilable, directions. I use these formulations about opportunities of being first, and about both expected and unexpected discoveries, as springboards in this chapter, in examinations of how the Arctic is figured as a site of alternatives and as a utopia in the original sense of the word: "the 'nowhere', the non-place [that] resides outside of history to extrapolate from it and comment

DOI: 10.4324/9781003355588-2

upon it" (Pfaelzer 284). An alternative, then, can be constituted by a small alteration of or addition to what is or was known about the Arctic that only incrementally adjusts the characters' and readers' perceptions, or by a complete reworking of Arctic space, such as is found in subterranean or lost-civilization novels.

In the first section, I discuss examples of how the 1845 Franklin expedition is reimagined when "history retires and fiction takes up the pen" as Henry Clay Fairman phrases it in the foreword to *The Third World* (6), a speculative novel that chronicles one survivor's discovery of the underground world of Polaria. As Jerome de Groot notes, history is inherently constructed as Other in relation to the familiar present, and the historical novel, like science fiction, builds on the reader's "interaction with a clearly unfamiliar set of landscapes, technologies and circumstances" (4). Alternative history, at focus in my discussions, is a speculative mode which pushes Otherness further.[1] Darko Suvin defines the genre "as that form of [science fiction] in which an alternative locus (in time, space, etc.) that shares the material and causal verisimilitude of the writer's world is used to articulate different possible solutions of societal problems" (149). The changes to the narrated world and history are in this formulation pervasive. Kathleen Singles similarly demonstrates how alternative histories pivot on a "point of divergence" from past events; they "feature a specific kind of deviation from historical record" that in radical works alter the course of history altogether (7). Singles' examples are Philip K. Dick's *The Man in the High Castle* (1962) which imagines a 1960s world in which Germany and Japan are superpowers following their victory in World War II, and, geographically closer to the discussion here, Michael Chabon's *The Yiddish Policemen's Union* (2007) that likewise depicts a different outcome of the war but revolves around the disintegration of Israel in 1948 and the emergence of a Jewish metropolis in Sitka, Alaska. While none of the texts I examine indicates that the known path of history changes, the authors embellish or subvert details in or aspects of history, affecting characters rather than prompting the reevaluation of the world and its structures.

In the second section I address nineteenth- and early twentieth-century texts that in various ways transform Arctic space. Moving from Jules Verne's *The Voyages and Adventures of Captain Hatteras*, which is a source of inspiration for many subsequent fictional forays into the Arctic, and which illustrates the interplay between known science and speculation, I turn to texts in which temperate lands and forgotten civilizations are hidden in or below the world's far north. The latter part of the nineteenth century and the beginning of the twentieth saw an abundance of such Hollow Earth and subterranean fictions and, as a result, an abundance of meanings.[2] In the US context, Nadia Khouri argues, the narratives appear as a reaction to fin-de-siècle capitalist society, highlighting "a tension between a primitive mode of accumulation and one of conspicuous consumption" (170). Examining the British market Bradley Deane notes that works "refigur[e] the frontier as an uncanny space in which the grand narrative of progress collapses to reveal a timeless model of imperial character" (206), and Elizabeth Hope Chang maintains that the "transatlantic" subgenre enables "pronounced attention to the operations of closed, near-planetary ecosystems" (388). The encountered culture is commonly opulent, with an abundance of precious metals and gems (not always recognized as assets by the inhabitants), it is lush and verdant in a drastic departure from the Arctic that surrounds and hides it, and although there are examples of civilizations that societally or culturally far surpass those in the Primary World, a common structure is one in which the visitors can conquer and colonize the lost world, or at least educate its inhabitants.

In the third section I interrogate how the Arctic in twenty-first-century novels becomes a stage for possible worlds or the double existence of reality and the supernatural. I approach Bracken MacLeod's *Stranded* with a starting point in cosmological theories applied in discussions about science fiction to account for simultaneously existing worlds and character doubles. Folklore and folktales play important parts in John Burnside's *A Summer of Drowning*, and Eowyn Ivey's *The Snow Child*. To varying degrees of explicitness, the authors test the limits of worlds by introducing the supernatural or inexplicable. The Arctic depicted in these novels is by no means unmapped, nor is it, in Burnside and Ivey, empty. Still, aspects of estrangement particular to the Arctic crucially contribute to blurred onto- logical and epistemological boundaries.

An Alternate Franklin Expedition

The fate of the last Franklin expedition has deeply engaged authors, and both realistic and speculative works fill the silence produced by the lack of concrete knowledge.[3] These indicate a will to imagine the everyday lives of the men and hypothesize about what caused their end beyond what is known from the sparse evidence that exists: only one document comprising two messages has been found. In 1859, William Hobson, a member of a rescue mission led by Francis Leopold McClintock and organized by Lady Jane Franklin, found this document at Victory Point on the northwestern coast of King William Island. The original message, written by Lieutenant Graham Gore on the standard form issued by the British Admiralty, tells of the wintering of *Terror* and *Erebus* at Beechy Island (although faultily noting the winter of 1846–47 instead of 1845–46), that Franklin is still in command and that all is well (McClintock 256). In a later message from April 1848, written in the margins of the same document, Captain James Fitzjames notes that the ships have been abandoned, that Franklin has died in June the previous year, and that 24 other crewmembers have likewise lost their lives. Almost as an afterthought, the expedition's second-in-command, Captain Francis Crozier has added "and start [on?] to-morrow, 26th, for Back's Fish River" (258).[4]

Even when the protracted silence and finds made suggested that success or even survival were unlikely, groups and individuals continued their search. "Franklin's presence in the Western imagination has *always* been a spectral one, even during the very period when search and rescue expeditions held out hope of locating him and his men alive," McCorristine notes ("The Supernatural Arctic" 62), and somewhat paradoxically, the discovery of three crewmen's bodies on Beechy Island in 1850 worked in an encouraging way. Appearing already in 1851, "The Extraordinary and All-Absorbing Journal of Wm. N. Seldon" exemplifies a narrativization of hope. The novella presents a number of details that ostensibly establish a factual content, such as a biography of Franklin which ends by mentioning rescue operations in 1848 and 1849 and a monetary award of 20 000 pounds that is collectable by anyone who is able to aid Franklin and his crew "and contribute directly to extricate them from the ice" (Seldon 10).[5] The novella imaginatively performs this extrication in the case of three American men, the eponymous Seldon, the tall and strong Jones and the pretty, young Wilson.[6] Compared to the paratextual biography and a short, anonymous introduction explaining that the narrative that follows "is in the handwriting of one of the three men" (Seldon 11), the journal has numerous formal mistakes and abbreviations that underscore the seeming authenticity of a document purporting to be written by a seaman.

The thrust of the narrative lies in the discovery of an unknown civilization, discussed in the next section of this chapter, and a few details only directly relate to the Primary World expedition. Already at the end of the journal's first paragraph, the men have reached the temperate land, but the reason they leave the ship, with "permission from Sir John," is to "find a pass for our vessel" (13). *Erebus* and *Terror* are locked in the ice at this point, but when the men are unable to find open leads in the water and attempt to return to the ships, the rest of the expedition is nowhere to be found. The novella does not, then, envisage the fate of the Franklin expedition broadly but shifts attention to men who are encouraged to go exploring the unknown region. Franklin features more concretely in the last paragraph when Seldon is back home in Michigan. It is then noted that "when we left Sir John Franklin, eight months ago, there was strong hopes of his soon getting free from the ice, and evidently a prospect of his finding out the north-west pass. He was gleeful and happy, as was also his adventurous crew" (36). The date and year are given as 15 December 1850. There is no mention of the location of *Erebus* and *Terror* when the three men leave, but apparently it is off the routes of the early rescue operations.

Franklin can thus be imagined as alive and well beyond the search area, and hope can remain for a successful end to the exploratory mission.

The expedition's disappearance is one of many Arctic mysteries in Ed O'Loughlin's *Minds of Winter*, and the novel's starting point is the Primary World puzzle of the Arnold 294, a chronometer that was listed as going north with *Terror* and *Erebus* in 1845 but found, "converted to a 'carriage clock'," at the Royal Observatory in 2009 (Potter 68). Although it is doubtful whether the object actually made the Arctic journey, O'Loughlin spins his tales around it, imagining ways in which it has traversed space and time, in the process forging links between a multitude of individuals, predominantly men, involved in Arctic and Antarctic expeditions. The intertwined stories start when Franklin is still Lieutenant-Governor of Van Diemen's Land in 1841 and move via rescue operations following the 1845 disappearance, Robert Falcon Scott's and Roald Amundsen's race to the South Pole, the fate of Inuit guide and translator Ipiirviq, to speculation around the identity of the man known as the Mad Trapper. Jack London makes an appearance in a story-within-the-story, telling polar adventurer Cecil Meares a tale about Arctic isolation and cannibalism. In the contemporary sections of the novel, O'Loughlin introduces his two purely fictional constructs: Fay Morgan and Nelson Nilsson who meet in Canada's Northwest Territories to investigate the fate of their family members. Like countless others before them, Fay's grandfather Hugh and Nelson's brother Bert have gone to the Arctic and disappeared.

Via the chronometer, time is a guiding element of the non-linear novel, highlighting larger contexts and connections as well as how the Arctic blurs temporalities. On board *Erebus* in Van Diemen's Land, Franklin's niece Sophia Cracroft thinks of Greenwich "where time was transubstantiated from the sky and consecrated in chronometers; [where] days were born and . . . returned to die" (O'Loughlin 37) and Fay has "a vision of clockwork, of wheels within wheels, the hint of bigger wheels lurking behind them" (299), suggesting inevitability and processes beyond human agency. The actual timepiece is also concretely worked into the narrative: Ipiirviq finds it among his wife Taqulittuq's belongings, and Fay sees it on the mantelpiece behind her grandparents in their wedding photo. It is suggested that Amundsen's *Gjøa* expedition returns it from King William Island and that it ends up in the hands of Meares. In 1911, at the start of the Antarctic *Terra Nova* expedition that would end with the death of Scott and the four men who walked to the South Pole with him, Meares reaches under the floorboards of the cabin at Hut Point and removes "an old hardwood case about eight inches square and six inches deep. A white-silvered clock face showed through its glass lid" (215). A few years later, the clock is briefly returned to Amundsen and accompanies him on the *Maud* expedition. In 1934, shortly before his death, Meares entrusts the chronometer to Fay's grandfather Hugh. Doubting whether "anyone is looking for it" Hugh gets the reply that "it could be looking for them." Meares continues: "I happen to know that it has a strong homing instinct. No matter where you send it, it always finds its way back" (446). As these examples illustrate, O'Loughlin consistently stresses the agentic function of inanimate objects as well as the connections these objects forge between individuals and time periods.

The starting point for all these interlinked stories, then, is the last Franklin expedition, and elements connected to it—individuals, events, documents—are found in the majority of the plot strands. O'Loughlin does not envision a different fate of the entire crew but extrapolates on the destiny of Crozier. A widely circulated belief is that he was among the last or the very last survivor, a belief underpinned by a report by John Rae, published a few years before McClintock's rescue mission. Rae, solitarily exploring parts of Arctic Canada, came into contact with Inuit hunters in 1854 who stated that they had been approached by a group of forty starving men four years earlier, led by an officer who matched Crozier's description: "a tall, stout, middle-aged man" (Rae 250–251). Beyond this point, nothing is known of this group of men, but critics have suggested that Crozier had skills that would have increased his chances of survival and previous experiences of winters in the Arctic, sailing under Captain William Parry on three expeditions in the 1820s and as second-in-command under Sir James Clark Ross on a mission searching for lost British whalers in 1835.[7] In O'Loughlin's novel, the quickly scribbled margin note in the document found at Victory Point is not Crozier's final act of communication. He leaves a letter to his friend Clark Ross dated 20 August 1848, and a message in a soldered metal tube is found by Amundsen, like Crozier a man with considerable experience of the Arctic, at Cape Chelyuskin, Siberia in 1918.

Beyond illustrating the agency of objects, the letter and message connect to functions of the Arctic in *Minds of Winter* that are at odds with each other: countless individuals go there only to vanish, and the busyness of the region means diminished opportunities to disappear. The letter to Clark Ross is written when Crozier is back at Beechy Island at the end of the summer and describes events that preclude the Primary World sightings of him by Rae and instead hints to the possibilities of achieving greatness by going further north. Just days before the crew leave the ships they are approached, Crozier writes, by a group of men whose amulets make his Inuit interpreter Johannes connect them to the Tunit: the people that preceded the Thule culture and Inuit in North America. As a seasoned traveler in the Arctic, Crozier has heard "that these old ones persisted in regions too bleak for the Esquimaux [on] fog-shrouded islands" a visit to which would mean "death for any man" (O'Loughlin 69). Not deterred, Crozier hopes that these individuals will be able to take him "to places beyond knowledge" (71). Echoing Shelley's Walton, Crozier imagines finding the open polar sea and something less tangible; a boon to humanity available only to the first non-Inuk in the highest Arctic. Crozier presses on further north, and the Arctic allows him to disappear.

The letter forms an important background to a further point of contact between Crozier and Amundsen, created by O'Loughlin's use of the latter's overwintering at Cape Chelyuskin and an incident in a magnetic observatory, which features as an almost insignificant detail in *Nordostpassagen*, Amundsen's own account of his exploration of yet unknown areas of the Arctic Ocean.[8] When describing the winter of 1918, Amundsen notes an uncharacteristic personal passivity resulting from injuries and accidents: "I had to remain inactive for weeks on end" (100, my translation). To fill his time, Amundsen retreats to an observatory built by *Maud's* crew, which he describes as a solid structure that neither takes in nor emits much air. Working alone, he does not notice the increasing difficulties he has breathing, but experiences "a crisis" in the evening which leaves him unable to read and makes his "pulse beat at the rate of a machinegun in the middle of an assault" (112, my translation). With legs that barely carry him, Amundsen struggles outside and back to the ship and laconically states that a ceiling valve is installed the next day which enables him to carry on his work. It is likely that the kerosene lamp used in the observatory caused a case of carbon monoxide poisoning.

O'Loughlin's Amundsen is as downtrodden and passive as his Primary World counterpart, a mood that is brought on by the lack of agency he perceives in relation to his fate and to how modern inventions exacerbate this lack. The death of Scott at the South Pole has left the Englishman forever young and adventurous in the public mind and "[w]ireless and telegraphy" threaten silence and the power to be what Amundsen perceives of as "the author of his own story" (O'Loughlin 303). The discovery of a message inside a tube in a stone cairn, marked by a Board of Ordnance sign that he recognizes from "a ruined hut at Beechy Island" (O'Loughlin 311), temporarily releases him from his apathy and is followed by days at the Cape during which Amundsen senses a presence in the dark and cold.[9] Bothered by the notion that he might be disturbed by the few individuals that share the Arctic location with him, Amundsen leaves *Maud* in the night for the observatory where, alone, he can read the message which in two senses of the word represents the past's "long-range communication" (315). Undated but undoubtedly signed by Crozier, the message gives coordinates to a place, Amundsen conjectures, in northern Canada, still, "Crozier was here, he thought. Here, thousands of miles from King William Island, on the opposite side of the Arctic Ocean" (316). Crozier communicates with him from a by-gone time and in a place he is not thought to have gone.

This temporal and spatial disorientation, along with blurred boundaries between real and supernatural, affect Amundsen both physically and psychologically. His heart races and his hands are frozen despite the warmth in the observatory as he tries to make sense of the message. A presence makes itself felt again outside the door, and first firing at it and then stumbling out into the snow, Amundsen is surprised to see that he has either lost or removed his boots, and he struggles to remember the ground rules for how to survive in the Arctic. He recognizes another feature that should not be visible in the newly fallen snow: "a tent-ring . . . like the circles he'd found once on King William Island, on the ice-bound coast near the magnetic north where his Eskimo guides were too frightened to go" (318). However, to follow the Tunit and the promises for new experiences they ostensibly tender is no longer possible; there are no more places beyond knowledge. The aftermath of the experience in and outside the observatory is rather characterized by despondency that partly ties back to Amundsen's wish for anonymity and thereby increased agency, partly to his sense that there are countless riddles he cannot solve. He cannot go back to being "unknown and free" (323) as he was before he decided to change the direction of *Fram* in 1910 and pursue the goal of reaching the South Pole, and he does not want to be responsible for what he has found, the code scribbled on the back of the Ordnance message undecipherable to him. Amundsen already knows that his present expedition is a failure and that "his luck had finally changed" (322). The Arctic as well as Antarctica have been spaces that have provided ways in which Amundsen can disappear and reappear, qualities that are now lost. Instead, the Arctic is busy with both figurative and literal lines of groups and individuals crossing each other.

Many of the storylines in O'Loughlin's novel are open-ended, reflecting the propensity of the Arctic to obscure answers to questions or render impossible the solution of mysteries, and lack of resolution becomes a narrative tool. Even the purely fictional Fay is incorporated in the pattern of non-resolution which aligns her with plot strands that are underpinned by documentary evidence. Fay is identity-wise unstable already when arriving in northern Canada, in fact going there in the first place to honor her mother's wish to return to the place of her birth. The death of her mother prompting the trip also has caused a mix-up with her bank that now has Fay registered as deceased. When checking into a hotel room booked for an occupant who has not showed up, the result is Fay's amused sense that she is "not really here" (190). Fay's research about her own family member in some instances works as a narrative device, shifting focus from one plot strand to another, but the reader is left with an epilogue in which a woman with "no identification of any kind on her" has been found dead in the snow (474). When Fay wonders what links individuals as disparate as Franklin, Ipiirviq and her own grandfather, pondering that it may be their very disappearance "in the ice" (298), she herself is moving towards a similar fate and towards becoming another chain in this ephemeral link.

The Franklin expedition, lost in the ice, is one crucial detail in the complex cultural construction of the Arctic that O'Loughlin sketches; in Dan Simmons' *The Terror*, it is central. The novel builds on documentary sources contemporaneous with the original expedition as well as later evidence and hypotheses in what I have elsewhere designated as the historical time track, but Simmons pads out the unknown fates of the crew members in fictional time and introduces a supernatural answer to many of the questions surrounding their fates in mythical time (Lindgren Leavenworth, "The Times"). At the start of the novel, in October 1847, two linked arrivals worry the crew aboard the ships, immobilized by the pack-ice. A young Inuk, whom the men call Lady Silence since her tongue has been removed, has been aboard *Erebus* for a few months. As she has arrived, so has a monstrous presence, now lurking below on the ice, attacking the men in the night. These appearances are seen against the backdrop of the generally threatening Arctic surroundings in which the ice and the cold throughout the novel exhibit an eerie agency. "*The Ice*," Dr. Harry Goodsir writes in his diary, "*will not give us up*" (Simmons 583) and the cold is intense: "teeth can . . . actually explode" in temperatures falling beneath – 50 degrees Fahrenheit (8). Sounds are distorted, making the movements of the ice resonate like gunshots and vice versa, and even the aurora borealis appears as monstrous, reaching for the ships with "[e]ctoplasmic skeletal fingers" (3). To Crozier, "*everything*" is threatening and unnatural from "the unrelenting cold [and] the uncanny lack" of animal life, to the badly soldered tins which may have poisoned the food, and "the summers that did not come" (189). The Franklin expedition has entered a forbidding realm where nothing behaves in an expected way, where the landscape and the climate plot against them.

Teasing out *The Terror*'s connection to the Gothic, Van Piercy draws attention to the reoccurring "enclosed spaces and loss of freedom" (546), manifested in small chambers, labyrinths, and subterranean passages, that correspond to a repression of the self and that exacerbate the anxiety in characters. In the Arctic, the frequently immobilized ships, the inherent threat of the landscape, and the intense cold mean a tight perimeter within which the characters can move, and the passages of water that open and close create a hard-to-navigate maze. With mistrust growing also between the men aboard *Erebus* and *Terror*, further circumscribing actions, they are easy prey for the fourteen-foot-tall creature seen variously as a preternaturally large polar bear, a god, a demon, or as it will henceforth be referred to, a *Tuunbaq*, allegedly belonging to Inuit mythology. Simmons' incorporation of Inuit cultures and knowledge as well as the monster's function are discussed in greater detail in coming chapters: suffice to say here that the

Tuunbaq, a "diegetic legend" (Thiess 229), is presented as the speculative solution to the Franklin mystery.

The Otherness of the Arctic and a time-specific male heroism are foregrounded in the Sunday sermon following the death of Lieutenant Graham Gore, the *Tuunbaq*'s first victim. Franklin takes as a starting point the story of Jonah and the whale and stresses that a strong faith is necessary to withstand the coming "winter in the belly of this ice" (Simmons 172). Something extraordinary is required of men who undertake a journey "beyond the farthest known edge of the world" to an inhospitable place, in all things far removed from the comforts of home, and who do so for the good of humanity. Designed to inspire courage and hope in the crew and help them remember their manhood, the gist of Franklin's sermon echoes Victor Frankenstein's admonishment of the crew of Walton's ship when mutiny foments. He draws their minds back to the motive for the "glorious" journey which will result in them being "benefactors of [their] species" and encourages them to "be more than men" (Shelley 217). In both novels the Arctic becomes an antithesis of home and a stage for conquests also of a more personal, affective nature. With reference to the passage from Shelley's novel, Francis Spufford argues that unrealistic or downright faulty perceptions of the Arctic played into the fate of nineteenth-century explorers. "Those . . . least able to perceive the Arctic as it was—indifferent rather than harsh, full rather than empty, a problematic dwelling space rather than a moral playground—were also least likely to survive there" (58). It is not only Franklin's sermon, but also his general attitude to the landscape and conditions: "ice was ice—something to be broken through, gone around, and overcome" (Simmons 76) that already at the outset align him with the less successful. Simmons' Franklin indeed sees the Arctic as an empty space with ill will seemingly directed at himself, and as a testing ground of moral and religious values.[10] He is consequently punished and when he is dragged under the ice by the *Tuunbaq* with his severed legs remaining on the ice above him, his final thoughts are used as an illustration of his paradoxical unpreparedness: "*I am in the sea. For the first time in my life, I am in the sea itself. How extraordinary*" (182).

Enter Crozier, who is imagined as simultaneously a more imaginative and pragmatic man than his superior, and thus, following Spufford, increasingly likely to survive. Simmons' 700-plus page novel in the main focalizes Crozier, which leaves ample room for depictions of the captain struggling in the cold and questioning previously held beliefs. Having been rejected by Sofia Cracroft three years before, Simmons' Crozier struggles with feelings of emasculation, which combined with his social class and Irishness, result in his sense of inferiority. His "melancholia [is] a secret weakness" (34) that he attempts to hide from the rest of the crew, and deal with himself through excessive drinking. However, the commoner Crozier is not fixed

in a role in the same sense as Sir Franklin, and he can more easily adapt
to the conditions in the Arctic and see it as a complex, already occupied
place whose landscape and inhabitants have agency that cannot be passively
yielded to the intruding visitor. However, to prosper in a supernatural Arctic
in which spirits have taken physical shape requires a sacrifice which Crozier
is prepared for because Simmons endows him with the gift of clairvoyance.
This speculative ability, creating ties to Inuit Angakoks, is apparent already
in Crozier's childhood, but it is put to specific ends in the static, vulnerable position he finds himself in. In his temporally jumbled visions, Crozier
sees Lady Jane Franklin sending repeated messages to the Admiralty, rescue
operations that have yet to take place, and a future version of himself lying
naked on a bed of furs next to Lady Silence. Untethered from history and
chronology, Crozier attains a bird's eye view of events that finally makes
him offer up his own tongue to be able to communicate with the spirits.

The sacrificial act signals Crozier's severing of ties with the expedition
and specifically with his ship with which he is initially figuratively fused.
In a reading of *The Terror* with a particular focus on the materiality and
physical embodiment usually repressed in historical novels, Derek J. Thiess
focuses on an instance in which this link is made especially apparent, in
which the captain "lays bare [an] immediate connection . . . between the
body and place" (226). With ice surrounding the ship and confined to it,
Crozier thinks that *Terror* "has become his body and his mind" (Simmons
34). As a body, the ship has a heartbeat, "[t]he orlop deck is the belly" and
the hold deck represents "the deep guts and kidneys." In a novel intensely
and viscerally preoccupied with body parts and bodily functions, the ship
here connotes both the familiarity and the fragility of the human body. As a
counterpart to Crozier's mind, likewise, to traverse the ship means moving
from "the sane part of himself" corresponding to the upper and "livable"
lower levels of *Terror* to the hold deck where the corpses of crewmembers
are kept. This, the "Dead Room, is madness" (35). Before making the sacrifice, the linkage between body, mind, and ship is absolute to Crozier and
provides both comfort and horror. In his new existence, when confronted
with the artefacts that he helped bring to the Arctic, he feels physically ill,
seeing with clarity the insanity of the expedition as such and its intention of
carrying England with it. When entering *Terror*, he perceives of it as devoid
of life and as haunted by the past ghosts of arrogance and greed. He has
severed the physical connection with *Terror* and what remains is only a
husk which he sets on fire in the ice.

These few examples from the vast body of fictions that re-imagine
various stages of the Franklin expedition illustrate the span in speculative
fiction and in alternative history: their points of divergence are variously
radical. O'Loughlin tells a story of disappearances and connections that
hinges on uncertainties and the construction that is history, Seldon invents

members of Franklin's crew and then releases them from the frozen-in ships, and Simmons' *The Terror* "reacts to the huge blanks in the historical narrative in a hyperactive manner, combining speculation with supernatural sensationalism" (McCorristine, *Spectral* 215). The texts move from hope of the crews' survival in Seldon's text, via a more pronounced critique of the arrogance of the project in Simmons', to a sense of business in the periphery that also means the end of speculation in O'Loughlin's. In *Minds of Winter*, a bartender watches news footage of the discovery of *Erebus* and remarks, bitterly: "They had to go and find her. They had to solve a perfectly good mystery" (470). This 2014 Primary World discovery and the finding of *Terror*'s wreck two years later: the result of archival and geographical research as well as a belated recourse to Indigenous knowledge, indeed solve part of the puzzle and may provide further material evidence of what actually happened, but fictional returns to the disappearance indicate how it holds a continuing allure. When seen as the pivotal moment for the imagination, the interest by extension also demonstrates the desire or necessity of keeping the Arctic both temporally and spatially a site in which the inexplicable holds a promise.

An Alternative Arctic

The last Franklin expedition is in two significant ways connected to the fantasy of the open polar sea: its goal of finding the Northwest Passage "revived the theory" behind it, and the failed attempts at locating *Erebus* and *Terror* seemed to suggest that the crew "sailed its bountiful waters searching for a way out" (Robinson 18, 15). Growing out of Dutch and British searches for a traversable northern route between the Atlantic and the Pacific oceans, the interplay between science and exploration is illustrated by sixteenth-century voyages such as the ones undertaken by William Barents and Henry Hudson, underpinned by theoretical reasoning by, for example, Petrus Plancius, and nineteenth-century expeditions, such as Elisha Kent Kane's, supported by ideas from the German armchair geographer August Petermann. In an overview of the history of scientific speculation, John K. Wright notes how hypotheses about open water, "sired by wishful commercial thinking and born to national ambition" (340), grew from geographical peculiarities, unpredictable ocean currents, winds, and the migration of animals. Adriana Craciun maintains that "the interior of the Arctic Ocean remained the least understood maritime space on the planet" when other coastlines were mapped by eighteenth- and nineteenth-century expeditions, and that the very notion of impassability raised "both practical and philosophical" issues, the latter questioning why "nature or God" would create such an impenetrable landscape, "lifeless and incapable of cultivation, improvement, even traversal" ("Frozen" 693, 695). There is, then, resistance to accept a frozen ocean and a consistent element of fantasy connected to the idea of a warm climate and open seas in the far north, encouraged by scientific speculation and only partially tempered by discoveries that suggested the opposite.[11]

The idea of an open polar sea fertilizes even more speculative theories of habitable locations either around the Pole or below ground. Alongside the jungles of Africa and South America, the polar areas are ideally poised for imagining such discoveries, especially in times when they were still literally *terrae incognitae* in Western exploration. Fictional narratives depicting hitherto unknown or forgotten lands in the Arctic and Antarctica reframe theories appearing already in ancient thought in which at the poles "openings existed for the departure of souls after death and their return at rebirth" (Leane 35). They were also often concretely influenced by the theories postulated by John Cleves Symmes (in turn influenced by Edmund Halley) that the Earth has a hollow core and that the poles represent entry points. Symmes' followers, Spufford notes, fall into two categories: those who believed in a hollow, habitable Earth and those who more modestly believed in open polar seas. "[F]or storytellers," Spufford continues, theories like these enabled "there to be *something* at the poles. . . rather than an expanse of ice significant only by geographical convention" (76). There are countless explicit references to Symmes' theory, and to the wider belief in polar openings in speculative fiction.[12] In S. Byron Welcome's *From Earth's Center* (1895), Symmes' hypothesis, by many seen as "unreasonable and a fallacy" (17) is refuted as the travelers about to find Centralia descend into the Earth's interior through a "polar whirlpool" (26), and as late as in Edgar Rice Burrough's "Tarzan at the Earth's Core" (1929/1930) the "ape-man" himself, believing that the idea of a habitable inner world "has been definitely refuted by scientific investigation," needs to reevaluate his convictions when he, through an opening in the Arctic descends into Pellucidar (Ch. 1).[13] Regardless of whether travelers reach the North Pole or a subterranean world, the highest Arctic is transformed and filled with narrative meaning, extending beyond ice.

There is a smattering of Hollow Earth fictions published in the first half of the nineteenth century that precede the great interest in lost or undiscovered civilizations that reaches its peak in the last quarter of the nineteenth century, in works that are commonly but anachronistically referred to as Lost World novels (after Arthur Conan Doyle's 1912 novel). In step with exploration and geological and archeological findings and theories, however, boundaries are pushed further, making authors take recourse to time-traveling and outlining multiple timelines; as Geoffrey Winthrop-Young observes, "the more the *terrae incognitae* are mapped, the more the lost kingdoms, races or species run out of hiding places" (111). In connection with Edward Bouvé's *Centuries Apart* (1894) in which a medieval society is found by an American expedition in the far south (also here thanks to an open polar sea), Elizabeth Leane observes that whereas time traveling in speculative fiction set elsewhere requires technological advances or physical mishaps—her example of the latter is the "bump on the head" required for Hank Morgan to travel centuries back in Mark Twain's *A Connecticut Yankee at King Arthur's Court*—"Antarctica functions as [the] time machine that makes the past simultaneous with the present" (163). The Arctic functions in a similar way regarding temporal uncertainty; the high latitudes too lack markers with which the passing of time is measured elsewhere.[14]

The large number of Antarctic and Arctic lost-civilization novels have as a common, unsurprising denominator that realism is maintained as long as travelers remain in mapped and well-known territory and that speculation increases when the unknown polar areas are reached. In William R. Bradshaw's *The Goddess of Atvatabar*, this process is seen also in stylistics. As Julian Hawthorne remarks in his enthusiastic introduction to the novel, the reader might just as well be enjoying "the reports of an Arctic voyage as recounted in the daily newspaper" in the initial stages of the journey and "within the realm of things already known or conceived of," but when intrepid explorer Lexington White reaches the subterranean world with its marvels and deeply attractive blue-haired, yellow-skinned goddess, "the style rises to the level of the lofty theme and becomes harmoniously imaginative and poetic" (11). Although some whimsies and eccentricities are apparent also in the portions of the text that narrate the planning of the trip, the outfitting of the ship, and the journey north—the bringing aboard of "*terrorite* guns" of the author's invention (Bradshaw 23); an astronomer named Starbottle—there is a marked difference between the prosaic explanations for earthquakes breaking up the ice and allowing the ship to pass, and the increasing astonishment and awe at the wonders that are encountered beneath, roughly, the North Pole. Among these are a lessened gravity, inventions enabling people to fly, 40-feet-tall mechanical cavalry ostriches, plants that are fused with animals, and even resurrection. Bradshaw's upsetting of physical and natural laws thus places sections set in Atvatabar far from the end of the speculative spectrum closest to the Primary World.

At the opposite end, in this section, we find Verne's *The Voyages and Adventures of Captain Hatteras*, which is closely modeled on Primary World polar exploration.[15] Edmund Smyth notes how the novel illustrates Verne's "responsible scientific speculation, extrapolating from contemporary social and scientific trends" (2), and Beau Riffenburgh how "close attention to geography and science constantly provide[s] a rationale for the apparently mysterious" (240). Several exploration narratives and reports from Franklin rescue missions were available in French at the time, and

Marie-Hélène Huet demonstrates how Verne "borrows extensively from [these] intent on integrating the most precise details" (156, 157). Also in the construction of his main characters—the eponymous captain who single-mindedly focuses on reaching the North Pole despite numerous obstacles, and Dr Clawbonny who supplies the crew and the reader with diverse scientific knowledge as well as thoughtful reflections on Arctic phenomena— Verne cleaves to traits touted as necessary for success in the Arctic. Loosely modeled on Franklin, Hatteras presses on towards his ultimate goal of the North Pole through mutiny and a shipwreck and across a cold, barren Arctic, empty of humans but populated by eerily cunning polar bears.[16] Clawbonny brings an array of scientific equipment and books that instantaneously transform him into "a physician, a mathematician, an astronomer, a geographer, a botanist, or a conchologist" (Verne 23); he is, Terry Harpold observes, "a man who knows how to use a library effectively" (35). While they thus complement each other, an effective contrast is also set up between Hatteras' obsession and the doctor's more pragmatic ability to, via texts, understand and explicate the new world they encounter.

The long history of exploration and the importance of claiming the North Pole for England join the captain and the doctor: both rally the crew with speeches about the courageous men who have gone before them. Clawbonny starts with tenth-century Icelandic and Greenlandic voyages and ends with the rescue missions sent after Franklin's expedition; Hatteras draws lines from Christopher Columbus to McClintock. While, as Katherine Bowers remarks, the lists emphasize that the expedition will "traverse waters haunted by previous [unsuccessful] expeditions" (72), Hatteras proudly notes the English names appearing at the later stages of exploration and the fact that the prize of claiming the North Pole is still there to collect. He concludes that "[i]f human foot is ever to reach the Pole, it must be the foot of an Englishman" (Verne 91). The North Pole as a point of national contention is highlighted with the entrance of the American Captain Altamont, whom the men have rescued and who shares Hatteras' singlemindedness. His abandoned ship at higher latitudes makes Hatteras pronounce, while "stung by the serpent of jealousy [that] safety lies to the north, always to the north" (250) and an uneasy alliance is formed to reach it. Unification is necessary as the dangers and uncertainty increase the further north the small group pushes, and the further into speculation the novel moves.

While the idea of an open polar sea agrees with the times' hypothesis, entering it makes Verne leave scientifically supported speculation and depict phenomena that elude even Clawbonny's book learning. The waters are transparent and lit up as if by electricity, giving the men the opportunity to see a variety of marine life, birds "of enormous size" fly overhead (397), and the air is unusually oxygenated, resulting in a "super-human energy; their ideas became more excited; they lived a whole day in an hour" (399). These positive effects are contrasted to more worrying signs, such as animals fleeing from the still distant North Pole in "repugnance" (402), and closer to their goal, the groups' small boat is taken by a "a whirlpool, a new Maelstrom" (407).[17] It is this forceful current rather than their own efforts that finally brings them to their goal: shot out of it, they find themselves, minus Hatteras, in calmer waters and gaze at a volcano which towers "like a lighthouse at the North Pole" (409). This Pole is thus far from an abstract point in the ocean or on the ice, instead it is clearly signposted for those who brave or are transported through the obstacles surrounding it.

Debates about what nation should lay claim to the prize are avoided when Hatteras, conveniently, is found uninjured on the beach below the volcano, but realizing the dream of an Englishman's foot as the first treading area around the Pole is simultaneously the start of his undoing. When Hatteras restlessly wanders the beach, Clawbonny hypothesizes that he may now "find the world too small" (421), and it is with a sense of relief Hatteras understands that one conquest remains: to plant his nation's flag at the precise coordinates of the Pole inside the crater. Throughout the narrative, Bridget Behrmann argues, the captain "creates his own heat, which seems to originate from somewhere deep inside" and it drives both his obsession and the material means for reaching the Pole to the point where "the volcano inside powers him inside the volcano" (4).[18] In the first imagined end to the novel, the leap would end with Hatteras' death (Huet 159), but in the published version, Captain Altamont hoists him from the crater. However, Hatteras' "mind is [left] at the top of the volcano" (Verne 428).[19] On the party's return to England, Hatteras spends the remainder of his life in an asylum, never speaking and in the asylum garden "always walking towards the North" (440) as if safety still lies in this direction. Hatteras' shattered sanity thus undercuts the success of the expedition, leaving him as another specter that haunts Arctic expeditions.

Among many followers of Verne, both Robert Ames Bennet and Vidar Berge recirculate the idea of an active volcano close to or atop the North Pole, but they also invest the Arctic with a populated land.[20] Published in 1901 and 1902 respectively, *Thyra: a Romance of the Polar Pit* and *Den hemlighetsfulla nordpolsön*, depict lush, green islands in the Arctic, inhabited by Viking descendants and prehistoric animals: locations as made for adventures and scientific discoveries. As Ben Carver notes, "[l]ost worlds needed to be well hidden in order to be 'found' in the imagination of the late nineteenth century" (and in the early twentieth) and "the island [is] the archetypal site" (155). As isolated microcosms, islands are ideal when imagining processes of preservation or variety, and the added geographical distance from the perceived center makes Arctic islands particularly hard to find. The novels by Berge and Bennet play with the tension between tradition and modernity, and both, Berge's novel explicitly, take inspiration from a failed polar expedition.

In 1897, the hydrogen balloon *Örnen* (the *Eagle*) carrying Swedish explorers Samuel August Andrée, Nils Strindberg, and Knut Frænkel ascended from Danskøya (Danes Island) in the western archipelago of Svalbard. The aim of the expedition was to sail north above the ice, claim the North Pole by dropping a buoy, and continue to the North American mainland. In the last years before the dissolution of the union with Norway, the actual or symbolic annexation of Arctic locations played an important role in the (re)building of a Swedish national identity, but factual information about the success or failure of the expedition ceased as the balloon left the field of vision of the amassed onlookers on Danskøya. Thirty-three years later, the men's bodies and the remains of a camp were found on Kvitøya (White Island), east of Svalbard, as unexpectedly ice-free waters enabled a naval landing by the scientific Braatvag expedition. The men's journals and notes, quickly edited and published by the Swedish Society for Anthropology and Geography in *Med Örnen mot polen* (1930), revealed that the balloon had not been airborne for more than little over two days.[21] The North Pole, consequently, had not been claimed by the daring Swedes and they had attempted a three-month-long trek back towards the mainland; an exhausting and futile endeavor as the ice periodically moved in the opposite direction, some days landing them further back than they started in the morning.

Following the Kvitøya discovery, the expedition members' project and destiny have been treated in several media formats, in narratives that to varying degrees rely on documentary evidence. Among these, *Den hemlighetsfulla nordpolsön* is a rare example of speculative fiction.[22] Following the trajectory from realism to speculation, the travelers are thinly disguised as Ander, Sindberg, and Wænckel, and the first chapters follow along a clearly identifiable historical time track depicting the planning for the balloon flight and its departure. Echoing Verne's listing of northern voyages pre-dating that of Hatteras', references are made to previous attempts to reach the Pole such as Nansen's *Fram* expedition, but with emphasis on suggestions for balloon flights. Among these are John Powles Cheyne's plans in 1876, which Huw Lewis-Jones notes seemingly "leapt straight from the pages of a Verne novel" (289), and the planned 1890 expedition by Gustave Hermite and Georges Besançon.

Coincidentally, the fictive balloon is airborne approximately the same time as *Örnen*, but instead of landing on the pack ice, Berge's expedition is forced down on a green island in the open polar sea. Upon landing in a meadow, the three men are surrounded by chirping birds and hear the distant sound of the surf of the open sea. Illustrations by Garibaldi Lindberg emphasize the impression of a seemingly welcoming Arctic, and one of the first depicts the men in the foreground, standing among grass, flowers, and lush trees. Two potentially more worrying features are also included: an active volcano in the background and a group of bearded, helmeted men carrying swords and bows. The illustration thus depicts the reason for life on the island, and the fictional travelers' first meeting with the Viking descendants who populate it. Once acquainted, one of the chieftains explains that a flood in the distant past has drowned the world except the beautiful island of Gimle, and the volcano, thought to be maintained by the fire-wielding giant Surtr, has kept the survivors alive when the waters once again froze around them. Berge consequently literalizes representations from Nordic mythology, in which Gimle is the home of the good and right-eous people after Ragnarök.

What John Rieder refers to as "fantasies of appropriation" that surface in novels about lost races and discovered civilizations have strong connections "with the political and economic acquisitiveness of imperialism" (40), and although *Den hemlighetsfulla nordpolsön* appears at the later stages of the genre's popularity and is strongly influenced by the adventure story, it aligns with a general trajectory in which the visitors implicitly or explicitly con-quer the far north. Berge's novel in part negotiates issues of encroachment and colonization by forging strong links between the three Swedes and the Viking descendants; as in other examples in the genre a "common ancestry is established indirectly by . . . historical, cultural [and] linguistic evi-dence" (Rieder 42). The story of Ragnarök is part of Ander, Sindberg, and Wænckel's own cultural background, and they are addressed in a shared language. There is also a connection through physical features, described in ways that echo the times' theories about racial biology: attention is drawn to the Vikings descendants' cranial shapes, their blue eyes, and blond hair (Berge 18). Still, they are clearly figured as less developed and consequently addressed in a traditionally imperialist manner. When the chieftain is unable to comprehend the flight of the balloon, for example, Sindberg takes recourse to an analogy with dandelion seeds. Blowing them into the air he pedagogically explains: "no bow has fired these, instead they float away by themselves. So have we too arrived through the air" (21).[23] Through the combination of superior technology and scientific knowledge, the explorers' leadership is naturalized rather than figured as imperial appropriation, and as representatives of modernity, Ander, Sindberg, and Wænckel in both work and adventures see themselves as improving life on Gimle. They build roads and Christian churches, solve age-old disputes, effect resolutions to love affairs, and kill (likely the last exemplars of) pre-historic animals such as pterodactyls and saber-toothed tigers.

The journey north and what turns out to be a permanent stay on the island simultaneously build on and explain Arctic phenomena, in the process giving credit to earlier hypotheses. Ideas about warm currents and an open polar sea are confirmed by the very existence of the island—"the renowned geographer Petermann," Ander states, "scorned and derided" by many in the scientific community, "now has been proven correct" (54)—and highlighted by the varied flora and fauna on it. A place is imagined in which the tropics and the north, prehistory and contemporaneity, are combined, with mammoths and sloths inhabiting the same forests, and with orchids growing among pine trees; the plant life especially is appreciated by "the countrymen of Linnaeus, the flower king" (178). But regardless of how powerful the men become on the island, they cannot leave it and bring results, including the feat of claiming the North Pole, back to Sweden because the strange winds that forced them down onto the island cannot be replicated and reversed. Despondently, they await the coming winter and an end to their work. As Surtr's volcano once saved the Viking survivors, however, it now comes to the aid of the balloonists because when darkness settles on the Arctic it steadily emits balls of fire that light up the sky. Ander, Sindberg, and Wænckel can put their fears to rest and continue to work in their isolated existence. "Such men," Berge enthuses, "do not have to pride themselves on descending from Vikings, they are themselves Vikings, themselves knights without fear or reproach, whose names their country mentions with pride" (62). Physical strength and sacrifice are transformed into intellectual counterparts that will ensure that the men will continue to bring honor to Sweden.

Five years passed between the ascent of *Örnen* and the publication of *Den hemlighetsfulla nordpolsön*, and I am by no means suggesting that Berge held out hope that the real explorers had survived. His novel is rather an attempt to extrapolate the silence that followed the last sighting of the balloon at Danskøya. In a careful examination of the plethora of texts appearing in the expedition's wake, Per Rydén argues that "you can and you should tell the story of August Andrée, Nils Strindberg and Knut Frænkel over and over again. Since there is something unknowable in the midst of the knowable, new stories are perpetually generated" (681, my translation). Berge's novel thus exemplifies authors' desires to fill gaps in history, much as the novels addressed in the previous section, and does so by downplaying the ice, cold, and the emptiness which is contingent on the absence of others like oneself.

Published the year before *Den hemlighetsfulla Nordpolsön*, and possibly working as a source of inspiration for Berge, *Thyra, a Romance of the Polar Pit* bears an implicit connection with the Andrée expedition: four polar explorers make use of a conveniently bypassing hot air balloon to speed up their journey north and when toasting to the abilities of craft, one of the travelers pronounces her as "truly an Eagle" (Bennet 15). With a firm grounding in the adventure genre, there are few traces of a scientific discourse in this novel, and the leap from the approximation of the Primary World to a Secondary is literally quick: when the expedition has progressed further north than Fridtjof Nansen, the first-person narrator contentedly notes that "[a]ll that the 'Fram' had won by months and years of northward creeping, our balloon had covered and outstripped by a few short hours" (12). The men land on an island close to the Pole and immediately help the eponymous Thyra to defeat a prehistoric cave-bear. Thyra belongs to a civilization of old Norsemen, the Runefolk, who are involved in continuous skirmishes with their relatives, the Thorlings. An added threat comes from a Paleolithic race of beast-like people. Unlike Ander, Sindberg, and Wænckel, the visitors cannot all claim an ancestral relationship with the encountered peoples and the text is characterized by what Rieder calls "the motif of the civil war" (40). The explorers are welcomed as potential saviors and "the civil war equivocates the adventurers' agency by turning adventure and conquest into alliance and rescue" (41). Potential transgressions are consequently naturalized as reasonable acts in protection of the Runefolk.

As in Berge's novel, the men are seen as deities descending to Earth, a view emphasized by their conveniently Æsir-sounding names: John Godfrey, Frank Balderston, and Thord Borson. The fourth man in the group, an African American sergeant, is notably not associated with deities; named Black and smoking a cigar he is instead perceived of as Surtr and consequently as an adversary of the Æsir. Bennet's novel is already in these aspects an overdetermined narrative, and relying on romance and adventure, it latches on to the ideals of physical prowess and courage that are noticeable already in "mid-Victorian" renditions of lost worlds: "timeless strongholds of primal masculinity" (Deane 206). Prehistoric animals are slain without compunction, heathen rites are dismantled, and the four men effect peace in and around the polar pit. Where Berge's balloonists transform into learned equivalents of Vikings, Bennet's rather embody the traditional conception: "raw strength, courage, instinctive violence, bodily size" (Deane 206) are characteristics of the primitive manhood that the novel champions and for which space is made in the northern periphery.

The earlier "The Extraordinary and All-Absorbing Journal of Wm. N. Seldon" illustrates a contrasting attitude to conquests and appropriation but here as well, an inhabited, verdant Arctic replaces the emptiness that follows an Arctic disappearance and attention is drawn to feats of discovery: the paratextual introduction proudly announces that the three men from Franklin's crew have encountered a civilization that "has never been spoken of" before and whose inhabitants after the men's visit "have learnt something of us" (Seldon 11). Adding seasons contrasting to the stereotypical image of the Arctic as caught eternally in winter, the encountered land is described as being in both a "perpetual summer" (11) and an "eternal spring" (20). The cold Arctic, consequently, has a marginal function in the narrative and the found civilization is rather its antithesis: there are colors in contrast to the monochrome icy landscape, heat instead of cold, and depth perspective instead of the flat view on the ice. Rather than initiating adventures, the three men stumble into them. Losing their way when on a hunt, for example, they suddenly find themselves in "the valley of death" which represents a stark contrast to the otherwise Edenic surroundings (34). The beautiful valleys and vistas are replaced with scenery that has "a goblin look" (28) and when they are attacked "as if pressed on by vampires" (31), they abandon their rational manners, jumping, screaming, and biting, before losing consciousness to a fever. The swamp they have wandered into thus holds a number of dangers associated with both Gothic Europe and the tropics and the ordeal temporarily transforms them, both physically and existentially; they need to be nursed back to health and a sense of self by tender women who come to their rescue. A later hunt conforms more closely to the masculine ideal and, indeed, to the Arctic, as they encounter, and "manfully" kill, several "white or polar bears" (34). The microcosm of the encountered country thus holds facets of otherwise geographically disparate adventure staples.

The discovery of an unknown land gives Berge, Bennet, and Seldon the opportunity to move away from the all-male exploration narrative. Indigenous to the speculative Arctic, the women are uncommonly beautiful and, in the novels by Berge and Bennet, blond and blue-eyed. The hyperbolic description of a chieftain's daughter in *Den hemlighetsfulla nordpolsön* asks the reader to imagine "a bedewed rosebud that tenderly opens its maidenly pure, not yet sullied petals . . . the innocent gaze of a small child, the chaste moonlight that falls through the branches in the grove" (Berge 27). The traits are tied to ideals in the travelers' Nordic home rather than being exotic or foreign, but despite this familiarity, the three balloonists never explicitly contemplate a relationship with the maiden nor with any of the other women they meet on Gimle, seen as noble but primitive ancestors. Although women are arguably 'civilized' in step with the men on the island, they are consistently limned in terms that connote a passive purity, not to be tampered with.

The situation is initially different in Bennet's novel, where the "Polar Valkyrie" is first encountered when fighting a bear. Being "six feet in height and beautifully proportioned" (30), the golden-haired Thyra displays great courage and skill.[24] Bera, half-sister to the King of the Thorlings is an attractive "Amazon" (41) and likewise displays great initial agency, and the physically small Jofrid has other powers, communicating with the Orm, a deity demanding sacrifices. These three women become the love interests of Godfrey, Borson, and Balderston, while Black, predictably, does not have a romantic liaison. The female characters' agency is then lessened as romances develop, especially evident in the cases of Thyra and Bera. The former is referred to as "an obedient child" (35) and, after a life of self-sufficiency, she needs to be protected in animal-attacks and battles. Bera, likewise, needs to change to become a believable and appropriate love interest, and after being saved from a bison by Borson, "the grim giantess" transforms into "a simple maid of sixteen" (147). Although couched in romance, the travelers thus profoundly influence the encountered culture, at least where expected or desired gender-performance is concerned, and bright conjugal futures explain why the explorers do not return from the discovered world.

Seldon's narrative provides a contrast to the focus on passive, northern beauty: the encountered people are instead presented as "part Indian and part Spanish," and the women in particular are unusually "passionate" (Seldon 19). "Fierce desire flames out of their dark-brown, gazelle-like eyes, and . . . nothing can be more exciting than their elastic movements," Wilson enthusiastically remarks. However, even though sexuality rather than innocence is foregrounded, it is connected to an uncorrupted state resulting from a lack of contact with the outside world. The women have "an unstudied grace" which aligns them with the "nymphs of the olden times" and Wilson argues that they are "civilized, though without our mannerish, artificial customs" (19). These women too are presented as belonging to an earlier time, not contaminated by the artifice of modernity. Since these earlier times are championed, Seldon, Wilson and Jones do not effect pervasive change in the encountered land; although they transfer knowledge about mechanics, the inhabitants have little interest in adopting a formal government or making other alterations that the travelers suggest; the latter conclude that the introduction of "education and law" would render the people "corrupted in a short time" (27). This assessment also pertains to the women: they need to remain unchanged as anything else would lessen their allure.

In terms of opportunities for scientific discoveries and adventures, Berge, Seldon, and Bennet present the discovered worlds as utopias in the contemporary usage of the word: as ideal or having significant advantages in comparison with Primary World societies. At the same time, the visitors remain at a superior distance from the encountered inhabitants, either encouraging moves towards modernity, or withholding information that would effect change. In Mary E. Bradley Lane's *Mizora: a Prophecy*, the inferiority of traveler Vera Zarovitch is in contrast drawn out through her association with a society that is seen as unequal, brutal, and ignorant, as well as through personal traits that pit her against the people she meets beneath the Arctic: not only short in stature, she is also "a brunette," "ill-formed and uncouth," and "apart from the groups of beautiful creatures like the genus of another race" (Lane, 17, 21, 16).[25] In the land of Mizora,

Science (capitalized throughout the narrative) has enabled procreation to be achieved through a never-explained process of parthenogenesis, crime is eradicated, education is furthered, and a multitude of inventions resembling contemporary dishwashers and vacuum cleaners carry out traditionally female duties. Men, belonging to an earlier phase in history that closely resembles the late nineteenth century, have been made obsolete through a process of eugenics that has also weeded out any undesired traits of a physical and intellectual nature. The result is that Mizora is populated by smart, statuesque, pale-skinned, and blond women.

Mizora is located not only in the distant Arctic, but underground and thus impossible to find on a map: while structures need to be introduced, the way there must also be signposted. A more consistent adoption of the travel narrative structure than in the previously considered texts, Verne's excepted, sees the protagonist leaving a clearly recognizable place and step-by-step acquainting herself with an increasingly less familiar environment. Earlier literary depictions of no-places also set a protocol for the dissemination of information about the encountered new culture. "By the nineteenth century," Darby Lewes maintains, "hordes of protagonists had encountered myriad isolated worlds and had enjoyed countless extended dialogues with legions of highly vocal natives, who expounded at length on the social and political customs of their utopian/dystopian societies" (12). Consequently, traveler and reader alike depart from the narrative's approximation of the Primary World into progressively more unfamiliar territory, jointly learn about the discovered civilization, and sometimes also return in a reversed trajectory.

The adoption of this structure does not mean, however, that Vera is presented, or presents herself, as an intrepid traveler with a clear design for her journey. Exiled to Siberia because she is suspected of subversive views, our Russian aristocrat protagonist escapes, is briefly marooned in an Inuit community, and then falls into Mizora through a whirlpool while alone in an open polar sea. It is thus a series of circumstances that leads her to the underground society: she even notes that "[h]ad I started out with a resolve to discover the North Pole, I should never have succeeded" (Lane 8). The encountered people are presented as considerably more advanced than the visitor and as a constant observer and listener to lengthy explanations, Vera can teach them very little. The brief stories she relays are rather echoes of the Mizorans' own dark past or serve as warning examples. Vera spends fifteen years in Mizora, and when she returns to the world outside, her appearance is unchanged signaling that the subterranean civilization is guided by different temporal laws. Despite time passing in the surface world, there is no readiness to accept or emulate the Mizoran structures and worldview. Wauna, who accompanies Vera back, is a curiosity, but her suggestions are not taken seriously and, weakened by what is to her an unhealthy environment, she dies, still searching for a way to return home.

Mizora belongs to an extensive body of utopias written by women in response to prevailing gendered structures or political movements.[26] In the time period 1870 to 1920, Lewes notes that "[m]ore than a hundred texts of astonishing diversity" were written by British and American middle-class women who each "at a particular historical moment imagined what men and women might be like in *un*customary societies" (1, 2). In Lewes' corpus, two works share *Mizora*'s placement of the action in the Arctic but represent different takes on gender issues. M. Louise Moore's *Al-Modad: Life Scenes Beyond the Polar Circumflex* (1892), according to Lewes' description, depicts a subterranean world "inhabited by a communal, technologically advanced society stressing education, sexual equality and sexual freedom [who] venerate Lo, a divine hermaphrodite who inspires goodness, simplicity and vegetarianism" (16, 18). In the satirical *Pantaletta: A Romance of Sheheland* (1882), gender reversal has resulted in a general dissatisfaction; the men are effeminate and enslaved, the women "have inherited with the pantaloons all the vices and wickedness of men" (Wood 176).[27] As in utopias broadly, the examples illustrate different views of feminism, politics, and social issues, and range from the somewhat realistic to the widely speculative.

As is commonly the case with polemical utopias, *Mizora*'s representations of a supposedly ideal social and intellectual paradise divide critics. Katherine Broad, for example, cautions against a blanket definition of the work as a feminist utopia and rather argues that the "ideals of Mizora hinge on repressive visions of reproductive and social engineering that undermine the radical potential of the text" (247). Carver, on the other hand, maintains that rather than "a programmatic utopia," it can be read as "an allegory of women recuperating the power of sexual selection and the restitution of a matriarchal society" (178). Critics of Lane's novel, then, have for good reason been interested in structures and processes in the utopian society and how these reflect or subvert Primary World issues of gender, eugenics, and social equality. The Mizoran setting, similarly, is commonly addressed to illustrate the close connections between "genetic engineering [and] forms of organic and horticultural cultivation" (Chang 393) or the "essentialist association" (Mahady 107) between women and nature that seemingly justifies solutions to the subterranean world's past problems. The placement of the world below the Arctic is seldomly remarked upon, the sense conveyed being that events could have taken place anywhere, provided that they remain hidden from view.

The journey through and descriptions of the Arctic which precede the discovery are frequently also elided. However, they provide a stark contrast to the detailed depictions in *Mizora* and the fact that Arctic is pronouncedly atopic, "not to be inhabited for long even in text" is telling (Lindgren Leavenworth, "Atopic" 7). A few pages only are devoted to Vera's year-long stay in an Inuit settlement and although she, "by birth [acclimated] to the coldest region of the temperate zone" (Lane 11), withstands the low temperatures and scarcity with relative ease by adopting Inuit clothing styles and eating habits, restrictions by the cold, wind, and ice make "existence a living death" (12). This Arctic is a negation of life, peopled by "*poor children* [who] struggle with cold and starvation" (11, emphasis added). Russia, Europe generally, and the US are later denounced as primitive in comparison with Mizora, but Inuit ("Esquimaux" in the text) represent an almost complete lack of progress. Carver, one of few critics commenting on the journey, notes that "the imagination of an alternative social arrangement" in Mizora is particularly effective because it is prefaced by this form of "time-travelling backwards along a natural-historical timeline of human evolution through less developed forms of society" (177). By moving further north, Vera descends a metaphorical ladder of progress to an atopic Arctic that she only temporarily and reluctantly visits.

To the south, then, resides "everything that was dear or congenial" (Lane 11), but not finding passage, Vera continues even further north. In the company of her Inuit hosts she encounters shores and open waters, vegetation, birds, and fish, and feels "the kindly greeting of a mild breeze" (12). Here, close to where north as a direction ceases to matter, Vera hopes that she "might meet in that milder climate some of [her] own race" (12): a desire to start the reversal of the evolutionary backwards movement. As her guides refuse to accompany her, she sets out alone in a canoe to follow this desire. Heidi Hansson argues that the time Vera spends with Inuit "prepares [her] for the mental reorientation" needed in the meeting with an alternative world, and that "loss of control" is a second requirement ("Arctopias" 74). This second facet, again reinforcing the chance nature of Vera's experiences, is produced when her small vessel approaches a part of the ocean that Inuit entirely avoid where it is first taken by a current and then caught in a whirlpool that leads to the subterranean world.

While Mizora's societal structure presents a stark contrast to those in the world at large, colors and abundance create a direct antithesis to the Inuit settlement. The portal leading underground is in the shape of "a curtain of rainbows fringed with flame" which contains "a thousand brilliant hues" (Lane 13): a heterogeneity distinct from the "never varied" (11) and monochrome landscape Vera has experienced in the Arctic, devoid of anything but flat expanses of ice and characterized by a lack of movement. The world beneath the surface enjoys Mediterranean temperatures, birds, flowers, and fruits in abundance, a far cry, then, from "the raw flesh and fat" Vera has subsisted on in the cold Arctic. Mizoran worldviews also completely reverse the previously outlined trajectory from advanced to primitive to the point where Vera comes to represent history and "the darkness of civilization" (90) and Mizora is the pinnacle of speculative evolution. But despite the fact that Vera returns to the surface world, and with a Mizoran in tow to boot, the critique of patriarchal and class structures they attempt to leverage leaves no discernible trace in the novel's approximation of the Primary World. What Vera continues to see as the ideal society remains hidden beyond the "dismal hills of snow and ice" of the Arctic (143).

This outcome to an extent gels with how Vera describes her chance discovery of Mizora, and the work's paratext indicates that there is even something haphazard about its dissemination. It is said to be an autobiographical manuscript "Found Among the Private Papers of the Princess Vera Zarovitch" which, broadly, signals a strategy for authenticating the speculative tale. I will return to this function of the paratext in the last chapter, but here just note that how *Mizora* has ended up in the reader's hands by chance, and how this echoes the despondency of the last chapter, form stark contrasts to how accomplishments of intrepid explorers are touted in *The Voyages and Adventures of Captain Hatteras* and *The Goddess of Atvatabar*, the novels that illustrate the span of speculation when imagining an alternative Arctic. Since Verne's novel is closely modeled on the history of Arctic exploration and includes lengthy enumerations of brave men as well as emphasis on the glory bestowed on individuals making new discoveries, his fictional explorers are likely to go down in the same annals of history. Huet notes how Hatteras throughout is against leaving material traces in the Arctic space, mainly to avoid rivals using helpful information, and she argues that the "extraordinary conquest . . . will leave no trace behind, except for the novel itself" (159). However, how results from the expedition are described in the last chapter leads me to another interpretation and one that also increases the speculation of the novel. Firstly, the report of the polar conquest has been "telegraphed over the United Kingdom" and Hatteras is hailed as the necessary "martyr" of the project (Verne 439). Secondly, there is Clawbonny's "account of the journey entitled 'The English at the North Pole', published the next year by the Royal Geographical Society." It is of course possible to read the title as a meta-comment, gesturing back to the book the reader is just finishing, but even so, the documented success of Verne's expedition is (or will be) internationally recognized and Hatteras is its undisputed hero.[28] In its contents, that is, Verne's novel represents a more conservative speculation than Vikings and heathen deities, to briefly bring back the texts by Berge and Bennet, but when effects in the approximations of the Primary World are considered, the works trade places on the speculative spectrum.

Bradshaw's *The Goddess of Atvatabar* combines these two aspects of speculation, starting already with the subtitle which proudly announces that the narrative, far from being a manuscript accidentally found, presents "the history of the discovery of the interior world and conquest of Atvatabar." Following prosaic descriptions of the voyage through an atopic Arctic, the ship *Polar King* starts descending into an oceanic abyss leading to Atvatabar and to fantastic adventures and romance, narrated in great detail. Mid-descent, however, terrified crewmembers leave the ship and return to the surface, and having made their way back home, they transmit news of the discovery of the subterranean world as well as of their intrepid leader. When one of the men returns underground accompanied by both British and American ships, he proudly announces that "[t]here is no man more famous to-day than Lexington White" (Bradshaw 237), and a newspaper account brought to Atvatabar states that "[t]he renown of Columbus and Magellan is overshadowed by [his] glory" (238). In Atvatabar, Lexington has risen to the status of king, with both military and political power. The novel itself—Lexington's first-person account of his adventures and success—is brought to the surface by the returning ships and he turns directly to the reader in the last chapter, seemingly promising a sequel. "[W]hen I again address you," Lexington states, "future experiences" are expected to be relayed, foremost among them descriptions of the "realms of Plutusia" (317), a second interior world surrounded by rumors. Atvatabar, made familiar through the lengthy descriptions, is only the first destination in a longer project of even more fantastical exploration.[29]

In an extended sense, the notion of the Arctic as a location suited to alternatives informs all the novels and short stories I discuss in this book, but the nineteenth- and early-twentieth-century texts addressed here fill what is perceived of as empty space in particular ways. Verne negotiates the abstraction of the North Pole and puts an end to the long history of attempts to claim it. Seldon, Berge, Bennet, and Bradshaw all use a lack of concrete geographical information to envision forgotten or hidden civilizations, and they depict an Arctic in which time has stalled and opened possibilities for civilizing missions as well as adventures. Lane's use of the underground is political, perhaps too pointedly so: no one is likely to ever find Mizora again. The impetus and inspiration vary, but jointly, the works show how the Arctic holds specific affordances for speculative fiction and, conversely, how speculative works draw from and contribute to discourses around alternative Arctic space.

Possible Worlds

In the twentieth-century novels I turn to now, the Arctic is no longer perceived of as empty, but instead presented as a site in which alternative ontologies can be interrogated; the authors depict both existential and concrete instabilities that come to the fore in or are produced by the

Arctic. In MacLeod's *Stranded*, human doubles appear in the midst of the Chukchi Sea, raising questions about which of them is real as well as about the reasons for the doubling. Burnside's *A Summer of Drowning* combines unreliable narration about disappearances with a particular view of a double-layered world, especially clearly seen in the white nights of the Norwegian Arctic, and Ivey's *The Snow Child* imagines a time outside time in Alaska, home to a girl that may be conjured forth by loss. I group together, then, one novel that would traditionally be seen as science fiction, one in which poetic ruminations combine with mystery, and one that intermeshes grief with folklore. All, however, are concerned with temporarily surfacing or periodically reachable other worlds that function as alternatives to the one we inhabit.

The most literal take on both effects and the idea of possible worlds is found in *Stranded*. One character asks his double to lift the hem of his shirt to make sure the same scar is found on them both (MacLeod 226), and this makes protagonist Noah Cabot remember "philosophy classes" in which "they'd talked about the best of all possible realities and 'many worlds' theory" and then admitting that "most of what he'd read had gone over his head" (227). Philosophy is but one field in which ideas of the existence of other worlds abound, as Marie-Laure Ryan demonstrates in a discussion about the intersections between theoretical physics and narratology, and in speculative fiction, the "many-worlds cosmology . . . provides a powerful way to dramatize the 'what if' mode of thinking . . . and creates narrative situations which would not be possible in a system of reality limited to one world" (668). Engaging with cosmologist Max Tegmark's taxonomy of parallel universes, Ryan investigates how ideas governing levels of varying probability have been utilized in speculative works, predominantly science fiction. The first level in the taxonomy, corresponding to depictions in MacLeod's novel, postulates that infinite space "has room for more than all the different possible combinations of elementary particles that make up the observable universe" and that it is probable "that the combination that describes our universe is realized more than once" (635). This opens for the idea that there are counterparts to our world and to ourselves, governed by the same physical laws yet potentially experiencing a different fate.

Despite the possibilities that a doubled universe or multiple worlds open in speculative fiction, strategies employed signal an awareness of, and ways around, unwanted complications. In what Ryan calls "wormhole narratives" there is a counterpart to the world from which the characters depart, often radically different from it, but the characters exist "in only one copy" (659). The second strategy is having each world contain material versions of the characters and when they travel into the other world, they take over the body that is there, vacated for the duration of the sojourn. This second scenario, Ryan argues, "creates a mind–body split" (659) that can productively be used for exploring existential and epistemological issues as the character inhabiting an evacuated body in another world brings with her or him specific and individual knowledge, experiences, and emotions. Both scenarios are designed to avoid that characters actually meet their own concrete doubles.

MacLeod, however, takes the more complicated route when on the oil platform Niflheim, crews from twin supply ships are staring at their own copies. Although some geographical confusion occurs in *Stranded*—at the end of the novel Noah is in a different part of the Arctic Ocean than he has thought—the premise is thus that doubles appear in the same world. There is a difference between the two ships, however, based in an accident during a previous trip resulting in two trajectories. In one Noah survives, in another his friend Connor MacAllister does. But the ramifications extend beyond these men's survival. A small-scale butterfly effect results in that the surviving Noah is seen as responsible for the accident in which Connor dies, and is, as a result, shunned by the rest of the crew. He has also lost his wife to cancer and is struggling to provide for his daughter. On the second *Arctic Promise*, Connor is alive and well and in his "version of history" (MacLeod 182) Noah's healthy wife has made a good life for herself and the couples' daughter following his demise.[30] When the two worlds intersect, Noah thinks that Connor's world is "the way the world is *supposed to be*—without me in it" (258) and tensions and conflicts in the novel revolve around questions of guilt and responsibility produced by the existential doubts. Reflecting the complexities around the many worlds theory, the open-ended novel does not resolve the conundrum of whether the two versions of history, equally real, exist simultaneously also outside of the Arctic and if the survival of one version means the death of another.

The questions raised by the existence of doubles and of parallel timelines are not specifically tied to the Arctic, but the fact that the discovery is made in an unfrequented periphery limits consequences to the characters directly affected by them. The erasure of boundaries "between original and reflection" (231) that is crucial to the central plot strand is also supported and foreshadowed by parallels in the Arctic climate and landscape. To judge distances is impossible, making the far-away seem close and vice versa, and time is at the same time "elongating, becoming meaningless" (158) and of the utmost importance given the two trajectories. There are also numerous references to the Arctic that harken back to the long tradition of presenting the area as unfit for human habitation or even existence, which further suggests that place importantly creates the right conditions for the split versions of past and present. "[T]his was not his place to be" (43), Noah thinks when a suddenly appearing fog initiates the strange events. The impossible turned into the possible has parallels in what Noah perceives of as supernatural transformations of the landscape: open water abnormally quickly turns to "old, consolidated ice" (62), which ties back to figurations of ice in the Arctic sublime: "ghostly and protean [ice is] appearing and disappearing in a matter of hours" (Loomis 102). The ice imprisons the ship Noah is on, which exacerbates the claustrophobic paranoia and anxiety produced by the doubles, and it eats away at structures, sinking ships and platforms alike. Noah is consequently left with the sense that the Arctic "was a place that consumed things. It broke them down and made them a part of itself" (315). Specificities of the Arctic thus crucially contribute to a dissolution between previously discrete boundaries, arrest movement, and violently incorporate visitors into itself.

Whereas MacLeod explicitly engages with the idea of co-existing worlds, Burnside's novel *A Summer of Drowning* does so in a subtle way, lying close to the Primary World end of the speculative spectrum. The protagonist Liv reflects on the titular summer, taking place ten years earlier when she was eighteen years old. Two local boys and a tourist drown during the course of the summer, and influenced by stories by an old neighbor, Liv goes back and forth on whether or not the *huldra* has been responsible for the deaths. The *huldra* is a well-known figure in Scandinavian folklore, going by slightly different names depending on geography and language.[31] In *A Summer of Drowning*, she is imagined as a beautiful woman, who lures men susceptible to her charms into the water. When Liv thinks about the stories she has been told, she imagines a young man being approached by the alluring *huldra*, "but if he could only look past this beautiful mask, he would see that, at her back, there is a startling vacancy, a tiny rip in the fabric of the world where everything falls away in emptiness" (Burnside 76). The image corresponds to customary depictions of the *huldra* as a beguiling woman with an emptiness or what seems like rotten wood where her back ought to be. However, Burnside draws out the implications of this absence and connects it to an existential instability that runs as an important theme throughout the novel. Living with her artist mother on Kvaløya off the coast of northern Norway, Liv is a self-professed loner, who continuously ponders the porous boundaries between what is real and what is imagined. "I was always aware of a gap—a dark, clean tear—in the fabric of the world" (321), she puts it, thus enforcing that how she imagines the physical appearance of the *huldra* is linked to a wider belief. Although the novel can be categorized as realistic fiction, infused with poetic reflections on the symbolic meaning of the *huldra*, it is this insistence on an unseen reality that makes me consider it as an example of speculative fiction.

Liv is to an extent an unreliable narrator, recounting memories from an unpleasant and therefore blurry summer a decade earlier and the novel's structure enforces a temporal instability that contributes to the oscillation between what can be determinately real and what is imagined. As David James notes, there is a "prioritization of transient moments" that from the

future point-of-view are "reassess[ed as] moments pregnant with implication or charged with proleptic insinuations of unsettling, and as-yet-
unexamined, recollections to come" (610). Remembering the pretty Maia,
for example, within the context of the drownings, makes Liv cast her in the
role of the *huldra*, and tales told by her neighbor Kyrre Opdahl become
portentous, bleeding into the real. Thinking back to her childhood and
imagining an even more distant past when her mother decided to relocate
to Kvaløya, Liv explicitly addresses how the island functions as "some parallel country" (Burnside 22) in which previous time periods can be accessed
and in which the traditionally measured time in the world outside carries
no meaning.

The fantastic world cannot be accessed in the same manner as the
different timescapes that seemingly coexist side by side. Astrid Bracke
suggests that "the strange does not penetrate the everyday, but rather
borders on it," and that the characters "cannot access it by their own
free will" ("Solitaires" 427). The world underneath or to the side of the
ordinary is in this way indicated to have an agency of its own, and Liv is
kept out of the place others are lured into by the *huldra*. It continues to
exist, however, also for Liv as an adult. In the last section of the novel,
focused on Liv's life in the present, she reflects on her current occupation
as a maker of unusual maps. The story about the *huldra* is seen as a first
"warning, a zone on the map that allows us to navigate an impossible
world" (Burnside 306) and the adult Liv creates images of "the unseen
. . . not as fantasy, but as invention—invention, in the old sense, which
is to say: revealing what there is, seen and unseen, positive and negative, shape and shadow, the veiling and the veiled" (323). Her maps are
designed to reflect two ways of perceiving or seeing the world. Liv takes
as an example a boy leaving the confines and security of a home in which
he has been taught to see the world in a certain way. For a while he tries
to keep to this way of perceiving his surroundings "but something creeps
in at the edge of his vision" altering his epistemology to the point that
the world of the *huldra* in fact is "the real world . . . that the farmhouse
and the village schoolroom try so hard to conceal" (324). Again, this
can at one level be read as an analogy of growing up and questioning
lessons taught by the parental generation, or perhaps rather questioning
how the truth of things remain hidden, or veiled as Liv would have it,
until the child is ready to face reality on his or her own. Importantly,
however, the adult Liv sets herself apart from others, precisely because
she has seen the unseen: that the world is the *huldra*'s world is not a realization she shares with others. The world of the stories and the fact that
although "the *huldra* [may not be] real . . . she exists" (77) remain Liv's
reality, much more relevant to her than what ordinary seeing allows her
to glimpse.

Equally important to stories is the agency of "the land from which the stories came" (171). To Liv, Kvaløya seems to hold both the present and the past. In James' reading of the novel, detailed "spatial description [is] a means of recuperating certain ways of being in, and acting toward, terrains where nature persists as a volatile presence" (605). In conjunction with the temporal instability, the "geologically austere, inhospitable landscape . . . may appear timeless, or out of time, yet is never motionless" (610). Particular Arctic conditions contribute to this motion and to a blurring of boundaries between reality and fantasy. The dark of winters and the light of the Arctic summers profoundly affect the island's residents, and especially conducive to catching sight of the *huldra* are "the endless, mind-stopping white nights of insomnia and wild imaginings" (Burnside 17). These white summer nights produce an otherworldly landscape in which the lines between what is real and what is imagined become almost indistinguishable. Burnside also draws attention to the starkness of the landscape, and the stillness, especially of summer nights, that "can make even the most pragmatic of souls think about spirits" (48). While many of these portrayals of the Arctic landscape are made in connection with the reactions of outside visitors, Liv is profoundly influenced by both the stillness and the changing light conditions. Arctic summer is a magical time, in several senses of the word: it conjures forth the supernatural and allows meetings between humans and otherworldly beings.

In a careful reading of Burnside's novel in tandem with Alaskan author Ivey's *The Snow Child*, Sara Helen Binney teases out the works' incorporation of folklore and their different connections to the Todorovian fantastic. Of salience to my discussion here is how both authors "keep their settings realistic [while] at the same time, they make the places strange" (Binney 5), Ivey by having the story narrated by characters who are strangers in the environment and Burnside by letting Liv describe Kvaløya and northern Norway for someone unfamiliar with the landscape. This, Binney maintains, "distances both the focalising characters and the implied reader from the place [and] creates a gap in knowledge, a space for a form of the marvellous which is not explicitly magical [but rather] a Todorovian fantastic hesitation" (6). Both settings, with their close connections to folklore and their particular Arctic conditions, sustain this hesitation whereby "a person who knows only the laws of nature, confront[s] an apparently supernatural event" (Todorov 25), thus landing neither text firmly in the genres of the marvelous or the uncanny. As noted, the unreal in *A Summer of Drowning* does not transform the world itself nor does Burnside set up a clear contrast between realism and magic. "Instead," Binney argues, "he describes a conception of nature which refutes that separation: nature is itself fantastic, containing both the magical and the rational, and refusing to choose between them" (13). The close connection, via folklore, between the *huldra* and the northern landscape imbues Kvaløya, and more importantly Liv's perception of Kvaløya, with the potential of the fantastic, highlighted by the unreality of the stillness of the white nights during which anything seems possible.

Facets in the possible world in *The Snow Child* point towards the marvelous and the uncanny but the novel does not fully realize either; the narrative sustains the fantastic hesitation. The story, set in the 1920s, reworks the Russian folk tale character Snegurochka (The Snow Maiden), read by one of the main characters, Mabel, within the novel.[32] Together with her husband Jack, Mabel has moved from Pennsylvania to Alaska, where they grieve the death of their baby. One evening, they fashion a child out of snow, which next morning is replaced by a girl who stays with the couple during the cold season, disappearing each spring. The child, Faina, is intimately connected to the Arctic: "she's made from this place, from this snow, from this cold" (Ivey 226), and for a long time, Mabel and Jack are the only ones who see her. There is a dreamlike quality to these meetings and Ivey represents these and other characters' conversations with Faina without the quotation marks that in other dialogues represent speech, in this way indicating that they may just as well play out in the characters' minds.

This uncertainty surrounding Faina's ontological status produces a gap in the text which cannot be conclusively closed even though the girl leaves concrete evidence of her existence in the form of dead animals and footprints in the snow, and late in the novel also a child of her own. Other characters meet and form connections with her, but these encounters as well occur in a hard-to-define space: they are not outside reality but have a quality that seems to destabilize it. Garret, who will become the child's father, is at home in Alaska and has a pragmatic attitude to both its challenges and affordances. When he first comes upon Faina in the late fall forest, a white swan has been caught in one of her traps and he watches her kill it. Her appearance and action change the forest for him and when he hears geese in the sky above him, "for the first time in his life, the sound frightened him" (293). Afterwards, he sees traces of her everywhere, always ahead of him. This encounter coincides with Faina's transition from childhood into adulthood, which seemingly binds her more tightly to material places. While she is a child, she moves in and out of Mabel's and Jack's lives, but as this freedom becomes curtailed it has consequences for both them and her. There is a strong sense that Faina is involuntarily hemmed in by motherhood and marriage, and to Jack her change symbolizes the loss of another child: the daughter that had been the "magic in their lives . . . . was gone, and Jack found himself mourning her" (351). This grief foreshadows the aftermath of the difficult birth, when Faina disappears in the winter night, this time for good, leaving her clothes and her baby behind but no footprints.

Although united in their love for her, Mabel and Jack see different reasons for Faina's appearance. To Mabel, the death of her child is a contributing reason for their move to Alaska where she will not be reminded, through laughter and play, of what she no longer has. But Mabel's personality makes her susceptible to an acceptance of the unreal: "All her life she had believed in something more, in the mystery that shape-shifted at the edge of her senses" (5), and Faina materializes as an answer to her desperate wish to again have a child. To her, Faina is a miracle, but Mabel's desire to mother a child cancels out the possibility of her seeing the girl as magical or marvelous. Plagued by the same grief, Jack sees himself as a more rational person than his wife, but experiences things working the Alaskan land that frighten him. The close association between Faina and the landscape features into his perceptions, as she "navigate[s] with ease . . . . the strange world of snow and rock and hushed trees" (95) that constitutes both an obstacle and a source of fear. As he follows her through the winter forests, the thought of finding nothing, "only insanity bared in the untouched snow," is the worst (97). While there are numerous references to the madness produced by darkness and isolation: the "cabin fever" that can produce visions of what people have "always wished for" (80), suggesting that Faina is produced by Jack's and Mabel's grief and longing, it is also clear that the girl in concrete ways inhabits the landscape, "[t]he snowy hillsides, the open sky, the dark place in the trees where a wolverine gnawed on the leg of some small, dead animal" (256). As Binney notes, Faina becomes "a cipher for the landscape itself" and both girl and place are "described as partly unknowable by Mabel and Jack" (9). The inherent Otherness that the Arctic presents to outsiders struggling to survive, to an extent naturalizes the Otherness of the girl. At the same time, it is the perceived realism of this Otherness that makes a reading of Faina remain in the mode of the fantastic hesitation since neither marvelous nor uncanny explanations suffice to account for her appearance and function.

MacLeod, Burnside, and Ivey occupy different positions on the speculative spectrum: the idea of doubles profoundly questions physical laws in the Primary World, whereas the blurring of boundaries between real and imagined caused by a different form of perception or by grief is subtle. Still, I have grouped the texts together because they question ontological and epistemological structures and do so via active use of the Arctic environment. In these novels, the Arctic is mapped, and, in the novels by Burnside and Ivey, it is peopled with neighbors and friends. Still, whether it is a temporary destination, a home, or the location for a new start in life, the Arctic contains within it, or temporarily makes accessible, an alternative world.

In the essay "The Glamour of the Arctic," based on his own experiences as a surgeon on a whaling ship in 1880, Arthur Conan Doyle described a region which held out the possibility of contacts with what lay beyond.

"You stand on the very brink of the unknown," he wrote, "and every duck that you shoot bears pebbles in its gizzard which come from a land which the maps know not" (325). Although boundaries of the unknown shift—with time or literary design—and although the unknown can be both actual and symbolic, it binds together the disappearances, discoveries, and possibilities discussed in this chapter. The Arctic is in this way an effective setting for imagining alternative histories, more successful ends to Primary World expeditions and explorations, and pebbles in the duck's gizzard may just as well come from warm beaches in the open polar sea as from subterranean shores, or perhaps from a place in between that which can be known and that which cannot.

Notes

1 As Geoffrey Winthrop-Young notes, taxonomic intricacies complicate discussions. Among "sometimes interchangeable, sometimes incompatible" terms describing the genre are "'uchronia', 'allohistory', 'parahistory', 'paratopia', 'allotopia', 'alternate history', the semantically more correct 'alternative history' … 'counterfeit world', 'counterfactual romance', 'what-if story', and so on" (105).

2 The novels and novella I address thus take their place in a significantly larger body of mid- to late nineteenth-century works illustrating the affordances of the Arctic for imagining lost civilizations. Some texts will be briefly referred to in the discussion, and among additional examples are George Sand's *Laura: Voyage dans le cristal* (1864), William J. Shaw's *Under the Auroras* (1888), John O. Greene's *The Ke Whonkus People* (1893), Charles Willing Beale's *Secret of the Earth* (1899), and Albert Sidney Morton's *Beyond the Palæocrystic Sea* (1895).

3 There are novels containing speculative elements building on or incorporating aspects of the Franklin expedition not included in the discussion here. Among them are Clive Cussler's *Arctic Drift* (2008), in which madness spreads on *Erebus* and *Terror* because of the bringing on board of ruthenium, an element that enables artificial photosynthesis. At the end of the novel, Franklin's corpse is found on *Terror*, still drifting with the pack ice, and can be returned to England to be interred next to Lady Jane's. Brian A. Hopkins' *Cold at Heart* (1998) mixes adventure and horror and features the Franklin expedition at the periphery of the narrative. Elizabeth McGregor's *The Ice Child* (2001) weaves together several plot strands mostly of realistic yarn but invents a cabin boy by the name of Augustus Peterman (no relation to the armchair explorer that will appear in the second section of this chapter) and sees Franklin-obsessed Doug Marshall find latter-day messages from the expedition. Aspects of Sten Nadolny's postmodern *The Discovery of Slowness* (*Die Entdeckung der Langsamkeit*, 1983) and Mordechai Richler's *Solomon Gursky Was Here* (1989) can also be designated as speculative fiction. For illuminating analyses of the latter two novels and their relation to the Franklin expedition, see McCorristine ("The Spectral Presence"), and Grace (209–213), respectively.

4   The insertion of the likely preposition is McClintock's.

5   The long and detailed subtitle similarly works to establish a frame of authenticity as it forges links with contemporaneous expedition and travel narratives: "one of a party of three men who belonged to the exploring expedition of Sir John Franklin, and who left the ship Terror, frozen up in ice, in the Arctic ocean, on the 10th day of June, 1850, to endeavor to find a passage for the vessel through the fields of ice by which she was surrounded; together with an account of the discovery of new and beautiful country, inhabited by a strange race of people; and an interesting and intensely exciting narrative of a sojourn of five months amongst them; their habits, customs, religion, &c."

6   There is no Seldon and no Jones in the actual expedition's muster, which lists mainly British crewmembers, but a Petty Officer John Wilson, aged 33 (Cookman 231).

7   Among critical works advancing this view is Michael Smith's 2006 *Captain Francis Crozier: Last Man Standing?* In 2021, Smith published a revised version of the biography, fleshed out with illustrations, and updated with information about the discoveries of *Erebus* and *Terror*; the revision is titled *Icebound in the Arctic: The Mystery of Captain Francis Crozier and the Franklin Expedition.*

8   O'Loughlin does not refer to Amundsen's untranslated exploration narrative in his acknowledgments, but to Tor Bomann-Larsen's biography *Roald Amundsen* (1995; in English translation 2006).

9   Primary World Amundsen stopped at Beechy Island to pay his respects at the beginning of his successful 1903 expedition in search of the Northwest Passage.

10 The characterization is in line with what is known of Franklin through *Narrative of a Journey to the Shores of the Polar Sea* (1823), chronicling his first Arctic expedition. Siobhan Carroll observes that "[i]n this account of their Arctic misadventures, Franklin and his men took pains to distinguish their responses to the environment from those of indigenous peoples [and] claimed to hold themselves separate from the landscape, regarding it, even at moments of great physical stress, as an object of objective scientific analysis and aesthetic contemplation" (*"The Terror"* 70)

11 The open polar sea features into a host of speculative fictions directed primarily to a younger, male audience; among them are several installments in the late nineteenth-century Frank Reade Jr-series (authored by "Noname"), and Thomas Wallace Knox's *Adventures of Two Youths on the Open Polar Sea: The Voyage of the "Vivian" to the North Pole and Beyond* (1885).

12 Not least in *Symzonia: A Voyage of Discovery* (1820), which through its title and in debates about authorship is closely linked to Symmes' ideas and person.

13 The novel conflates Burrough's popular Tarzan-series with his heptalogy about a hollow earth. I address an even later narrative that engages with polar openings in the concluding chapter: Steven Utley and Howard Waldrop's short story "Black as the Pit, from Pole to Pole" (1977).

14 In Edmond Hamilton's short story "The Daughter of Thor" (1942), depicting a radical German invasion and control of Norway, the Arctic-as-time-machine gets another inflection, when the protagonist Mart Fallon, an American pilot, discovers a "blind-spot valley" (19) in "the vast, uninhabited wilderness that is North Norway" (15). In what turns out to be an earthly Asgård, ten years

equal a thousand in the outside world; it is a discrete "space-time sphere" in which the Æsir, "but one of the Norse races" in a distant past founded their home and used "the cosmic forces" (26) particular to the sphere to develop supernatural abilities and battle skills. The year of publication makes the short story pronouncedly political, and Hamilton imagines that deities are on the side of the righteous in the war, finishing with a vision of the Norwegian people finding inspirations in stories about the returned Æsir to continue the fight, and the proleptic assessment that "the tyrants [will] be overthrown" (47).

15 The novel was originally published in two parts *Les Anglais au pôle Nord* and *Le Désert de glace* (1864) translated as *The English at the North Pole* (or *A Journey to the North Pole*) and *The Desert of Ice* (or *The Field of Ice*). I use the 1876 version of the novel (translator unknown) for my discussions here.

16 Like Franklin, Hatteras has previous, disastrous experiences of Arctic exploration behind him. His first voyage, in 1846, is halted at the seventy-fourth parallel north and Hatteras "carried his temerity so far that henceforth sailors were averse to undertaking a similar expedition under such a leader" (Verne 93). Six years later, a small expedition he commands reaches further north, but a harsh overwintering leads to that "Hatteras alone returned to England" (94).

17 A whirlpool or cataract is a well-circulated motif in speculative fiction, and constitutes the bulk of Edgar Allan Poe's "A Descent into the Maelstrom" (1841), set off the coast of northern Norway. Although the maelstrom has the power to draw everything into it: "fragments of vessels, large masses of building-timber and trunks of trees, with many smaller articles, such as pieces of house furniture, broken boxes, barrels and staves" (Poe 243), it does not lead anywhere in particular. Rather the teller of the story, his black hair turned white by the harrowing experience, narrowly escapes the certain death of it.

18 Behrman's analysis is underpinned by Michel Butor's discussion in "Le point suprême et l'âge d'or à travers quelques œuvres de Jules Verne" (1960).

19 In an aside, Lionel Philipps draws attention to Verne's wordplay in the original: "(In French, 'perdre le Nord' [losing the North] means to go crazy): We know that Hatteras loses his, by struggling so much to keep it" (30).

20 No information about author Vidar Berge is available, and the name is likely a pseudonym. Discussions about the novel in this section are in part based on my article "Andrée på äventyr" ([The Adventures of Andrée] Lindgren Leavenworth 2018).

21 A translation into English by Edward Adams-Ray was published already in 1931. The London edition bears the descriptive title *The Andrée Diaries being the Diaries and Records of S. A. Andrée, Nils Strindberg and Knut Fraenkel Written during their Balloon Expedition to the North Pole in 1897 and Discovered on White Island in 1930, together with a Complete Record of the Expedition and Discovery; with 103 Illustr. and 6 Maps, Plans and Diagrams.* The New York edition published a year later has the title *Andrée's Story: The Complete Record of His Polar Flight.*

22 Another is Leon Lewis' *Andree at the North Pole* (1899) in which Andrée, Strindberg, and Frænkel encounter antagonist Pirr Garvel, coming from a people thought to be "vastly superior" to the travelers' "own in science and progress" (25). Although this novel quickly veers into the speculative, an

introduction, photographs, and numerous footnotes with references to Primary World articles give it an ostensibly authentic frame. In Willis George Emerson's *The Smoky God* (1908) a Norwegian fisherman finds an advanced civilization via an Arctic opening and remains convinced that Andrée, Strindberg, and Frænkel "are now in the 'within' world, and doubtless are being entertained . . . by the kind-hearted giant race inhabiting the inner Atlantic Continent" (174–175).

23 All translations from the Swedish are mine.

24 Thyra is thus a statuesque woman, but the visitors, all "trained athletes," are her match, three of them "over six feet two" and Borson "seven and a half feet tall" (1).

25 *Mizora* was serially published in the *Cincinnati Commercial* 1880–81 and when published in book form, it was introduced by the paper's editor who noted the curiosity the original appearance had caused but also that "the author ... kept herself in concealment so closely that even her husband did not know that she was the writer who was making this stir in our limited literary world" (Halstead 5). The 1890 edition of *Mizora: A Prophecy*, used here, gives the author as Mary E. Bradley, but she is commonly referred to as Mary E. Bradley Lane. In the introduction to a 1999 edition of the novel, with the alternative and plot-spoiling subtitle *A World of Women*, Jean Saberhagen notes that "how the author's married name was uncovered" remains a mystery, as does the identity of the author herself (v). Although using the earliest text, I will refer throughout to the author as Lane to align my discussion with contemporary critics'.

26 Jean Pfaelzer groups Lane's novel together with Charlotte Perkins Kilman's *Moving the Mountain* (1911) and *Herland* (1915), noting that the works "appeared during fervent activity for women's suffrage, the eight-hour day, women's educational reform, and contraception" (282).

27 Lewes includes *Pantaletta* in her discussion because of the author's name, but there are suggestions that the author was male, likely US journalist William Mill Butler. *Nequa; or, the Problem of the Ages* (1900) is not mentioned in Lewes' discussions, perhaps because of conflicting views of authorship. The author's name (as well as the first-person narrator's) is Jack Adams, whereas the copyright holders are Alconoan O. Grigsby and Mary P. Lowe. The narrative itself engages with assumed gender identities in its denouement: Adams reveals that he is in fact a woman, Cassie Van Ness, and that she can no longer abide by the "the arbitrary rulings of either church or state," but instead meet her betrothed, ship captain Rafael Ganoa—one of very few who have not realized her true gender—"as an equal" (386).

28 Different translations of Verne's novel introduce additional complexities, and the title is not always included, substituted with a vaguer reference (see, for example, the 1875 edition of *The Fields of Ice*, 268).

29 *The Goddess of Atvatabar* is, however, Bradshaw's only novel.

30 In what Noah refers to as a general "cognitive dissonance" the difference between himself and Connor on the one hand, and the rest of the crew on the other, stands out. "*They each lacked a reflection. Instead, they had each other's ghosts*" (McLeod 224).

31   *Huldra* is used in both Swedish and Norwegian; *ulda* in the Sami languages. In Iceland, the *huldufólk* (hidden people) bear strong resemblances to *huldra*, as do beings such as the *skogsrå* and *vittran* in Sweden. In all cases, the creature entices humans away from their ordinary reality.

32   Repeatedly used in Russian culture, in, among other things, a play and an opera (by, respectively, Aleksandr Ostrovsky and Nikolai Rimsky-Korsakov), the folktale has inspired several Anglophone authors. Angela Carter includes the short vignette "The Snow Child" in her collection *The Bloody Chamber and Other Stories* (1979) and parts one and two of Ivey's novel are prefaced by epigraphs from Arthur Ransome's *Little Daughter of the Snow* (1916; also included in its entirety at the end of the novel), and Freya Littledale's *The Snow Child* (1979), both of which adapts the folktale for children.

2 Preserved in Ice

At the end of July, Shelley's Walton finds himself stationary, caught in the Arctic ice and surrounded by fog. When the fog lifts, he and his crew see an equally static and boundless landscape, "vast and irregular plains of ice, which seemed to have no end" (25). The only movement is that of a dog sled moving across the ice and carrying, unbeknownst to the crew, the Creature. Arrested by the Arctic ice, all the men can do is watch it disappear. Shortly afterwards, the ice breaks and Victor Frankenstein drifts towards the ship on a large floe, is taken onboard and tells his strange tale. The similarity between this tale and the attempt to conquer the Arctic, Katherine Bowers argues, "shifts Walton's [Romantic] perception of polar space" to one that rather foregrounds the Arctic sublime, and after this point, "ice serves metaphorically for the limits of civilisation, empire, and science" (75). While ice comes to represent the northern boundary for humanity's literal progress, it also preserves scientific discoveries as well as alluring marvels beyond its rim. With Victor's principal story concluded, Walton is again "surrounded by mountains of ice, which admit no escape" (Shelley 215), but, coinciding with Victor's last hours, the ice breaks up anew, and is this time "driven with force towards the north" (218), which opens possibilities to return south, to return home. Although the novel itself suggests that Walton's story indeed reaches England, Walton himself does not within the text, and the Creature pushes onwards to build a "funeral pile" even further north (224). Various processes in *Frankenstein* are in this way contained within, concluded in, and preserved by the Arctic.

My discussions in this chapter are tied to how images of the literal or figurative static nature of the Arctic are extrapolated in various ways in speculative fiction. This involves examinations of a set of persistent Arctic tropes: those of dearth, immobility, immutability. "In the Western imagination," John McCannon notes, "the polar world has featured as a realm of crystalline purity, as a grey kingdom of frozen death . . . as eternal and unchanging" in descriptions of place as well as in ruminations of a more

DOI: 10.4324/9781003355588-3

existential nature (7). Effects of concrete stasis are seen in the mummified remains of John Torrington, William Braine, and John Hartnell, three of the first fatalities of the last Franklin expedition, discovered almost perfectly preserved in the Arctic permafrost. Exhumed from their graves on Beechy Island at least twice, once in 1852 and once in 1984, the bodies illustrate how mysteries of the past can be solved with the aid of the Arctic environment.[1] Further, Francis Spufford contends with a starting point in these two exhumations,

> the preserving ice does something curious to history. It does not distinguish between the recent dead and the remote dead; all are glazed over alike, and in a place, furthermore, where the signs of *period* by which we make familiar judgements of historical time are almost completely absent.
>
> (163)

The few signs of time passing in the material Arctic space are put to specific ends in speculative fiction. In Chapter 1, the Arctic worked like a time machine that transported protagonists to other realms in fictions about (re)discovered civilizations; immutability produced alternative spaces. In the fictions I address here, the Arctic figures as a productive repository of the past with manifestations that influence or interact with characters in the forms of ghosts and monsters, but which also constitute threats to humanity which are (re)awakened in thaws. In Michelle Paver's *Dark Matter*, a captain taking an expedition to Svalbard says that they are "so far north that 'dead things' last for years" (40), a pronouncement that sums up effects of stasis in all the fictions I discuss in this chapter. In Paver's novel, dead things pertain figuratively to a past of violence and resource extraction, but also to a manifestation of these traumas in the form of a ghost. Arctic icescapes and forests also preserve monsters and bring forth the monstrous, allowing visitors brief glimpses of what has been repressed and symbolically dead, sometimes also within themselves. In Algernon Blackwood's novella "The Wendigo," a hunting party encounters an atavistic being "that had survived somehow the advance of humanity" (130), beyond the boundary of where humans are meant to go. Again, there are links between this view of the Arctic periphery harboring an alternative space and the possibility to discover forgotten civilizations addressed in Chapter 1, but the lushness and possibilities for expansion commonly encountered in those narratives find contrasts in darkness, disorientation, and shrinking personal space. Rather than forgotten or hidden, the Wendigo and its monstrous kin have simply remained in the periphery: they resist transgressions into their domains and punish failed attempts at orientation and adaptation.

In the speculative encounter between characters and the Arctic ghosts and monsters, pasts are conjured forth that illuminate time-specific fears and anxieties, often resulting in ideological critiques. In Shane McCorristine's discussions about actual mummified remains in the context of nineteenth-century polar exploration, he highlights moments in which what is seen as long dead seemingly comes to life, frightening crews with sounds and visions and destabilizing the pragmatic grounds for forays into the Arctic. "[T]he moral dimension of scientific practice hits home," he argues, "when this *something* becomes *somebody*" (*Spectral* 198). The frequently female mummies that explorers brought home "disturb," he continues, "because they are the actors of colonial haunting par excellence; rarely mentioned at all in narratives of Arctic exploration, they come from the dark depths beneath the icy surface." The past, almost perfectly preserved by the ice, is in these instances forcibly returned to the present, where it figuratively thaws and reawakens, calling into question an array of practices. And while not commonly included in Primary World materials, speculative fiction makes ample use of the destabilization between the past and the characters' present, refusing to let "injustices or memories rot in the ground" (46). In the forms of ghosts and monsters, they illustrate past traumas or policed boundaries, forcing temporary visitors to the Arctic to reevaluate or face what is taken for granted or what is impossible at home.

In the first section of this chapter, I address how processes of catching sight of ghosts are hampered by particular Arctic conditions; I examine how the trauma that produces them impacts their legibility and how Arctic or Subarctic locations or conditions function to produce or exacerbate the characters' loneliness, madness, and fear. In the second section, I transition from the often-occluded sightings of uncanny ghosts to examine marvelous monsters and supernatural beings that have concrete influence on the fictional world, killing or physically transforming characters. In this section I also widen my scope from *Frankenstein*'s frame story to address the one-way journey north that the Creature leads Victor on, and the function the Arctic has in the novel's thematization of punishment. In speculative fiction about ghosts and monsters, then, the Arctic preserves the past or is depicted *as* the past. These static qualities paradoxically induce an array of instabilities in the characters; they lose their physical or psychological foothold and must come to terms with different ontologies to keep their sanity and appease or conquer ancient beings to survive. In the third section, which also functions as a bridge to the environmental concerns in focus in the next chapter, I turn my attention to how the past is unlocked by melting ice, with ramifications that extend beyond the scientific protagonists. In speculative fictions that bring into literal view ancient species or pathogens that constitute local or global hazards, the notion of Arctic preservation is consequently juxtaposed to the threat or promise of thaws.

Ghosts

In this section, my focus is on specificities of the Arctic that have bearing on the appearance and function of ghosts and on what actual or psychological conditions set the stage for the protagonists' encounters with them. The ghost stories are imbricated in a wider mesh of both fictional and nonfictional texts in which loneliness in the peripheral Arctic has detrimental effects on the psyche of the visitor, untethered from an identity grounded in the stability of home. Separated from family and friends, indeed from the romantic, inspired reader he is at home in England, Walton has trouble reconciling his dreams of discovery with the static reality in the ice. He writes to his sister of a loneliness stemming from the absence of someone "whose tastes are like [his] own" (Shelley 19), and that his dreams of what will be accomplished in the Arctic "want (as the painters call it) *keeping*" (20).[2] Even though Walton is surrounded by other men, there is an absence of an equal who can contribute a sense of proportion, needed to harmonize his desires with the choices he must make. The lack of such an equal, before the appearance of Victor Frankenstein, leaves Walton without support to "regulate [his] mind." Desires and ambitions thus combine with loneliness to produce the conditions for a madness particular to the Arctic icescape.

In ghost stories, characters' unstable psychological states intertwine with difficulties of seeing or understanding the emergence and function of the revenant and result in narratives that oscillate between the uncanny and the marvelous. Julie Ann Stevens notes the sideways glances required to catch sight of ghosts, how they occupy shadowy or dark corners (of houses and minds alike) and how they "haunt all places disturbed, following in the wake of war, or dispossession, or suppression" (11). Luke Thurston draws attention to "the literary ghost . . . as an intrusive, illegible 'guest' element at odds with a 'host' structure of discursive legibility," that is, how the ghost interrupts ordinary understandings (6), and with a starting point in trauma theory, Arthur F. Redding argues that fictional ghosts appear "in the aftermath of persistent violence" that has disrupted ways in "which human beings stitch together a coherent understanding of the world" (4). Past trauma, be this individual or collective, inhibits or complicates narration, and the ghost becomes a mouthpiece "speaking that which cannot be spoken" (Redding 4). In my readings, I draw out the implications of the difficulty of catching sight of ghosts, and of how the Arctic past or present impacts their articulations.

The failure of the last Franklin expedition disrupted legibility insofar as it cast doubt on motives behind exploration broadly and as the few traces found did not provide conclusive answers to what actually happened. This void seemingly opened a door to supernatural speculation, among its instantiations the ghost of a girl who presents a particularly convoluted process of seeing and hearing messages from beyond. Louisa Coppin of Derry City, who died only three years old, appeared only to her siblings, who in turn reported their communications with who they referred to as Little Weesy. In 1849, the older sister Anne ostensibly received instructions from the ghost and drew a map indicating that searches for the expedition's ships should be made around Victory Point. The drawing influenced Jane Franklin to gather funds for the *Prince Albert* rescue mission, launched in 1850, and have it follow the relayed instructions. As McCorristine notes, this is "the first documented time a person asked a dead person or spirit about Franklin" (*Spectral* 166), but it takes its place in a wider network of female clairvoyancy and mesmerism that surrounds the disappeared expedition. In connection with this gendered shift of power, however, Spufford notes that women's visions were especially effective because of "assumptions about female ignorance" which held that an uneducated female mind was "a *tabula rasa*, a mental snowfield" that required "an inexplicable power" behind its formulations (133). Uneducated women were thought to have no factual knowledge of or information about the Franklin expedition and their pronouncements were therefore seen as necessarily coming from a more authoritative source. And if women generally were seen as especially susceptible to missives from afar or beyond, a girl's mental state was a snowfield indeed.

In Ed O'Loughlin's *Minds of Winter*, additional layers of decoding and figuratively seeing Little Weesy are found in a storyline that centers on Ensign Joseph René Bellot, whose faith in authorities crumbles when it becomes apparent that he has been made to follow instructions from a child who never set foot in the Arctic. On the second *Prince Albert* rescue mission, in 1851, Bellot is responsible for taking exact measurements and creating trustworthy maps, tasks he deems especially important since the men onboard speak of optical illusions such as the Fata Morgana, Cape Flyaway, and the Croker Mountains that have misled explorers to the point of ruining their reputations. Bellot is kept out of discussions, however, and continuously thwarted by William Kennedy, the ship's captain who does not seem to want a scientific charting of Arctic areas. An over-land trek results in sleeplessness, starvation, and almost complete disorientation, and at the end of this agonizing experience, Kennedy reveals that they have all along been led by Little Weesy's map. Bellot is not the only one struggling to understand the function of this particular ghost and all the men who are directly influenced by her communications are at a great distance from her, both spatially and metaphysically. The narrative then backtracks to Kennedy's visit to the Coppin household where the ghost is seen as physically present—each night, the family saves "a place at table for Weesy" (O'Loughlin 116). Like other adults, Kennedy does not see the ghost himself but is convinced by Anne's past sightings. As the most sensitive of the siblings, she reacts oddly to what is said about her sister and has an episode after which she tells Kennedy that the ghost is gone. The children's father believes that Little Weesy has joined Franklin and his crew "and that if they are found she will be at rest" (123). The ghost's communication is seen to carry weight because there is no familial connection between the Coppins and the Franklins, and because the young children are thought to know very little of the potential tragedy: her pronouncements, unattached to sources of reliable information must have a sanctioned, and male, origin. In O'Loughlin's version, Bellot becomes collateral damage in the process of heeding the authoritative instructions. Hindered from mapping the Arctic and terrified of being associated with the supernatural, he retires from public view and in an extended sense becomes one of the many who go to the Arctic only to disappear.

When considered as one strand in the complex spectral weave that surrounds the disappearance of Franklin's 1845 expedition, Little Weesy's communication illustrates the same kind of hope that underlies the Seldon narrative addressed in Chapter 1 as it implicitly signals that she communicates with still living members of the expedition. In this larger context, the hope makes this ghost peculiarly visible, despite needing her siblings' mediation. The information she relays initiates and influences rescue missions, and she thus becomes connected to a level of agency, unusual in connection with ghosts. Rather than being attached to place, she manifests the national trauma caused by a disappearance in the Arctic and she is suggested to depart to be with Franklin and his crew, isolated in the far north, and potentially further, to another realm.

The realm beyond death is actively sought by the titular figure in Arthur Conan Doyle's short story "The Captain of the 'Pole Star'," a ghost story that explicitly engages with processes of catching sight of the ghost, here the product of a personal trauma.[3] The narrative is structured around sets of juxtapositions between home and away, and between rationality and irrationality, the latter respectively embodied by the ship's doctor John McAlister Ray, who cannot see the ghost, and its captain Nicholas Craigie, who can. Presented as part of a journal written by Ray, the narrative starts on September 11 in an unknown year off the coast of Svalbard, on a ship frozen in the pack ice. Repeatedly questioning whether anyone will read his journal, let alone believe in its contents, the rational doctor describes experiences that take place in a little over a week, and that lead him to partly question previously held assumptions about absolute boundaries between natural and supernatural.

Ray's irrational foil Craigie has without concrete reason kept his ship in northern waters beyond the end of the whaling season and has gone from being respected to being feared. He exaggerates the isolation of the Arctic by confining himself to his small cabin during his bouts of a black mood, and the crew's stories about him indicate that he is actively seeking death. Anxious to return home, the crew are consequently both worried about being led into danger and wary of voicing their concerns to an unreliable commander. Many of them are also deeply superstitious, perceive of the ship as haunted, and interpret sounds as the moaning of specters. The doctor notes a superstitious "epidemic" plaguing the crew and resorts to giving "out rations of sedatives and nerve-tonics with the Saturday allowance of grog" (Doyle 337–338). To Ray, however, it is the unusual, stationary situation that causes the deepest unease, exacerbated by a "deathly silence" (341). "It is only here in these Arctic seas," he writes, "that stark, unfathomable stillness obtrudes itself upon you in all its gruesome reality" (346), opening for possibilities to ponder that which seems impossible at home.

The contrast between home and way is also emphasized by arrested images of women. Ray keeps a "vignette" of his fiancée Flora on his watchchain (336) and at the foot of Craigie's bed is a "water-colour sketch" of a female face, intriguing in its "mixture of character and weakness" (343). In his reading of the short story, McCorristine demonstrates how the materiality of objects like these "mediate processes of intimacy" that are interrupted or forestalled; the "link between the male and the female remains tenuous due to the physical and emotional separation between home and Arctic" (*Spectral* 192). But to the concrete images, McCorristine continues, is added a "spectralisation of sexuality, its sublimation into sounds, images and rumours," notable when crewmembers insist that they both see and hear something inexplicable. At midnight, the second mate and the harpooner have heard sounds reminiscent of "a bairn crying [or] a wench in pain" and they see a "white figure moving across the ice-field" that they adamantly protest is not of the natural world (Doyle 338). These sightings increase apprehension on board the ship, not least because they cannot be written off as a hallucination or illusion by a single witness. Rather, reports accumulate about "something uncanny . . . flitting round the ship" in the night, "greetin' and ca'ing in the darkness like a bit lambie that hae lost its mither" (344). Not only women, but also children and lambs—vulnerable beings that have no place in the isolated and dangerous Arctic setting—are thought to produce the sounds the crew hears as eerie echoes of home.

The living Flora awaiting Ray at home exerts a vicarious form of agency; signifying a future promise, she constitutes a link to sanity for him. Without her, Ray writes, he would be susceptible to the same erratic and despondent behavior as the captain and "care very little whether the wind blew from the north or the south to-morrow" (337). It must be, Ray further hypothesizes, "[s]ome great sorrow" that has "blighted" Craigie's existence and made him into what he is. While the precise nature of this sorrow is not revealed to Ray in the Arctic, a concluding note penned by his father includes a reference to a report testifying that Craigie's "betrothed had died under circumstances of peculiar horror" years earlier (350). When this ghost of Craigie's beloved appears in the Arctic, she remains distant and creates illegibility in more ways than one. The nature of the trauma that has produced her remains unexplained, as do the reasons for why she has become untethered from the site of her demise. Instead, Doyle focuses on what consequences the ghost's appearance has on the small, male world aboard *Pole Star*, and how rational science and spiritualism juxtapose Ray and Craigie.

   While Ray progressively sees more and hears more than his rationality can explain, Craigie is from the outset actively looking for the ghost and for ways to join her. Early on, and anticipating the crew's assessment, he proclaims that he has "more to bind [him] to that other world than to this one" (336), and he consistently gazes at the ice through his looking glass. One early evening, Ray comes upon the captain on deck and observes how he after scanning the horizon finally appears to see something that ignites in him "horror, surprise, and something approaching to joy" but which is also retreating from him (340). To catch "a last glance at the departing object," Craigie attempts to climb higher on the bulwarks, but lacks the physical strength to do so. When Ray protests that he has seen nothing, Craigie concludes that a head-on look at the ghost has been made possible only because of "the glass . . . and then the eyes of love." While there is something frightening about the ghost, Craigie pronounces it a welcome and exclusive sight, signaling a possibility to finally rest in that other world. When the wind indeed starts blowing from the north, and a lead to the south opens in the water, the captain jumps off the ship and disappears, desperate, is seems, to stay in the Arctic. When his dead body is found, his face bears "a bright smile" (350) suggesting that the sorrow, at last, has been lifted from him. By his dead body, the doctor is then one of few on *Pole Star* who does not see the ghost, interpreting the white shape hovering over Craigie as "a snow-drift" (349). To the crew, on the other hand, the ghost temporarily comes into focus as she hovers over the locus of her haunting; they swear that the form "started up in the shape of a woman, stooped over the corpse and kissed it, and then hurried away across the floe." To the superstitious crew, the departure of both the ghost and Craigie ends the brief disturbance to the fabric of life.

   Ray, on the other hand, does not have a belief in the supernatural to fall back on, and experiences that do not have a rational explanation leave him foundering. "I shall not continue my journal" reads the opening sentence to the last paragraph of the short story (350). Further narration is no longer meaningful or trustworthy as Ray has started to question his assignation of madness and superstition to the captain and the crew respectively. Throughout, Ray has tried to dissect the reports of supernatural events and attempted to link them to the isolated and dangerous conditions but in the abnormal silence of the Arctic he has himself heard a "ghastly scream" one night and thinks he perceives the sounds of the dead captain walking the deck (346). Ray is in this way left when he is *en route* home, his worldview shaken. Again, the concluding note fills an important function. Firstly, Ray's father indicates that credence should be lent the story since his son is "a strong-nerved and unimaginative man, with the strictest regard for veracity" (350). Secondly, the testimony regarding the horrible death of Craigie's betrothed supports how past trauma bleeds into the characters' present. To Ray's fantastic narrative is added a statement of his trustworthy character as well as an explanatory background. Three rational men thus agree that a ghost may very well have appeared in the Arctic, where the absence of sound and movement creates the right circumstances, and the note lets Ray catch at least figurative sight of it.

Paver's *Dark Matter* revolves around a broader conception of both actual and metaphorical emptiness and, as noted in the introduction to this chapter, Svalbard is described as literally preserving the past: dead things do not decompose at an expected rate this far north. To protagonist Jack Miller, this concrete quality easily slides into the symbolic, and it tenders promises of experiences uncorrupted by modernity. By joining a meteorological expedition, Jack hopes to experience immediate emotions and be able "to see clearly for the first time in years. Right through to the heart of things" (Paver 41). The expedition is thus expected to strip life down to essentials and provide access to a sharpened metaphorical vision. However, a preserved past also means preserved evidence of previous visitors and activities that interferes with Jack's desire for unmediated emotions and sights. Far from being unsullied by human contact, the Svalbard beaches are littered by remains of previous expeditions. Jack hopes that the (fictional) bay of Gruhuken, their destination, will prove different, but there as well, objects and structures evidence a past marked by human greed. The expedition he takes part in himself is not designed to overexploit Svalbard, but when Jack first lays eyes on the name of Gruhuken on a map, he writes in his journal: "I want it to be ours" (18). This early comment, gesturing to a seemingly innocuous version of greed, plays into how a long history of resource exploitation in Svalbard is figured as a past trauma, and how an individual trauma in this history produces a ghost.[4]

I have previously analyzed Paver's novel with a starting point in how specificities of the Arctic "blur the boundaries between previously discreet categories" such as day and night, inside and outside ("Abnormal Fears" 463), and examined how this resistance emanating from what I describe as a queer Arctic results in Jack's both physical and psychological disorientation. For my purposes here, focusing on processes of catching sight of and understanding the ghost that prowl the beaches of Gruhuken, I return to the significance of how a material past makes its way into the present. Among instances that illustrate these dissolved boundaries is Jack's bodily incorporation of the past via water tasting of seal blubber. The long history of intense seal hunting in Svalbard is one example of what Nicole M. Merola sees as the novel's representations of "inhuman ecologies," and by drinking the water, Jack " 'incorporates, though he cannot metabolize, the violence of marine mammal deaths" (31). Despite Jack's desire to distance himself from the destructive tradition, he unwittingly becomes part of it. A corresponding example comes in the form of an old trapper's hut on Gruhuken's beach. Jack describes it as permeated with despair: "as if the desperation of those poor men had soaked into the very timber" and the expedition members decide not to use it (Paver 65). A material object in this case becomes a repository for past emotions, and these are in time also concretely transferred to Jack: when he burns the timber from the hut, a storm forces the smoke back down the chimney. Jack inhales the desolate past preserved in and by the Arctic environment.

Gruhuken is thus from the start haunted by a violent and traumatic past, and what Jack perceives of as abnormalities, such as the simple absence of "an hour or so of twilight," contribute to estranging it further (135). Sightings of the ghost are initially tied to an abnormality also connected to light: the appearance and disappearance of the sun. On 16 August, newly arrived at Gruhuken, the expedition members experience the first dark, that is, when the sun sets for the first time after the Arctic summer. At the end of a solitary walk, Jack returns to see a figure standing, back turned, by an old bear post that remains in front of the newly built cabin. Two months later, the sun rises and sets for the last time, and again, Jack remains outside after having taken the meteorological readings. For no immediately discernible reason, he is afraid, and then sees movement among the rocks. A form has "hauled itself from the sea" (106) but the silence is absolute and unnatural, and Jack understands that he has "just seen a ghost" (109). What is visible, however, is in both instances only the ghost's form. The phrase "wet round head" is repeated in Jack's descriptions (106, 176, 242), as are references to the male figure's posture with one shoulder higher than the other and hanging arms; Jack also notes that "something about the tilt of his head" is odd and unappealing (83). The ghost, that is, evades a straight look, even when placed right in front of Jack.

Jack's frail mental state, which deteriorates when he is left alone at Gruhuken, gestures to that the ghost may have a Todorovian uncanny explanation, and thus remain invisible to anyone but Jack himself. The uncanny effect is to an extent destabilized by descriptions Jack accesses through a notebook left behind by Gus Balfour, one of his scientific colleagues, and that illustrates that both Gus and the third member of the expedition, Algie Carlisle, have experienced identical sensory impressions: seeing knives, smelling paraffin, and being bound. However, these experiences do not provide a view of the ghost either and are rather described as "*walking nightmare*[s]" (156) and "*hallucinations*" (157). Gus and Algie are wary of admitting a concrete presence at Gruhuken and paradoxically prefer to doubt their mental stability. Expected effects of Arctic isolation—"*Rar. Ishavet kaller.* Cabin fever. Nerve strain" (24)— are to all three men exacerbated by place-specific dissolutions of boundaries that hinder orientation. When Jack no longer has the company of Gus and Algie, he holds on to what have become meaningless temporal markers that he "impose[s] . . . like a grid on the formless dark" (129), and he keeps to a regimented schedule of meteorological duties, even though he has concluded that visitors' and expeditions' ceaseless measuring and categorizing are but futile attempts "to render bearable this vast, silent land" (194). This structuring of Jack's existence is coupled with actions and notions that limit him further, metonymically representing his besieged body and afflicted psyche. The absolute dark of a late fall in the High Arctic makes Jack suspect that he is alone to an extent beyond the immediate situation: "maybe there is nothing beyond those windows. Maybe there is only you in this cabin and beyond it the dark" (136). The fear this notion produces makes him cover the windows with blankets. When he suspects that the ghost can get into the cabin, he isolates himself further to the bunk room, also here nailing blankets to the wall, in effect creating "a padded cell" (226). The ghost's perimeter of influence expands, shrinking Jack's.

The ghost's increasingly material presence is foreshadowed by Jack's early attempts to rationally account for oddities at Gruhuken and which foreground how past traumas linger in objects and landscapes. Among these is the idea of "place memory" (111), signifying how intensely violent emotional events leave an echo in objects or landscapes for perceptive listeners. Jack's reaction to the bear post is particularly portentous. Close to it, he seems to perceive "an auditory imprint, a lingering trace of some act of savagery which was once perpetrated here at Gruhuken" (157), and when the ghost appears in the post's place, the residual echo from the past seeps forth "like blood staining a bandage" (178). In a dream which precedes Jack's shutting down and closing out the world, he is tied to the bear post, tortured and burned alive, as was once, he has been told, a man whose claims on Gruhuken were opposed by a mining company. The violence and trauma of the past, inextricably linked to a history of disputed ownership in Svalbard, have remained in the physical object of the bear post and are repeated in the terrifying dream. Assuming the position of the unfortunate man, however, does not mean that Jack is allowed a clear view of the ghost, quite the contrary. The nightmare rather becomes another process of enforced metabolization in which Jack involuntarily gets access to the ghost's perspective and experiences without fully understanding what to make of them. Oscillating between uncanny and marvelous, Paver's ghost story becomes another example of the Todorovian fantastic.

Dark Matter shares with Yrsa Sigurðardóttir's *I Remember You* ideas of eerie continuation, which in Paver's novel loop back to the repeated reference to Svalbard as a location in which neither symbolic nor actual matter decomposes. Assuming the position and perspective of the ghost in the nightmare makes Jack fear that he will also transition into its role and take over its function: that the haunting of Gruhuken will continue. "To be conscious in eternal night" would be a logical punishment for encroaching on Gruhuken, he thinks, and "pray[ers] for oblivion" would go unheard (231). Jack escapes both this fate and the Arctic but remains convinced that Gruhuken continues to be haunted. On a beach in Jamaica, he keeps his distance to the water, "the same sea" that surrounds Svalbard, and that is perceived as a conduit to the isolated bay and "what walks there in the dark" (251). The idea of inheritance, of a perpetuated circle of haunting, is literalized in *I Remember You* which ends with the ghost of one of the protagonists, Katrín, protecting "her home [where] nothing would disturb her . . . again" (Sigurðardóttir 391). Like Jack, Katrín and her companions Garðar and Líf have come to a peripheral island as outsiders and have attempted to order and understand the surroundings, but this denouement indicates that Katrín not only comes to see the location as hers, but has inherited from the already present ghosts, an anger directed at intrusions.

Sigurðardóttir effectively uses the isolation of Hesteyri in Iceland's Westfjords, the approaching cold and dark season, and the unpreparedness of a mismatched group to blur boundaries between imagination and reality. And several aspects combine to place the characters in similar positions as the visitors to the Arctic in the previously discussed texts. Hesteyri is unfamiliar to the characters, and primitive in comparison with Reykjavik, without electricity or reliable cell phone reception. Katrín, Garðar, and Líf come there to escape the instability occasioned by the 2008 financial crisis in Iceland, seeing the restoration of a dilapidated building as a slim chance for a more stable future. However, in contrast to the protracted and futile process of catching sight of the ghost in *Dark Matter*, Katrín sees "a pitch-black shadow" standing out against the "dim surroundings" (15) already when landing on the beach. A series of occurrences then convince them that they are not alone: crosses from the nearby cemetery are moved into the backyard, seashells appear in heaps or as forming words, they hear sounds of sobbing, and catch unpleasant smells. When they see a figure standing in an unusual pose "with his cap-covered head hanging down to his chest and his arms dangling . . . . as if the person had surrendered to the injustice of the world," Katrín understands that the figure is a child (119). In fact, the house is haunted by the ghosts of two children, their deaths sixty years apart, and there is something eerie about the building itself, visible across the fjord. The boat captain transporting them to Hesteyri suggests that the "desperation" of many who have drowned in the cold, violent waters has become attached to "the last thing they ever saw in this life" (369), a pronouncement that echoes Jack's theory of place memory, and more broadly connects to how past traumas produce not only ghosts but loci of fear and loneliness.

While some incidents in Sigurðardóttir's novel can be interpreted as consequences of the small group's vulnerability, and in particular those in which one character alone perceives the smells and sounds and sees traces of wet feet on the floorboards, other events shorten the route towards an acceptance of the existence and influence of the supernatural. To the captain's gesturing to a widespread belief that the location is haunted is added a film the group finds, in which a previous renovator of the house has come to realize that he will never leave the island and is "saying his final goodbyes" (185). Fear mounts among all three characters simultaneously, exacerbated by these other pieces of evidence that something is wrong at Hesteyri, and on the film, they recognize a shadowy figure in the background as the boy they have seen. As if this realization opens a literal door for the marvelous, Katrín and Líf shortly afterwards see "pale, yellowish fingers" wrapping around a corner in the house, sense an odor "of kelp and rotten meat" and hear a "terrifying voice, now raised in anger: *I said I'm not finished*" (192). The boy who has died over half a century previously, trying to escape the cold under the floorboards of what used to be his home, is intent on driving all visitors away, or destroying them: Katrín's last sensation while she is still alive is feeling small "hands, cold as ice" strangle her (362). Whether or not she assumes the place as the next ghost in line or joins the boy specters is uncertain, but in Sigurðardóttir's speculative Westfjords, ghosts have a dangerous level of agency.

The last speculative fiction I will discuss, Sarah Moss' *Cold Earth*, illustrates how processes of catching sight of ghosts are also actively addressed within the narrative. As in the novels by Paver and Sigurðardóttir, disturbances of a resting place are central when a small archeological team arrives in West Greenland at the end of the summer. They have come to excavate a site that was home to the original Greenlanders, a colony of Norsemen from Iceland, that inhabited the area between the tenth and fifteenth centuries, and whose disappearance reads like an Arctic precursor to Roanoke. In the non-fictional *The Frozen Ship*, published three years before the novel and addressing polar narratives broadly, Moss draws attention to the mystery surrounding this and the Eastern settlement "disappearing . . . perhaps unnaturally into the Arctic mists," the historical details "offer[ing] a compelling mixture of homeliness and strangeness, a kind of domestic Gothic" (56). The reason for past (possible) trauma is debated: it could have been an epidemic, conflicts, climate change, or a combination, but when the priest Ivar Bardarson, sent in the fourteenth century from a Norwegian diocese to examine why tithings were no longer forthcoming, he found "buildings . . . intact and seemingly inhabited [yet] no sign of anyone present or recently departed" (36).[5] Archeological finds indicate that the settlement was populated after Bardarson's visit, but there are signs of yet another hasty departure with foodstuffs still in larders, and personal effects left behind. The archeological work that has shed light on but not conclusively answered the question of the settlements' disappearances is continued in fictional form in *Cold Earth* and is intertwined with the elements of a ghost story.

The novel is told in sections of first-person narrations from the six members of the party, all addressed to living or dead loved ones at home. Like the journal format in the texts by Doyle and Paver, the address is well suited to depict individual attitudes towards the excavation and to increasingly strange occurrences, as well as illustrating the protagonists' mounting fear. There is an ominous sense that the letters may not reach the addressees due to a possible contagion spreading in the world the group has left (I discuss this aspect in more detail in Chapter 3), and when communications from the outside world cease, life in the camp becomes contained and claustrophobic. The expedition is ill-planned and the members of the group, not close to begin with, become increasingly vulnerable due to mistrust and paranoia. As their resources are dwindling and winter approaches, they find more and more similarities between their own situation and that of the disappeared settlement.

Nina, whose first-person sections start and finish the novel, is to an even greater extent than the others an outsider in the isolated valley. She is working towards a doctorate in English literature and has an interest in the dark undertones to Norse folktales, but she is of little practical help in the dig, preferring not to come too close to the human remains that are preserved in the frozen ground. She acutely feels that the group encroaches on the past and on place, disturbing both despite their attempts to not leave permanent traces. And then she starts having nightmares. In the first, Nina sees a church with its roof set on fire, trapping men inside, and how the settlement's women are brought aboard intruders' ships. Subsequent dreams place her inside the church and outside it in the aftermath of the fire. To an extent, the nightmares correspond to speculations in the contemporary group about what has possibly happened to the original settlers, which finger very real intruders as the culprits. Later dreams, however, move the action to a neighboring village and introduce a less concrete reason for the settlement's undoing, with something unearthly emitting disturbing sounds. In a vain attempt at defense, the men of the village are all killed, and Nina sees "something pale flapping up the hill. Whatever

came to the dark hillside has gone. For now" (88). The intrusion of something unnatural on the settlement is paralleled by how the everyday of the
contemporary dig is shaken when Nina's nightmares seem to migrate into
her awake state. Matter is seemingly affected—an inexplicable tear in a
tent, a stone thrown with no discernible hand behind it—and the rest of the
group is influenced by the disturbances.

Initially, the archeologists feel close to the people whose disappearance
they investigate, because the actual landscape and conditions under which
they live seem unchanged. Lines between past and present are becoming
indistinguishable, and the group concludes that they are "haunted by the
people [they are] excavating" (144). Nina, however, indicates that what
both settlers and archeologists have done is to disturb "something that's
always been here" (78) and that there are consequently hauntings both
in the past and in the present. There is a possible third layer of haunting
as well; already in the second dream, Nina is convinced that the priest
caught in the burning church can see her, and although she in later dreams
understands that she is invisible, her presence still frightens the early
settlers. Frustratingly, she cannot leave this past although all she wants
is *"to come back home"* (33): a desire for both a geographical and temporal return. Nina remains an observer, never privy to the whole truth
about what happened to the first Greenlanders, and without power to
avoid proximity to the dead in her dreams. Encased in a small space, she is
among the dead of the village and her *"fingers find the papery smoothness
of a frozen face, the prickle of eyelashes and then the open ice-cube eyes"*
(100). The agency she exerts in her waking state, keeping careful distance
to the human remains, is overthrown.

. As the process of literally digging up the past continues, the other
members of the group also begin to experience things they cannot completely align with reality. At first, it is Nina's night-time cries and her conviction that something has been disturbed that unsettle them, and then her
conviction that past is affecting present in a literal sense. "[T]hey come in
the night. The dead ones" she tells them (120), with bloody faces and the
agency to enter her tent, and the group's explanations to sounds they all
hear become increasingly untenable. In his letter to family at home, Jim
admits that there are "ghosts we're all beginning to believe in" (226) and
Catriona writes to the woman she secretly loves that "there is someone or
something here with us, moving things" (259). Although Nina remains
the only one who sees the ghosts, the majority of the others are concretely
affected. In tandem with an increased sense of isolation and vulnerability
to hunger and cold, a sense of group hysteria develops. Rather than being
physically harmed by the ghosts, the characters turn on and hurt each other.

Delineating a Scottish Gothic, Timothy C. Baker notes a trajectory going
from Doyle's ghost story to Moss' (and to John Burnside's *A Summer*

of Drowning, discussed in Chapter 1), in which "absence [becomes] a sort of presence" in the northern locations (149). In "The Captain of the 'Pole Star'," the lack of sound and movement in the icebound ocean provides a point of entrance to the supernatural and in *Cold Earth*, the characters resist notions of haunting until the specificities of the static and quiet Arctic take precedence. Jim, for example, reflects that unexpected sounds and movements perceived are so "slight" that they would be impossible to "notice anywhere busier" (Moss 225). "The North," Baker argues, "becomes a setting for haunting purely because whatever is there, it seems, must be imagined: superstition and imagination become credible in a world where they have no material counterpart" (149). Moss' archeologists are preoccupied with the past to the point that it bleeds into the present and erodes differences. The seasonal changes even further contribute to an emptying of material space, sparse to begin with, "like creation on rewind, back towards darkness and the void" (Moss 184). Baker suggests that the lack of "clearly delimited geographic boundaries" in northern or Arctic locations "often functions as a metonymic representation of a lack of fixed boundaries between life and death" (151, 152), and in Moss' novel, the specific location ceases to matter with the onset of winter and the dwindling of resources. Hovering in a liminal zone between life and death, between past and present, the characters come to a standstill, no longer concerned with the mystery they have come to Western Greenland to solve.

Whereas vampires and spirits reside in the south and east, "[g]hosts in Europe are northern," argues Peter Davidson (144), and "the revenant narrative . . . is a product of occluded weather and broodings upon the fate of the dead" (145). The lack of boundaries between day and night—what I see as one facet of the queer Arctic—seemingly produces a "zone between the living and the dead" (146), a liminal space where the departed and the past seem close to or even indistinguishable from the living present. With the exception of Little Weesy, who in my reading increases legibility, the ghosts make the targets of their visitations ontologically uncertain, a destabilization which is exacerbated by the characters' vulnerability, distanced from home and in an Arctic space that refuses to let go of the past. Liminality and peripherality thus join the five ghost stories addressed in this section. But added to these abstract notions are also specific Arctic traumas that migrate into the characters' present and that open for a critique of events, practices, and histories. Although O'Loughlin's rendition of spectrality in connection with the Franklin expedition zeroes in on effects on Bellot, it more broadly participates in an interrogation of how polar exploration haunts the present and haunts the Arctic. With more specific geographical and historical foci, the hard-to-see ghosts in Moss' novel gesture to uncomfortable parallels between the distant past and the archeologists' present, and Paver's ghost is a result of a history of environmental trauma in Svalbard, one individual tragedy in a destructive practice.

Monsters and Monstrosity

Etymologically unsurprisingly, monsters constitute a contrast to hard-to-see ghosts, showing themselves as signs of reminder and warning. By their difference, they indicate what is normal and benevolent, but "the rhetorics of horror," Ken Gelder notes, also "provide ways of defining . . . what should be seen (and what should remain hidden)" (1). This often-made observation is particularly compelling when monsters move from a temporal or spatial periphery to the center, or when characters confront monsters that appear in their own environment. What then threatens a known social structure stands out as the Other that needs to be combatted or excluded: "this naming of difference as evil," Rosemary Jackson argues, "is a significant ideological gesture" (52). The identified monster destabilizes boundaries of knowledge and the self and brings to light what is historically and culturally repressed, in a more symbolic and wider sense than ghosts that are tied to specific events and traumas. But if monsters, as Jefferey Jerome Cohen suggests, are products of time-specific cultures, and if cultures can be understood by "the monsters they engender" ("Monster Culture" 3), what monsters are produced by an Arctic that is stereotypically viewed as empty and outside time? The speculative novels I discuss in this section in the main present characters who are distanced from their own social structure and the monstrous that is engendered within it, instead venturing into what they perceive of as a static Arctic void. With Victor Frankenstein's Creature as the exception, the monsters are not brought north by the visitors in the sense of being manifestations of repressed fears or desires as ghosts often are. Instead, they are tied to Indigenous cultures, to myth and folklore, to earlier time periods, and to the Arctic or Subarctic landscape.

In addition to highlighting the marvelous, that is, depicting how the inexplicable finds physical, manifest form, the texts examined in this section also illustrate how two very different forms of the Arctic—vast icescape and claustrophobic forest—are figured as repositories for the past, and as effecting a profound personal change in the protagonists. Blackwood's novella "The Wendigo" effectively illustrates the uncomfortable coexistence of stasis and transformation, and how purported civilization has pushed the north in front of itself, and with it all that eludes rationalization. In the aftermath of events, these are the concluding thoughts by the protagonist Simpson:

Out there, in the heart of unreclaimed wilderness, they had surely
witnessed something crudely and essentially primitive. Something that
had survived somehow the advance of humanity had emerged terrific-
ally, betraying a scale of life still monstrous and immature. He envisaged
it rather as a glimpse into prehistoric ages, when superstitions, gigantic
and uncouth, still oppressed the hearts of men; when the forces of nature
were still untamed, the Powers that may have haunted a primeval universe not yet withdrawn.

(Blackwood 129–130)

Set in northwestern Ontario, the novella falls slightly outside my geographical scope, but the great, cold northern forest harboring and making
accessible a terrifying prehistoric past, as well as the cannibalistic monster
with a heart of ice connect to discourses around horror and monstrosity in
the Arctic more broadly. "The Wendigo" also introduces sharp contrasts
between home and away, as well as destabilizations and transformations
that are highlighted in specific ways by the Arctic. The enormity of the
forest that Simpson enters is pitted against the "little toy woods" (90) of his
Scottish home, and the scope of the former suggests that "there might well
be depths of wood that would never in the life of the world be known or
trodden" (91), a description that easily lends itself to a figurative reading.
The hunting party Simpson belongs to only temporarily visits this uncontrollable wilderness, and remains at its periphery, but to enter the forest
still entails a "shifting of personal values hitherto held for permanent and
sacred" (81). Although this kind of shift can be accommodated or even
welcomed, the novella depicts a radical and far more detrimental psychological change when the party's guide, Défago, is carried off by a Wendigo.
    In Margaret Atwood's delineation of how the Wendigo has been
appropriated from Algonquin myths, the monster's main function is to
"incarnat[e] the concept . . . of going crazy in the North—or being driven
crazy by the North" (*Strange Things* 62), and in the most frightening scenario, the transformed individual has somehow called forth the Wendigo
within him- or herself.[6] Défago is from the outset described as "deeply
susceptible . . . to that singular spell which the wilderness lays upon certain lonely natures" (Blackwood 72), and is particularly vulnerable when
traveling through the forest. To Simpson, who does not have the same sus-
ceptibility, there is a prolonged moment of disorientation when attempting
to follow the Wendigo and its prey, in which sensory perceptions relay
"uncommon things to his brain" (98) and in which a nightmarish mood
limits his powers and agency. Simpson's disorientation and distrust in his
rational self is momentary, however, whereas Défago is permanently altered
in both body and mind. When found, Défago's facial features are contorted
and animalistic, his memories and ability to speak are gone, his "entire

structure threaten[ing] to fly asunder and become—*incoherent*" (125). The imminence of incoherence caused by the Arctic, here in its Wendigo embodiment, echo in all the fictions addressed in this section.

But the many iterations of the Wendigo also open for readings in which the monster is anything but called forth from within. Marlene Goldman, for example, sees the monstrous being as a manifestation of past trauma, with stories specifically "register[ing] the ongoing impact of imperialism" on Indigenous peoples (168), and Jackson Eflin, investigating a recent resurgence of Wendigo stories in contemporary popular culture, notes that "the memory of the Wendigo and all it represents haunts the collective unconscious of America, a howling reminder of colonial dispossession" (9).[7] A function akin to these instantiations targeting encroachment and loss, but with greater emphasis on environmental issues, is filled by the *Tuunbaq* in Dan Simmons' *The Terror*.[8] Siobhan Carroll, examining the novel in the context of the ecological uncanny—the uncomfortable recognition of "the human in the natural and *vice versa*"—describes it as a "tale of a punitive ecological response to the British Empire's penetration of the North", and in which the *Tuunbaq* figures as an instrument of determent ("*The Terror*" 67, 73).

No exact correlation exists between Simmons' *Tuunbaq* and deities or spirits from Inuit myths, but it is incorporated into a long fictional history that foregrounds protection of the Arctic. The maritime deity Sedna, in Simmons' version, initially creates it to punish other spirits, but when this plan backfires and the *Tuunbaq* turns on its creator, she banishes it "to the coldest, emptiest part of the crowded Earth—the perpetually frozen region near the north pole" that Inuit agree to not permanently populate, nor use for excessive fishing or hunting (Simmons 708). It is foreseen, however, that the arrival of the *kabloona*, "the pale people," into this domain will signal "the beginning of the End of Times" when Indigenous language and knowledge will be forgotten and the "cold, white domain will begin to heat and melt and thaw" (710). The Franklin expedition thus represents an early step in the process of appropriation and exploitation of the Arctic and the ecological disconnect that will follow, and what is at the beginning an unruly spirit that can be appeased with respect for the Highest Arctic, turns into a monster in the eyes of the crew when it exacts its revenge.

From the perspective of the visitors, then, the marvelous is made manifest when the *Tuunbaq* approaches the frozen-in ships, and the boundaries between monster and landscape are blurry. Able Seaman Charles Best's narration of the attack on Lieutenant Graham Gore emphasizes the *Tuunbaq*'s intimate connection with the Arctic landscape, echoing how the ice previously has been described, with "pressure ridges appear[ing] as if by magic . . . sometimes moving faster than a man can run" (59). Best repeats the phrase "the ice just rose up" to explain his impressions, and then the ice takes "*shape*. A white shape. A form" (151). Whereas Franklin and Commander James Fitzjames insist that Gore has been attacked by a polar bear and that the witnesses' horror makes them exaggerate its size, Best urges them to accept that what they have encountered cannot be rationally explained. Again, the Arctic landscape is invoked as "the thing . . . surrounded" Gore and after killing him "just went back down into the ice—like a shadow going away when the sun goes behind a cloud" (152). Gore, in this retelling, has been punished by an embodied Arctic and anxieties build even higher among the men onboard *Erebus* and *Terror* who sense there is no longer any safe space.

Crozier is the only survivor in Simmons' novel, and his success hinges on his ability to understand the nature and ramifications of the expedition's encroachment and a certain justification for the *Tuunbaq*'s actions. To a far greater extent than the others in the crew, he *sees* the *Tuunbaq*. The first sighting is a result of his clairvoyance, an ability that links the character to the Primary World's foregrounding of extrasensory perception in the search for the expedition's lost ships, and which ties into both past and future. In this premonition, he is a naked child kneeling in a church preparing to take Communion, but the figure posing as the priest is preternaturally large, towering over the boy and "has no Wafer in his hand. He has no hands. Instead, the dripping apparition leans over the altar rail, leans far too close, and opens its own inhuman maw as if Crozier is the Bread to be devoured" (359). The regression into the child state is indicative of Crozier's vulnerability in the Arctic and to the *Tuunbaq* and the mere action of participating in Communion is taboo, as to everyone in Crozier's family except his Catholic grandmother it is considered "pure transubstantiated cannibalism" (358). The vision signals Crozier's ability and willingness to go against what is expected and condoned, and receiving the Eucharist foreshadows a literal transformation. When Crozier, wide awake, finally faces the Arctic *Tuunbaq*, the change from priest into a monster is reversed with the *Tuunbaq*'s "[f]ur dripping like a priest's wet and clinging white vestments [and its] predator's eyes searching for his soul" (746). At this point in the novel, Crozier has come to see ostensibly innocuous exploration as an intrusion in the Arctic and on its Indigenous peoples, and he has formed a close relationship with Lady Silence, the Inuit woman who arrives to the ships concomitantly with the monster. In a reversal of Holy Communion, Crozier offers up his own tongue to be able to communicate with the *Tuunbaq* and by extension with the land itself. The extrasensory gift of clairvoyance is exchanged for one that aligns Crozier with Indigenous spiritual practices and ties him even closer to the Arctic.

By conflating discourses circulating around the Franklin expedition with contemporary environmental concerns, the *Tuunbaq*, following Cohen, embodies two "cultural moment[s]" at once, substituting "a time, a feeling, and a place" ("Monster Culture" 4) with times, feelings, and places. To the crews of *Erebus* and *Terror*, the *Tuunbaq* is a monster because it upsets known science and because it is conflated with the sublime Arctic land-scape that already has punished them. When foregrounding the process of environmental degradation of the Arctic that the Franklin expedition initiates, it is a lamentable monster because it confirms that the end times are approaching. As a portent of future destruction, the monster appears (or returns) to prompt a reevaluation of "how we perceive the world, and how we have misrepresented what we have attempted to place," Cohen argues, asking, as many monsters do, "why we have created them" (20). Although Cohen does not explicitly refer to *Frankenstein* in "Monster Culture," it is of course in this novel the question is most loudly posed, and from a rare perspective articulated by the being that is created: "Why did I live?" (Shelley 138).[9] This question reverberates in the many adaptations and reanimations of *Frankenstein*, and answers to it illustrate how this promethean myth too responds to a plethora of cultural moments.

In Shelley's novel, the readiest answer is Victor Frankenstein's quest for scientific glory and renown, which shifts the assignation of monster to the human creator who not only ignores consequences for the world outside his laboratory, but also eschews further responsibility for what he has made.[10] The conflation of monster and creator is well-explored territory in the vast body of scholarship surrounding Shelley's novel, with attention paid to formal details, such as how a lack of "differences in tone, diction and sentence structure" between Victor and the Creature blur boundaries that the narrative initially tries to uphold (Newman 146), as well as to how the customary function of the monster—to signal "what we must on no account allow ourselves to become"—turns into a horrifying illustration of "what we are" (Griffin 72). While unstable demarcations and transform-ations such as these are important to my readings not only of *Frankenstein* but of the other novels discussed in this section, I will briefly stay with the close association between the Creature and arcticity, as well as in the con-crete function filled by the Arctic.

In his comprehensive, contextualizing study of Shelley's novel, *Ariel Like a Harpy*, Christopher Small demonstrates how "[w]inter accom-panies the Monster . . . ice and snow are in truth congenial to him, they are his proper environment" (46). Easily read as a metaphor for an unfeeling nature, indeed for monstrosity itself, cold acquires literal meanings as the novel progresses, and follows the development of the Creature. Created on a rainy November night, the Creature's first months are spent in the cold, and, reflecting his initially uncorrupted state, he searches for shelter, learns to make fire, and welcomes the warmer seasons. Thinking back on these early days, the Creature tells Walton that "when the images which this world affords first opened upon me, when I felt the cheering warmth of summer . . . I should have wept to die" (Shelley 225). Disavowed by Victor and influenced by the hostility and suspicion he is met with by others, the Creature "becomes more monstrous [and] his surroundings are more frozen" (Small 46), a development that culminates in the Arctic. In the Creature's own assessment of his difference, attention is drawn not only to his advanced agility and tolerance for a "coarser diet" than that of others, but to his ability to withstand "the extremes of heat and cold" (Shelley 123). Victor's corresponding vulnerability to cold is established already in the sections of *Frankenstein* set on Mont Blanc and on Orkney, yet he responds to the Creature's challenge. "Follow me" the Creature writes on rocks and tree trunks: "I seek the everlasting ices of the north, where you will feel the misery of cold and frost, to which I am impassive" (208). Victor follows, intent on revenge, moving "northward" and into temperatures "almost too severe to support" and into lands that are empty of both people and sustenance (208–209). Neither the Creature nor Victor share Walton's idea of a tropical polar paradise, instead they venture into an Arctic that promises no comforts, a place of exile for them both.

The recourse to a geographical periphery features already when the Creature asks Victor to create for him "a companion . . . of the same species" as himself (146). But exchanging South America, where the Creature and his mate would live a "harmless" life (148), for the Arctic underlines the importance of drawing Victor and his destructive practices away from humanity. As Beth Newman suggests, frame narratives derive their efficacy "by promising something powerfully horrifying at their center" but they also gesture to "the barriers that protect us from it" (159). The frame story and the Arctic fill the same function in this regard: in the periphery, damage will be confined to the characters immediately affected by events. A final standoff between Victor and the Creature is forestalled, however, Victor never quite catching up and the Creature returning for his pursuer too late. In Small's reading, "nature itself, by splitting the ice between them at the climax of the chase, clearly forbids" such a final encounter (187). Jonathan Bate approaches the linkages between the Creature and nature from a slightly different perspective, seeing in *Frankenstein* how ideas "of [the] Enlightenment or modernity [position] the natural man as a sign of its own alienation" (45). The Arctic becomes a locus of agency also in his analysis, but rather than aligning with the Creature, it thwarts the superiority of Victor and science more broadly. "Enlightenment mastery is based on *division*" and categorization, Bate argues, whereas "the Arctic [is] *a place where divisions do not hold*" (54). Gesturing to formulations in Barry Lopez's *Arctic Dreams* around how dissolved categories of "time, season, light and spatial relations" upset notions taken for granted in lower latitudes, Bate thus suggests that the Arctic itself stands in opposition to the novel's denouement, while at the same time being the logical end point of the narrative.

When the unusual trajectory of the one-way journey north does not function as punishment, it commonly relies on a significant change in the protagonists, such as Crozier's physical transformation in *The Terror*. In Adam Nevill's dark and violent *The Ritual*, which depicts a hike gone grievously wrong, protagonist Luke emerges both figuratively and literally naked from the Arctic Swedish forests at the end of the novel. Although he follows a "thin line [through] the landscape of stone and reindeer moss" that indicates that someone in the past has escaped "the dreadful forest," Luke is left on this barely perceptible path rather than seen returned to safety (Nevill 416). Having faced a number of horrors among the trees and also gone through a "final reckoning of himself" (Nevill 369), Luke is vastly different from who he was when he entered the forest; like in many other examples in the horror genre, layers of what is seen as civilization are peeled off to enable characters to access suppressed traits or abilities.

A process of identity disintegration is underway already at the start of the narrative, when four British men are quickly getting lost in Muddus (in Sami Muttos) national park. Attempting to reestablish a friendship of their youth, the men are strangers to each other and unwilling to cooperate. Anxieties brewing in the group make them quick to turn on each other, and as past wrongdoings come to light all four lives are revealed as failed or incomplete. This vulnerable group tries to make its way to safety, but the agentic forest leads them astray from planned paths and straight lines, and the meager light let in by canopy creates the impression that they are "descending into an environment that was only getting darker and more disorienting" (Nevill 17). The resistance to orientation is then coupled with increasingly strange occurrences. There are animal carcasses strung up impossibly high between trees, and in the attic of a dilapidated building the men find evidence of further animal sacrifice. The forest outside is at this point decidedly different from where they entered the national park: "rotten. And lightless" and the finds in the house suggest to the men that it is the natural environment that "made these people crazy. Because . . . people are [not] supposed to come here" (50). In this prohibitive space, the injured, dehydrated, and exhausted men press on in what they hope is the right direction to exit the forest and madness increasingly makes itself felt. Luke feels that "[h]is personality was disappearing, paring itself down to instinct and fear" (195), a process that mixed with nightmares eventually takes him "near the very end of himself" (316). At this proximity to an existential end, Luke is also the sole survivor as his companions have one by one been taken by what resides in the forest, leaving behind tents full of blood and turning up "wet and spread about the trees" like the animals they have previously seen (224). Until their last moments, the men catch no

more than fleeting glances of something impossibly large moving through
the forest and hear its bellows, but in a last stand-off, Luke glimpses its
dark shape, goat-like legs, and then "[a] thick-haired face, black, with a
wet bovine muzzle" (411). Although Luke is able to injure this monster, via
a combination of truck and Swiss army knife, the sense is that it and its kin
will continue to roam the forest, keeping intruders out.

Nevill's monsters, or more precisely old gods, have a long presence in
the disorienting forests, it is indicated, and the revelation that they are
this time called forth by three teenaged members of a black metal band,
Blood Frenzy, highlights how different times produce monsters that speak
to specific cultural moments. The old gods have a supposed connection
with the Wild Hunt in Scandinavian folklore, presaging a catastrophe or
upheaval, and the teenagers want to overthrow a civilization consisting
of "Christians, and immigrants and social democrats" (325), that in
their view has relegated the old gods to a cultural periphery. It is the
group's dissatisfaction with the current cultural climate that ostensibly
produces the monster, that is, and through sacrifices they aim to instigate
a new Ragnarök which will allow access to wilder, untamed forces also
within themselves. Nevill presents the teenagers' corrupted view of both
undesirable demographics and heathen cults as the main, but somewhat
naïve, evil, but this assignation is complicated by a juxtaposition between
atavism and civilized modernity which runs throughout the novel. The
forest is consistently contrasted to the well-ordered social democracy that
the protagonists have experienced before their hike, and the increasingly
horrific details gain traction precisely because of their impossibility in
a civilized world. When Luke in the end takes recourse to a "hot red
place of instinct and rage" to avoid becoming a final sacrifice (370), he
reflects the crumbling boundaries between cultured behavior and primal
emotions but also, uncomfortably, feels reassured by discovering that this
part of himself, previously hidden under a veneer of civilization, is still
there. Luke's transgression of personal boundaries makes him respond
with violence, which places him in closer proximity to the monster within
himself.

In *Frankenstein*, the notion of transgression is highlighted by Shelley's
use of Samuel Taylor Coleridge's *The Rime of the Ancient Mariner*, which,
in addition to providing a narrative structure in which a tale is told to a
stranger, is alluded to throughout the novel. In Walton's second letter, sent
before he has left Russia, he assures his sister that he "shall kill no albatross" on his voyage (Shelley 21); he will not risk the good luck he feels
blessed with before his voyage has even commenced. Victor's reanimation
of dead flesh, on the other hand, violates the rules of nature, and he is from
the start aware of correspondences between his own and the Mariner's guilt
and lapsed responsibility.[11] The killing of this particular albatross uproots

him and makes him function as a needed sign of warning to Walton, when parallels grow between their respective projects.

There is a plethora of figurative albatrosses killed in the speculative fictions discussed in this chapter, and although not all characters are compelled to endless wanderings, words of warning echo through them. In discourses around Arctic exploration broadly, the central transgression is undoubtedly the practice, but even the notion of, cannibalism. Reports of Primary World cannibalism among Franklin survivors were relayed to John Rae by Inuit in 1854 causing an uproar in the British public (and, famously, in Charles Dickens), and Leopold McClintock's *Fox* expedition four years later was not only a rescue mission but an attempt to, to the greatest extent possible, restore Franklin's reputation.[12] The message found in 1849 usefully showed that Franklin had died long before the taboo had been practiced. Also in Simmons' *The Terror*, the captain is exonerated by dying in time, but Caulker's Mate Cornelius Hickey, one of the human antagonists who leads a band of mutineers, engages in cannibalism in visceral detail. The Franklin expedition as such is punished for pressing too far into the Arctic, protected by the *Tuunbaq*, and on a smaller scale, Hickey is punished for transgressing laws concerning the consumption of human flesh. With the rest of the mutineers gone (escaped or eaten), Hickey finds himself together with his lover Magnus Manson in a pinnacle on the ice, surrounded by a dizzying array of objects. When Manson freezes to death, Hickey is disturbed by the companion's lifeless stare and removes his eyes, thinking that he can remedy this "later when He brought Magnus back" (Simmons 678), thus gesturing to a sense of megalomania that oversteps yet other boundaries. Hickey no longer fears the *Tuunbaq* but believes he can "order it into nonexistence and banish it to the farthest reaches of the universe with a sweep of his gloved hand" (679). When the *Tuunbaq* approaches, it keeps a distance to Hickey (while without compunction biting the head off Manson), as if the dying Hickey's departing spirit is to be avoided. Hickey remains immobilized in the small boat, unable to blink, even as "his blind eyes shattered from the cold" (682).[13] In contrast to the *Tuunbaq*, whose monstrosity becomes debatable when seen in the context of environmental degradation of the Arctic, there are no redeeming qualities in Hickey.

Cannibalism features also in Jules Verne's *The Voyages and Adventures of Captain Hatteras* but is rather used as punishment for the transgression constituted by mutiny. The main culprit is Mate Richard Shandon, who leaves the heroes of the narrative unable to leave the Arctic or progress further north. When Johnson, the boatswain, recounts events, Shandon's evil ways are highlighted by how he encourages the men he now commands to believe "that the time of suffering and privation had gone by;" he allows the stove to burn around the clock and freely distributes food and drink

(244). This excess makes Johnson exclaim: "May they be punished as they deserve!" (237). In the penultimate chapter, the five men who have successfully reached the North Pole are slowly making their way south. On Devon Island (in what is now Nunavut), they find human remains and conclude that Johnson's prayer has been answered. Their punishment does not only come in the form of death, but in their undisputed connection with cannibalism: "they had been obliged to eat human flesh" (436).[14] The literal collapse of boundaries between self and other illustrates a step beyond the peeling off of layers of civilization, and the perpetrators are depicted as monstrous indeed.

Policing geographical boundaries, the monsters in the texts by Blackwood, Simmons, and Nevill remain in the Arctic, continuing to function as deterrents for future transgressions. Stefans Spjut's *Stallo*, which conflates Sami mythology with the contemporary Nordic interest in trolls, provides a contrast, as it depicts how marvelous beings rather push their way into view, migrating into the consciousness and mundane life of humans.[15] That these humans are at home in the Swedish Arctic also presents a contrast to the previously discussed texts, and the plot revolves around information-gathering about the disturbance to what they see as reality. The process of documentation starts with a Hasselblad camera, and a flight across Rapadalen (in Sami Ráhpavágge), in Sarek national park.[16] Gunnar Myrén, the photographer, has moved his family to the north of Sweden because of an initial interest in "the dramatic play between light and darkness" above the polar circle (72), and among his many attempts to catch the sublime vistas, he takes a picture of a bear carrying something on its back. The creature is small and monkey-like, and in their attempt to decode the image, the family finally settles for the initially impossible: "[t]he thing clinging to the bear was a troll . . . . something that will not allow itself to be categorised" (79). But while this particular being may elude categorization, Gunnar's granddaughter Susso, the novel's protagonist, commences an ambitious project to map the movements and understand the function of the trolls, or Stallo.[17] Her attention is turned from the barren mountainside where the troll first appears to the "deep, wild forest, ancient and full of dead wood" (154), which, Sofia Wijkmark remarks, becomes a "dark and chaotic site of the uncanny" (121). Susso also draws from and contributes to an also chaotic array of information gleaned from interviews, additional photographs, video recordings, and websites. Little by little, she understands that trolls have always populated the world and that they, by being pushed further north by modern inventions, have literally fallen out of view. The lack of concrete previous evidence "is at the core of the detailed realism that enhances the uncanniness of the fictional universe" (Wijkmark 117), but the fact that the trolls are once again made visible does not diminish the horror they produce.

Contributing to this horror are sets of characteristics that, indeed, make the trolls elude "the classificatory 'order of things'" (Cohen 6), both when seen in isolation and when approached as a cryptozoological species. Ten-foot-tall, immensely strong Stallo coexist with tiny ones, the latter often functioning as bait when luring children away from safety. All trolls can shapeshift, assuming their animal shape when they die, and some appear as (almost) human. Added to these physical properties, "a radical and uncanny intimacy" (Wijkmark 121) is also established as the trolls can telepathically influence humans and even breed with them, which brings about another kind of category crisis. The increasingly blurred boundaries between the human world and that of the trolls that Susso's research illuminates is further emphasized by how humans actively work as helpers for the giants, abducting children who calm and entertain the monstrous beings. In the appropriation of Sami narratives, Spjut in the latter aspect introduces a variation on the propensity of the "evil ogre" to prey on the Sami and eat "human flesh," preferring that of children (Cocq 91). Coppélie Cocq observes that Stallo scenarios in the Sami tradition reflect various external threats or challenges experienced by Sami communities, and that when taking human mates, for example, Stallo often provide contrasts to "the proper relations between family members" (186). The monster's function as regulation and warning becomes less effective when lines blur between Stallo and humans in Spjut's novel, and the way in which child victims become adult perpetrators along with references to more generally shared motivations rather draw attention to the potentially monstrous within the human. Also, in contrast to Sami stories in which Stallo are commonly defeated thanks to superior human cunning, Spjuth is more pessimistic about containing that which is Other, or perhaps rather questioning if it can and should be contained or suppressed. Always threatening to become even more visible, Stallo in the novel push a boundary of visibility southward, and the painstaking documentation fills a similar function as tales and legends migrate into reality.

At the end of each text discussed in this section, the monsters continue to exist and threaten, despite attempts to vanquish them, or to dispel their power by understanding them. Possibilities thus remain for the monsters to endlessly reappear, filling new functions in new contexts. That the Creature is still "living" at the end of *Frankenstein* is crucial, Small maintains, as he then "brings back with him from darkness and distance some of the Arctic desolation into which he vanished" (329) and enables further parallels to be drawn between humanity and the monsters we create. Culturally and temporally distinct answers to the original question can be provided by the delayed end, as well as to the interlinked questions about existence and purpose, sparked off by the Creature's readings of Milton, Plutarch, and Goethe: "Who was I? What was I? Whence did I come? What was my destination?" (Shelley 131). The disorienting qualities of the Arctic help transfer the urgency of the questions also to human protagonists; they need to be answered to counter the deep ontological doubts produced in the meeting with the monster, or with the darker sides of their own identities.

The monsters' "externally incoherent bodies [that] resist attempts to include them in any systematic structuration" (Cohen 6) is what most powerfully occasion ontological quandaries, but the incoherence is also reflected in how the human protagonists become hybridized, doubled, or fragmented. In *Stallo*, the problems of classification are actively discussed, and hybridization is worked into the narrative through the monsters' abilities to control human minds and bodies. The *Tuunbaq* in Simmon's novel is variously seen as a polar bear, as belonging to "some ancient species" preceding bears, and as "a demon" (370, 126), but it also appears in the form of a priest and, as what results of its attacks most clearly indicates it is, a predator. Crozier's assessment of the monster, going from a conviction that it is "an animal, nothing more "(593) to understanding its function in the environmental context, means that he abandons previously held beliefs and goes through a physical transformation to be able to communicate with the embodied spirit world. The confused glimpses of the monster in *The Ritual* underline size and strength, but the disorienting forests are also home to physically hybridized beings. In the attic of the building the men enter is found a goat-like figure with sown-on human hands, whereas another, powerful entity comes in the form of an old woman with hooves instead of feet. It is also this novel that presents the most radical fragmentation of the protagonist's psyche, taking him to, or beyond, the limits of himself.

Thaws and Hibernation

In the "uncoupling of monstrosity from appearance," Jeffrey Andrew Weinstock argues, new monsters appear that more clearly speak to present anxieties and concerns (276). He delineates four salient manifestations that shift focus to uncontrollable agents: the hard-to-identify psychopath or terrorist, financial or political greed, viruses affecting local or global populations, and a vengeful nature. Scenarios featuring these threats underline that the monstrous is found in "the intention and desire to harm the innocent," (280) and the latter two especially are tied to an "epistemological anxiety related to visibility" and identification; regarding viruses and the environment it is possible to "determine the monster's presence [only] through its effects" (287). I will return to narratives depicting nature striking back in Chapter 3—and echo Weinstock's caveat that anthropogenic climate change is sometimes hard to interpret as an antagonist exacting vengeance on the sinless—but am in this section particularly

interested in how twenty first-century speculative fictions extrapolate
the invisible threat of thawed toxins and viruses in the Arctic environment. While this chapter may seem to have moved full circle from invisible ghosts to concretely manifest monsters and back to the imperceptible,
there is nothing uncanny about the toxins let loose in Juri Jurjevics' *The
Trudeau Vector* and reawakened century-old virus in Robert Masello's *The
Romanov Cross*. These novels rather align with Verne's brand of scientific
speculation, as theories for the survival and use of the agents are painstak-
ingly outlined, and as detailed explanations are given for how experiments
find a natural home in the remote Arctic. Secrets buried or forgotten in the
ice are consequently used as a speculative but credible threat to humanity
in both novels. Masello then pushes speculation further by engaging with
rumors of a still-living Anastasia Romanova, intertwining her survival
with that of the virus, and his emphasis on thawing processes that lead to
changed ecological patterns and a destabilized geology bridges this chapter
and the next.

I start, however, by addressing James Rollins' *Ice Hunt*, a novel situated
far from the Primary World end of the speculative spectrum in which
ancient monsters are found beneath the surface of the Arctic Ocean, in the
abandoned subglacial Ice Station Grendel. These monsters are anything
but hard to see: "pale white and smooth-skinned, like the beluga whales
that frequented the Arctic, and almost their same size, half a ton at least"
(Rollins 110). They are coupled to monstrosity not only by the character-
istic of exaggerated size, but also by "raking claws" and an "elongated
maw, stretched wide to strike, lined by daggered teeth." But when first
encountered, they are frozen into giant blocks of ice and thus determined to
pose no immediate threat to the team of American scientists who enter the
ice station. Rather, they can be studied, and Dr Henry Ogden (a modern-
day Clawbonny), is there to offer explanations to their origins and preservation. Drawing links to the *Ambulocetus natans*, the walking whale that
existed in the early Eocene, he speculates that this, much later creature, is
a result of a migration from southern waters. "Once here," he ponders,
"they developed Arctic adaptations. The white skin, the gigantism, the
thicker layer of fat" (112). As explanation to why the species has remained
unknown, the remoteness and inaccessibility of the Arctic "at the end of
the world" (35) are invoked, and further still "the bottom of the Arctic
Ocean, a region barely glimpsed at all" (112).[18] The Arctic thus comes to
constitute a vantage point for the study of hitherto unknown life forms
and a lockbox of preservation of secrets. Or perhaps these life forms are
not unknown, but rather forgotten? To a scientist of Nordic descent, the
frozen shapes remind him of "Norse carvings of dragons. The great wyrms
curled in on themselves" (151). Combined with the station's name, the
implication is that Vikings have encountered the beings and worked them

into their mythology, in turn migrating into *Beowulf*. "There's no telling how long these things have been around," Dr Ogden muses, "occasionally brushing into contact with mankind, leading to myths of dragons and snow monsters" (360).[19] Unfortunately, the encountered specimens prove Ogden right by being awakened from their periodic dormant state. Literally thawed, they are "damn hungry" (215) and become agents to be vanquished in the mayhem that follows.

The grendels' hibernation process, likened to that of Arctic frogs, is another adaptation to the Arctic environment, moving between the deathlike state and life according to vast cycles of freeze and thaw, and it connects with another speculative plot strand which focuses on experimentation on humans. Based on the idea that the genetic ability of the frogs is "found in *all* vertebrate species," Dr Ogden concludes that scientists previously occupying the base have likely sought "[i]*mmortality*" by using the grendels' genetic abilities (271). Significantly, the victims of the experiment, like the grendels frozen in blocks of ice, are all indigenous to the Arctic, and, uncomfortably for the contemporary group, the experiments have been conducted by their own nationals and not by Russians as they have expected or hoped. Protagonist Matthew Pike (a Fish and Game Officer slightly out of place in the predominantly scientific and military cast of characters) is informed that an American military unit was sent to Lake Anjikuni Village, Nunavut, in 1936 to collect human objects for experimentation. This was seen as an easy assignment since "[w]ho would miss a few isolated Eskimos" (398). The narrative proper is prefaced by a fictional article reporting the disappearance of the village's inhabitants, a vanishing that in Primary World discussions commonly is deemed an urban legend, but in the concluding author's note, Rollins makes broader connections to American experiments conducted on minority groups and otherwise vulnerable demographics.

The cryogenic suspension of Inuit is deeply disturbing, but horror is intensified at the end of the novel when effects of the injection of the grendel "elixir" are described (472). Craig Teague, a character that turns from sympathetic protagonist to antagonist, is expecting the world to end and, alone in a small ocean-going vessel, in order to survive in a frozen state, he subjects himself to similar experimentation that has been carried out on Inuit. Too late, he realizes that the state he enters is "*not* sleep," rather he stays conscious, cold to the bone, "[d]eaf, dumb, blind" and unchanging (472). "Deep in the black depths of the Arctic Ocean, one thought persisted as madness ate at what was left of him. *How long? How long is eternity?*" While Teague comes to personify transgressions into ethically unsound territory, and is punished accordingly, the description of madness and isolation exacerbate the victimization of the Inuit test subjects.

Arctic Cold War tensions and sovereignty disputes echo in *Ice Hunt*, in the form of local clashes between Russians and Americans who vie for control over the station, or who eschew responsibility for past destructive practices. In *The Trudeau Vector*, an international community initially rather celebrates the distance "from distorted values and divisive pressures" of the scientists' home nations (Jurjevics 168), and they congregate at a research station in the Canadian High Arctic. Positioned "on the edge of creation," the location is eminently suited for biological research (253). The sprawling plot, however, soon introduces Cold War echoes also in this novel. In brief summary, a biologist detects a missile beneath the ice and, fearing that the scientific work will be interrupted by military involvement, the station's director exposes her and two colleagues to lethal algae before they can contact the authorities. Protagonist Jessica Hanley, an epidemiologist, travels north to solve the mystery but arriving at the station are also Russians with the aim of retrieving their missile and investigating the deaths of almost a hundred crewmembers aboard one of their submarines. One of their agents has carried freeze-dried algae put in talcum powder onboard, and unwittingly released the toxin.

I read the *use* of lethal algae in the string of deaths as the element of speculation in what is otherwise a straightforward crime-novel. That the algae can suspend animation for periods of time and withstand temperatures far below freezing, on the other hand, is carefully explained by the novel's host of Clawbonnys, who point to the plant/animal hybrid's counterparts in frogs, beetles, and even mammals (the Arctic ground squirrel). The scientific interest in the algae and other Arctic life forms is in the novel focused on potential uses of hibernation in the pharmaceutical industry, but it predictably backlashes. Existing below the ice, the algae cannot survive in conditions required for human life, rather oxygen and light cause them to destroy the human host whose body they are released into. Paired with discussions about giant worms able to metabolize the sulfide produced by underwater volcanoes, the *Fusarium* fungi, and saxitoxins, the detailed explanations to the fatal workings of the algae are not far-fetched. The suspended animation of the algae also reveals that the threat to humans is not confined to the present-day setting of the novel. The research station is established close to "the northernmost place of human occupation in Arctic Canada" (145) and almost perfectly preserved bodies of late nineteenth-century Aleut at the original excavation site make the scientists "rule out a bioengineered microbe because . . . it dropped by here a century ago and annihilated the local shaman" (351). As with viruses and other biological hazards, algae have a certain periodic agency, but the threat they constitute is exacerbated by human involvement.

The algae's and other life forms' adaptation to Arctic conditions underline human vulnerabilities in a novel teeming with depictions of the effects of the cold. "At fifty-eight below freezing, and no wind at all, ordinary tires shatter," Hanley is told as she arrives at the station, "human cells rupture, metal breaks like glass, glass disintegrates like rust" (106). Early in the novel, a character ridden with guilt over the initial deaths brings on his own by simply going outside and removing his clothes. In his last moments, with the glass in his spectacles cracked from the cold, he wonders if "since all the fluids [in his body] were frozen, by standing he had broken his spine" (13). Rather than adapting, humans in the Arctic attempt to create tolerable conditions and below the domes of Trudeau, efforts are made to construct a sense of normalcy; systems maintain the illusion of daylight in the Arctic winter and darkness in the summer. Sleep patterns are still off, however, the days elongating, and Hanley is informed that it is not uncommon that people who spend an extended time at the station (and in the Arctic generally) "go zombie" (262). Both mentally and physically "[t]hey slow down," confining their attention to what is immediately ahead of them and "[d]evelop a shuffling gait" (262, 263). The vastness of the ice stretching out in all directions powerfully influences this need to focus on smaller, closer things, and paradoxically leads to a sense of acute claustrophobia. Combined with the biological threat, Jurjevics' Arctic is a frightening wasteland containing only small artificially constructed pockets in which humans can survive.

In trying to tease out what has caused the algae to reappear, parallels are drawn to other pathogens that have been shown to survive in dormant states, and a brief reference is made to work carried out by the "Hultin Expedition" (Jurjevics 305) engaged in researching the 1918–1919 pandemic, the most lethal outbreak of influenza A in known history. Pathologist Johan Hultin took a particular interest in Brevig Mission in Alaska (previously Teller Mission) where, during a span of five days, 72 out of 80 Inuit and missionary residents died. Tissue samples from remains exhumed from the permanently frozen ground in 1997 have helped shed light on the geographical and historical contexts of the violently virulent strain and the particular fatality it held for Inuit (see Taubenberger et al).[20] The presence of this virus in the Arctic gets a speculative twist in Masello's *The Romanov Cross*, and is connected to the persistent rumors that Princess Anastasia survived the Bolshevik assassination of her entire immediate family at Ekaterinburg on July 17, 1918. In the novel she is instead helped by a follower of Grigori Rasputin and taken to a remote island off the coast of Alaska, where believers in the holy man have established a colony. Anastasia becomes the "sly mechanism" that makes the virus migrate to an almost entirely "isolated rock," while being immune to it herself (Masello 190). In the 2011 setting, several characters converge on the island as the permafrost has begun to melt, exposing the buried bodies, the treasures accompanying them in their graves, but invisibly also the virus.

When antagonistic killers are seemingly innocuous algae or a thawed virus, the traditional role of the detective is assumed by a scientist. Masello, like Jurjevics, uses an epidemiologist as protagonist, and with "compromised credentials" to boot (66), Frank Slater has neither much to lose nor a chip to bargain with when he is dispatched to (fictional) Port Orlov in Northwestern Alaska. The effects of climate change in this location have resulted in a precariously leaning "Inuit totem pole" (50) in the town square and in "things that were buried . . . coming to the surface. Things like old caskets" (52). As it is known that the individuals inhabiting St Peter's Island have died from the influenza and been interred in these caskets, thawing permafrost is a cause for great, perhaps global, concern. Before his journey to Alaska, Slater visits the Armed Forces Institute of Pathology in Washington DC to access the samples taken from one of the first US soldiers succumbing to the pandemic: like Inuit remains at Brevig Mission, crucial to the sequencing of the viral genome leading to subsequent vaccines. Slater believes that "in order to fully engage in battle, he needed some visceral sense of his enemy" (66), and through the microscope he stares at "an ancient battlefield" encased in glass but on an adversary that transcends time: "it was the same foe he would soon confront in the Arctic" (68). The virus, invisible to the naked eye, is seen and identified, and Slater is ready for the fight.

The probable speculation of a thawed strain of the virus competes with sightings of a woman on St. Peter's Island who should no longer be alive, thus ushering in more radical speculation. Both treasure hunters and scientists encounter the woman accompanied by a pack of wolves who are the only other inhabitants on the island, and whose numbers never alter: like the woman they seem to be "stranded somewhere between this world and the next" (98). In the sexton's register, chronicling the burials at the island cemetery, Kozak, a Russian member of the scientific team reads about her toil in burying one body after another and finally letting the cross accompany the body of Sergei, the man who helped her escape, into his grave. "[M]*ay its chains no longer bind me to this earth. I long to be released, but I fear that its blessing has now become my curse*," reads the notation in the register (378). The signature below it tells Kozak who has written the section and he feels "the same eerie chill he had felt as a boy when it was the *rusalka* he had imagined coming back from the dead."[21] To the Russian, Anastasia's uncertain fate puts her on par with the folkloric beings, and in his mind she has, indeed, hovered in a liminal space between life and death. In the novel's denouement, the body of an old woman, whom Kozak unhesitatingly identifies as Anastasia, is discovered. In line with the scientific thrust of the narrative, Slater prepares to gather her DNA for further analysis, but (also in line with this thrust), the still-living Anastasia is consumed by flames when a toppling candle ignites the kerosene that she has doused herself in. The church on the unsteady, thawing ground crumbles over her body, conclusively putting an end to further attempts to prove her identity.

This tension between speculation and scientific explanations is constant in the novel, underpinned by parallels between past and present. While Anastasia's unnaturally long life span remains within the realm of the radically speculative, the recessive strain of hemophilia that she carries is used as an explanation for her imperviousness to the virus. A doctor caring for Anastasia and her sister Tatiana when they have been ill with the influenza notes how healthy and strong individuals succumb to the viral infection when their immune systems turn on themselves. The young and strong are killed, whereas the "frail and pampered princesses" live (427). A reference to "cytokine storms" killing healthy individuals is then made in the following chapter when Slater is exposed to the released H1N1 influenza virus (433). A previous bout of malaria has weakened him, which paradoxically mitigates the symptoms and saves his life. The constant in this balancing act between speculation and science is the warming climate, and the novel ends on a rather grim note that gestures to further disastrous effects of the Arctic melt. The Armed Forces Institute of Pathology has removed all signs of human life and habitation on the island and covered the cemetery with cement. Slater also observes "huge, empty cylinders of malathion, an organophosphate widely used in places like Central America where DDT had lost its sting" indicating that the ground in the now uninhabited Arctic periphery has been saturated with a particularly potent poison (461). These tactics, Slater thinks, will prove ineffectual: "The warming climate would eventually shift the earth again, and crack the cement." While the radically speculative survival of Anastasia will remain buried, the threat of a returning influenza continues to hover over St. Peter's Island, with ramifications extending globally.

Masello's emphasis on effects of climate change loudly echoes Primary World concerns about pathogens awakening in thawing permafrost and as is the case with the monsters discussed in the previous section of this chapter, iterations of minute or invisible Arctic threats reflect the time and culture that create them. The earliest text in my sample that references a microbial threat, Wilford Allen's short story "The Arctic Death," published in 1927, starts with how "an epidemic of unparalleled deadliness [has] spread fan-like out of the Arctic" (770). This threat, however, becomes connected to ideas of conquest, the ideal starting point of which is the area around the North Pole, and it is engineered by an alien race. The short story thus quickly leaps from invisible to visible threat, but the finale seems to foreshadow Weinstock's assessment that fears of viruses reflect the dread "that we may already be infected without knowing it" (286). It does so with a twist, however. One of the human characters takes on the role of a virus by infiltrating, or infecting, the alien interconnected intelligence. The struggle this human virus incites within its host puts an end to the alien design for Earth, but when the intelligence leaves, it is still infected, the consciousness of the scientist departing with it.

In Peter Høeg's *Miss Smilla's Feeling for Snow* (*Frøken Smillas fornemmelse for sne*, 1992), the murder of the small boy Isaiah and his father before him, become connected to an isolated, glaciated island off the coast of Greenland. Embedded in the glacier is an ancient meteorite which holds within it not only evidence of "the encounter between stone, inorganic life, and higher organisms" (Høeg 404), but also a threat to human life in the form of a parasite that the father and son have unwittingly carried with them. The otherwise realistic crime novel is pushed into the realm of the speculative, while the denouement also effectively highlights a long history of colonial oppression of the Greenlandic Inuit. In the most recently published text employing the threat of released pathogens, Sequoia Nagamatsu's 2022 *How High We Go in the Dark*, what becomes known as the Arctic plague is unleashed as scientists unearth the mummified remains of a pre-historic girl in the Batagaika crater in Siberia. Research is carried out "to understand what's coming out of the ice as it melts" one scientist explains, as ultimately, "whatever is in the land will make its way to cities, to oceans, to our food" (Nagamatsu 19). Responding to the threat of Arctic melt in ways similar to Masello, Nagamatsu highlights the instability and interconnectedness of ecosystems, but the novel's year of publication makes it difficult to not also draw parallels to the global anxieties connected to the COVID-19 pandemic.

In J. M. Sidorova's *The Age of Ice* (2013), protagonist Prince Alexander Velitzyn is conceived on a slab of ice, in an ice palace erected on the orders of Empress Anna Ioannovna. With this beginning to his life, Alexander is impervious to cold, icy to the touch and aging but slowly. He becomes the reader's guide through history, participating in such diverse events as The Seven Year's War of 1756–63, Joseph Billings' late eighteenth-century search for the Northwest Passage, the Napoleonic and World Wars, and the 1968 student uprisings in France, moving largely unaltered through time. Sidorova uses both figurative and literal properties of ice throughout the narrative, ranging from its encasing and arresting abilities to its cracks and melts, in illustrations of characters' fluctuating emotions as well as of the rise and fall of political structures. Her protagonist is moved by a desire to, like Shelley's Creature, find an answer to a central question: "Was I less alive? I seeded crystals. I made icicles endure like diamonds" (92).[22] Although ice is negatively connoted in the bulk of the novel: "a chrysalis of degradation" that blots out identifying marks and differences (69), the final chapter, set in 2007, gestures to detrimental effects of its disappearance. At this point, Alexander sees anthropomorphized ice as having "lost the battle" against human-driven accelerated warming: "He lies, bleeding water out of his mortal wounds" (387). To save ice, once his foe, Alexander plans to go as far north as possible and "spread [his] arms for an embrace" (388), in the hopes that his own cold will slow or stop the Arctic melt, or that he will take the place of ice itself.

By embodying ice, Sidorova illustrates how it (or he) allows access to the past, a function that the Arctic broadly performs in the fictions discussed in this chapter. As a repository of the past, the Arctic manifests past trauma in the form of ghosts, as a space beyond the known, "where maps run out, ships slip moorings and navigators click their compasses shut" (Kearney 3), it becomes the home to monsters, policing boundaries to lower latitudes. In Vicki Jarrett's *Always North*, which features as a consistent companion in the next chapter, protagonist Izzy thinks that "[i]ce is memory" (192); it holds in itself not only terrifying or romantic remnants of the past, but also evidence of a long history of human impact. Seen in works discussed in the last section of this chapter, as in the concluding part of *The Age of Ice*, sometimes stereotypical renditions of stasis are now upturned by a melting Arctic.

Notes

1 The first un-interment, performed by Captain Edward A. Inglefield, is described in a letter to Rear-Admiral Francis Beaufort which Owen Beattie and John Geiger excerpt in their book *Frozen in Time* (187). Beattie performed the 1984 exhumation, the results of which led him to hypothesize that lead poisoning was a strongly contributing cause of death, and that the badly soldered Goldner's tins were the main culprits in the general fate of the Franklin expedition.

2 Walton's sentiment finds a Primary World echo in a letter sent by Crozier to his friend and superior James Ross, once the last Franklin expedition was underway. He writes: "All goes on smoothly but James dear I am sadly alone, not a soul have I in either ship that I can go and talk to. 'No congenial spirit as it were'" ("Letter"). Walton's unstable psyche finds another parallel in that of Captain Hatteras in Jules Vernes' novel (discussed in Chapter 1). Hatteras' polar madness is similarly produced because he is surrounded by men who do not share his exact ambitions.

3 In addition to the fiction discussed here, Doyle used his Primary World experiences on an Arctic whaler in the short story "The Man from Archangel" (1885), the poem "The Athabasca Trail" (1914) and, to a more limited extent, the short story "The Adventure of Black Peter" (1904).

4 The comment is repeated: "I want Gruhuken to be *ours*" (66) with the emphasis brought on by Jack's building knowledge of past expeditions as well as by the feeling that he and his colleagues are not alone in the bay.

5 In "The Glamour of the Arctic," Doyle cites the small Ice Age as a reason for the outside world's lack of definitive information about the colony's fate, if not necessarily for its demise. A productive "haze," which Doyle prefers to all-encompassing knowledge, means that the colony's descendants can be imagined as still existing in Greenland, with later generations perhaps joining with "Skraelings" (the Old Norse and Icelandic term for the Thule people, preceding Inuit in Greenland), resulting in "a race of tow-headed, large-limbed Esquimaux" (325).

6 In William H. Blakes "A Tale of Grand Jardin" (1915), which shares several similarities with Blackwood's novella, "those who die insane without the blessing of a priest become wendigos" (151).

7 With a starting point in "the doubled relationship between creature and creator," Goldman also draws attention to parallels between Wendigo stories and *Frankenstein* (173). She notes how Victor "ends up losing his mind and personality and destroying his family members and those he loves most" just like the victims of the Wendigo, and the cognates between the two narratives "signal a related desire to explore the pathological will to consume that characterizes western culture" (173).

8 In the article "Arctic Terror," which addresses the adaptation of Simmons' novel in the 2018 AMC TV-series, Anita Lam reverses the perspective, arguing that the Wendigo (or in her article Windigo) represents the monster within: "the Windigo's cannibalism metaphorically represents the devastating effects of the icescape on the minds and bodies of foreign explorers" (196).

9 In a later text, Cohen expounds on the Creature's verbosity and on his complaints that "Victor refuses to hear" ("Promise" 462).

10 While the term "monster" is employed throughout Shelley's novel, it is predominantly connected to how the perception of others controls the assignation. When Victor and Elizabeth visit the kind-hearted Justine at the prison, for example, she clarifies that her confession to the murder of Victor's brother has been a lie but that she is pressed to hold on to the story: her "confessor," she exclaims, "threatened and menaced, until I almost began to think that I was the monster that he said I was" (88). The Creature goes through a similar process of internalizing others' views, with Victor's disavowal representing the first step. Progressively, the Creature's self-perception comes to hinge on his physical difference from others; when he catches sight of his own reflection in a small body of water, he sees only "miserable deformity" (117) and becomes convinced of being, precisely, a "monster" (116).

11 A stanza (lines 446–451) from Coleridge's poem comes to Victor's mind on the morning after having brought the Creature to life (Shelley 60).

12 In Tina May Hall's *The Snow Collectors* (2021), Lady Jane Franklin's attempts to conceal any potential evidence that her husband ate human flesh drive the plot. The message in the margins of the document found at Victory Point is in this novel scribbled not by Fitzjames or Crozier but by a member of a hitherto unknown rescue operation, dispatched for precisely this reason.

13 This sequence of events is one of many in which Simmons attempts to present answers to remaining mysteries. Members of the *Fox* expedition discovered

two human skeletons inside a boat, one of which was thought to have been "destroyed" after death by "large and powerful animals, probably wolves," whereas the other was "in a somewhat more perfect state" and was "enveloped in clothes and furs" (McClintock 294). The remains were never identified.

14 In the 1875 translation of *The Field of Ice*, the horror of cannibalism is exacerbated by the mutineers possibly eating of their still-living partners in crime: "the poor wretches had been feeding on human flesh, perhaps while still warm and palpitating" (263).

15 Spjut's novel is also translated as *The Shapeshifters* and is followed by *Trolls* (*Stalpi*) in 2017, and by the recent, as yet untranslated, *Rovet* (2022) that curiously repeats some characterizations and events from *Stallo*. Other examples of contemporary written Nordic fiction focused on trolls are Joanna Sinisalo's 2000 *Not Before Sundown* (*Ennen päivänlaskua ei voi*), in which trolls are affected by climate change and migrate into urban areas, and John Ajvide Lindqvist's 2006 short story "Border" ("Gräns") in the collection *Let the Old Dreams Die* (*Pappersväggar*), in which the extrasensory abilities of the troll protagonist make her effectively patrol both national and personal borders. These examples all illustrate how trolls and humans, often uncomfortably, share the same space.

16 Like Muddus, Sarek is part of the world heritage site Laponia.

17 Stallo (or Stállu) is the North Sami spelling. Other variants are Stalo and Stállo.

18 The Arctic as a peripheral freezer features also in Lincoln Child's *Terminal Freeze* (2009), in which a saber-toothed tiger is thawed to catastrophic effects, and in D. J. Goodman's *Arctic Gauntlet* (2017), in which a host of maritime dinosaurs turn on visitors. Rather than featuring in scenarios of adventure, like the prehistoric animals inhabiting some of the discovered civilizations discussed in Chapter 1, reawakened predators become the main antagonists in the contemporary novels. In George B. Tuttle's "The Roc Raid" (1970), enormous flying creatures attack humans and cattle, and even lift off a circus elephant. They depart from and return to "a 'blind spot' between Point Barrow and Spitzbergen" where several ancient species have survived (87).

19 The hypotheses concerning periodic contact with humankind is proven correct when a diary kept by a crewmember of the American ship *Jeanette* is found at the ice station. It recounts how survivors split up into three groups after abandoning the sinking ship and that one of these small crews think themselves saved by the discovery of "carcasses of some strange sea beasts, preserved in the ice" (402). Salvation then turns to nightmare as "the dead awoke and attacked our sleeping party." Rollins thus takes as his starting point the Primary World sinking of *Jeanette* in 1881, as well as the fact that one of the three boats used to try to reach safety was lost.

20 Bodies of coal miners exhumed near Longyearbyen in Svalbard have likewise helped map the virus sequence (see Oxford 2000).

21 In Slavic folklore, the rusalka is a female entity, often malicious toward humankind and frequently associated with water. References to another being, the Kushtaka, forge closer connections to Arctic legends and align more closely with Anastasia's fate. The Kushtaka signify how "an unhappy soul, still

nursing some grievance on earth" is prevented from following "the staircase of the aurora borealis into heaven" and instead remain among the living, the spirit being "half-human and half-otter" (Masello 198).

22 Alexander meets Mary Shelley, of course, and accredits himself with providing her with inspiration for *Frankenstein*, specifically by telling her "about *polynyas* and ice drifts, about the deep freeze that lures you into his cradle" (268).

3　Arctic Futures

The idea for *Frankenstein* was born in 1816, the year without a summer. The eruption of Mount Tambora in Indonesia the previous year had had catastrophic local effects, killing at least 60 000 but perhaps as many as 120 000 individuals, and volcanic ash released into the atmosphere affected the global climate, causing rainfalls, storms, and dropping temperatures. The dark and damp atmosphere at the Villa Diotdati in Switzerland where Shelley started to articulate her ideas likely worked as an influence on sections of the novel set in cold climes such as on Mont Blanc and Orkney, and of course on the Arctic frame story. But Shelley's engagement with altered temperatures and their effects ran deeper, Siobhan Carroll maintains, and both "discontinuities and . . . eerie similarities" can be discerned between the period's debates and controversies and today's focus on anthropogenic climate change ("Crusades" 212). The year without a summer, Carroll demonstrates, became a watershed in a history of ideas in which a perceived cooling of Earth's temperature was seen as either connected to growing, unruly polar ice or, anticipating contemporary concerns, to deforestation and intensified agricultural processes that altered local landscapes and microclimates. A distant, non-human antagonist was welcomed as it shifted attention away from irresponsible human practices closer to home, and a host of wild geoengineering ideas were formulated in which polar ice was either to be fought and diminished or moved to the tropics to create a globally balanced climate. At the same time, human intervention in nature was perceived with skepticism, an attitude that involved exploration of the polar areas as well; Carroll consequently notes that "[t]o describe a polar expedition in 1818, as *Frankenstein* does, is thus to engage with the highly controversial topic of ecological crisis" (219).[1] Victor Frankenstein not only illustrates the hubris connected to transformation—with bioengineering replacing geoengineering—but creates a being that from the start is suited to a future, cold world. Placing both the start of the narrative and its denouement in an atopic space beyond the political or cultural power

DOI: 10.4324/9781003355588-4

of a nation state also furthers Shelley's engagement with ideas of responsibility in times of far-reaching crises and the novel, Carroll persuasively demonstrates, partakes in a discourse through which we can apprehend "an uncanny reflection of our own struggles to discern the nature of, and decide on the proper response to, alterations in the global climate" (225). Finding new actuality because of engagements with how it reflects its times' responses to global changes and to foreshadowed ends, *Frankenstein*'s Arctic frame story works as a springboard in this chapter for discussions about environmental instabilities and upheavals in speculative visions of the future.

Two human-driven processes place the Arctic at the center of contemporary environmental instability: the Arctic Paradox, which refers to how ocean currents propel toxins northward and affect environments at the furthest distance from sites of pollution (see Cone), and Arctic amplification, through which diminishing sea ice results in temperatures warming at an accelerated rate in the Arctic (see Previdi et al.). A recent United Nations report indicates that even if the 2015 Paris Agreement commitments are met, winter temperatures in the Arctic will rise by 3–5°C (9°F) by mid-century.[2] In short, we see the fastest climatological changes taking place in the Arctic, and consequences are or will be global. On one level, then, the Arctic migrates from periphery to center, but lingering tendencies to see the Arctic as atopic space rather than place, and the resilient view of the world's far north as both literally and figuratively static, slow or prohibit perceptual and concrete change. Firstly, when distant destruction takes place in what is regarded as "spaces frequently imagined as belonging both to a collective humanity and to 'no one'," it is difficult to identify "who can intervene in the environmental degradation" (Carroll, *Empire* 188). Secondly, and paradoxically, "anthropogenic climate change, most evident in the Arctic, can be still purportedly refuted, as the perception of that region is one as frozen and unchanging for eternity" (Stenport and Vachula 284). These challenges to change again connect the poles; as Elizabeth Leane remarks, the presumption is "that the ice itself will be preserved for all eternity" and there is a general resistance against accepting the fact that Antarctica "like the rest of the world, is subject to change, and that humanity's own actions are in all likelihood rapidly accelerating this change" (176). Each day brings reminders of how the poles literally diminish: as I write this, alarm is being raised concerning environmental tipping points such as the collapse of the ice sheets of Greenland and West Antarctica. "The melting poles" that have "function[ed] as symbolic canaries in the mine of climate change" (Bracke, *Climate Crisis* 106) are growing ominously quiet.

While tipping points, in which a final, sometimes small alteration sets off a far-reaching domino effect, fit uncomfortably well into what Rob Nixon calls the "spectacle-driven" (6) contemporary media climate and answer to public demands for the instantaneously dramatic, there are significant challenges inherent in capturing the "slow violence . . . of delayed destruction that is dispersed across time and space" and that disenfranchises already vulnerable communities (2).[3] Along with political and economic strategies to mobilize action, Nixon continues, a central question becomes "how to devise arresting stories, images, and symbols adequate to the pervasive but elusive violence of delayed effects" (3). It is, of course, with these imaginative possibilities I am concerned, among them examples from what is today a robust body of climate fiction, and more broadly with how fictions constitute particularly productive spaces in which to explore and extrapolate the ramifications of the slow violence of anthropogenic climate change. Speculative and realistic works respond differently to the challenges inherent in the temporal and spatial scope of climate change, but Frederick Buell foregrounds the affordances of the former. Speculative fiction, he argues, "acts as an imaginative heuristic for exploring today's omnipresent, fundamental, multiple risk space," and by "condens[ing] narratives out of the complex penumbra of shifting possibilities," it captures contemporary instabilities more effectively than realist forms ("Global Warming" 277). Environmental collapses are commonly also combined with or followed by other crises: apocalyptic visions engendered by a plethora of Primary World risk scenarios, such as nuclear threats, economic crises, overpopulation, terrorism, and pandemics.

This chapter is concerned with imagined futures in contemporary fictions and with depicted processes resulting in profound changes to Arctic environments. My readings trace renditions of climate change, of material more-than-human entanglements, and of the (post)apocalypse. In relation to near or far future climate change I address how the Arctic's oscillation between being perceived as atopic space and affectively connoted place plays a part in attitudes to accelerated warming and attempts to combat it. Taking inspiration from ideas in the environmental materialist turn, specifically critics' stress on the need to see the human as always already part of more-than-human nature, I explore how the Arctic features into the sense of precarious and vulnerable interconnectedness between all life on the planet. And by examining different strategies and narrative perspectives employed when depicting end-of-times scenarios, I highlight how and why the Arctic functions as a last outpost after a complete global collapse. Environmental concerns tie the sections together and Vicki Jarrett's *Always North* weaves in and out of the discussions, thematically connecting and providing transitions between representations of climate change in near and far futures, material interconnections between the human and animal, and temporal instabilities connected to (post) apocalypse.

Close and Distant Climates

In the earlier texts in my sample, there are few examples of futuristic images of the Arctic, arguably because the area remains an estranged space: room can be made for discoveries and innovations without altering the temporal setting. In one of few examples, Emma Louise Orcutt's *The Divine Seal* (1909), the reader is introduced to a twenty-second century governed by sound democratic principles in the four republics that now constitute the world, a culture of lively commerce and technological innovation, and to a changed climate which has opened for new discoveries in the Arctic. The thrust of the narrative (which quickly veers into romance) lies in finding the Heclades, "an island or continent in the Polar Sea, rich in minerals, fertile, and of wonderful civilization" (Orcutt 3), references to which have literally been unearthed via archeological work in the recently resurfaced Atlantis. Permanently open polar waters enable the search for the fabled land but although "the western shores and isles of Alaska are magnificent in verdure and climate" and redolent with scents "from orange fields and spicy fields" (5) the icy areas further north have preserved the marvelous: the aim of an international expedition going north is to find the esoteric tomb of Zallallah and what turns out to be a tropical destination hiding in the ice is ruled over by Ozomoth, half man, half serpent. In one of few readings of the novel, Michelle Kathryn Yost concludes that *The Divine Seal* "demonstrates the frustration felt by the public at the failure of so many Polar expeditions, but belief in the promise of technology" (183–184).[4] Development has progressed in the speculative future world, that is, but the poles remain unreachable until the twenty-second century, constituting the last resistance to humanity's ambition; it is only through climate change that the expedition can reach the Arctic and the secrets hidden there.

Avoiding future settings, imagined ice-free conditions appear in other examples of the early fiction in my sample, either in the form of the permanently available open polar sea, or as temporary states created by unexpected natural events. Jules Verne's *The Voyages and Adventures of Captain Hatteras* illustrates the latter when a storm dislodges the pack ice. The result, a new "ocean stretch[ing] beyond the line of vision" (393) is naturally welcomed by the explorers pressing on for the North Pole. In the later novel *The Purchase of the North Pole* (*Sans dessous dessous* 1889), Verne returns to the idea of an ice-free polar area but focuses on the idea of artificially and permanently changing the climate. By firing an enormous cannon from the top of Mount Kilimanjaro, the idea is to tilt the axis of the world and thereby create a warmer climate in the far north, a projected result that ties back to earlier Primary World fears of a cooling word and to Romantic "crusades against frost" in which humans united could "forge a new cosmopolitan utopia" (Carroll, "Crusades" 212). An ice-free Pole will in Verne's fictional scheme also enable access to vast coal deposits; the story is one among many that foregrounds the riches of minerals and natural resources in the Arctic and hinges on greed to drive the plot. In this form of early geoengineering narratives, Steve Asselin demonstrates, "anthropogenic climate change is not the inadvertent effect of capitalistic ventures but the very goal of such enterprises" (443). Some inevitable consequences in Verne's novel are lamentable: "[t]he astronomer might lose a few of the familiar constellations; the poet might lose the long winter nights and the long summer days that figure so frequently in modern verse" but these are outweighed by "the advantages that would be enjoyed by the majority of the human race" (*Purchase* 361). It is not, then, the Arctic only that will be affected, but a less variable global climate, which would be the result of a successful detonation, is seen as a boon to humankind. This form of climate manipulation has as an associated ideological consequence that "people no longer simply *inhabit* climate, but . . . become *consumers* of climate" (Asselin 444). In Verne's novel, as in Mark Twain's *The American Claimant* (1892) and Faddey Bulgarin's early *Plausible Fantasies or a Journey in the 29ᵗʰ Century* (Правдоподобные небылицы 1824), all addressed by Asselin, the Arctic as well as global temperatures are figured as commodities, made available through deliberate human intervention in weather and climate patterns.⁵ Commodification of the Arctic in these nineteenth-century narratives is in part tied to the lingering tendency to see the Primary World's high latitudes as empty space and it is its transformation into a warmer, more accessible area that opens for the possibility of the Arctic becoming place.⁶

In later examples of speculative climate fiction, a common strategy to highlight effects of disasters that start in the Arctic is to transform locations that are at least potentially more well-known to the reader. In J.G. Ballard's *The Drowned World* (1962), for example, solar storms and rapidly melting ice caps at the poles are the two "gigantic geophysical upheavals" that have transformed the globe in an unspecified, hot future. The Arctic has become "a subtropical zone with an annual mean temperature of eighty degrees" (21), resulting in decades of human "poleward migration" (22). However, the novel itself does not migrate to the Arctic, instead the effects of a rapidly warming climate are visualized by how London has become submerged. A drowned Leicester Square and treasures from museums, brought to the surface by divers or made accessible by damming the extensive lagoons, illustrate the impact of flooding on human-made structures and cultures that the main characters still affectively relate to. And even in works that more overtly reflect the centrality of the Arctic to environmental collapse, effects of such catastrophes are moved elsewhere: "polar novels" Adam Trexler maintains, "struggle to connect change to more familiar and affective places" (82).[7] In Jarrett's *Always North*, a detailed description of a climatological and environmental collapse in the Arctic Ocean is represented as a terrible sound in a stark environment devoid of human habitation, in fact one in which "[h]umans don't belong" (Jarrett 72). It is followed by a relocation to the Scottish Highlands where effects of the collapse are described, accompanied also by reports of the destruction of structures and areas that are likely more well-known to the reader, such as Dubai's Burj Khalifa and a fire-ravaged Manhattan. The disembodied sound, coming from an Arctic that is torn apart, is substituted with descriptions connected to vision—among them footage of London's Canary Wharf burning—and to material, physical consequences for people inhabiting exposed areas. The lingering perception of the Arctic as peripheral and empty consequently introduces an additional level of complexity to the challenges inherent in depicting climate change.

Laline Paull's *The Ice*, Tobias Buckell's *Arctic Rising*, and Emmi Itäranta's *Memory of Water*, in focus in this section, inhabit different positions on the speculative spectrum, with Paull's employing a near-future setting and dealing with a slightly accelerated raise of Arctic temperatures, Buckell's set fifty years into the future in which climate change is still being discussed and combatted, and Itäranta's depicting global flooding in a far future Finland. In *The Ice*, the Arctic melt means increased opportunities for tourism and greedy business and although Svalbard is rapidly changing, it constitutes one of the last sites in which visitors can establish a connection with emotions perceived to be lost in modernity. In Buckell's novel, the Arctic is a new bustling world center which is still being explored by new arrivals and a site for conflicting responses to climate change. In *Memory of Water*, however, the Finnish Arctic is home to protagonist Noria and generations before her. In my readings, I consequently address how the Arctic oscillates between being perceived as space and affectively connoted place, but a concern in all three novels is how a warming world affects the Arctic, and how a melting Arctic affects the world. The deliberate human actions, seen in earlier geoengineering schemes, are substituted with slow but inescapable anthropogenic impact.

Commodification, however, is noticeable here as well. In *The Ice*, Svalbard has been made available for both consumption and corruption as the newly opened "TransPolar Route" (Paull 3) across ice-free channels in the Arctic has shaved off transportation time not only for legal goods but for guns run from Asia to Africa. As the novel opens, however, stress is on how climate change has opened the area for tourism. Svalbard is apprehensively thought to be transforming into "the Ibiza of the north," offering attractions such as "[t]he midnight sun [and an] exotic locale" but importantly also a chance to experience "the fragility of the region" (31).

An imminent ecological collapse has become a selling point, and there is a rush to take the last opportunity to see the vulnerable area ahead of others.

However, expanded access also means diminishing possibilities for Arctic tourists to see what they have come for: fauna in general, but especially "the great apex predator, the polar bear" (2) that gives the increasingly heavily trafficked fjords a wide berth. The novel starts on *Vanir*, a luxury cruiser full of disappointed passengers. Seemingly mocked by promotional materials that have promised them not only the sight of the predator but glittering cold, the passengers experience weather "dank as an English summer" and repair to the salon where they peruse footage by previous visitors—unbeknownst to them "several years old"— among them images of their own ultimate goal, a polar bear after it has made a kill (1, 2). When *Vanir*'s captain follows information from an illegal drone and enters a fjord otherwise off limits, he breathes a sigh of relief when the passengers at last see and feel what they have come for. A large "white god" has positioned itself "on the most photogenic port side of the Midgardbreen glacier" and cameras click frantically along the bow (5, 4). The shining pelt that makes the polar bear particularly authentic to the tourists, however, appears that way because of the "greyish tinge" of the snow (4). In the bear's youth, by contrast, when the snow was "clean and white" the pelt showed as "pale yellow." A long history of anthropogenic impact on the planet, with pollution as one consequence, is condensed into how this local, Arctic symbol appears, and it is caught on film by temporary visitors in the Arctic.

An inquest into the death of Tom Harding provides a structure for the novel's oscillation between past and present, and it is held in London. This structuring device highlights how the novel's main characters too are outsiders, drawn to Svalbard for different reasons and representing different attitudes to preservation and commodification. To protagonist Sean Cawson, the Arctic has exerted a persistent pull ever since his childhood, signifying the comingled feelings of attraction and fear and the promise of life-altering experiences. In part, Sean's attraction to the Arctic is bound up with the history of exploration, and particularly with twentieth-century anthropological expeditions. An admiration for inter-war polar travelers such as Knud Rasmussen and Peter Freuchen has drawn Sean and Tom together during their time in Oxford, but the friends' paths diverge with Tom earnestly working "to save the world" and Sean striving for riches and for putting "his name on the map" (62). When Sean, backed by sinister businessman John Kingsmith, develops Midgard Lodge—an exclusive retreat in an isolated Svalbard bay that ostensibly encourages ecologically sound thinking in the privileged visitors—Tom functions as the green alibi, whose role is to ensure that detrimental effects of developments in the "fragile, sublime, vulnerable environment" are minimized (70). Without Tom's knowledge, Sean has been allowed by the Norwegian authorities to keep a small but well-equipped military unit at Midgard that Kingsmith uses to ensure free passage for ships carrying weapons to areas of conflict. While Svalbard, and the Arctic broadly, are thus of strategic and ideological importance to Sean and Tom, it remains an atopic space, a stage on which confrontations come to a head.

Actual and symbolic polar bears become pawns in this game of control and, like the Arctic, they are used to highlight characters' varying needs and desires. In the next section, when I explore how speculative fiction can aid in envisioning material interconnections between humans and, in this case, animals, I am aided by Stacy Alaimo's stress on "ethical and political possibilities" that come to the fore when "the human is [seen as] always intermeshed with the more-than-human world" (2). Paull's novel too gestures to a need for material and ethical entanglements between humans and polar bears, but primarily uses the animal to signify a connection to a primal, undestroyed environment, logical in a novel building on Primary World climate anxiety. Two situations stand out in this regard: the brief contact between the cruise passengers and the bear, and a solitary canoe trip undertaken by Sean. What the tourists desire and have dearly paid for is in a tantalizingly close past: an Arctic that tenders a promise of connection with the primitive, and when their gaze is met by the bear's, the humans finally experience the desired "euphoric jolt of fear" (Paull 5). Instead of seeing how climate change entangles the predator's vulnerable existence with their own lives, lengthening the "jolt" of dread and extending its significance, the passengers regard both bear and emotion as needed but temporary links to what they perceive to be lost in the modern world. The connection is also cut short because the bear senses the calving of an iceberg from the glacier and takes off. The movement of the ice dislodges Tom's body from a cave within it, an event that is also caught on film, and the passengers' exhilarating experience ends with a return to decidedly human preoccupations.

Also to Sean, who has a longstanding and concrete connection to the Arctic, the polar bear comes to represent the possibility to access emotions and a sense of immediacy unavailable elsewhere. After Tom's death, Sean embarks on a solitary canoe trip in waters he knows very well and becomes aware that he is followed by a large polar bear, bearing a "duelling scar" (50) similar to the specimen photographed by the cruise passengers.[8] In the bear's actions, Sean interprets human manipulation—it is "willing [Sean] to panic and make a mistake"—and like the tourists, he experiences "a jolt of fear" (51). But instead of a disturbance caused by a natural event, approaching motorboats drive this bear off, and the close encounter with potential death makes Sean "feel more alive than he had done in years" (52). Tourists and Sean alike take from their brief and interrupted moments in a concrete contact zone a new appreciation for life that has little to do with the precarious situation the wild predator is in but is rather intimately tied to a stereotypical primitivism.

Ethical questions related to the past, present, and future responsibility for the planet are instead linked to dead polar bears in *The Ice*, already beyond the actual contact zone. At the inquest, Tom's former lover Ruth Mott recounts an autopsy she has performed on a polar bear carcass and draws attention to the myriad instabilities that follow climate change. Tattooed with a symbol showing it had come from East Greenland and traversed an immense distance, Ruth hypothesizes that it had either come "around the North Pole clockwise, *or* the polar currents are already so disrupted by climate change that it came counter-clockwise" (271). Her testimony follows that of a scientist who vehemently argues that it is impossible not to see the collapsed Svalbard cave as anything but "a direct consequence of climate change" and that all lives on the planet are "in a burning building together" (260). The disoriented dead bear and the impassioned call for a recognition of interconnectedness gesture to the need for material links between the destinies of human, animal, and planet, still, the polar bear in the novel is restricted to two Primary World functions: a link to supposedly uncorrupted nature, distinct from human culture, and as a victim of anthropogenic climate change. In this order, they slot into how commodification and exploitation of the Arctic gradually give way to emphasis on the will or need to (re)assume responsibility, and polar bears (dead or alive) become implicit agents in the novel.

The ice of the novel's title similarly performs an agentic function, particularly in regard to Sean's search for atonement. Already in Sean's childhood, in a home for boys, he is drawn to a painting that makes him forget his own predicament and transfer "his consciousness into the ice" (49). In *Arctic Dreams*, which Paull includes in a bibliography at the end of her novel, Barry Lopez mentions Frederic Edwin Church's large oil painting *The Icebergs* (1861) which, through a series of purchases and inheritances, vanished from public view for over a century but ended up in the Rose Hill estate close to Manchester, later turned into a remand home. That the painting's location was unknown for such an extended time, Lopez notes, is one "oddity" (247) about it, and another is that the poor reception at its original unveiling made Church add a "trace of man in it" (246): part of a ship's mast is inserted in the foreground in an otherwise "empty" landscape.[9] In *The Ice*, it is not inconceivable that Sean gazes at just this painting, and the human-made trace is significant, as Sean imagines his father as a victim of the shipwreck and that the loss of him has caused his mother's troubled state. Sean's conclusion is that "[t]he ice had taken his family and he must go there to get them back" (Paull 49). The "there" of the ice is at this point abstract, but Sean's early, uncorrupted, fascination with the north does not cease and the Arctic becomes, to him, an at once "beautiful and terrifying lover" (48). With an initially similar attitude to the Arctic, Tom argues that it "shows you your soul, even if you think you don't have one" (70), and Sean's process of catching sight of who he truly is entails movements through stages of corruption. Professionally, Sean's triumphs are undermined by the immorality of gun running, and personally, corruption comes in the form of adultery. At the end of the novel, Sean thinks that to reestablish relationships with his ex-wife and daughter he must "come back from the ice" (362), and he gives testimony at the inquest that incriminates both himself and Kingsmith. Sean thus personifies larger processes of accountability needed to if not reverse then at least stall human-driven destruction of the Arctic.

Representing more radical speculation, Buckell's *Arctic Rising* is set fifty years into the future, and climate change has transformed large parts of the world into extended atopias. Areas in the southern hemisphere are, if not yet uninhabitable, plagued by soaring temperatures and unpredictable storms, and Thule, an "artificial … island" (Buckell 4) of ice around the North Pole is maintained in the warming waters by cables bringing cold up from the ocean floor. Heidi Hansson discusses Buckell's novel as illustrating "a new kind of writing about the Arctic where the Arctic is central rather than peripheral" not only because it extrapolates the role the area plays in contemporary Primary World debates, but also because the significantly altered map of the world has made it into a central economic power ("Arctopias" 76). "Once-tiny towns [that] were barely presences at the turn of the century" have developed into central hubs for commerce and the circumpolar nations are "Arctic Tiger[s]" wielding global power (Buckell 32). Melting ice resulting in arable land and easier access to oil and minerals has also, ostensibly in a favorable way, affected Indigenous communities in this future Arctic. In Greenland, for example, "a natural resources superpower" (159), Inuit have refused to again "become minorities in their own country" (96) and instead profit from the extraction industry.

Buckell's future is thus a construction based on past climate change, still, the plot revolves around its ramifications as well as possibilities to slow or reverse its continuing effects. Protagonist Anika Duncan is an airship pilot for the United Nations Polar Guard, and she is shot down after detecting nuclear radiation from a freighter moving into out-of-bounds waters. Anika's ensuing investigation into actions and plans that threaten the Arctic leads her to Thule, and to the Gaia Corporation. Gaia presents itself as an environmentally friendly company working to slow down the warming of the climate by artificially creating clouds that deflect sunlight: as such, it is supposedly constituted by "nice people" (177). Against them are pitted those who fear the changes that would follow the atmospheric project, but also individuals representing either the view that the problem is too large to be resolved or a general mistrust of climate change. Impatient with individuals not seeing the catastrophic ramifications of climate change, Gaia's executives have devised airborne reflective spheres that together form a giant mirror that can either deflect or focus heat. A "weaponizing [of] the upper atmosphere" (185) naturally constitutes immense power, threatening in the wrong hands: as in many novels depicting technological advances, military applications of benevolent innovations loom large. Polarizations in the contemporary Primary World debate are in this way reflected and create several potential antagonists in the novel; conflicting ideologies represent a significant obstacle to the resolution. The initial projected use of the mirror is to "cool the planet again" (252) and allow time for potential solutions to the climate crisis, but material effects would be clearly visible in the Arctic as its economy would crumble. The destruction of the mirror at the end of the novel paradoxically upholds a status quo; as Ben De Bruyn argues, Anika "uses a disquieting solution to geopolitical strife to counteract a disquieting solution to ecological upheaval" (49). Threats of military involvement and war, aspects that play a large role in Anika's and several other characters' past, in this way outweigh the necessity of slowing climate change.[10]

As a setting in this ecological thriller, the Arctic becomes an experimental space not only for technology but for a new geography. Thule, "[a] petri dish of a country" (Buckell 104) is an integral part of Buckell's future speculation, importantly not connected to or representing an existing location. De Bruyn remarks that the "formerly nonhuman world" around the Pole "is being integrated into an all-too-human world of market forces and resource extraction" (48) and the future microcosm of Thule reflects, in speculative form, the relocations caused by climate change in the Primary World. This radical change to Arctic space is explained to the useful figure of the outsider through extended dialogues or via extradiegetic narration. The distancing effect that results from these info-dumps is paralleled by how, to Anika and the other main characters on temporary visits, Thule remains an experimental blueprint that they can draw inspiration from rather than forming affective bonds with. Anika's spy-friend Roo, for example, plans to convince disgruntled Thule inhabitants to accompany him back home to "the Caribbean where it isn't the Wild West like up here" and put their knowledge about "factories and greenhouses" to use (Buckell 333, 332). Buckell's future Arctic in this way remains an atopia, an unstable location that illustrates possibilities and signal warnings.

The first-person perspective and reflective form of Itäranta's *Memory of Water* provides a contrast to modes of telling rather than showing, and the novel depicts the effective immediacy of an irreversibly altered environment. To protagonist Noria Kaitio, Arctic Finland is home, a place which, despite environmental challenges and unstable political structures, she has deep, affective ties to. Indigenous to this speculative future, Noria reflects on the past destruction that has made her present difficult and her future uncertain, as if in communication with someone who inhabits the same world. This address, Katherine Farmar notes, results in that "certain aspects of the world are left a little vague," but also in an engaging exercise in which "the reader must interpret the evidence of Noria's life in the same way that Noria interprets the artefacts she discovers from the past— our present." Just as Noria and her friend Sanja try to understand previous uses of near-indestructible objects they find in the community's large "plastic grave" (Itäranta 55), the future world, both locally and globally, is slowly decoded via details in the mundane lives of the characters. Pieces of clothing illustrate effects of raised temperatures, off-hand comments about modes of transport and communication highlight an unequal distribution of technology, placenames like "New Piterburg [and] Mos Qua" (46) describe cultural changes to the southeast, and a future version of China has ascended to a position of superpower.

The vagueness and imprecision that create both estrangement and a productive similarity between the reader's and Noria's processes of knowledge building have a concrete, and far more detrimental, counterpart that results from a lack of reliable information and stable communication channels in the future post-collapse world. With Ursula Heise's call for "eco-cosmopolitan environmentalism" (*Sense of Place* 210) as a backdrop, Katarina Leppänen sees in *Memory of Water* a "dystopian future" in part resulting from "the individual's [in]ability to connect . . . the local and the global" (430). At the basis of Heise's call is a positively connoted "deterritorialization . . . that [is] premised no longer primarily on ties to local places but on ties to territories and systems that are understood to encompass the planet as a whole" (*Sense of Place* 10). Processes of deterritorialization are thus reliant on the "connectedness of societies around the globe," which in post-disaster novels have crumbled together with the environment. In *Memory of Water*, the breakdown in technology and the depletion of fossil fuels that make travel difficult mean that Noria can only speculate about a globally uniform climate disaster and there are slim chances for organizing a resistance to oppressive water politics also on the local level. A slow unearthing of clues to the Twilight Century, lying between the past-world of which Noria has been told and her unstable and dangerous present, combine with the incomplete or sketchy references to life in this future to point to additional obstacles in the process of re-creating the world.

As a subset of climate fiction, what Astrid Bracke terms "flood fictions" are especially effective "synecdoches for" contemporary environmental instabilities ("Flooded Futures" 279). The long figurative association floods have with ends and beginnings in Western thought combines with concretely rising waters and eroded coastlines in the Primary World to make a watery future easily imagined, and flood fictions thus respond particularly well to the "representational and imaginative challenges" inherent in depicting the slow violence of anthropogenic change (279). Rising waters in the contemporary flood fictions Bracke discusses trans- form terrestrial space and threaten "narratives, books, and knowledge" in a process that reflects "the wider collapse of (Western) civilization" (284). In Itäranta's vision of a future Finland, agentic saltwater is par- ticularly threatening—the ocean is an expansive "shroud" harboring "silent ghosts of lives past" (Itäranta 64)—but like freshwater, it is also figured as a vulnerable archive of the past. Rather than only obliterating knowledge in Itäranta's novel, water also preserves it. Freshwater does not bend to human will and design and it "carries in its memory every- thing that's ever happened in this world" (90). Arctic ocean ice is similarly "carrying the memories of the past-world locked within" (41), among them recollections of the intense oil wars that played a central part in the global destruction. Both archives of knowledge are threatened in Noria's present, however, with freshwater withdrawing in a catastrophic reaction to anthropogenic impact and polar ice "slowly giving in to water and melting into its embrace" in the increasingly hotter climate (41). As the last in a long line of tea masters, Noria is both protector and servant of water, and assumes responsibilities not only related to the ceremony of her guild, but also to remember what the waters know.

There are naturally many connection points between the apocalyptic and postapocalyptic narratives which I turn to in the third section of this chapter, and the climate fictions discussed here. Itäranta's novel in par- ticular pivots on a global environmental collapse which has put a per- manent end to many human practices and profoundly altered human existence and it shares an "insist[ence] on the power of agency [and] of narrative itself to inspire action" with other examples of contemporary postapocalyptic works (De Cristofaro 15). In the recent anthology *Images of the Anthropocene in Speculative Fiction*, *Memory of Water* is the first example of a body of texts that intertwines depictions of global destruc- tion so vast that "there is no nature left, only the environment" with "the major and universal role of storytelling" (Dědinová et al. 2). Awaiting pun- ishment for violating the water laws, Noria starts writing in the last of the tea masters' books to preserve her own story and her own self, to avoid her truth and identity from being appropriated or annihilated. She joins her memories to her present to tell her version of what is now lost under water and what starts as a slow trickle of words becomes a spring "burst[ing] to the surface" (Itäranta 254). The act of storytelling recuperates power and shares with water the sense of something "always flowing and changing, never static, trapped, or dead" (Dědinová et al. 2): it connects Noria to a larger context and to a further future. By relaying her story, which holds within itself the knowledge from the generations of tea masters that have proceeded her, others will be able to "carry the story forward. Perhaps some small stretch of the world will be more whole after them" (Itäranta 259).

The foregrounding of Noria as a small but significant part of a greater story plays into the novel's didactic message about accountability and action, repeatedly relayed through water imagery and extended to include past-world choices. Noria imagines how the "dry scar" of a riverbed was once full of water, and how it may function as a conduit between temporalities and responsibilities, with the potential to inspire change (26). An individual in the past may look into the flowing waters and "the present-world, the world that is [could] bleed into theirs, the world that was." What Noria wishes for is a two-way communication between her contaminated present and the past-world and the choices made in it, but she concedes that whereas one individual from the past world may go home and act differently, another may not: "I can't tell which one of them is real and which one is a reflection in clear, still water, almost sharp enough to be mistaken for real" (26). Although the novel promises a faint hope of finding the truth about past destruction and present oppression, Itäranta consistently emphasizes the unreliability of human choice: it is as difficult to catch or predict as water.

While the material affordances and vulnerabilities of the Arctic may be apparent, the challenge in both Primary World discussions about climate change and in fictions that narrativize it is to turn the area from space to place, or to demonstrate how Arctic instabilities affect the world at large. Both Paull and Buckell use the Arctic as a starting point for global alterations, illustrating how their future worlds will or have become "as extreme and unpredictable as the poles have long been to most Westerners" (Bracke, *Climate Crisis* 130). With an only slight temporal shift—described on the dust jacket as "the day after tomorrow"—Paull articulates close connections between biosystems, presenting the sudden calving of icebergs as "a tiny stitch in a larger pattern" (11) that include flooding in the Maldives, a lack of snow in European ski areas, and unpredictable winds which cover London with dust from the Saharan desert. Buckell depicts a precarious global balance in part through his multicultural cast. The nations of the far north are the winners in his vision of the future, but Nigeria and the Caribbean, homes to Anika and Roo respectively, are on the losing side, reeling from the disastrous effects of rising temperatures in the southern hemisphere. In both novels, the Arctic functions as the canary in the mine to borrow Bracke's phrase, rather than becoming place and home, an affective location for the lives and deaths in it. Itäranta sets *Memory of Water* in a Finland she knows well—her Arctic is imagined because of its futurity—and makes it home to Noria and generations before her. In this future, it is the largely unreachable outside world that is transformed into atopic space, and it surrounds an Arctic that still, precariously, sustains an affective bond.

Human–Animal Entanglements

To narrativize climate change is one way to make it graspable, but as all life and matter on the planet is or will be impacted by environmental upheaval it also, in the words of Donna Haraway, "matters what stories tell stories" (39). Along with other critics in the environmental materialist turn, she gestures towards the need for alternative perceptions of the world in order to generate new, productive forms of knowledge. Haraway proposes that "tentacular thinking" complements or replaces anthropocentric (two-armed) understandings that have proven destructive to the planet in order to tell new stories (30–57).[11] Alaimo introduces trans-corporeality, "material interconnections of human corporeality with the more-than-human world" (2) that make it impossible to separate human from nature or environment, and she uses climate change as an unusually clear example of "a swirling landscape of uncertainty" that demands alternative perspectives and ethics (20). What both theorists call for is a heightened attention to forms of agency occluded in constructivist divisions between humans and nature, and the consequences of such agencies.

Although I will not engage deeply with ecocritical or new materialist theory, I take inspiration from these calls for perceptual change and examine how speculative fiction, released from Primary World limitations, performs specific cultural work when questioning human-centered paradigms, and makes room for "wider groups of human beings, plants and animal species, geophysical events, weather, and technology" (Trexler 74) that constitutes the more-than-human world.[12] The novels in focus in this section, Sam J. Miller's *Blackfish City* and Jarrett's *Always North*, present a planet on or past the brink of environmental tipping points where questions of ethics and anthropocentrism are highlighted. They effectively illustrate how speculative fiction contributes images of how humans and animals are or become materially entangled to a wider discussion about how alternative perceptions and agencies are needed to understand and combat an array of destructive anthropocentric practices. Neither of the authors dislodges the human from her privileged position—Jarrett rather foregrounds anthropocentrism—but both ask and give rise to questions about consequences of continuing to see the human as distinct from the more-than-human.

In Miller's novel, the function of the fictional city of Qaanaaq and the centrality of storytelling highlight interconnectedness as a salient theme that frames more manifest forms of entanglements. A century from now, global devastation caused by climate change and attendant wars and societal collapse have made Qaanaaq, floating "[e]ast of Greenland, north of Iceland" (Miller 5), into one of the last refuges on the planet. Initially constructed as a perfect ecosystem and run by Artificial Intelligences to avoid human flaws impacting the day-to-day, existence in Qaanaaq is still fraught as warring factions fight for control and as society is becoming increasingly segregated. To this microcosm of the world, refugees have "brought their ghosts . . . . Soil and stories and stones from homelands swallowed up by the sea. Ancestral grudges. Incongruent superstitions" (8). The past, both the true and the false, has migrated north with the people remembering and telling the stories, and has transformed space into affectively connoted place. Everyone tells a different story, a heterogeneity that is mirrored in the broadcast *City Without a Map*—"[a]n elliptical, incongruent guidebook for new arrivals" as well as for long-time inhabitants (5)—which gives information and relays rumors about the history and present of the place in different languages and voices. Featured as stand-alone chapters, or interspersed in chapters in which main characters are focalized, the literary device provides a shorthand to the community into which the reader is relocated, and its personal address—"Here you are. Here we both are" (40)—imbricates both characters and readers. Marie Stern-Peltz comments that "*City without a Map* makes the point again and again that there is no such thing as a perfect system; only a human, flawed world endlessly shaped and reshaped by the stories we tell" and that themes of "interdependence and interconnectivity" are foregrounded not only by the broadcast but by the city itself. Disjointed both in how it is inserted into the novel itself and through its different languages, dialects, and address, the broadcast becomes the voice of the multicultural city, enforcing how seemingly disparate lives are connected.

Like other cities in urban fantasy, Qaanaaq becomes akin to a character, more precisely an antagonist against whom listeners to the broadcast are encouraged to rise.[13] Stories and memories, when traded, merge individuals, and as one voice proclaims: "Gather enough stories and soon you're not alone; you are an army" (Miller 224). Inciting protest and revolt against the flawed systems, *City Without a Map* thus calls for a future in which all agents are accountable. The central characters in the novel each have their own relationship with the city that alternately hinders or facilitates their literal and figurative progress, and discrete perceptions of the city are highlighted by occupations: one character scales buildings, another bisects areas. When these relationships with and perspectives of Qaanaaq align, chances for successful outcomes increase. Knowledge of both the affordances and limitations of Qaanaaq thus underpin Miller's central themes of reconnection.

A central storyline in the novel is focused on the re-establishment of family ties and it is coupled with concrete entanglements in the form of nanobonding. This is an experimental process which radically reestablishes ties between humans and animals, and in an extended sense attempts to reforge the severed ties between culture and nature: a disconnect that underlies the catastrophic climate change in the past of the novel. In this process, humans are injected with nanites—tiny AIs in the bloodstream—that produce a symbiotic connection with an animal, or more precisely, that enable humans to "*control their animals through thought alone*" (73). Valentina Romanzi's reading of the novel, which like mine sees a thematic linking between the depiction of Qaanaaq and this process, is based in Rosi Braidotti's transhumanist and posthumanist lines of thought and highlights how nanobonding exemplifies "a technologically mediated encounter between a human and an animal *zoe*-form" (79), the latter defined as "the non-human, vital force of Life [which] cuts across and reconnects previously segregated species, categories and domains" (Braidotti 60). The arrival of one of the nanobonded, Masaaraq, starts the narrative in *Blackfish City*: she comes to Qaanaaq with an orca, Atkornatok, swimming next to her boat, and the intense connection is later described as shifting Masaaraq's motivations, behaviors, and desires to the point where she no longer is "entirely human" (Miller 186). Romanzi argues that rather than reiterating the past "power imbalance" that followed the divide between humans and animals, Masaaraq and Atkornatok "are fully-fledged *zoe*-forms working in tune with each other by leveraging their radical differences. What results is a posthuman assemblage" (80).[14]

There are, however, complexities attached to how nanobonding concretizes more-than-human entanglements to highlight the need for joint responsibility for the environmental present and future, and the process puts all involved at risk. Stern-Peltz maintains that it at once imagines "a form of community which goes beyond the human, where the risk to animals and the natural world cannot be as easily ignored as it is today" while simultaneously demonstrating "the potential power of an extreme form of vulnerability." While a division between herself and the orca is inconceivable to Massaraq—"me and Atkonartok are all we have"—the symbiosis is both "frightening" and "exhilarating" (Miller 227). Risks involve a loss of individuality and sanity but are countered by a close physical proximity with the partner in the symbiotic relationship, and by a strong connection with the ancestral past which only Indigenous Arctic communities in the novel uphold (something I return to in the concluding chapter). Masaaraq's journey to Qaanaaq is initiated when she returns to her village after a hunting trip only to find most of its inhabitants killed and her wife and children gone: a result of growing suspicions and hostility towards people who "shouldn't have existed" (141), and one catastrophic event in a history of "nanobonder genocide" (183). Both the hostile attitude to the nanobonded and effects of involuntary separations demonstrate that the process, in Miller's speculative future, while offering hope for future sustainable relations, is also dangerous to communities and individuals.

The complexity of entanglements and the reliance on an anthropocentric perspective are highlighted in Miller's descriptions of the reestablished symbiosis. When Masaaraq arrives, there is a "polar bear . . . in chains" on the deck of her boat with a "metal cage over its head and two smaller ones boxing in its forepaws" (Miller 2). The bear was bonded to Masaaraq's son Kaev, and the long separation has had detrimental consequences. The human, also at a distance from community and ancestors, struggles with physical and mental tics, and the animal, without the concrete connection with its human partner, needs to be caged or restrained. When they are in close proximity for the first time, and look into each other's eyes, Kaev immediately sheds his feelings of being imprisoned in a body that does not obey him, and his insecurity concerning communication. Together, they act "in concert in ways that had nothing to do with language, planning, rational thought" and become "[o]ne animal" (132). Their concerted actions are violent, avenging Kaev's long, enforced existence as the losing fighter in rigged bouts, which means that the human's anger and frustration incite and organize a combination of defense and attack. In this instance, the bear comes to represent how physical strength and instinct are inspired and regulated by human emotions: "A bonded animal is only as tame as its human" (189). At the end of the novel, the bear's will is the driving force, but human emotion and control are still central to the denouement. Despite the pronouncement that "[a]nimals exist in the moment" (133), the bear sees in Masaaraq only the human that has kept him in chains and attacks her. Kaev lacks the calm that can balance the one organism they have become, and the metaphysical connection is materially manifested as he sees his own hands as "huge, thick with white fur, capped with long black blade-claws" ready to strike his unconscious mother (318). Atkornatok instinctively and without being either helped or hindered by Masaaraq defends the human she is bonded to and drags the dead body of the bear out to sea.

I am not tasking Miller with representing precise environmental materialist notions of more-than-human entanglements that erase distinctions between categories and annul defined responsibilities in the symbiotic relationship. The narrative perspective, after all, rests with the human characters in *Blackfish City*, and it is to a large extent human emotions and reactions that drive the action. However, the novel signals that the nanobond provides crucial possibilities and even necessities in its encouragement of new forms of knowledge and agency that are required to build a better, more ethically sound future. The speculative process thus effectively destabilizes previous hierarchies and interrogates consequences of new agencies in ways that are exclusive to speculative fiction.

Jarrett is more pessimistic about human capabilities to responsibly care for the planet, and an environmental tipping point is in focus in a 2025 temporality in *Always North*, produced by ethically questionable and destructive practices in the Arctic. The novel's seismologist protagonist Isobel, or Izzy, takes part in an ocean bed survey of the High Arctic that masquerades as science but is really searching for oil in areas that are ostensibly protected by a fictional 2020 global agreement. Five years later, however, "big money has found a way. As it always has. Always will" (Jarrett 8). Izzy cannot find either ethical or financial justification to not take part in the survey, but reasons that the information she helps gather is passive and neutral until someone else uses it. At the same time, the Arctic impresses her as central to how "the world [is] working," that the "frozen region is a vital piece of the engine that drives the world along" (15). To stall this machine will have irreversible consequences, and at the time of the survey, climatological instabilities have already changed the Arctic: there are only a few polar bears left on the planet, and high-latitude temperatures fluctuate wildly. In this unstable and vulnerable environment, infractions in the seabed continue, until interrupted by a "sound of the world ripping open" (110). The sound from a breaking Arctic ends the long history of human impact on nature and compresses destruction into one moment that separates before from after.

The moment of ecological collapse is imbricated in a wider examination of time in the novel, and a pronounced difference is established between human and non-human paradigms. Specificities of the Arctic work to introduce this divide and the distinctly human organization of time. On board *Polar Horizon* and disoriented by the Arctic summer light, Izzy and the crew insist on ordering time into measurable and recognizable units, and they indicate a general loss of agency and power if this human propensity is neglected: "If we don't measure, divide and account for time then what is it to us? What are we to it?" (Jarrett 49). Izzy jealously thinks about how human-measured time is progressing normally in other parts of the world, with each day bringing "a clean slate," whereas the lack of differentiation in the Arctic entails that "there are no real tomorrows and there can be no forgiveness" (69). The destabilization of human conceptions of chronology is thus indicated to have far-reaching consequences, and one character argues that "a before and an after [are] fundamental to everything we are" and that in the human software "linear time is the operating system" (75). The non-human world is run according to a different protocol, as bears and other animals are hypothesized to only experience an eternal present: "Everything that happened, is happening, will happen, is always happening" (245–246). Conceptions of time in this way separate the human from the more-than-human world, reflecting myriad practices that rely on divisions.

Izzy's time-specific memories, accessed through her journal—the sections of the novel set in 2025—play a central role in an experimental merging of temporal perspectives, designed to isolate and access the precise moment before the irreversible environmental collapse. In what is shakily identified as 2045, Izzy is recorded when reading the journal, and the recording is then played back to members of *Polar Horizon*'s crew to stimulate dreams and unconscious memories.[15] When listening to her own voice, Izzy is reminded of the unreliability of memory as she does not quite recognize events. She describes the process as one in which she is "looking over [her] own shoulder" (159), emphasizing how linear time has progressed, partially separating her from who she was. These returns to versions of the past constitute part of a process that in ethically uncomfortable ways concretize material entanglements: one in which the past which humans remember needs to be combined with the eternal present of a polar bear.

The combination of environmental collapse and the Arctic does not make the centrality of a polar bear particularly surprising, but many forms of this animal populate the novel and conjure a host of meanings. A stuffed toy named Snowball is tied to memories from Izzy's childhood, a carved figurine that she is given as an object of protection is linked to an Inuit tupilaq. Memories of an apathetic sow that Izzy sees at a zoo as well as environmental protesters dressed as polar bears carrying placards reading "*Homeless, please help*" (21) draw attention to processes of relocation and displacement. The latter connects with Octavia Cade's observation that polar bears are often featured "as refugees" or "unwelcome migrants," from the diminishing Arctic in speculative fiction.[16] A similar motif is addressed by both Bracke and Heise in discussions about a 2010 commercial for electric cars in which a polar bear leaves its unstable Arctic habitat, travels a great distance, and finally finds itself on a driveway in a suburban area where it hugs the car owner who has made an environmentally responsible choice. The commercial, Bracke argues, "neatly greenwashes what is essentially a polluting industry" (*Climate Crisis* 105) while Heise, by juxtaposing it with Zacharias Kunuk and Ian Mauro's documentary *Qapirangajuq: Inuit Knowledge and Climate Change* (also from 2010) illustrates how cultural specificities influence the polar bear's meaning. In the documentary, an increasing number of polar bears close to human communities are seen by interviewed Inuit as a sign of conservationist and monitoring practices that negatively impact Indigenous lives. Consequently, "from a Euro-American perspective [the polar bear] seems to transcend its local environment to signal the urgency of global ecological crisis [but it has] a quite different and far less transcendently planetary meaning in the local environment itself" (*Imagining Extinction* 243). Jarrett utilities the many instantiations of polar bears to signal how it is appropriated to serve different ends, echoing Primary World practices and attitudes, and there are tensions between local and global also in her novel.

Neither displaced actual bears nor bears in more symbolic form have prepared Izzy for seeing a specimen in the wild and once she does, the male predator "is terrible in his whiteness" (Jarrett 54).[17] Far from the passive or controllable previous instantiations, this bear "is in charge of . . . speed, distance, time" in an Arctic that has already destabilized human conceptions around these categories, and Izzy thinks, "I doubt he will forgive us our trespasses" (55). These awe-inspiring qualities combine with incongruities or even impossibilities; the captain on the survey vessel adamantly argues that it is the same specimen that decades earlier killed his brother, and with an eerie cunningness, the bear uses the sound of a breaking world to come onboard the boat to drive the intruders away.

Izzy's life-long entanglement with bears as an idea is replaced by a concrete connection when the wild bear, captured once boarding the boat, is held in a cabin above hers. Izzy imagines how the bear settles down in a sleeping posture identical to her own, and how their joint "dreams [are] drifting down like snow and settling in stratified layers" (234). These blurred lines between animal and human bodies and minds foreshadow the bear's function in the postapocalyptic world: as the only surviving specimen he will go from local to global as the agent that will contribute the eternal present in the process designed to reverse the destruction. Cryogenically suspended—his already unnatural lifespan artificially and involuntarily prolonged—the bear's brain is materially connected to those of crewmembers present at the ecological collapse. The bear is untethered from place and forced to align with the unfamiliar concept of linear time: bolts and wires concretely tie him to the destiny of the planet, darkly twisting the fact that he was always already part of a vast more-than-human entanglement. The melding process involving crewmembers has been unsuccessful, and Izzy decides to make a final attempt at achieving the "temporal transfer" (305) at the very end of the novel, when the world is literally burning around her. No longer separated by a deck, Izzy climbs onto the table, fits herself into the unconscious embrace of the bear, and thinks: "[w]e stay where we are, where we were, where we never were and will always be, curled together, spines nestled one within the other, floating on a frozen sea" (308). While the jumbled temporalities suggest that Izzy has been freed of the human notion of linear time, her attempt at a complete entanglement may be too little, too late to save the world, and the novel's final sentence: "I close my eyes and let go" is difficult to read as signaling possibilities for a human future.

In contrast to Miller's novel in which entanglements, despite challenges arising from them, still point to how the human productively can be seen as a node in a network, Jarrett paints a dark picture of violent and exploitative material connections that rather underlines how the human continues to be seen as distinct from non-human nature. There is an inescapable logic that leads from depictions of the ocean bed finally crumbling under the onslaught of encroaching humanity to the polar bear as an abused and exposed testing animal, at the mercy of human desperation. That all events are connected like a line of dominoes is also underlined when Izzy wonders what point in time she should really go back to in order to avoid anthropogenic destruction of the planet. Doubtful as to whether the moment before the sound heralds a broken Arctic is far enough, she thinks she ought to go "further back to when the North was still an impenetrable mystery, or further still to before humanity decided mysteries were there to be solved, exterminated, the last of them hunted past the point of extinction. Or to before we burned the first tree, putting our warmth above its life" (261). It takes a global environmental collapse for Izzy to reach this insight about humanity's complicity in its own destruction and the realization rather works as a dystopic caution. When read against Haraway's and Alaimo's ways of becoming-with that do not systematically and detrimentally privilege the human, *Always North* twists notions of more-than-human entanglements into dark but effective counterparts.

At the End of Time

"Apocalypse," writes Lawrence Buell, "is the single most powerful master metaphor that the contemporary environmental imagination has at its disposal" (285). An imagined apocalypse can concentrate the slow violence of climate change into one, clearly demarcated event, shattering societal, economic, and cultural structures, leaving either a utopian clean slate or a dystopian wasteland, but equally often, a radical environmental tipping point remains hidden in the past of the speculative world and readers and characters alike are left searching for meaning among the rubble. The latter structure produces elisions and often influences narrative style—effects recognizable from Itäranta's *Memory of Water*—and forms of incompleteness discussed in this section alternately connect gaps with the lack of reliable information and communication, or with more comprehensive ontological doubt. Climate change reappears in some of the texts in focus, with ramifications that concretely affect the characters, but the Arctic is also seen as a refuge from other disasters decimating life on the planet.

My examples range from possibly apocalyptic in Sarah Moss' *Cold Earth*, via apocalyptic in Lily Brooks-Dalton's *Good Morning Midnight*, to postapocalyptic in Marcel Theroux's *Far North*, that is, I use the term postapocalyptic to tease out the characters' temporal location in relation to the global disaster. Other critics argue, for good reason, that we are already living in or after apocalyptic events. Teresa Heffernan, for example, uses the term postapocalyptic to signal that we "live in a time . . . after the faith in a radically new world, of revelation, of unveiling" (6), and Frederick Buell ends his comprehensive *From Apocalypse to Way of Life* by arguing that "literature today represents a deepening environmental crisis as a context in which people dwell and with which they are intimate, not as an apocalypse still ahead" (321–322). Claire Curtis uses apocalyptic and postapocalyptic to distinguish works that "focus on the event itself," from those in which "the event is the causal precursor to starting over" (6), and Briohny Doyle sees "postapocalypse as a contemporary modification of apocalypse which withholds revelation in favour of playing out scenarios of human survival in the ruins of the old world" (100). Regardless of terminology, these and other critics examine the uncertain status of the end, or the potential meaningfulness of the end, in relation to the shift in meaning from religious revelation to secular catastrophe.

Beginnings, moments or periods of disruption, and aftermaths are in this way salient to (post)apocalyptic writing, and I return, here, to the moment of ecological collapse in Jarrett's *Always North*. Intertextually indicating an apocalyptic portent, the sound that heralds the Arctic breaking and with it the world is described as:

> Not a bang or a whimper but a rending, a tearing of this time, this now from everything that will follow—the infliction of a wound that can never heal. It is a sound to make you weep and fall to your knees, to pray to any god that might hear you to make it stop, to take you back, just a few seconds to where this sound is not happening. But knowing your pleas will not be answered. This is happening, this will always be happening and there will be no end to it.
>
> (Jarrett 108)

This moment is a nexus in several destabilizing processes in the novel, connected to time itself, identity, and the coherence of the world. Descriptions of it are inserted before the narrative proper starts, in the 2025 timeline (when it actually occurs) and as memories in the time after the ecological collapse. These returns facilitate the navigation of the apocalyptic structure in which "[t]he writer and the reader must be both places at once," that is, simultaneously both before and after the radical disruption, "imagining the post-apocalyptic world and then paradoxically 'remembering' the world as it was, as it is" (Berger 6). By prefacing the entire narrative, "this present moment . . . the last that can ever exist before this new thing, this irredeemable thing, happens" (Jarrett 1) is evoked as the point around which everything pivots, and the oscillation between 2025 and 2045 illustrates how postapocalyptic fiction "takes us after the end, shows the signs prefiguring the end, the moment of obliteration, and the aftermath" (Berger 6). The before is continuously present in the after in Jarrett's novel, but the after is also foreshadowed in the before.

Jarrett makes inventive use of the printed-out manual to Proteus, the software program used to detect oil in the seabed, to intertwine unstable temporalities and repetition with the destruction of the planet. This manual is pointedly never used by the scientists in the novel because to do so "would be seen as an admission of weakness, the same way as asking for directions reveals you're lost" and instead Izzy keeps her journal on the back of the pages, "recording [her] reality on the flipside of the official version" (Jarrett 42). The reversed chapter heads of the manual that Izzy describes are repeated in the novel. The first backwards heading is INSTALLATION and it is followed by the exact latitude and longitude of the location in the Arctic Ocean. Chapters then proceed through stages such as CONFIGURATION and ALARMS & WARNINGS until the moment of ecological collapse. A relocation to 2045 (and to peopled areas in Scotland) follows, in which the devastation of the world is described, and the narrative then returns to the "before" and to the Arctic, with events ominously shaded by knowledge of the fictional future. The first chapter in this section of the novel is entitled REBOOT and the previous careful notations about exact location and time are substituted with the vague "Arctic Ocean" and time markers that move from July, to summer, to only the year, and finally end altogether. After the last chapter, SYSTEM CRASH, the narrative again shifts to the postapocalyptic 2045. In a novel engaged in a committed critique against anthropocentric practices the headings easily lend themselves to readings of the manual as instructing humanity in how to take responsible care of the planet. But, again, no one ever reads the manual.

How environmental destruction features as one consequence of late modernity and capitalism aligns Jarrett's novel with a body of contemporary apocalyptic novels that Diletta De Cristofaro discusses with a focus on the salient feature of "critical temporalities." In novels such as David Mitchell's *Cloud Atlas* and Jeanette Winterson's *The Stone Gods*, experimentation with temporal levels, fragmentation, and elision "expose the hegemonic apocalyptic temporality at the core of Western modernity as a narrative enmeshed with power structures, thus framing the contemporary apocalyptic imagination as a critique of the ideological foundations of Western modernity" (10). The notion of the meaningful end, found in the teleological structure of religious apocalypse, is resisted or debunked in this critique, and Jarrett's novel is the clearest example in my selection of postapocalyptic novels of how the resistance leads to a pronounced dystopia.

None of the novels I address reflect temporal instabilities through radically experimental form, but they continue from the challenges inherent in capturing the immense scales of time in the slow destruction of the planet seen in climate fiction, as well as from the blurred Arctic temporalities I discussed in connection with ghosts and monsters in Chapter 2. In *Cold Earth*, the growing similarities between past and present produce ontological and epistemological doubt in the characters, and in *Good Morning, Midnight*, the unfathomable end of times gets an individual inflection, intertwined with the logical end of the protagonist's life. *Far North* oscillates between past and present, but while both temporalities are set after the global collapse, Theroux introduces a smaller, individual apocalypse that results in a re-take on the before and the after. With a continued focus on the Arctic, I explore how "[p]ostapocalypse . . . is not a teleological end point but is positioned as transitional and haunted by memories of the pre-catastrophe world" (Doyle 101). How place literally or figuratively becomes space is central to the trajectory of destruction, but there are also tendencies to resist this transformation in the texts I discuss, and attempts to reforge connections with Arctic landscapes.

Moss' *Cold Earth* presents a scenario of a possible contagion spreading through Europe and North America, rumors of which circulate in the archeological camp in Western Greenland. Headlines about an airborne virus disturb the first narrator, Nina, already at Heathrow, and she muses:

> It is usually a mistake to think about the news, I know, but worse when travelling, and a particularly bad idea to think about people you love and the news at the same time when you're nowhere near either of them. There's something about dislocation that makes the news seem horribly probable in a way that it doesn't at home.
>
> (Moss 2)

The tension between home and away is underlined by the epistolary form of the novel in which the characters move between chronicling their experiences at the Arctic excavation site and memories or fantasies of what is going on in the outside world. The novel's "focus becomes not the stories told about those who have already died, but the stories formed in relation to the experience of death" (Baker 156). The characters speculate about what caused the demise of the original settlers, such as an attack from invaders, climate change, and an epidemic, scenarios that reflect their own fields of archeological expertise and, in turn, inform their suspicions about what might be happening at home. When informed by two shepherds, their only visitors, that there is indeed a "sickness" affecting the outside world, the archeologists struggle to accept that they "are better here" (Moss 176). The "dislocation" Nina and the others experience makes them focus on what Timothy C. Baker terms "[t]he horror of the world-without-us" (151) and on the similarities between past and present that forge links between the disappeared settlement and themselves. The bay, at "the end of the road" (Moss 182) is hemmed in by the ocean and Nina thinks that it must have been seen by the Greenlanders as both a horror and a boon, bringing "them everything from plague and terrorists to glass and the latest fashions" (74). To the contemporary group as well, both possible salvation and potential threat come from the sea, and their periphery is further isolated when information slows down and then stops. Satellite connections become increasingly more unstable, webpages are no longer updating, and it starts to dawn on the group that the plane that is to collect them once the dig is concluded may not come. A salient fear in postapocalyptic fiction, Heather Hicks argues, "is the *loss* of a global perspective," (7) illustrated by how defunct technology isolates characters from information about the world beyond their own patch of space. With resources dwindling, the group members turn on each other, in Jim's formulation, because they are "so scared of cold and hunger and of what cold and hunger might do to us all" (Moss 251). The world shrinks as do possibilities to picture life going on elsewhere. When Jim tries to imagine his return to where "you can see threes and sculpture and parking lots and crowds of people" he checks himself, wondering "[i]f crowds are something people are still prepared to risk . . . . If there are still enough people to make crowds" (225). The letters present a certain chronology, and become shorter and shorter, reflecting the lack of energy and imagination as the group starts to be seriously affected by starvation and hypothermia and give up hope of being rescued.

The Arctic becomes a vantage point for the characters from which to contemplate "the dread of obliteration" in both the past and the present (Monaco 1011). Only faint traces are left of the lost history of the original Greenlanders and several processes in the Arctic landscape, moving from late summer into the cold fall, work to remove signs of human presence and of life itself. As Carroll notes, different forms of resistance have contributed to broadly transforming the Arctic to an atopia in times of exploration. "Signs were torn down by the elements; discoveries were challenged by other explorers; and the histories of expeditions were lost along with the men who perished," she observes (*Empire* 20). In Moss' novel, the possible contagion in the outside world works to establish connections between Arctic processes of disintegration and a potentially global collapse; there is a need to be remembered, to survive. When Nina ostensibly returns to Greenland with Yanni's ashes at the end of the novel, she insists that "we were there. We are history too" (Moss 278) yet she can no longer see signs of the group's presence. An earlier hypothesis that the Greenlanders were so environmentally conscious that evidence of them is hard to find becomes applicable on the contemporary group: ecological thoughts thus combine with the transformative environment to foreground nature and obliterate signs of human presence.

Moss does not give a conclusive answer to whether the world outside the isolated bay has ended or not. In the last chapter, in the form of a letter from Nina to Yanni, the expedition leader, there is a tentative return to some kind of normalcy. In it, Nina recounts reading another letter in the comfort of her London home, preparing a sumptuous evening meal, this one sent by Yanni's mother and centering on a request to spread his ashes at the campsite.[18] Yanni has frozen to death on the beach before the rest of the group is airlifted out, it seems, and Nina's last correspondence can in part be read as her acceptance of his never-explicit apology for having put them all in harm's way. Critics commonly see the concluding chapter as "open-ended" while still suggesting that aside from Yanni, the rest "are able to return to their former lives" (Baker 157, 156), or as "an epilogue" in which "readers vaguely learn" about the aftermath (Monaco 1025), but it is also possible to see it as untethered from the previous narrative—as wish fulfillment or a final dream on Nina's part. Her first long letter which opens the novel ends with her increasing frustration at not being believed when she tells her colleagues about ghostly presences, and with her mounting horror at the nightmares that have made it into her awake state. Addressing her boyfriend in London, she finishes:

> I am very sorry to let you down, but I can't keep going anymore. There are dead people in my mind and rotted flesh on my fingers. Open mouths and clawing hands. Bone feet in my shoes and crying voices. It's dark here, cold and dark, and strange sounds come carried on the wind.
>
> (Moss 103)

In the subsequent letters, Nina's trustworthiness and mental stability are repeatedly questioned, and form a backdrop to the other letter-writers' worries about their own and others' future. Ruth's letter, to her therapist, ends with a faint hope, nothing more, of being able to return home, and Jim's with the conviction that "[t]he plane's not coming" and a message to his family: "with the last beat of my heart and the last breath in my body I loved you all" (252). Catriona's narration is addressed to a female friend whom she realizes she loves deeply and romantically, and she ends her letter: "You won't even see this, probably. But it would have been too sad, to leave it unsaid" (263). In his very short letter, Ben is "not saying goodbye" (271) but cannot form a coherent image of who might be reading his words. Yanni's letter, preceding Ben's, is difficult to interpret. He takes responsibility for the ill-planned expedition and for endangering the others, but also recounts a nightmare in which he kills a woman, so vivid that he cannot for certain determine what has and what has not happened. He remains convinced, however, that they "are all going to die" in Western Greenland (265). That Nina, the only character who is heard from again, textually evinces a mental breakdown makes it possible to read the narrated return to normalcy as a dream, or even as her dying thoughts.

I see the ambiguous ending related to how, as in other examples of postapocalyptic fiction, the actual catastrophe "is often a gap in the plots, thus undercutting the power of the end to make sense of history" (De Cristofaro 20). In *Cold Earth*, the lack of reliable information about exactly what (if anything) has happened in the world outside produces a focus on personal history, a sometimes unreliable reckoning of lives the characters have had at home. Also in *Good Morning, Midnight*, information about the precise nature of the secular apocalypse is sketchy—all that is said is that "the last news from civilization, over a year ago, had been of war" (Brooks-Dalton 5)—and in the silence that follows, the end of times acquires meaning through being intertwined with the end of a human life. As in Moss' novel, the Arctic on one level becomes a place of safety, at a distance from potential ongoing battles, and left at the (fictional) Barbeau Observatory on Ellesmere Island when the rest of the personnel are finally evacuated is only Augie Lighthouse, an aged astronomer. Doyle notes that "scattering effects of catastrophe mean that texts often focus on small groups, individuals, and local responses" (103), and *Good Morning, Midnight* depicts, in terms of characters, a tiny environment. Remaining at Barbeau are only Augie and a child, Iris, who he reluctantly attempts to take responsibility for, but who may just as well be a figment of his imagination. In his isolation, Augie ponders questions of a personal nature that are raised by the inevitability of what is coming: the end of him as well as of humanity.

The transition from global to local establishes close ties to the climate fictions addressed in the first section of this chapter (with *Memory of Water*, which could also be categorized as postapocalyptic, as the clearest example), and to strategies of narrating forms of slow violence. In *Good Morning, Midnight* the further narrowing down to the perspective of an individual is offset by one that concretely incorporates a global perspective: the view of Earth from outer space. In the novel's other storyline, six astronauts aboard the spacecraft *Aether* are returning from an exploratory voyage to the moons of Jupiter, a mission that has "[s]hown them how tiny, how exquisite, how inconsequential they really were" (Brooks-Dalton 25), and how Earth, from this new perspective appears as "[a]n enormous round oasis in the midst of a parched black desert" (217). However, human-made lights go out one by one, and the oasis is growing ominously silent. Mission Specialist Sullivan, or Sully, is focalized in these sections of the novel, and after many failed attempts to establish contact with Earth, she finally and briefly reaches Augie. While he cannot contribute information about the global catastrophe, they talk about things she struggles to recall after her long sojourn to Jupiter: "She wanted to remember how it felt to be held by Earth" (229). To Augie, Sully's voice represents the final contact he will have with humanity. With the isolation of the Arctic comparable to the isolation of space, Augie and Sully ruminate on love and regret, past choices, and future uncertainties.

Augie is literally "[t]he last man on earth" (231), a relatively unusual figure in postapocalyptic fictions, but one that enables a "focus on experiences of solitude, the disruption of closed order, crises of identity, and the encounter with a reality that eludes human understanding" (Mussgnug 334).[19] In contrast to other instantiations of the trope, Augie is not a strong, masculine hero but a feeble old man, and the identity crisis he experiences revolves around questions of the fate of his life's work and his questionable decisions as a parent. At the end of a long scientific career, Augie has "imagined that what he left behind would endure for centuries. In this way his own mortality had seemed inconsequential" (Brooks-Dalton 17). He has not been afraid to die, but with the demise of humanity it inevitably follows that no one will be left to read his papers, or teach his findings.[20] "The immensity of a civilization's end" becomes understandable to Augie only through the consequence of the "recalibration of his own importance" (18). In addition to a heightened focus on aspects of his life that have been less successful than his career, the recalibration makes Augie turn his attention from the stars to the land.

The future Arctic, "with great shelves of ice that never melted and the ground that never thawed" (7), provides a stability that Augie on one level finds reassuring, it represents a constant in a world that is going through profound change. On another level, lack of change and response makes him doubt his own significance and even sanity: "The land did not care for him and there was nowhere else to go" (4). Brooks-Dalton depicts a long process in which Augie comes closer to and understands the land, and the child, Iris, is instrumental in the process, not only because the responsibility for her is what concretely anchors Augie to place, but because she shows him the way. Iris has a deep knowledge, Augie reflects, "about the wolves, the musk oxen, the hares" (141); she becomes an embodiment of the field guide she reads. Iris also helps Augie see how the cyclicality of seasons grounds people in the landscape. In previous years, Augie has left the Arctic each summer because the stars become invisible, but now, "[s]ince the evacuation, since Iris, he had felt more earthbound than he had in years" (157), and he can easily imagine and look forward to life returning to the Arctic with the summer.

While Iris encourages Augie to form solid attachments to the material Arctic and in a more symbolic sense to the humanity he has paid little interest in the past, her ontological status in the novel is uncertain. She is simply there at the observatory after the evacuation, just as communication with the world outside their small Arctic location ceases, and she appears to Augie as "hollow" (14) and "feral" (115), as a stray that does not mind, but neither welcomes human contact. Still, at "the edge of humanity, measured in both time and space" she is the one thing that keeps Augie alive (118). Rather than signifying vulnerability, this child gives Augie the purpose and reason to stay alive for one last act of communication with the world outside the Arctic and above Earth, with Sully, whose first name is Iris. The child may thus be read as conjured up by Augie's need to insert himself into a context that still matters, to establish a final point of contact with a daughter he has never acknowledged as his own. When the last transmission is cut off, Augie is gripped by a fever and "struggle[s] to understand what he had known all along" (234). His last question to the child Iris is: "Why are you here?" Getting no reply, he closes his eyes. When he opens them, Iris is gone.

When read as illustrating Augie's need for attachments to the earthly world, and the last conduit to them, the child's disappearance may signal his death, or a transition into a space in-between life and death. I suggest this, because it is followed by a last illustration of Augie's linkage to the material Arctic, which moves beyond Brooks-Dalton's otherwise realistic depictions. From time to time, Augie has spotted a polar bear and gone from a desire to, like it, only experience basic "instincts . . . . never love, never guilt, never hope" (7), to sympathizing with its vulnerability and "loneliness" (82). Perceptions of the bear in this way reflect the changes Augie goes through, encouraged by Iris, and there is always a careful distance between human and animal. After Iris' disappearance, Augie encounters the bear again, when it is dying in the snow. Augie does more than close the distance to it, he inserts himself in its passive embrace. "No longer an interloper, but a part of the landscape" (239), Augie listens to the faint beating of the bear's heart, and that is the last description of his final day in the Arctic. As John Berger notes, "the end of the narrative [seldom] coincide[s] with the end of the world" in apocalyptic fictions (6), but like Jarrett, who similarly finishes with a human in the involuntary embrace of a polar bear, Brooks-Dalton comes close to doing so, especially if this last scene is seen to play out if not after death, then in a liminal place. By drastically narrowing the apocalypse from global to individual, the end of a human life really does mean the end of the world.

In *Good Morning, Midnight* I consequently read the young Iris less as an actual child than as an agent that raises questions of meaning-making in the shadow of the end. She functions to both push Augie onwards and find purpose in his last year, and to nudge him back into the past to see the processes and decisions, among them the refusal to acknowledge parenthood, that have led him to an existence that is isolated even before the global collapse. At the same time, she functions as a child at precise moments when Augie confronts his loneliness and identifies the cure for it: "*Perhaps this is how fathers feel*" (161), he thinks when he realizes he has passed on the prosaic knowledge of making an evening meal. As the storylines converge around Iris as a conduit for communication, and connect the Arctic to outer space, Sully remembers growing up without a father (left only with his interest in the stars) and laments the fact that the never identified man she has talked to will remain "a disembodied voice, a spectral wanderer. He would die alone" (231). She, in turn, has a strained relationship to her own child, and in contrast to Augie no possibility to reassume a sense of parental accountability. Relationships between parents and children, regardless of how concrete or unsuccessful they are, thus feature as a major component of the novel's interrogation of what makes us human, and as in many other postapocalyptic works, as well as in some examples of climate fiction, these relationships become embodied representations of the lapsed responsibility of preceding generations.

Parenthood is intertwined with questions of survival and remembrance in Theroux's *Far North*, set in an unspecified future in which the world is reeling from climate instabilities and associated unrest. Protagonist Makepeace Hatfield stewards the depopulated settler town Evangeline in Siberia and is, like her Arctic surroundings, cold, hard, and distant: "[t]hese are not soft-hearted, womanish times" (22). In her shut-off and lonely existence, Makepeace meets Ping whom she first takes for a young boy. Like Makepeace herself, however, Ping passes as a man because of threats of sexual violence in the postapocalyptic world, and she is not only a woman, but pregnant. The future that seems promised by the pregnancy brings about a change in Makepeace, and she later describes "a streak of fond soil" inside herself "that Ping put roots into" (86). The roots interrupt Makepeace's identification with what she sees as "a broken age" (15) in which both humans and nature are "decaying back into wilderness" (28), and the hope of a new generation brings new possibilities and vulnerabilities. The death of both Ping and the baby unmoors Makepeace; it is a scaled-down catastrophe that translates the slow violence that has destroyed the natural environment and eroded social structures into a personal apocalypse. Yet, it instills in her a realization of larger contexts and a desire to leave marks on the world. Her own child, the result of "a hasty intimacy" (283) in a prison camp is such a mark, and her recollections constitute a legacy for a future generation.

The legacy Makepeace herself has been left is bleak, with her Quaker parents leaving the US full of hope but ending up embittered by the experience. What in previous periods would have been prefaced by "a warrant from a king [to] set sail to found a colony in some emptier space" (48), Makepeace thinks, is really a desperate flight from the ravages of climate change and associated collapses, while simultaneously, "the End Times," seem to have been expected or even "secretly long[ed] for" (110) in her parents' faith. What is right, an ideological True North, becomes corrupted in a world that has "gone so far north that the compass could make no sense of it, could only spin hopelessly in its binnacle" (271), and the descent into disorder and destruction includes betrayals by Makepeace's own father. These processes of destabilization, but especially the results of her parents' relocation—what Makepeace refers to as "a bunch of New Jerusalems . . . in the frozen north" (57)—makes De Cristofaro foreground the novel as an example of how "the convergence between colonial occupation and the ideology of progress derive[s] energy from the apocalyptic imagination" (96) in which exploitation of natural resources, economic strategies, and ideas of empty lands are seen to point towards a preordained end. *Far North*, De Cristofaro argues, "interrogate[s] colonial discourse and its contemporary permutations and legacies" by several modifications. Makepeace summarizes her parental generation's ideological project as "hooey" (Theroux 57) and stresses that what the settlers get is none of the riches of the Arctic, but literally and figuratively only its "thin topsoil" (51).

Propelled by the death of Ping and her child, Makepeace leaves behind remnants of unsustainable and unrewarding colonization and a slow but steady erosion of the meanings of True North and sets out to learn "what had happened to the world in [her] absence" (33). As a tourist from the far north, Makepeace journeys through a small religious community, a labor camp, a poisoned city inside what is known as the Zone, and an army base, before closing the loop with a return to Evangeline. The Arctic through which she moves is likened to "a beaten horse, limping with old injuries, and set on throwing its rider" (99) and the destinations are peopled by what Curtis refers to as "[t]he necessary Other: the groups of people who do not react so well to the cataclysm" (8). Threats of violence and sexual abuse compete with depictions of "ordinary cruelty" (Theroux 25) that follows in the wake of upheaval, and a diminishing supply of sustenance and culture. In a fragmented way, Makepeace's encounters and discussions with individuals representing different ideologies and worldviews in the varied locations echo the "countless extended dialogues with legions of highly vocal natives" (Lewes 12) that characterize the nineteenth-century lost-civilizations novels discussed in Chapter 1; they allow for diegetic explanations of the current situation. But added is the implied threat of the extinction of humankind: Makepeace's individual journey becomes metonymic for how humanity needs to amass knowledge anew, coalesce impressions, and rebuild what is possible of life.

These processes of salvage are concentrated in Makepeace's consistent gathering of books. In contrast to other apocalyptic scenarios, flooding in particular, the materiality of books is not at risk in Theroux's future Arctic, but the human focus on survival has rendered them unnecessary as anything else than kindling. That Makepeace sets the books she finds "aside for someone" in the future (Theroux 5), aligns with frequently returning "anxieties over the survival and manipulations of archives after the catastrophe" as well as with the associated emphasis on "the transformative power of narrative" (De Cristofaro 24). At the end, Makepeace has "2,075 [books] stacked up in the armoury and 177 . . . laid by in the house" (Theroux 285). The narrative she writes, planned to be gifted to her own child, is put with the rest of her collection where it will function as "a little prayer against annihilation" (288). These acts of preservation and insurance against being forgotten become particularly important when seen against other forms of knowledge that have already been lost, a loss that transforms the landscape. "*This was a place once*" (183), Makepeace thinks, as she searches for names of hills and rivers. Throughout *Far North*, Makepeace resists this transformation of place into space, believing that her own story, in some way, will make a difference.

This belief, and an associated conviction that something will remain after the end, compete with the dystopic depictions of both past destruction and more recent, dangerous forms of knowledge. Shamsudin, who will father Makepeace's child, argues that past measures taken to slow or reverse climate change were ineffective, and even that lowered carbon emissions sped up the process: "in trying to do the right thing, we had sawed off the branch we were sitting on" (139). In the poisoned city Polyn 66, experiments have been conducted that bring to mind the hubris of Victor Frankenstein: "how to breathe life back into a corpse, how to double the lifespan of a person, how to engender a child without the act of kind" (197). These instances indicate the lack of a didactic message in *Far North*, and align with Doyle's assessment that, "the alternative worlds of postapocalyptic literature are not presented as educational, a map to salvation via the threat of extinction" (111). On an individual level, however, there are tentative steps in the opposite direction, produced foremost, and unsurprisingly, by Makepeace's own pregnancy. Before it, the thought that "something will go on" unsettles her; rather than seeing a continued existence of humanity, she envisions "dark, slippery, once-human things . . . waiting to hatch out of the ark" (Theroux 184). When she returns home to have her child, the vessel withstanding the deluge has come to contain something else. Makepeace sees animals she does not recognize in the Arctic environment and becomes convinced "that they were salvaged from a busted ark . . . . a whole menagerie crawling and hopping north, tracing the route of the rivers that flowed to the cold" (284). New, unknown forms of life replace old, or start inhabiting previously empty locations, and the final end is postponed.

Although there are significant differences in how the apocalypse is depicted in the novels by Moss, Brooks-Dalton, and Theroux—ambiguous,

cataclysmic, or as an inevitable consequence of slow violence, respectively—
all depict how "something remains *after the end*" (Berger 6), that is, as
examples of postapocalyptic fiction, they belong to "a discourse that
impossibly straddles the boundary between before and after some event
that has obliterated what went before yet defines what will come after"
(19). The letters in *Cold Earth* are effective in the temporal structure often
employed in postapocalyptic fiction in which the before and the after need
to be portrayed and imaginatively inhabited. Makepeace oscillates between
her present and the past which events bring to mind, and the journey motif
puts her in contact with individuals who need or can provide explanations
for the gradual collapse: the past is forever present in *Far North*. Brooks-
Dalton seems to cancel out the idea of before and after by intertwining
the end of humanity with the natural end of a human life. Still, in the last
chapter of *Good Morning, Midnight*, Sully leaves *Aether* to descend to
Earth in a pod. "Even if this was the end," Sully thinks, she is glad to return
"home" (253). This final scene illustrates that despite the suggestion that
what will come after will be very brief, there is still time for one last look at
a planet that has been completely silent and dark for some time.

The ice that began to thaw in the previous chapter reveals, in this one, a
deep-seated anxiety connected to what its disappearance means, not only
for the polar areas but for the planet. Conversely, a warming climate permanently shifts associations to the Arctic and Antarctica. In Benjamin
Morgan's words, "regions that had for centuries dramatized the fragility
of human life have, in a few short decades, been refigured as representing
the Earth's profound vulnerability to collective human agency" (3). This
Primary World shift in perception, he goes on to suggest, "means that the
Arctic has begun to do a very different kind of cultural work . . . requir[ing]
new] conceptual frameworks and vocabularies." The novels examined in
this chapter take part in the refiguration and respond to the call for alternative ways of perceiving and describing the Arctic. Tackling the representational challenges inherent in depicting the slow violence of climate change,
they offer images of temporally near and distant environmental collapses,
possibilities for new paradigms that decenter the centrality of the human,
and (sometimes thwarted) attempts to make sense of the end of the world.

Notes

1 With attitudes shifting in the decades following the original publication,
resulting in a "renewed, but qualified, trust in the stability of climate" Carroll
traces the changes Shelley made between the editions, observing that "[i]f the
1818 version of *Frankenstein* hinted at a potentially-immanent apocalypse that
science might need to combat, the 1831 edition . . . shifts responsibility for

the human race's possible annihilation more squarely onto Victor's shoulders" ("Crusades" 224, 225).

2 The numbers are in comparison with 1986–2005 levels. See Schoolmeester et al. 2019.

3 Kyle P. Whyte points out that how climate change is envisioned calls to mind losses already experienced by Indigenous peoples, produced by "forms of colonialism: ecosystem collapse, species loss, economic crash, drastic relocation, and cultural disintegration" (226).

4 Yost also addresses the recirculated idea that the subterranean Arctic originates humanity and preserves, by virtue of its peripherality, the secrets of the human soul's divinity, and she suggests William F. Warren's *Paradise Found* (1885) as a likely inspiration (182).

5 In the last chapter of *The American Claimant*, the appropriately named capitalist protagonist Sellers by letter instructs a friend to "buy Greenland and Iceland at the best figure you can get now while they are cheap. It is my intention to move one of the tropics up there and transfer the frigid zone to the equator. I will have the entire Arctic Circle in the market as a summer resort next year" (Twain 272). This plan, as the one in Verne's novel, comes to naught, whereas in Bulgarin's novel the far-future Arctic is already what Sellers envisions: "a seaside paradise—with no apparent consequences for the rest of world from the increased heat or ice-melt" (Asselin 441).

6 Planned geoengineering is found in one of the plot strands in James Rollins' *Ice Hunt*, discussed in Chapter 2, and features as an instrument of revenge. Admiral Viktor Petkov's father has died at Ice Station Grendel, and based on his research, Petkov aims to effect climate change through a nuclear detonation. The waters of the Arctic Ocean are expected to transform into cold precipitation, slowly turning into glaciers with the result "[a]fter fifty thousand years, a new ice age would begin" (Rollins 140). Petkov's father's demise in the ice will thus be extended globally. However, a partial detonation does not definitively upset climate patterns; the ice cap is "re-formed" the following winter attesting to the resilience of the Arctic (470).

7 An unstable Arctic is a temporary destination only in Ian McEwan's *Solar*, in which physicist Michael Beard goes to Svalbard "*to see global warming for himself*" (59), before retreating to a more reassuring location.

8 Given the early assessment "that the animals had all but vanished" (2), the bear is likely one and the same.

9 Lopez adds that "hanging without a frame in a stairwell" at the home, *The Icebergs* was not perceived of as an original and was "signed by one of the boys" (247).

10 That the Arctic remains altered by climate change and a nexus for future power struggles and conflicts "is helpful," De Bruyn notes, "as it creates further opportunities for novelistic exploration" (48). *Arctic Rising* inaugurates a series and is followed by *Hurricane Fever* (2014), set in Buckell's native Caribbean.

11 Non-mimetic forms of storytelling are important in Haraway's call for profound change and her inclusive label "SF" comprises "science fiction, speculative fabulation, string figures, speculative feminism, science fact, so far" (2).

12 Discussions in this section in part draw on my article "Human–Other Entanglements in Speculative Future Arctics" (co-written with Van Leavenworth, 2022).

13 After aggregating definitions of urban fantasy, Stefan Ekman identifies "the Unseen" as a salient ingredient in works in the genre. "Dark, labyrinthine, or subterranean settings . . . obscure our view," he notes (463), and narratives are peopled by "social outcasts we consciously look away from, [by] people from society's margins [and by liminal] characters who have license to move between margin and center" (463, 465). In *Blackfish City*, previously Unseen demographics push their way back into view.

14 In the city, Romanzi sees a similar "idea of an assemblage: Qaanaaq is still becoming—that is, it is still forming its identity as a community of individuals" (81).

15 "It's June, or July perhaps," Izzy reflects in the first chapter set after the before. "I'm reasonably sure the year is 2045" (117). Strict timekeeping is impossible or no longer matters in the devastation after the disruptive moment.

16 *Always North* is one of the written fictions Cade discusses, along with Kerrin P. Sharpe's poem "The Bear" (from the 2018 collection *louder*) and Yoko Tawada's *Memoirs of a Polar Bear* (2016).

17 The description reads like an echo from Herman Melville's chapter "The Whiteness of the Whale." The repetition of the phrase "*Call me Isobel*" (152) establishes another link to *Moby-Dick*, in which Ishmael too exists in two versions, with the narrator recalling himself in the before.

18 As Anna Auguscik observes, to scatter Yanni's ashes across the site "contributes to his worst nightmare" (217). Of all the characters, Yanni is the most adamant that the contemporary group leaves no traces, yet his remains, as it were, may be the only ones that remain in Western Greenland.

19 Shelley's 1826 *The Last Man* is among Florian Mussgnug's examples, as are M. P. Shiel's *The Purple Cloud* (1901) in which explorer Adam Jeffson against all advice travels to the Arctic, discovers the North Pole, but then releases toxic gasses that spell the end of humanity.

20 The space mission provides a similar perspective on how human discoveries require "a wider audience" to become meaningful and on how the "blackness" of space, like the end the dark Earth signifies, turns "ambition [into] flimsy vanity" (27).

Conclusion
Writing and Imagining the Arctic

The speculative fictions analyzed in this book span from Mary Shelley's 1818 *Frankenstein* to Vicki Jarrett's 2019 *Always North*, and from the figure of Prometheus, highlighted in Shelley's subtitle, to Proteus, a software program in Jarrett's novel. Shelley's use of motifs connected to the Promethean myth is well explored territory, with critics tracing nineteenth-century attitudes to ways in which "the powers of nature might be appropriated for humanity" (Spufford 59) in technological and scientific pursuits, as well as variously interpreting the punishment for hubris. Jarrett's brief reference to Proteus is enmeshed within her broader critique of anthropocentric practices, gesturing to how hubris has already taken humanity past the point of redemption. In Greek mythology, Proteus was a deity connected to bodies of water who had the ability to shape-shift. Positive connotations to mutability and adaptability were coupled with Proteus' ability to reluctantly prophesize about the future. In *Always North*, the Proteus software is used to explore the Arctic ocean bed, to decode it in ways that allow access to the last oil reserves on an overtaxed planet. It gathers data, is fed old data, and spits out a prediction about where to find the precious remnants of the fossil fuel, but it is human interpretation of the results, of course, that determine how to proceed. Despite the inanimateness of Proteus, it seems to signal warnings. Before going live, trial runs signal some problems in the operation of the system and the momentary black screens give protagonist Izzy a sense of "foreboding" (Jarrett 53), later exacerbated by inconsistent noise interruptions in the data read-outs as well as from the ice itself, the latter foreshadowing the terrible sound that represents the final ecological collapse. The hubris starting with how Prometheus in an extended sense brought knowledge, science, and civilization to humanity—in *Frankenstein* encapsulated by the act of bringing life into dead flesh—results in a global collapse in Jarrett's novel engaged with the vast ramifications of anthropogenic climate change.

In this final chapter, I conclude discussions by addressing strategies employed when writing and imagining the Arctic that have not been fully

DOI: 10.4324/9781003355588-5

explored in the preceding chapters. Although I will return to many of the speculative fictions already addressed, I will also comment on a few texts that have not previously entered discussions, but that nevertheless effectively illustrate the challenges and affordances that the Arctic brings to the field of speculative fiction, and conversely, what speculative fiction brings to the Arctic. Narrative techniques and representations of Indigenous Arctic peoples in my material are especially at focus in this chapter. Although representations of Indigenous characters (or lack thereof) are of relevance to discussions in previous chapters as well, not least where I have discussed authors' inventions of empty Arctic space that can be filled and manipulated, Indigenous questions and identities are moving to a more central place in contemporary, often environmentally oriented texts. I thus revisit novels and short stories previously analyzed for what they can tell us about the function of the Arctic in connection with alternative histories, ghosts, thaws, monsters, and more-than-human entanglements to illustrate how inside perspectives productively complicate the Arctic as a construction. I end by addressing how past and present constructions of Arctic space function in the context of climate change; the way the Arctic has migrated from periphery to center in debates is an important starting point for my overall project.

My focus on these strategies and constructions is coupled with attempts to, in a more traditional fashion, sum up my overarching claims and heighten the attention to how fantasies invited by Arctic instabilities are put to particular use in speculative fiction, and how speculative fiction, in turn, destabilizes perceptions even further. By approaching speculative fiction as a field of cultural production, with works clustering around events, perceptions, and questions, I have traced how the Arctic functions in the texts, and how renditions of the Arctic are affected by variously radical speculative elements. The selected texts occupy different positions on the spectrum of speculation with some comprehensively transforming Arctic locations and introducing fantastic events and beings in them; others are only incrementally removed from Primary World conditions. With primary sources weaving in and out of discussions, I have also demonstrated how elements in each text can be variously speculative. Representations of the Arctic can consequently within a single text fluctuate between the two extremes of the spectrum.

Emerging from my readings are three main functions of the Arctic: as antagonist, as last outpost or repository, and as a victim, predominantly of anthropogenic climate change. These functions, which sometimes coexist in the same text, in turn produce connotations to destabilizations of categories and individuality, to stasis and dearth but also to hopes and promises, and to a sense of precarious more-than-human interconnectedness. The Arctic as antagonist is found in fictions that cleave to the Primary World exploration tradition, but also in texts in which the boundary to lower latitudes is policed by monsters. As an obstacle to spatial progress, the Arctic is then a foe to be vanquished or outsmarted, but one that frequently locks visitors into a static state. In the form of vast icescapes or dark forests, the Arctic is also as disorienting as the marvelous beings that reside there. With ice as the foremost emblem of preservation, secrets of both the past and the present remain in the Arctic, but even ice-free Arctic landscapes are sometimes figured as refuges for what has become impossible elsewhere. The Arctic as a lockbox of secrets is used in scientifically and environmentally oriented novels, and in some imaginings, the Arctic is the last livable place in the midst of global upheavals. Central among these is climate change, and the Arctic alternates between being depicted as a vulnerable, soon-to-be ghost and, again, as exacting revenge on humanity. These functions of the Arctic return in different guises when traced in texts published during two centuries, and they are connected to broader societal and ideological changes. In the late nineteenth century, for example, beliefs and allegiances shifted as a result of scientific developments, industrialization, and political movements and, as I discussed in Chapter 1, led to a slew of texts in which an alternative Arctic both critiques and offers shelter from developments in the Primary World. Late twentieth- and early twenty-first-century texts similarly respond to unsustainable forms of rapid development and coupled with the steady migration of the Arctic to a position of geopolitical significance, works predominantly concerned with environmental issues (discussed in Chapter 3) illustrate that the northern polar area again constitutes a needed alternative space.

The main functions of the Arctic are produced by the overarching tendency to see the vast area as a blank space. The notion of emptiness in the sense of uninhabited locations—recall Walton's stress on the importance of "tread[ing] a land never before imprinted by the foot of man" (Shelley 16)—is of course deeply problematic in Primary World contexts, whether the fantasy of absence is used to rationalize conquest or colonization, or to provide a stage for ideological positioning or identity creation. These contestable processes, building on a downplaying of the heterogeneity and busyness of the vast region, find their way into speculative fiction as well, but what is blank and void (what is space rather than place) also provides endless fodder for the imagination. In "Desert and Ice: Ambivalent Aesthetics," geographer Yi-Fu Tuan makes a distinction between "[h]omeplace, which nurtures biological life [and] alien space [which is] life-negating in severity and yet inspiring" (149). In the limiting environment of polar icescapes, he continues, "homeplace is the hut and immediately beyond is alien space" (154). As Elizabeth Leane remarks, the latter formulation stresses how place "is squeezed to nothing" in polar regions, and "the border between In Here and Out There—hut and environment, body and landscape, self and other—becomes precariously fragile" which results in images of Antarctica and the Arctic as sites of "amoebic shapelessness and changeability" (11, 54). These mutable qualities, extending into ontological and epistemological instabilities, draw authors' imaginations north in the first place, and how the Arctic is textually represented is similarly a question of molding and manipulation.

The construction of the narrative in *Frankenstein* is itself illustrative of manipulation, but with an initial focus on the process of monstrous creation. Walton takes notes without Victor's awareness; they are simply a continuation of a practice he has already started, and which follows the protocol of exploration. But when Victor realizes that his story has found its way to paper, he asks to read it and, Walton remarks in what reads as a meta-comment, "corrected and augmented them in many places" with the explicit aim to give "life and spirit to the conversations he held with his enemy" (Shelley 213). The reason for amendments and additions, Victor claims, is that he does not want "a mutilated" version of his story to "go down to posterity." Into Walton's notes, that is, Victor injects descriptions and extrapolations that fit his objectives, and the story the reader has just perused is a result of this manipulation. Walton's letters, whose specific formulations have functioned as starting points for many of my analyses, are ostensibly more immediate; in these we rather see how ideas and preconceptions of the Arctic are tempered or overthrown by Walton's experiences in the ice. The examples that now follow illustrate other processes of manipulation as well as strategies employed to create a sense of immediacy, both important to how the Arctic is written.

Ed O'Loughlin's *Minds of Winter* includes a tale-within-the-tale that explicitly illustrates how images of the Arctic are ordered, reordered, and made to fit different motives and ends, and how stories are disseminated via sometimes very complex processes. Waiting for a wireless message at a hotel in Victoria, British Columbia, Cecil Meares tells Hugh Morgan a story about a 1904 encounter with Jack London, the latter at this time a war correspondent for the *San Francisco Examiner* dispatched to Manchuria to cover events in the Russo-Japanese War. In what is represented as an excerpt from a never completed autobiography, London, or "the writer" (O'Loughlin 253), interferes as Japanese soldiers attempt to execute what they deem to be a spy and then sit at the man's, or Meares', hospital bed through the night. London recounts a story he has been told by a Russian, referred to by the ubiquitous Ivan, in the heyday of the Klondike Gold Rush and that he plans on making into a short story. The never-named Meares interjects with questions or by trying to anticipate plot twists, and the narrative is once interrupted by a return to Morgan and Meares in the now of the plot in *Minds of Winter*; the chapter also ends in this temporality, with both men pondering the consequences of details in the tale.

Somewhere along the Rat River, the writer tells the man in the hospital bed, Ivan has come upon what he recognizes from his own culture as "a hermitage or mission" (265). Inside he encounters two men, Cuthfert and Weatherbee, ravaged by scurvy and frostbite, who nevertheless offer him exceedingly sweet coffee, a meaty stew, and bread freshly baked using torn-out pages from a Russian Bible as baking paper. The men show Ivan logbooks that they have found which have little meaning to them and that are illegible to the Russian, not schooled in the Roman alphabet. Further, they produce a soldered tube bearing the Board of Ordnance sign, and an old, engraved revolver. The objects that carry little meaning or value in the isolated existence by the river turn out to have been unearthed from two old graves outside the hermitage. Following an after-meal skirmish that sees Weatherbee dead and Cuthfert dying, Ivan re-inters the objects, barring the revolver, in one of the graves, noting in this process that one of the corpse's "lower body, from the waist down" is missing; the men, he conjectures, had found "a way to beat the scurvy" (279). Rather than taking an interest in this tale of cannibalism, Meares focuses on the found objects, especially since London's notes enable him to remember that the revolver is engraved with F. R. M. C.—observant readers of O'Loughlin's novel have already come across the initials of Franklin's second-in-command: Francis Rawdon Moira Crozier (65)—and in how this relayed story can turn out to be a piece of the Franklin puzzle. To avoid others detecting the same clues, Meares persuades London to remove the elements that he claims overburden the tale with an outdated sense of the "Gothic [and] supernatural" (283). A pared-down story, he suggests would be "starker [and] more modern" and would allow London to focus on "the cracks in a character [and on] how we rely on a very thin layer of civilization to hold us together" (283, 284).

Throughout *Minds of Winter*, O'Loughlin makes use of the fact that Meares' "life . . . was largely a blank space" (298), but that what is known makes it possible to imagine him at specific places at designated times. Like the chronometer that features as an agent connecting times and places in the novel, Meares fills the function of drawing elements of the plot together and affecting history. Although the dates do not align in this example, London's short story "In a Far Country" (published four years before the imagined encounter with Meares) is a tale with no traces of cannibalism but rather what O'Loughlin's Meares suggests: a modern tale with a focus on what Arctic isolation does to men who are incompatible with each other and unable to adapt.[1] Vaguely speculative elements feature in the published short story: Weatherbee is driven to try "to resurrect the spirits that slept in the forgotten graves" (London 86) that are left undisturbed outside the cabin and is haunted by the result. Emphasis, however, is on how "the Fear of the North" mentally alters the men and sharpens the animosity that exists between them from the start—it makes them lose "all semblance of humanity, taking on the appearance of wild beasts" (92). In the fictional London's plan for the story are elements which the fictional Meares finds too detailed and "far-fetched" (O'Loughlin 283); there are answers to questions—such as the design of the cabin: "one of the many mysteries which lurk in the vast recesses of the North" and the making of the graves: "whose hand had piled the stones?" (London 77)—but the imagined removal of these produces a productive focus on Arctic isolation and its consequences. When seen in relation to "In a Far Country," the layered story in *Minds of Winter* is thus an effective illustration of how narratives are ordered to gel with expected discourses, and how both answers and individuals are allowed or encouraged to disappear to make sure that these discourses are maintained.

The majority of the characters in the works I have examined travel to the Arctic on journeys that are designed to include a return to the point of origin—in geography as well as in identity. The nineteenth- and early twentieth-century texts I discuss in Chapter 1 are closely modeled on travelogues or maritime diaries resulting from Arctic expeditions, and depict heroic explorers searching for the open polar sea, the Pole, or the Passage, but commonly finding, instead, civilizations hiding in the periphery. Authors of speculative novels like these are explicitly engaging with a writing tradition in which events and impressions are embellished, and in the polar context influenced by expectations connected to the Arctic sublime. Like their Primary World counterparts, narrators and focalized characters emphasize the scientific mission to bring a trustworthiness to their descriptions, an emphasis notable also in formal details such as notations of latitudes and longitudes, dates, and temperatures, inserted as guidance at the start of chapters or sections. In examinations of paratexts that frame lost-civilization novels, David Seed notes that "they do indeed function as thresholds by mediating between the reader's familiar world and attendant assumptions about reality, and the events narrated which will challenge those assumptions" (138). Titles, forewords, afterwords, and notes are thus designed to arbitrate between realism and speculation and the atopic Arctic serves as a quickly traversed stage on the journey.

Filling a function akin to Walton's letters in *Frankenstein*, paratexts may also explain how narratives about lost civilizations and subterranean societies reach an audience. In these cases, manuscripts are often unexpectedly found and edited, or stories are told to sometimes suspicious compilers. Henry Clay Fairman's *The Third World* (1895), exemplifying the process of discovery and manipulation, starts in the aftermath of the Franklin expedition and is prefaced by an author's note detailing historically verifiable events and the commercial importance of the Northwest Passage. Once information about the disappearance of the ships, rescue missions, and hypotheses, is exhausted, the introduction veers into the imagined. Although "history retires and fiction takes up the pen" at this point (Fairman 6), the tone of the narrative does not change, rather the author's note goes on to explain that an exciting discovery has been made by a Norwegian sailor in 1859. He has found a cave, a grave containing two bodies whose preserved state seems to be "in harmony with the Arctic environment" and a compass with the inscription " 'The Terror' " (6). The real prize, however, is a journal by the last surviving crewmember, referred to by Fairman as simply "the Survivor." It begins as many other tales of fantastic discoveries: "I believe that my adventures are without a parallel in the history of mankind," notes the Survivor, and then states that he "write[s] a book that none but [him]self can ever read" (7). Readers with an interest in a fictional first-person account of life on *Erebus* and *Terror* and an explanation (likewise fictional) for what actually befell the last Franklin expedition will be disappointed when the editor removes the Survivor's "detailed account of the voyage, loss of the ships, and death of [everyone] but himself" (8) and instead lets the journal resume in Northern Greenland, where the Survivor has been brough by an Inuit rescuer (I discuss their short time together below). The Survivor's initial travails in the Arctic are briefly chronicled, but the bulk of the text describes how he finds considerable treasures, not to mention conjugal bliss, in a subterranean civilization where he also plans to live out the rest of his life. Wanting to protect the riches of Polaria, he "advise[s] the King to close the corridor" (313) leading to the society but counterproductively leaves the journal, which arguably works as an effective map, above ground.

Fairman ends his foreword by stating that the journal "speaks for itself" (6), thus casting no doubt on the veracity of the personally held journal; he functions merely as the mediator ensuring that readers are informed of the historically confirmable context, that they are "spared" prosaic details about life on *Terror*, and that the text reaches an audience. In *The Smoky God* (1908), author Willis George Emerson takes a more active part, describing how he has transcribed the story of yet another discovery of a subterranean society in the far north, all the while pronouncing himself "a disbeliever" (12). There are repeated references to this disbelief, a warning that the "eloquent madness" of Olaf Jansen (another enterprising Norwegian) may have led him astray (12), and an insistence upon the reader's agency in the process of drawing conclusions from the story. Geographical and scientific questions abound, but, he writes, "[t]he reader may be able to answer these queries to his own satisfaction, however far the chronicler of this narrative may be from having reached a conviction" (13). This uncertainty is repeated in the afterword—Emerson reports what he has been told but has no first-hand information—but competing with the two positions of eyewitness and chronicler are also numerous footnote references to exploration narratives, philosophical treatises, natural histories, and pseudoscience. Emerson employs an "unusually insistent framing," Seed remarks, and the notes in particular "constantly re-position the narrative's relation to other texts and thereby also give readers confusingly disparate signals about its status" (156). The radical speculation of Jansen's two years among giant inhabitants in the Earth's interior is not lessened by the consistent paratextual dialogue with other works, but the numerous quotations purport to establish plausible ground for how Primary World conditions are merely extrapolated. Observations by John Barrow, Fridtjof Nansen, and a host of other Arctic explorers are combined with references to the Grimm Brothers' folk tales and hypotheses in William F. Warren's *Paradise Found*. Together, narrative and paratext thus align with the broader discourse in which the Arctic tests boundaries for what is possible.

Speculative fictions mimicking Primary World exploration narratives thus present an alternative geography of the Arctic and fill a figurative or literal emptiness with discoveries that either offer visitors opportunities for adventures and power, or that by their difference illustrate critiques of Primary World ideological or societal structures. Howard Waldrop and Steven Utley's short story "Black as the Pit, from Pole to Pole" (1977) is an unusually late example of experimentation with Arctic space: "a postmodern homage to the hollow-earth tradition" (Leane 65). Revolving around the continued existence of Shelley's Creature—who moves from north to south through the hollow earth and encounters a host of characters and entities from the writings of H. P. Lovecraft and Edgar Allan Poe—the short story replaces the epistolary frame of its source of inspiration with an intertextual weave, and it begins with an end. "It ends here, Victor Frankenstein," the Creature thinks, in a geographical counterpart to "the nothingness" from which he has been "summoned" (Waldrop and Utley 220). The self-immolation suggested at the end of *Frankenstein* is not needed in this continuation as the Creature will not be found "[a]t the top of the world" and as he has only posed a threat to Victor. Coming to in the snow, the Creature feels like he did in "the night of his first awakening" (221), the sense conveyed being that Victor's process of creation and the Arctic fill similar functions: they both leave the Creature without possibilities to orient himself. Moving into a strange landscape and approaching the polar opening, the Creature sees possibilities to enter a land as unnatural as he perceives himself, and remove power from Victor, the memory of whom continues to haunt him. By following the Creature's journey from the Arctic to Antarctica, the short story becomes a condensed comment on how ideas in the early and mid-nineteenth century come together. John Cleves Symmes' theories and John Rae's attempts to gather information about the disappearance of Franklin's crew are put next to Shelley's writing of *Frankenstein* and Poe finding inspiration in the voyages of Jeremiah Reynolds. "Mocha Dick, the great white whale" swims southern waters long before Herman Melville is born, and Arthur Gordon Pym finds an existence outside Poe's novel, driven by a "burning desire . . . to go to sea" (223).[2] By collapsing boundaries between fact, fiction, and metafiction, the short story effectively illustrates the conflation of several discourses, mobile spheres of meaning that can unproblematically collide and fertilize each other in speculative fiction.

Adaptations and continuations of *Frankenstein* demonstrate the malleability of the promethean myth, but in contemporary versions of it, the Arctic is disappearing from narratives, which instead come to revolve more tightly around genetic experimentation and other threats of category collapse. The function of the Arctic as signaling both symbolic and actual properties of desolate wastes and representing the ends of influence of human science is negated, of course, as the polar areas are moving to the center of discussions about environmental and cultural (un)sustainability. Just as effects of climate change are perceived as being more effective in the mobilization of action if moved to lower latitudes (I discussed this in Chapter 3), geographically transposing *Frankenstein* gives rise to foci more suited to the contemporary condition. Contemporary retellings also involve the notion of creator in specific ways, like in Waldrop and Utley's short story concretely incorporating Shelley into the speculative fictions. In Jeanette Winterson's *Frankissstein: a Love Story* (2019), the doubling of the original author—the nineteenth-century Mary Shelley in Geneva and the twenty-first-century reincarnation, the transgendered Ry Shelley—respectively highlight processes of creating and letting go of the monster and how AI questions the limits of reality. Victor's sanity has been shattered in this novel and, held at Bedlam mental hospital, he is in a symbolic but constant pursuit of the Creature fleeing from him. The Arctic features in the background as Walton has returned to England a hero after having discovered the Northwest Passage, and recounts to a Bedlam doctor his encounter with Victor Frankenstein in the Arctic icescape. "In this man," Walton says, "the long unravelling of life is tightly wound, and he has but one thought, one wish, one pursuit. Day and night are the same to him. He haunts himself" (Winterson 182).

The substitution of more symbolic readings of the doppelgänger-motif with concretization is even more pronounced in Peter Ackroyd's *The Casebook of Victor Frankenstein* (2008). Here, it is not only the Arctic sections of the novel that are transposed to London, but also the continental European episodes, replacing Shelley's icy imagery with a watery one. In a detour from the British context, however, Victor joins Shelley and her companions in Switzerland and is paradoxically present at the birth of *Frankenstein*, and the novel becomes an extended reflection on processes of intertextuality and the blurred lines between literary history and fiction. Lines then blur also between creator and Creature, with the latter confessing that "I am wedded to you so closely that we might be the same person" (Ackroyd 252), and dissolve altogether with the indication that the Creature is wholly a figment of Victor's imagination. In this convoluted narrative, there is clearly no place for either the Arctic or an epistolary structure and the novel moves entirely within Victor Frankenstein's troubled mind: "I commune with everything I see as something not apart from but inherent in my own nature" (126). In addition to quoting from texts by the authors present at Villa Diodati, there are structural and thematic echoes of later Gothic texts like Robert Louis Stevenson's *Strange Case of Dr Jekyll and Mr Hyde* (1886) and Bram Stoker's *Dracula* (1897), signaling the influence of a wider field of speculative fiction.

Emphasis on unreliability is heightened by the employment of the seemingly unmediated journal format in the contemporary novels in my sample, and dubiousness turns to dystopia in Jarrett's *Always North*. In Chapter 3, I discussed how the increasingly spare and erratic notations of precise locations at the start of chapters reflected a rupture of human linear time, but this rupture also has bearing on the contents of Izzy's journal—the 2025 sections of the novel—and, importantly, how they are perceived. When the journal is used in the 2045 sections, members of the original crew listen to Izzy's recordings of it in order to return to the moment when the ecological apocalypse is preventable. Both when rereading her notations and when listening to her own recordings, Izzy becomes aware of the mutability of human memory, and of the crucial difference between who she is at the time of listening and who she used to be. Her recollections are "changed somehow by the reading process, reshaped by the remembering. There are layers and folds . . . . Evolution and mutation" (Jarrett 157). Izzy's comments on her own narrative works metatextually, and encourage returns and reappraisals of what has previously been narrated. In the larger context of Jarrett's critique of destructive anthropocentric practices, these destabilizations of meaning, identity, and even purpose are intertwined with a collapsing Arctic. "Ice is memory," Izzy thinks (192), but the archive of the solid Arctic is destroyed. As it breaks and melts, all that is left is uncertainty.

Less experimental ideas of ordering, of attempting to control time, and of presenting a cohesive identity are found in Michelle Paver's *Dark Matter*, and it is rather a resistance emanating from a still solid Arctic that causes the protagonist's growing madness. In Primary World exploration narratives, journal-keeping was used as "a personal metronome," Leane argues, and helped explorers in polar areas handle "the absence of familiar patterns of night and day [that] would have been confusing in a deep bodily sense" (156). These facets of what I term a queer Arctic disrupt or hinder processes of orientation in Paver's novel, as seen in my discussions in Chapter 2, but like in Jarrett's novel, the journal format also allows protagonist Jack to return to a previous textual version of himself, finding that he can either not recognize this instantiation, or that it has been exceedingly naïve. But Paver adds an additional level of complexity and unreliability by incorporating two separate journals written by Jack, and a third narration that can be read as depicting his immediate thoughts. The first journal (the bulk of the novel) ostensibly provides direct contact with Jack's growing fear and disorientation, but it ends with Jack's conclusion that there is no longer any point in continuing: there is "[n]othing left to write" (Paver 232). The two chapters that follow are materially different—in another font—and consist of a string of present-tense sentences that describe immediate emotions, sensations, and actions, and include Jack's profession of love for his colleague Gus. This last admission is followed by Jack noting (or thinking): "I'm glad I haven't written about it in my journal. I couldn't bear if you read it and turned away" (235). The suggestion is that Jack, circumscribed by social and cultural codes and by discourses in which the Arctic provides a stage for the enactment of masculinity and heteronormativity, has edited himself. In the novel's last chapter, there is an explicit return to a journal format, but rather than being used to order time and identity, Jack employs it "to give an account of [him]self" (244). Now residing in Jamaica, he is pleased with "predictable" work at a botanical garden and reassured by "the same length" of the nights in the tropics (247). The monochrome and silent Svalbard has been replaced by intense colors and the uninterrupted noise of birds and insects, and Jack's disintegration, caused by the Arctic, has been reversed.

The dissolutions so central in Paver's novel are one among several attributes that have helped shape popular conceptions of the Arctic and they combine with coldness, pristineness, and a peculiar combination of abundance and scarcity to further constructions of Arctic spaces and places. I turn now to how the Arctic as construction emerges in specific ways in texts that feature an inside perspective. I will begin, however, by developing the discussion about the conspicuous absence of Indigenous Arctic peoples from the nineteenth-century texts in my sample, an elision particularly glaring in text portions that delineate the travelers' journey north in the lost-civilization novels discussed in Chapter 1. In the novels by Vidar Berge and Robert Ames Bennet, the explorers literally descend into forgotten civilization, bypassing land travel and potential encounters with Indigenous communities altogether, and in William Seldon's novella, it takes but a paragraph for the three protagonists to leave Franklin's ships and discover a lost world. Although Dr. Clawbonny is able to (as with all topics) discourse at length about "Esquimaux" ways of life, the lack of their presence is rather affirming that Jules Verne's explorers in *The Voyages* and *Adventures of Captain Hatteras* are "the first ever to set foot on [an] unknown shore" (283).[3] In Mary E. Bradley Lane's *Mizora*, Inuit become intertwined with the atopic Arctic, and despite staying with them for a year, Lane's protagonist does not correct her Mizoran companion's assessment that they must be "animals" (143). Inhabitants found and engaged with in the Arctic periphery are instead either reassuringly familiar to the visitors, or so fantastical that the category of human dissolves altogether.

The first chapters of Fairman's *The Third World* unusually feature Inuit Loolik as a central character, but the author's note, briefly discussed above, clarifies that the Survivor, like other Arctic explorers, has accepted the help from Loolik "by dire necessity" as no one else is around to rescue him from the wreckage of Franklin's ships (6). This necessity aside, Survivor is impressed with Loolik's ability to thrive in the Arctic and decides "to display the same indifference to danger that marked the conduct of my Esquimau friend" (8). The two men land on more equal footing when they approach the northern boundary of Loolik's previous journeys and discover new land in the highest Arctic. When Loolik's knowledge of place ends, more stereotypical roles are assumed with Survivor as "Robinson Crusoe" teaching Loolik, "his man Friday," to read and to embrace the Christian faith (12). Loolik thus serves as a guide to skills and knowledge required in an Arctic that Survivor is only partly inured to through his time on *Terror*, a service Survivor then magnanimously reciprocates by civilizing the "savage" (11). Also problematic is that Loolik's function is temporary: he dies when Survivor has learned enough to act independently and even if a period of deteriorating sanity follows the severing of "the last link" to humanity (20), Survivor alone, and unencumbered by the need to share the glory, discovers the subterranean civilization of Polaria.

That the long history of contact between explorers and members of Arctic Indigenous cultures are elided in speculative fiction that depicts heroic quests and startling discoveries is not surprising, since these texts draw from discourses surrounding Primary World, nineteenth-century exploration. In a British context, Jen Hill remarks, exploration of the Arctic was seen as "morally stainless," because of the perceived emptiness of the region and results in "a 'white' history about white Englishmen in a white space" (9). And even when contacts are worked into narratives, intrepid travelers (in fictional as well as in documentary texts) are depicted or depict themselves as entering communities that know nothing of the world outside their own location in the Arctic. The fact that these communities "had been entangled with western material cultures and ontologies since, at least, the sixteenth century" makes gestures to originality belated indeed (McCorristine, *Spectral* 60). Adriana Craciun draws attention to this "larger historical frame" in analyses of the pronounced lack of acknowledgment of or faith in "Inuit geographical accuracy" when examining the aftermath to Franklin's last expedition ("Disaster" 202). When search parties received information that crucially went against what was expected or desired—and that indicated chaos, immorality, cannibalism—testimonies were suppressed.[4] The Arctic, consequently, has consciously been kept empty on both symbolic and actual levels, the emptiness and silence serving a multitude of ends.

The increased presence of Indigenous perspectives and characters in the contemporary texts in my sample are naturally connected to how Arctic peoples and their heterogeneity in histories, traditions, and views, have gained visibility and agency in post- or neo-colonial contexts, in complicated and variously successful processes to achieve independence, and in initiatives furthering both nature and cultural preservation. From the occasional and one-dimensional portrayal in early literature, there is a greater variety in representations. I want to note again, however, that my examples remain written by outsiders to whom the Arctic is imagined, not home, and that views of Arctic indigenes are sometimes used predominantly to underline the cynicism of antagonists. In Laline Paull's *The Ice*, for example, sinister businessman Kingsmith masks his profit-driven adventures in Greenland as future improvements of life for Inuit who rather than "being nostalgic for Arctic Past" want items associated with "Arctic Future. . . TVs, iPads, foreign travel, all the rest of it. You can't keep *kids* in the last century" (Paull 204, emphasis added). Although the sentiment may connect to a realistic view of Indigenous individuals—as John McCannon puts it, few would likely oppose a more comfortable life or prefer to "exist as ethnographically 'authentic' artefacts in a gigantic open-air museum" (294)—Kingsmith insists, like many of the nineteenth-century fictional travelers, on placing Inuit further back on an evolutionary time scale.

Dan Simmons gestures to the longer history of contact between members of Franklin's crew and Inuit in *The Terror*. He utilizes Inuit oral history when staging the location of the lost ships and emphasizes the function of Inuit traditions and myths particularly in the formulation of a future apocalypse. As an example of alternative history, *The Terror* also provides opportunities to question discourses connected to masculinity by incorporating female voices. Simmons' annexation of Inuit knowledge and storytelling, and how these aspects are combined with an ostensibly female perspective is not without problems, however. Derek J. Thiess argues that "[t]o place what is legendary (even if appropriated) alongside the [historical] material is to give it a life that colonialism would deny it" (233), but this process in Simmons' novel problematically hinges on the necessity of a close, personal relationship between main protagonist Crozier and Inuit Lady Silence. The name is forced upon the latter by Franklin's crew, ostensibly because of her inability to speak, but it resonates, Van Piercy notes, "with what little interest" they and nineteenth-century explorers (and later followers) broadly, "have for listening to the indigenous people" (548, 549). Silence should therefore be understood as both a concrete practice and as an extended metaphor for how women generally and Inuit women in particular are controlled and constructed through a male perspective.

In the bulk of the novel, consequently, Crozier cannot and will not hear Lady Silence. Figuratively, this extends to denying her an identity as human: "she has too much of the savage about her" (10) and rather brings to his mind a "furry animal" (107). She is metonymically connected to the Arctic—her eyes "as black as the holes in the ice through which [the crew] lowered their dead"—and closely associated with the *Tuunbaq* (94). In short, Lady Silence is unnervingly Other, and, like the Arctic landscape itself, resisting attempts at being understood. But she is paradoxically also highly sexualized: "in one chapter there are eight references to her naked body in as many pages" (Lindgren Leavenworth, "The Times" 205). Her communication with the *Tuunbaq* is by an onlooker rendered as "a passionate and open-mouthed kiss," and it ends "with the suddenness of the climax of wild lovemaking" (Simmons 292). These depictions align with stereotypical notions of Indigenous women as closely (in this case intimately) connected to both myth and nature, and the narrative perspective means that Lady Silence has no possibility to question or invert the gaze.

What is required for a change in perspective is Crozier's symbolic death and re-birth into a new existence. After having nearly perished at the hands of the mutinous Cornelius Hickey, Crozier is tended to by Lady Silence, or Silna as her real name is, and he emerges like a "baby bird" (688) in a "place [that] might be anywhere" (717). Chapters outlining his recovery alternate with ones in which, Siobhan Carroll argues, Inuit myths "tak[e] up the structural prominence previously enjoyed by 'scientific' commentators" ("*The Terror*" 73). Problematically, however, the power to comment never quite leaves Crozier. He remains the focalizer through which the knowledge and prowess of Silna are recounted with increasing respect, and although he introduces affect as a complementary lens through which to view the world, it is strongly paired with his previous scientific rationality. Since Silna lacks a tongue, she is incapable of verbal communication, instead using gestures to indicate emotions and desired actions. But these attempts to give her a figurative voice are undercut by communication in the form of dreams and relayed in a sphere that continues to be divorced from the world around her and Crozier. The novel in this way traces a series of transformations that see Crozier move from an outside to an inside perspective as regards Inuit mythology and Indigenous knowledge, without completely relinquishing his narrative power.

Less controversial uses of Indigenous characters are found in contemporary crime novels, and they share the stage with "environmentalists, park wardens and scientists [who take] the place of traditional detectives" when changes to Arctic ecologies or climate become central to plots (Hansson, "Guilt" 16).[5] In the novels revolving around scientific speculation discussed in Chapter 2, the protagonists are epidemiologists who examine effects of lethal algae or try to hinder viruses from thawing, and Inuit characters play prominent roles. In Robert Masello's *The Romanov Cross*, Frank Slater teams up with Nikaluk (or Nika) Tincook, a major of a town close to the unfortunate island that is the novel's main setting, and in Juri Jurjevic's *The Trudeau Vector*, Jessica Hanley works closely with Jack Nimit, an engineer. While neither Nika nor Jack are protagonists on par with Slater and Hanley, they provide opportunities to address Indigenous questions and perspectives in the otherwise speculatively scientific plots.

Nika in Masello's novel sees the threat of a thawing influenza virus from a local perspective: its potential effects will have immediate consequences for her longtime home. Her anthropological expertise in the research that is designed to prevent such an outcome is coupled with "a powerful spiritual urge, one that connected her not only to the Inuit people but to the worldview that they maintained" and she is described as unwilling "to deny the possibility of things simply because our ordinary senses could not see or hear or smell them" (Masello 192). While this may seem a stereotypical characterization, Nika usefully embodies the tension between speculation and scientific fact that propels events in the novel and that in other plot strands is arrived at through parallels between past and present. To Nika, the past is rather associated with a sense of lapsed responsibility and a history of trauma, which combine in a terrifying dream she has when she is infected with the influenza virus. In a state that seems "real, but unreal" (445), she travels to her ancestral village where all she finds are dead humans and animals. There are signs of both violence and disease, gesturing to a past of hostility towards Inuit as well as to the catastrophic effects of the influenza on the Indigenous Arctic peoples. The only still-living inhabitant of the village, an old woman, repeatedly assures Nika that "[y]ou will save us" (447, 448). In a novel intensely focused on processes of seeing, Nika's project, once she emerges from the dream (and the infection), becomes one of heightening or re-focusing attention to both visible and invisible aspects of her culture. This historical and cultural grounding in the Arctic that Masello depicts (and that other characters only visit temporarily), makes the novel's denouement dystopic. As I discussed in Chapter 2, the ground of the island on which the virus has survived is saturated with poison and covered with cement, but the climate change that has released the threat to begin with will render both these solutions temporary. Trauma is thus likely to appear in a new guise, predominantly affecting the permanent residents of the location.

The specific past trauma of forced relocation is foregrounded in *The Trudeau Vector*, via Jack's recollections of growing up on Ellesmere Island. Existence there, he tells Hanley, was marked by poverty, substance abuse and violence, and by a loss of connection with a cultural past and the Indigenous language. "We weren't exactly the nomadic noble savages, leading hard yet perfectly balanced lives in the unforgiving, beautiful Arctic," he remarks, and adds that the relocated families had no desire to live that far north: "But the farther north you have inhabitants, the more territory you can claim" (Jurjevics 278). The High Arctic Relocations that Jack alludes to commenced in 1953 and were ostensibly designed to offer Inuit from Port Harrison, Quebec, and Pond Inlet, Baffin Island a more secure future. In analyses of the process and its lingering effects, Janice Cavell notes how Inuit in the 1980s reported that "their relocation—or exile, as some preferred to call it—had resulted not from a misguided attempt at benevolence but rather from a secret plan to reinforce Canadian sovereignty in the all but uninhabited High Arctic by using them as 'human flagpoles' " (119).[6] Referencing this history, Jack has no desire to return to Ellesmere Island, and instead gestures to an improved situation for Inuit; as he notes, "Canada's returned some of our territory" (Jurjevics 279) and at the end of the novel he heads for Nunavut, "the new Inuit territory" (506).

These references to Primary World processes of concretely constructing areas in the Arctic in *The Trudeau Vector* find a fictional counterpart in manipulations of limited Arctic spaces. The research station is constructed to make a minimal imprint on the natural environment, but also protects the scientists from the cold world outside—described as "hell with the fires out" (316)—and its systems that maintain daylight and darkness "encourage normalcy" (187). When the visitors need to leave this sphere, they are forced to don "[t]he Trudeau suit" which constitutes a personalized "microenvironment" (99). Jack, however, eschews the suit, leaving the station clad only in "his native furs and leggings," because he feels "homesick" (146). Rather than merely connoting a stereotypical resilience, these descriptions reflect how the theme of adaptation propels the plot. However, the rootlessness that results from the forced relocations also continues to affect Jack, and neither the periods outside the stifling, artificial environment of the research station nor the promise seemingly tendered by a future in Nunavut provide a complete alleviation of the homesickness.

Lionel Davidson's *Kolymski Heights* (1994) shares several similarities with the novels by Jurjevics and Masello, as it revolves around ideas of hibernation and thaws. Its speculative element comes in the form of a bioengineered hybrid in which genes from a 40 000-year-old Cro Magnon, an early European Neanderthal, and primates are combined.[7] Of interest to discussions here, however, is that the novel represents a rare example of an Indigenous protagonist. Johnny Porter (born Jean-Baptiste Porteur) is a member of the Tsimshean First Nations, more specifically Gitksan, from Subarctic British Columbia.

Porter is academically brilliant with degrees in biology and anthropology, but it is his linguistic prowess and ethnicity that make him especially useful to the CIA in a plot revolving around military applications of advanced, speculative technology. In his early academic work, Porter has noticed the profound differences between K'San and Nisqua, spoken by groups that are closely related but "almost unintelligible to each other" (70). Yet, he notes that the Gitskan's and the Nass' "stories . . . were identical almost to the smallest detail." This observation initiates wider processes of both linkages and differences. In Siberia, Porter moves between ethnic disguises, but, although one non-Indigenous character emphatically tells him: "You *are* of the north" (244), convincing Indigenous interlocutors that he is one of them is more difficult. "The Yukagir had not thought him a Yukagir, or the Evenks an Evenk," Porter reflects (217). Moving "a world away" from home (181), identity becomes a careful and fluctuating construction for him. While the successful resolution of the plot relies on the common ancestry in many indigenous Arctic peoples that enables Porter's disguises, Davidson also gestures to political rifts between groups, and to the heterogeneity of histories.

Sam J. Miller's *Blackfish City* features a family of Indigenous Arctic ancestry as protagonists and the novel presents, in speculative form, processes of appropriation but also resistance to a long history of disenfranchisement. The main setting also gestures to this history as the fictional, floating city of Qaanaaq takes its name from a village in West Greenland that in the 1950s became the new home to Inuit being forcibly relocated when the villages Pituffik and Dundas were appropriated for the building of the American Thule air base. Processes of past, forced relocations echo on a global scale as the city, among the last livable places in Miller's future, becomes a permanent or temporary home to "exiled kings and political prisoners and wide-eyed children" (Miller 325), but its construction also draws attention to artificiality and a detrimental separation of humans and the natural world (325). The speculative experiment of nano-bonding (discussed in more detail in Chapter 3) is designed to overcome this separation, and the entanglement of human and animal is represented as being something "the Western world had lost sight of" but that Inuit have "relearned" (144). Inuit children are paired with animals at a young age, the choice determined by "community need and availability" (228) and this community and ancestors also provide reasons why the nanobond process can be survived and be successful.[8] One of the protagonists, Masaaraq, explains that "we never lose the people we love . . . which is why the nanites didn't kill us, didn't drive us mad, gave us this gift, this curse" (144). Designed to reforge a connection with the natural world and counter the dystopic development in the fictional future, the nanobond still make Inuit distinctly different, and the gift or curse make them be perceived by some as "demonic [and] undermining Caucasian hegemony" (73). Views like these underpin the rootlessness of the nanobonded Inuit and cause the separation or destruction of families. These dystopic elements mainly reside in the background to the central plot, and it is rather restrengthened bonds with the natural world that represent hope in the novel. The lesson relearned by Inuit, that is, points forwards to forms of community that were already there, but have the potential to appear in new guises, suited to the particular challenges of this far-future Arctic.

A handful of novels in my sample feature characters that are at home in the Arctic, but still go through processes or have dispositions that introduce destabilization and disorientation. In John Burnside's *A Summer of Drowning*, for example, an alternative world opens up next to the ordinary one, with effects that comprehensively change the protagonist's outlook. Emmi Itäranta presents Arctic Finland as home to her protagonist Noria in *Memory of Water*, which creates an effective immediacy when outlining the consequences of global climate change and attempts to halt it. In a rare reflection on the need to name that which is in the process of being lost, Noria describes how what to her is "The Dead Forest" has replaced the previous "Mosswood," a name that, in turn, has been introduced at a point "when words for such greenness were . . . needed" (203). In an even more distant past, when forests were so ubiquitous that they were unmarked, it "had not had a name at all." In Marcel Theroux's *Far North*, in which the Arctic represents both the end and the beginning to second-generation immigrant in Siberia, Makepeace Hatfield, an opposite trajectory is presented as features of the landscape that once had names, in the now of the novel are becoming blank spaces. Both examples capture the slow violence of climate change and highlight the Arctic as construction, or more precisely, the Arctic as in a process of constant re-construction.

Michel Faber's short story "The Fahrenheit Twins" depicts what may be termed speculative indigeneity, a character construction that opens for a shifted perspective of the Arctic as either home or Other. The children of the title, Tainto'lilith and Marko'cain, are the result of a meeting between their mother Una and a member of the Guhiynui, a fictional people residing in a remote Russian archipelago. Looking nothing like their tall, German mother, the twins are "shaped and coloured . . . by a sub-Polar archipelago;" place itself seems to have given them straight, black hair and dark eyes "with something of the seal about them" (Faber 233). They are in tune with nature rather than with the sciences propagated by Una and her husband Boris, and as often as they can escape the "domed monstrosity of concrete," filled with European knickknacks and "attached umbilically to a generator" (236), that is supposed to be their home. The death of their mother then precipitates a "a quest for origin and anxiety about destination" (Zlosnik 67) as the twins are tasked with finding a suitable burial place. On this quest they come across the now abandoned Guhiynui settlement and a building that is another reminder of processes of culturally appropriating or adapting the Arctic. The same kind of decorations and furnishings as in the twins' own home is found in the building along with "the heady perfumes of a long-lost Bavaria" (Faber 268) and a large painting of their mother in the arms of someone who decidedly is not Boris. This image is the only connection the twins form with their paternal line, but the "cultural hybridity" of both the painting and the building forges close links to them (Zlosnik 72).

With names suggesting that they represent the start of something new, the twins throughout the short story manipulate knowledge they receive and amass their own. When they head into the cold expanse of the Arctic, they rely on their close connection with place to let them know what needs to be done, but the reader is from the start led to see the twins as rootless and unsure of where they have come from; they ponder "who on earth their mother might be" (Faber 237) and are estranged from Boris who, likely in reference to their heritage, sees them as "little primitives" (246).

The lack of parental guidance and support creates a void in the short story and is coupled with the twins' isolation. But, Nicholas Prescott argues, it combines with absence as a narrative element in a wider sense: "absence of resolution, absence of logic, absence of information, the absence of comforting or quotidian explanations" to produce a "curious and compelling kind of dread" associated with the uncanny (101, 97). The Arctic in which the children grow up plays a pivotal role in the evocation of the uncanny as it lacks boundaries, markers with which to judge distances, and since it is cast in an "almost perpetual … twilight" (Faber 231). The distance from "the green parts of the world" initially also ensures that Tainto'lilith and Marko'cain remain "a secret" (234), but both this secret and their abilities to orient themselves are threatened as they journey to the end of land. They start to lose their bearings and when no longer understanding the workings of the compass, they conclude that "north [has] lost its meaning" (250). Reaching the ocean means reaching new sensory impressions, different from the "circumambient silence" that has characterized their lives and given them the impression that they are the only living things. On the shore, in contrast, the twins are "swallowed up by a larger life" (252). The Arctic that their parents have constructed for them can no longer support their search for identity, belonging, and knowledge. The short story ends with the twins making plans for the future that entail leaving the Arctic. Everything to the south of "the icy zenith of the world" (231) constitutes a lower latitude sublime, inspiring both fear and possibilities.

Instabilities and incongruities of the Primary World Arctic have worked as consistent sources of inspiration for authors who have manipulated Arctic geographies, inhabitants, and histories. But contemporary climate change introduces uncertainties that trouble the use of the previously so productive aesthetics of the Arctic sublime. No longer serving to highlight the fragility of human life and frozen permanence, the Arctic is becoming increasingly vulnerable to human actions: it turns "from solid to liquid" (McCannon 280). Reframing the Victorian ideological and aesthetic formulations, Benjamin Morgan argues that:

> If the Arctic was long imagined as an overpowering environment where human capacities could be tested and masculine national character could be dramatized, it now resonates in a very different register. . . . the story that the Arctic now tells us seems to have less to do with ideologies of the nation-state, and more to do with the ways in which extranational networks of humans and nonhumans distributed across the entire planet will be affected, unequally, by the changes that are manifested most evidently at the earth's ice caps.
>
> (3)

This disorienting change introduces complexities in both contemporary Primary World debates and in how the Arctic continues to be imagined. Heidi Hansson and Anka Ryall note that combined with resource extraction and cultural loss, climate change signifies "rapid changes in both [the Arctic's] physical state and in the way it is perceived, creating imbalances and blind spots in our understanding of the processes involved" (3). Adding to these actual and perceptual challenges is the self-evident fact that the Arctic will remain geographically distant for most people—it will stay space rather than transforming into place. Fiction is an important carrier of ideas that have informed and continue to inform the way we think about the Arctic, but also plays a crucial part in breaking up static or unchanging images; it figuratively transports readers to the Arctic (or the Arctic to readers). Fiction does not do away with blind spots, nor does it concretely initiate actions needed to affect change, but it is an indispensable source of new perspectives, structures, and worldviews. Fiction makes visible the Arctic as construction, and how this construction needs to be amended or altered in order to accommodate a complex reality.

Speculative fiction releases authors from the constraints of everyday reality in particular ways but, as I have demonstrated, this freedom is especially effective when it is paired with a continuous engagement with the

Primary World Arctic. While arcticity and arcticness are worked into a wide array of works, located in what is traditionally defined as the genres of fantasy and science fiction, the novels, novellas, and short stories I have discussed cluster around aspects of the actual Arctic—specific locations and climates, historical or contemporary incidents, uncertainties, and traumas—and maintain the dynamics of discourses. I have thus mapped and examined examples of speculative fiction to illuminate what non-mimetic literary forms contribute to past and present discourses, themes, and motifs, and to how the new Arctics added to the textual tradition complement or complicate already-existing constructions.

One last return to the novels that bookend my selection illustrates how speculative Arctics come into being at discrete moments in time, and thus reflect both Primary World concerns and imaginative possibilities. As the only possible setting for the telling of the marvelous tale, the solid Arctic in *Frankenstein* is a construction born from geographical uncertainty. It acquires a figurative agency by providing a limit to human science, and a literal agency by halting the characters in their tracks, making sure that they remain in the periphery. To Shelley, then, the Arctic functions as a site removed from the everyday, one in which consequences of promethean science (biological and geographical) can be contained. In *Always North*, Jarrett's Arctic is a thoroughly mapped and central part of the machinery that makes the world function. This enhanced visibility of the Arctic makes it vulnerable to exploitation of various kinds, the most detrimental being the protean transformation of the still-distant ocean bed in the search for the last precious drops of oil. As a construction coming into being in times of climate anxiety, the agency of this Arctic has a global reach: when this Arctic breaks apart, it initiates the collapse of the vast network that is the world.

Notes

1 London's short story is mentioned in O'Loughlin's acknowledgments, thus encouraging a parallel reading.
2 The intertwining of fictional universes means answers to conundrums in them. Emerging from the hollow earth at the southern polar opening, Leane observes, the Creature is "covered in white volcanic ash" and becomes the author's "solution to the giant white figure that Pym encounters at the end of Poe's novel" (66).
3 A slightly different formulation is found in Leon Lewis' *Andree at the North Pole*, in which the quest for the illusive North Pole is based on a conviction that there exists "a branch of the human family, a sister nation" there, importantly, "as far removed from the Esquimaux as possible" (26).
4 In Parks Canada and The Arctic Research Foundation's eventually successful attempts to locate *Erebus* and *Terror*, there is a "high profile 'vindication' of Inuit accuracy and knowledge," Craciun notes, which "appears as a conventional

component of the larger narrative of discovery, appropriation and settlement that the Harper government nostalgically revived" ("Disaster" 202–203).

5 Hansson's examples of Indigenous protagonists in crime fiction include Aleut detective Kate Shugak in Dana Stabenow's series set in Alaska, Anna Magnusson, a Sami prosecutor in Lars Petterson's books set in Kautokeino and Kiruna, part-Inughuit Smilla Qaavigaq Jaspersen in Peter Høeg's *Miss Smilla's Feeling for Snow* (1992) and part-Inuit Edie Kiglatuk in M. J. McGrath's trilogy *White Heat* (2011), *The Boy in the Snow* (2012), and *The Bone Seeker* (2014). To these examples can be added Olivier Truc's Sapmi-trilogy (*Le Dernier Lapon* 2012, *Le Détroit du loup* 2014, and *La Montagne rouge*, 2016) which features Sami police officer Klemet Nango investigating a series of crimes connected to a long history of colonial oppression.

6 The quoted expression is from the article "Human Flagpoles" by John Amagoalik (*Toronto Star*, 4 July 1991).

7 Joseph Stalin is in this novel actively encouraging speculative experimentation. Embalming has preserved the body of his predecessor Lenin, but Stalin becomes interested in having his own "hibernated so at some future time it would be of greater benefit" to the people (299). Further experimentation is sparked off to enable the mining of riches beneath the frozen Siberian ground, work deemed unsuitable for humans. By the time the protagonist arrives in Siberia, the experiment has resulted in apes, closely resembling humans, that have the ability to talk and work in the demanding environment. The Arctic, consequently, is a place in which "[a]n intelligent ape was of use" (305).

8 The main characters are bonded to an orca, a buzzard eagle, and a polar bear, powerful predators that represent life in the ocean, in the sky, and on land. As if to deflate this stereotypical assignation, Miller depicts how Masaaraq and Ora's daughter Ankit as an adult chooses to be bonded to a monkey because these species "are survivors" (230). Masaaraq is perplexed by the choice, noting how the boats that make up Qaanaaq are "full of functionally extinct predators—I could have gotten you a tiger, or a wild boar, or a sea snake."

Works Cited

Speculative Fiction

Ackroyd, Peter. *The Casebook of Victor Frankenstein*. Chatto & Windus, 2008.

Adams, Jack. [Alconoan O. Grigsby and Mary P. Lowe]. *Nequa; or, the Problem of the Ages*. Topeka, KA: Equity Publishing Company, 1900. *Project Gutenberg*. Accessed 2 January 2023.

Adolph, Anna. *Arqtiq: A Study of the Marvels at the North Pole*. 1899. *Project Gutenberg*. Accessed 2 January 2023.

Allen, Wilford. "The Arctic Death." *Weird Tales*, June 1927, vol. 9, pp. 769–780. *Internet Archive*. Accessed 2 January 2023.

Ballard, J. G. *The Drowned World*. 1962. Fourth Estate, 2014.

Bennet, Robert Ames. *Thyra: A Romance of the Polar Pit*. 1901. Dodo press, 2009

Berge, Vidar. *Den hemlighetsfulla nordpolsön*. [The Mysterious North Pole Island]. Stockholm: Wilh. Siléns förlag, 1902.

Blackwood, Algernon. "The Wendigo." *The Lost Valley and Other Stories*. Alfred A. Knopf, 1917, pp. 71–132.

Blake, William Hume. "A Tale of Grand Jardin." *Brown Waters, and Other Sketches*. The Macmillan Company of Canada, 1915, pp. 144–161.

Bradshaw, William R. *The Goddess of Atvatabar*. New York: J. F. Douthitt, 1892.

Brooks-Dalton, Lily. *Good Morning, Midnight*. 2016. Weidenfeld & Nicholson, 2017.

Buckell, Tobias. *Arctic Rising*. 2012. Tor, 2013.

Burnside, John. *A Summer of Drowning*. 2011. Vintage, 2012.

Burroughs, Edgar Rice. "Tarzan at the Earth's Core." *The Blue Book Magazine*, September 1929–March 1930. *Project Gutenberg Australia*. Accessed 2 January 2023.

Davidson, Lionel. *Kolymsky Heights*. 1994. Faber & Faber, 2015.

Doyle, Arthur Conan. "The Captain of the 'Pole Star'." 1883. *"Dangerous Work" Diary of an Arctic Adventure*. Edited by Jon Lellenberg and Daniel Stashower. The British Library, 2012, pp. 333–350.

Emerson, Willis George. *The Smoky God*. Forbes & Company, 1908. *HathiTrust*. Accessed 2 January 2023.

Faber, Michel. "The Fahrenheit Twins." *The Fahrenheit Twins*. 2005. Canongate, 2006, pp. 231–276.

Fairman, Henry Clay. *The Third World: A Tale of Love and Strange Adventure.* Atlanta: The Third World Publishing Co., 1895. *HathiTrust.* Accessed 2 January 2023.

Hamilton, Edmond. "The Daughter of Thor." *Fantastic Adventures*, August 1942, pp. 10–47. *Internet Archive.* Accessed 2 January 2023.

Høeg, Peter. *Miss Smilla's Feeling for Snow.* 1992. Translated by F. David. Harvill Press, 1993.

Itäranta, Emmi. *Memory of Water.* Harper Voyager, 2014.

Ivey, Eowyn. *The Snow Child.* 2012. Tinder Press, 2014.

Jarrett, Vicki. *Always North.* Unsung Stories, 2019.

Jurjevics, Juris. *The Trudeau Vector.* 2005. McArthur & Company, 2006.

Lane, Mary E. Bradley. *Mizora: A Prophecy.* 1880–81. New York: G. W. Dillingham, Publisher, 1889. *Project Gutenberg.* Accessed 2 January 2023.

Lewis, Leon. *Andree at the North Pole: With Details of his Fate.* 1899. Forgotten Books, 2017.

London, Jack. "In a Far Country." *The Son of the Wolf: Tales of the Far North.* Boston and New York: Houghton, Mifflin and Company, 1900, pp. 21–51. *HathiTrust.* Accessed 2 January 2023.

MacLeod, Bracken. *Stranded.* Tor, 2016.

Masello, Robert, *The Romanov Cross.* 2013. Vintage, 2014.

McEwan, Ian. *Solar.* Jonathan Cape, 2010.

Miller, Sam. J. *Blackfish City.* Ecco, 2018.

Moss, Sarah. *Cold Earth.* 2009. Granta, 2010.

Nagamatsu, Sequoia. *How High We Go in the Dark.* William Morrow, 2022.

Nevill, Adam. *The Ritual.* 2011. Pan Books, 2014.

O'Loughlin, Ed. *Minds of Winter.* Riverrun, 2016.

Orcutt, Emma Louise, *The Divine Seal.* The C. M. Clark Publishing Company, 1909.

Paull, Laline, *The Ice.* 4th Estate, 2017.

Paver, Michelle. *Dark Matter: A Ghost Story.* Orion, 2010.

Poe, Edgar Allan. "A Descent into the Maelstrom." *The Complete Works of Edgar Allan Poe.* Volume 2. Edited by James A. Harrison. Thomas Y. Crowell & Company, 1902, pp. 225–247.

Rollins, James. *Ice Hunt.* Orion, 2010.

Seldon, William. N. "The Extraordinary and All-Absorbing Journal of Wm. N. Seldon." Detroit: E. E. Barclay, 1851. *Wright American Fiction.* Indiana University, 2019. Accessed 2 January 2023.

Shelley, Mary. *Frankenstein; or, the Modern Prometheus.* 1818. U of Chicago P, 1982.

———. *Frankenstein; or, the Modern Prometheus.* 1831. Penguin, 2003.

Sidorova, J. M. *The Age of Ice.* Scribner, 2013.

Sigurðardóttir, Yrsa. *I Remember You.* Translated by Philip Roughton. 2012. Hodder & Stoughton, 2013.

Simmons, Dan. *The Terror.* Little, Brown and Company, 2007.

Spjut, Stefan. *Stallo.* Translated by Susan Beard. 2012. Faber & Faber, 2016.

Theroux, Marcel. *Far North.* 2009. Faber and Faber, 2010.

Tuttle, George B. "The Roc Raid." *Magazine of Horror*, vol. 6, no. 1, 1970, pp. 82–114. *Internet Archive.* Accessed 2 January 2023.

Twain, Mark. *The American Claimant.* New York: Charles L. Webster & Company, 1892. *HathiTrust.* Accessed 2 January 2023.

Verne, Jules. *The Fields of Ice.* Translator unknown. 1866. London: George Routledge and Sons, 1875. *HathiTrust.* Accessed 2 January 2023.

Verne, Jules. *The Voyages and Adventures of Captain Hatteras.* Translator unknown. 1866. Boston: James R. Osgood and Company, 1876.

Verne, Jules. *The Purchase of the North Pole.* Translator unknown. 1889. New York: Vincent Parke & Co., 1911.

Waldrop, Howard and Steven Utley. "Black as the Pit, from Pole to Pole." 1977. *Lovecraft's Monsters.* Edited by Ellen Datlow. Tachyon, 2014, pp. 219–256.

Welcome, S. Byron. *From Earth's Center.* Chicago: Charles H. Kerr & Company, 1895. *HathiTrust.* Accessed 2 January 2023.

Winterson, Jeanette. *Frankissstein: A Love Story.* Jonathan Cape, 2019.

Wood, Mrs. J. *Pantaletta: A Romance of Sheheland.* New York: The American News Company, 1882.

Secondary Sources

Alaimo, Stacy. *Bodily Natures: Science, Environment and the Material Self.* Indiana UP, 2010.

Amundsen, Roald. *Nordostpassagen: Maudfaerden Langs Asiens Kyst 1918–1920.* Kristiania: Henrichson og Lies Boktryckeri, 1921.

Asselin, Steve. "A Climate of Competition: Climate Change as Political Economy in Speculative Fiction, 1889–1915." *Science Fiction Studies*, vol. 45, no. 3, 2018, pp. 440–453.

Atwood, Margaret. *Strange Things: The Malevolent North in Canadian Literature.* Clarendon, 1995.

———. "True North." *Writing with Intent: Essays, Reviews, Personal Prose, 1983–2005.* Carroll & Graf, 2005, pp. 31–45.

Auguscik, Anna. "The Death of the Archaeologist: Imagining Science, Storytelling and Self-Understanding in Contemporary Archaeofiction." *Writing Remains: New Intersections of Archaeology, Literature and Science.* Edited by Josie Gill, Catriona McKenzie, and Emma Lightfoot. Bloomsbury Academic, 2021, pp. 203–223.

Baker, Timothy C. *Contemporary Scottish Gothic: Mourning, Authenticity, and Tradition.* Palgrave Macmillan, 2014.

Bate, Jonathan. *The Song of the Earth.* Picador, 2000.

Beattie, Owen and John Geiger. *Frozen in Time: Unlocking the Secrets of the Franklin Expedition.* Bloomsbury, 1987.

Behrmann, Bridget. "Éclat: Duality and the Absolute in *Voyages et aventures du capitaine Hatteras.*" *Verniana*, vol. 7, 2014–2015, pp. 1–15.

Berger, James. *After the End: Representations of Post-Apocalypse.* U of Minnesota P, 1999.

Binney, Sara Helen. "How 'the Old Stories Persist': Folklore in Literature after Postmodernism." *C21 Literature: Journal of 21st-century Writings*, vol. 6, no. 2, 2018, pp. 1–20.

Bloom, Lisa. *Gender on Ice: American Ideologies of Polar Expeditions*. U of Minnesota P, 1993.

Botting, Fred and Justin D. Edwards. "Theorising Globalgothic." *Globalgothic*. Edited by Glennis Byron. Manchester UP, 2013, pp. 11–24.

Bowers, Katherine. "Haunted Ice, Fearful Sounds, and the Arctic Sublime: Exploring Nineteenth-Century Polar Gothic Space." *Gothic Studies*, vol. 19, no. 2, 2017, pp. 71–84.

Bracke, Astrid. *Climate Crisis and the 21st-Century British Novel*. Bloomsbury Academic, 2018.

———. "Flooded Futures: The Representation of the Anthropocene in Twenty-First-Century British Flood Fictions." *Critique: Studies in Contemporary Fiction*, vol. 60, no. 3, 2019, pp. 278–288.

———. "Solitaries, Outcasts and Doubles: The Fictional Oeuvre of John Burnside." *English Studies*, vol. 95, no. 4, 2014, pp. 421–440.

Braidotti, Rosi. *The Posthuman*. Polity Press, 2013.

Broad, Katherine. "Race, Reproduction, and the Failures of Feminism in Mary Bradley Lane's *Mizora*." *Tulsa Studies in Women's Literature*, vol. 28, no. 2, 2009, pp. 247–266.

Brontë, Charlotte. *Jane Eyre*. 1847. W. W. Norton & Company, 2001.

Buell, Frederick. *From Apocalypse to Way of Life: Environmental Crisis in the American Century*. Routledge, 2003.

———. "Global Warming as Literary Narrative." *Philological Quarterly*, vol. 93, no. 3, 2014, pp. 261–294.

Buell, Lawrence. *The Future of Environmental Criticism: Environmental Crisis and Literary Imagination*. Blackwell, 2005.

Byron, Glennis. "Introduction." *Globalgothic*. Edited by Glennis Byron. Manchester UP, 2013, pp. 1–10.

Cade, Octavia. "To Bear Witness: The Polar Bear as Refugee in Speculative Fiction." *Clarkesworld* 191, August 2022. https://clarkesworldmagazine.com/cade_08_22/. Accessed 2 January 2023.

Carroll, Siobhan. *An Empire of Air and Water: Uncolonizable Space in the British Imagination, 1750–1850*. U of Pennsylvania P, 2015.

———. "Crusades Against Frost: *Frankenstein*, Polar Ice, and Climate Change in 1818." *European Romantic Review*, vol. 24, no. 2, 2013, pp. 211–230.

———. "*The Terror* and the Terroir: The Ecological Uncanny in New Weird Exploration Narratives." *Paradoxa*, no. 28, 2016, pp. 67–89.

Carver, Ben. *Alternate Histories and Nineteenth-Century Literature: Untimely Meditations in Britain, France, and America*. Palgrave MacMillan, 2017.

Cavell, Janice. "'Consolidation and Control of All Eskimo Income': The Motive for the 1953 High Arctic Relocation." *Journal of Canadian Studies*, vol. 55, no. 1, 2021, pp. 118–151.

Chang, Elizabeth Hope. "Hollow Earth Fiction and Environmental Form in the Late Nineteenth Century." *Nineteenth-Century Contexts*, vol. 38, no. 5, 2016, pp. 387–397.

Cocq, Coppélie. *Revoicing Sámi Narratives: North Sámi Storytelling at the Turn of the 20th Century.* 2008. Umeå University, PhD dissertation.

Cohen, Jeffery Jerome. "Monster Culture (Seven Theses)." *Monster Theory: Reading Culture.* Edited by Jeffrey Jerome Cohen. U of Minnesota P, 1996, pp. 3–25.

———. "Postscript: The Promise of Monsters." *The Ashgate Research Companion to Monsters and the Monstrous.* Edited by Asa Simon Mittman and Peter J. Dendle. 2013. Routledge, 2016, pp. 449–464.

Cone, Marla. *Silent Snow: The Slow Poisoning of the Arctic.* Grove Press, 2005.

Conrad, Joseph. *Heart of Darkness.* 1899. W.W. Norton & Company, 2006.

Cookman, Scott. *Ice Blink: The Tragic Fate of Sir John Franklin's Lost Polar Expedition.* John Wiley and Sons, Inc., 2000.

Craciun, Adriana. "The Disaster of Franklin: Victorian Exploration in the Twenty-First-Century Arctic." *Arctic Modernities: The Environmental, the Exotic and the Everyday.* Edited by Heidi Hansson and Anka Ryall. Cambridge Scholars Publishing, 2017, pp. 191–212.

———. "The Frozen Ocean." *PMLA*, vol. 125, no. 3, 2010, pp. 693–702.

Crozier, Francis. "Letter to James Ross (1845 July 9)." *Life and Death in the Arctic.* www.canadianmysteries.ca. Accessed 2 January 2023.

Curtis, Claire P. *Postapocalyptic Fiction and the Social Contract: "We'll Not Go Home Again."* Lexington Books, 2010.

Davidson, Peter. *The Idea of North.* Reaktion Books, 2005.

Deane, Bradley. "Imperial Barbarians: Primitive Masculinity in Lost World Fiction." *Victorian Literature and Culture*, vol. 36 no. 1., 2008, pp. 205–225.

De Bruyn, Ben. "The Hot War: Climate, Security, Fiction." *Studies in the Novel*, vol. 50, no. 1, 2018, pp. 43–67.

De Cristofaro, Diletta. *The Contemporary Post-Apocalyptic Novel: Critical Temporalities and the End Times.* Bloomsbury Academic, 2020.

Dědinová, Tereza, et al. "Introduction." *Images of the Anthropocene in Speculative Fiction: Narrating the Future.* Edited by Tereza Dědinová, Weronika Łaszkiewicz and Sylwia Borowska-Szerszun. Lexington Books, 2021, pp. 1–24.

De Groot, Jerome. *The Historical Novel.* Routledge, 2010.

Dillon, Grace L. "Imagining Indigenous Futurisms." *Walking the Clouds: An Anthology of Indigenous Science Fiction.* Edited by Grace L. Dillon. The U of Arizona P, 2012, pp. 1–12.

Doyle, Arthur Conan. "The Glamour of the Arctic." *"Dangerous Work" Diary of an Arctic Adventure.* Edited by Jon Lellenberg and Daniel Stashower. The British Library, 2012, pp. 319–325.

Doyle, Briohny. "The Postapocalyptic Imagination." *Thesis Eleven*, vol. 131, no. 1, 2015, pp. 99–113.

Eflin, Jackson. "Incursion Into Wendigo Territory." *Digital Literature Review*, no. 1, 2014, pp. 9–19.

Ekman, Stefan. "Urban Fantasy: A Literature of the Unseen." *Journal of the Fantastic in the Arts*, vol. 27, no. 3, 2016, pp. 452–469.

Emmerson, Charles. *The Future History of the Arctic: How Climate, Resources and Geopolitics are Reshaping the North, and Why It Matters to the World.* 2010. Vintage, 2011.

Farmar, Katherine. "*Memory of Water* by Emmi Itäranta." Review. *Strange Horizons,* 15 August, 2014. http://strangehorizons.com/. Accessed 2 January, 2023.

Fredriksen, Lill Tove. "Imagination and Reality in Sami Fantasy." *The Arctic in Literature for Children and Young Adults.* Edited by Heidi Hansson, Maria Lindgren Leavenworth and Anka Ryall. Routledge, 2020, pp. 135–145.

Gelder, Ken. "Introduction: The Field of Horror." *The Horror Reader.* Edited by Ken Gelder. Routledge, 2000, pp. 1–7.

Gill. R. B. "The Uses of Genre and the Classification of Speculative Fiction." *Mosaic,* vol. 46, no. 2, 2013, pp. 71–85.

Goldman, Marlene. "Margaret Atwood's *Wilderness Tips*: Apocalyptic Cannibal Fiction." *Eating Their Words: Cannibalism and the Boundaries of Cultural Identity.* Edited by Kristen Guest. State U of New York P, 2001, pp. 167–185.

Grace, Sherrill E. *Canada and the Idea of North.* 2001. McGill-Queen's UP, 2007.

Griffin, Andrew. "Fire and Ice in *Frankenstein.*" *The Endurance of Frankenstein: Essays on Mary Shelley's Novel.* Edited by George Levine and U. C. Knopflmacher. U of California P, 1979: pp. 49–73.

Halstead, Murat. "Preface." *Mizora: A Prophecy.* 1880–81; New York: G. W. Dillingham, Publisher, 1889. *Project Gutenberg.* Accessed 2 January 2023.

Hansson, Heidi. "Arctopias: the Arctic as No Place and New Place in Fiction." *The New Arctic.* Edited by Birgitta Evengård, Joan Nymand Larsen and Øyvind Paasche. Springer, 2015, pp. 69–77.

———. "Guilt in the Ice: Crime Fiction, Arcticide and the Anthropocene." *Chatter Marks,* no. 1, 2019, pp. 15–18.

Hansson, Heidi and Anka Ryall. "Introduction: Environmental, Exotic and Everyday Arctic." *Arctic Modernities: The Environmental, the Exotic and the Everyday.* Edited by Heidi Hansson and Anka Ryall. Cambridge Scholars Publishing, 2017, pp. 1–13

Haraway, Donna. *Staying with the Trouble: Making Kin in the Chthulucene.* Duke UP, 2016.

Harpold, Terry. "Verne's Errant Readers: Nemo, Clawbonny, Michel Dufrénoy." *Verniana,* no. 1, 2008–2009, pp. 31–42

Hawthorne, Julian. "Introduction." *The Goddess of Atvatabar.* New York: J. F. Douthitt, 1892, pp. 9–12.

Heffernan, Teresa. *Post-Apocalyptic Culture: Modernism, Postmodernism, and the Twentieth-Century Novel.* U of Toronto P, 2008.

Heise, Ursula K. *Imagining Extinction: The Cultural Meanings of Endangered Species.* U of Chicago P, 2016.

———. *Sense of Place and Sense of Planet: The Environmental Imagination of the Global.* Oxford UP, 2008.

Hicks, Heather J. *The Post-Apocalyptic Novel in the Twenty-First Century: Modernity Beyond Salvage.* Palgrave MacMillan, 2016.

Hill, Jen. *White Horizon: The Arctic in the Nineteenth-Century British Imagination.* State U of New York P, 2008.

168   *Works Cited*

Holland, Patrick and Graham Huggan. *Tourists with Type Writers: Critical Reflections on Contemporary Travel Writers*. Ann Arbor: Michigan UP, 1998.

Huet, Marie-Hélène. "Winter Lights: Disaster, Interpretation, and Jules Verne's Polar Novels." *Verniana*, no. 2, 2009–2010, pp. 149–178.

Huggan, Graham. "From Arctic Dreams to Nightmares (and back again): Apocalyptic Thought and Planetary Consciousness in Three Contemporary American Environmentalist Texts." *ISLE: Interdisciplinary Studies in Literature and Environment*, vol. 23, no. 1, 2016, pp. 71–91.

Höglund, Johan. "Indigenous Hauntings: Nordic Gothic and Colonialisms." *Nordic Gothic*. Edited by Maria Holmgren Troy, Johan Höglund, Yvonne Leffler and Sofia Wijkmark. Manchester UP, 2020, pp. 125–146.

Jackson, Rosemary. *Fantasy: The Literature of Subversion*. 1981. Routledge, 2003.

James, David. "John Burnside's Ecologies of Solace: Regional Environmentalism and the Consolations of Description." *Modern Fiction Studies*, vol. 58, no. 3, 2012, pp. 600–615.

Johnstone, Tiffany. "'To Help You Find Your Way Home': Michael Kusugak's Reimagining of Fear and Danger in the Canadian Arctic." *The Arctic in Literature for Children and Young Adults*. Edited by Heidi Hansson, Maria Lindgren Leavenworth and Anka Ryall. Routledge, 2020, pp. 122–134.

Kearney, Richard. *Strangers, Gods and Monsters: Interpreting Otherness*. 2003. Routledge, 2005.

Keskitalo, Carina. "International Region-Building: Development of the Arctic as an International Region." *Cooperation and Conflict*, vol. 42, no. 2, 2007, pp. 187–205.

Khouri, Nadia. "Lost Worlds and the Revenge of Realism (Les Mondes perdus et la revanche du réalisme)." *Science Fiction Studies*, vol. 10, no. 2, 1983, pp. 170–190.

Lam, Anita. "Arctic Terror: Chilling Decay and Horrifying Whiteness in the Canadian North." *Horror Studies*, vol. 11, no. 2, 2020, pp. 187–204.

Leane, Elizabeth. *Antarctica in Fiction: Imaginative Narratives of the Far South*. Cambridge UP, 2012.

Leffler, Yvonne and Johan Höglund. "The Past that Haunts the Present: The Rise of Nordic Gothic." *Nordic Gothic*. Edited by Maria Holmgren Troy, Johan Höglund, Yvonne Leffler and Sofia Wijkmark. Manchester UP, 2020, pp. 11–28.

Leffler, Yvonne. "The Gothic Topography in Scandinavian Horror Fiction." *The Domination of Fear*. Edited by Mikko Canini. Brill, 2010, pp. 43–51.

Lenz, William E. "Poe's 'Arthur Gordon Pym' and the Narrative Techniques of Antarctic Gothic." *Cea Critic*, vol. 53, no. 3, 1991, pp. 30–38.

Leppänen, Katarina. "*Memory of Water*: Boundaries of Political Geography and World Literature." *European Review*, vol. 28, no. 3, 2020, pp. 425–434.

Lewes, Darby. *Dream Revisionaries: Gender and Genre in Women's Utopian Fiction 1870–1920*. The U of Alabama P, 1995.

Lewis-Jones, Huw. "'Balloonacy': Commander Cheyne's Flight of Fancy." *Polar Record*, vol. 44, no. 231, 2008, pp. 289–302.

Lindgren Leavenworth, Maria. "Abnormal Fears: The Queer Arctic in Michelle Paver's *Dark Matter*." *Journal of Gender Studies*, vol. 26, no. 4, 2017, pp. 462–472.

————. "Andrée på äventyr: verklighet och spekulation i Vidar Berges *Den hemlighetsfulla Nordpolsön*." [The Adventures of Andrée: Reality and Speculation in Vidar Berge's The Mysterious North Pole Island.] *Tidskrift för Litteraturvetenskap*, vol. 48, no. 3, 2018, pp. 39–49.

————. "Orientation and Disorientation in Realistic and Speculative Young Adult Fiction." *The Arctic in Literature for Children and Young Adults*. Edited by Heidi Hansson, Maria Lindgren Leavenworth and Anka Ryall. Routledge, 2020, pp. 217–229.

————. "The Atopic Arctic in Lost World Novels." *Translocal: Culturas Contemporâneas Locais e Urbanas*, no. 5, 2020, pp. 1–10.

————. "The Times of Men, Mysteries and Monsters: *The Terror* and Franklin's Last Expedition." *Arctic Discourses*. Edited by Anka Ryall, Johan Schimanski and Henning Howlid Wærp. Cambridge Scholars Publishing, 2010, pp. 199–217.

Lindgren Leavenworth, Maria and Van Leavenworth. "Human-Other Entanglements in Speculative Future Arctics." *Fafnir—Nordic Journal of Science Fiction and Fantasy Research*, vol. 9, no. 2, 2022, pp. 118–133.

Loomis, Chauncey. "The Arctic Sublime." *Nature and the Victorian Imagination*. Edited by U.C. Knoepflmacher and G. B. Tennyson. U of California P, 1977, pp. 95–112.

Lopez, Barry. *Arctic Dreams*. 1986. Vintage, 2014.

Mahady, Christine. "No World of Difference: Examining the Significance of Women's Relationships to Nature in Mary Bradley Lane's *Mizora*." *Utopian Studies*, vol. 15, no. 2, 2004, pp. 93–115.

Marcus, Alan Rudolph. *Relocating Eden: The Image and Politics of Inuit Exile in the Canadian Arctic*. UP of New England, 1995.

McCannon, John. *A History of the Arctic: Nature, Exploration and Exploitation*. Reaktion Books, 2012.

McClintock, Sir Francis Leopold. *In the Arctic Seas: a Narrative of the Discovery of the Fate of Sir John Franklin and his Companions*. Philadelphia: Porter and Coates, 1859.

McCorristine, Shane. *The Spectral Arctic. A History of Dreams and Ghosts in Polar Exploration*. UCL Press, 2018.

————. "The Spectral Presence of the Franklin Expedition in Contemporary Fiction." *Critique*, vol. 55, no. 1, 2014, pp. 60–73.

————. "The Supernatural Arctic: An Exploration." *Nordic Journal of English Studies*, vol. 9, no. 1, 2010, pp. 47–70.

McGhee, Robert. *The Last Imaginary Place: A Human History of the Arctic World*. Oxford UP, 2005.

Medby, Ingrid A. "Preface—'Arcticness and Change'." *Arcticness: Power and Voice from the North*. Edited by Ilan Kelman. ULC Press, 2017, pp. v–vii.

Mendlesohn, Farah. *Rhetorics of Fantasy*. Wesleyan UP, 2008.

Merola, Nicole M. " 'for the terror of deadness beyond': Arctic Environments and Inhuman Ecologies in Michelle Paver's *Dark Matter*." *Ecozon@: European Journal of Literature, Culture and Environment*, vol. 5, no. 2, 2014, pp. 22–40.

Monaco, Angelo. "Archives of Environmental Apocalypse in Sarah Moss's *Cold Earth*: Archaeology, Viruses, and Melancholia." *ISLE: Interdisciplinary Studies in Literature and Environment*, vol. 29, no. 4, 2022, pp. 1010–1029.

Morgan, Benjamin. "After the Arctic Sublime." *New Literary History*, vol. 47, no. 1, 2016, pp. 1–26.

Morice, Francis David. *The Olympian and Pythian Odes of Pindar: Translated into English Verse*. London: Henry S. King & Co, 1876.

Moss, Sarah. *The Frozen Ship: The Histories and Tales of Polar Exploration*. BlueBridge, 2006.

Mussgnug, Florian. "Naturalizing Apocalypse: Last Men and Other Animals." *Comparative Critical Studies*, vol. 9, no. 3, 2012, pp. 333–347.

Newman, Beth. "Narratives of Seduction and the Seductions of Narrative: The Frame Structure of *Frankenstein*." *ELH*, vol. 53, no. 1, 1986, pp. 141–163.

Nixon, Rob. *Slow Violence and the Environmentalism of the Poor*. Harvard UP, 2011.

Oxford, J. S. "Influenza A Pandemics of the 20th Century with Special Reference to 1918: Virology, Pathology and Epidemiology." *Reviews in Medical Virology*, vol. 10, no. 2, 2000, pp. 119–133.

Oziewicz, Marek. "Speculative fiction." *Oxford Research Encyclopedia of Literature*. 2017. DOI: 10.1093/acrefore/9780190201098.013.78

Pfaelzer, Jean. "The Changing of the Avant Garde: The Feminist Utopia (La transformation de l'avant-garde: l'utopie féministe)." *Science Fiction Studies*, vol. 15, no. 3, 1988, pp. 282–294.

Philipps, Lionel. "The Filiation from Cyrano to Verne: An Exacting Poetics that Birthed French Science Fiction." *Rediscovering French Science-Fiction in Literature, Film and Comics: From Cyrano to Barbarella*. Edited by Phillipe Mather and Sylvain Rheault. Cambridge Scholars Publishing, 2016, pp. 21–39.

Piatti-Farnell, Lorna. "Arctic Gothic: Genre, Folklore, and the Cinematic Horror Landscape of *Dead Snow* (2009)." *Studies in European Cinema*, vol. 18, no. 1, 2021, pp. 76–85.

Piercy, Van. "An Icy Allegory of Cultural Survival: Gothic Themes in Dan Simmons's *The Terror*." *21st Century Gothic: Great Gothic Novels since 2000*. Edited by Danel Olson. The Scarecrow Press, 2011, pp. 539–551.

Potter, Russell, "A Horological Mystery." *Visions of the North*, Thursday, May 21, 2009. https://visionsnorth.blogspot.com/2009/05/horological-mystery.html. Accessed 2 January 2023.

Prescott, Nicholas. "Echoes of Poe—Absence and the Uncanny in 'The Fahrenheit Twins' and *The Courage Consort*." *Michael Faber: Critical Essays*. Edited by Rebecca Langworthy, Kristin Lindfield-Ott and Jim MacPherson. Gylphi Limited, 2020, pp. 95–112.

Previdi, Michael, Karen Louise Smith, and Lorenzo M. Polvani. "Arctic Amplification of Climate Change: A Review of Underlying Mechanisms." *Environmental Research Letters*, vol. 16, 2021, pp. 1–25.

Rae, John. "Arctic Exploration, with Information Respecting Sir John Franklin's Missing Party." *Journal of the Royal Geographical Society of London*, vol. 25, 1855, pp. 246–256.

Redding, Arthur F. *Haints: American Ghosts, Millennial Passions, and Contemporary Gothic Fictions*. U of Alabama P, 2011.

Rieder, John. *Colonialism and the Emergence of Science Fiction*. Weslyan UP, 2008.

Riffenburgh, Beau. "Jules Verne and the Conquest of the Polar Regions." *Polar Record*, vol. 27, no. 162, 1991, pp. 237–240.

Robinson, Michael. "Reconsidering the Theory of the Open Polar Sea." *Extremes: Oceanography's Adventures at the Poles*. Edited by Keith Rodney Benson and Helen M. Rozwadowski. Science History Publications, 2007, pp. 15–29.

Romanzi, Valentina. "Plural Identities in Sam J. Miller's *Blackfish City*." *ContactZone*, no. 2, 2020, pp. 68–86

Ryall, Anka, et al. "Arctic Discourses: An Introduction." *Arctic Discourses*. Edited by Anka Ryall, Johan Schimanski and Henning Howlid Wærp. Cambridge Scholars Publishing, 2010, pp. ix–xxii.

Ryan, Marie-Laure. "From Parallel Universes to Possible Worlds: Ontological Pluralism in Physics, Narratology, and Narrative." *Poetics Today*, vol. 27, no. 4, 2006, pp. 633–674.

Rydén Per. *Den svenske Ikaros*. [The Swedish Icarus]. Stockholm: Carlssons, 2003.

Saberhagen, Jean. "Introduction." *Mizora: A World of Women*. 1890. U of Nebraska P, 1999, pp. v–xii.

Saxo Grammaticus. *The Danish History*. Translated by Oliver Elton, 1905. *Project Gutenberg*. Accessed 2 January 2023.

Schimanski, Johan, and Ulrike Spring. "Explorers' Bodies in Arctic Mediascapes: Celebrating the Return of the Austro-Hungarian Polar Expedition in 1874." *Acta Borealia*, vol. 26, no. 1, 2009, pp. 50–76.

Schoolmeester, Tina et al. *Global Linkages—A Graphic Look at the Changing Arctic*. UN Environment and GRID-Arendal, 2019.

Seed, David. "Framing the Reader in Early Science Fiction." *Style*, vol. 47, no. 2, 2013, pp. 137–167.

Singles, Kathleen. *Alternate History: Playing with Contingency and Necessity*. De Gruyter, 2013.

Small, Christopher. *Ariel Like a Harpy: Shelley, Mary, and Frankenstein*. Gollancz, 1972.

Smith, Andrew, and William Hughes. "Introduction: Defining the ecoGothic." *EcoGothic*. Edited by Andrew Smith and William Hughes. Manchester UP, 2015, pp. 1–14.

Smyth, Edmund J. "Verne, SF, and Modernity: An Introduction." *Jules Verne: Narratives of Modernity*. Edited by Edmund J. Smyth. Liverpool UP, 2000, pp. 1–10.

Spufford, Francis. *I May Be Some Time: Ice and the English Imagination*. Faber and Faber, 1996.

Stenport, Anna Westerstahl, and Richard S. Vachula. "Polar Bears and Ice: Cultural Connotations of Arctic Environments that Contradict the Science of Climate Change." *Media, Culture & Society*, vol. 39, no. 2, 2017, pp. 282–295.

Stern-Peltz, Marie. "*Blackfish City* by Sam J. Miller." Review. *Strange Horizons*. 11 February, 2019. http://strangehorizons.com/. Accessed 2 January 2023.

Stevens, Julie Anne. "Introduction." *The Ghost Story from the Middle Ages to the Twentieth Century*. Edited by Helen Conrad O'Briain, and Julie Anne Stevens. Four Courts Press, 2010, pp. 11–15.

Sugars, Cynthia. *Canadian Gothic: Literature, History, and the Spectre of Self-Invention*. U of Wales P, 2014.

Suvin, Darko. "Victorian Science Fiction, 1871–85: The Rise of the Alternative History Sub-Genre (La science-fiction victorienne, 1871–1885: l'émergence du sous-genre de l'uchronie)." *Science Fiction Studies*, vol. 10, no. 2, 1983, pp. 148–169.

Taubenberger, Jeffery K., et al. "Discovery and Characterization of the 1918 Pandemic Influenza Virus in Historical Context." *Antiviral Therapy*, vol. 12, no. 4, 2007, pp. 581–591.

Taylor, E. G. R. "A Letter Dated 1577 from Mercator to John Dee." *Imago Mundi*, no. 13, 1956, pp. 56–68.

Thiess, Derek J. "Dan Simmons's *The Terror*, Inuit 'Legend', and the Embodied Horrors of History." *Journal of the Fantastic in the Arts*, vol. 29, no. 2, 2018, pp. 222–241.

Thurston, Luke. *Literary Ghosts from the Victorians to Modernism: The Haunting Interval*. Routledge, 2012.

Todorov, Tzvetan. *The Fantastic: A Structural Approach to a Literary Genre*. Translated by Richard Howard. 1970. Cornell UP, 1975.

Trexler, Adam. *Anthropocene Fictions: The Novel in a Time of Climate Change*. U of Virginia P, 2015.

Tuan, Yi-Fu. "Desert and Ice: Ambivalent Aesthetics." *Landscape, Natural Beauty and the Arts*. Edited by Salim Kemal and Ivan Gaskell. Cambridge UP, 1993, pp. 139–157.

Weinstock, Jefferey Andrew. "Invisible Monsters: Vision, Horror, and Contemporary Culture." *The Ashgate Research Companion to Monsters and the Monstrous*. Edited by Asa Simon Mittman and Peter J. Dendle. 2013. Routledge, 2016, pp. 275–289.

Wheeler, Sara. *The Magnetic North: Travels in the Arctic*. 2009. Vintage, 2010.

Whyte, Kyle P. "Indigenous Science (Fiction) for the Anthropocene: Ancestral Dystopias and Fantasies of Climate Change Crises." *Environment and Planning E: Nature and Space*, vol. 1, no 1–2, 2018, pp. 224–242.

Wijkmark, Sofia. "Nordic Troll Gothic." *Nordic Gothic*. Edited by Maria Holmgren Troy, Johan Höglund, Yvonne Leffler and Sofia Wijkmark. Manchester UP, 2020, pp. 103–124.

Winthrop-Young, Geoffrey. "Fallacies and Thresholds: Notes on the Early Evolution of Alternate History." *Historical Social Research*, vol. 34, no. 2, 2009, pp. 99–117.

Wolf, Mark J. P. *Building Imaginary Worlds: The Theory and History of Subcreation*. Routledge, 2012.

Wright, John K. "The Open Polar Sea." *Geographical Review*, vol. 43, no. 3, 1953, pp. 338–365.

Yost, Michelle Kathryn. *American Hollow Earth Narratives From the 1820s to 1920*. 2014. The University of Liverpool, PhD dissertation.

Zlosnik, Sue. "Globalgothic at the Top of the World: Michel Faber's 'The Fahrenheit Twins'." *Globalgothic*. Edited by Glennis Byron. Manchester UP, 2013, pp. 65–76.

Index

Note: Endnotes are indicated by the page number followed by "n" and the note number e.g., 63n27 refers to note 27 on page 63.

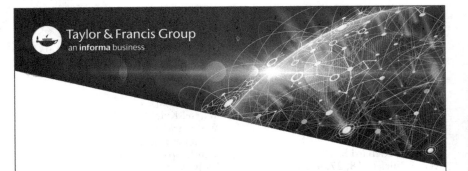

9781032409665